The Kennedy Boys

Finding Kyler

The First Novel

SIOBHAN DAVIS

www.siobhandavis.com

Printed by Createspace, An Amazon.com Company
Paperback edition © January 2017

ISBN-13: 978-1539331650
ISBN-10: 1539331652

Editor: Kelly Hartigan (XterraWeb) editing.xterraweb.com
Cover design by Fiona Jayde www.fionajaydemedia.com
Image © istockphoto.com
Formatting by The Deliberate Page www.deliberatepage.com

The Kennedy Boys

Kaden
The Mastermind

Keven
The Hacker

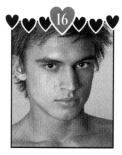

Kyler
The Thrill Seeker

Kalvin
The Player

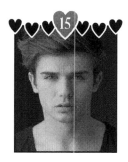

Keanu
The Poser

Kent
The Delinquent

Keaton
The Joker

Note from the Author

I have written this book in American English, as is my usual style; however, when Faye first arrives in Massachusetts, her speech and thought patterns are quite "Irish." As she acclimates, her language changes when she grows accustomed to how American teens speak. I haven't dwelled too much on this as it's not pivotal to the story, but I still wanted to make it appear somewhat authentic. I spent three months in Cape Cod when I was twenty (during summer break from college) and I've based Faye's transition, in part, on my own experience. In a lot of cases, I think you can guess the meaning, but if you get stuck, I've listed some of the Irish colloquialisms Faye uses in a glossary with their equivalent meaning. Where a word or phrase can have several meanings, I've listed the one that's most relevant to the context.

The glossary is at the back of this book.

Chapter One

"You can't be serious?" I rub a tense spot between my eyes as I level an incredulous look at the bald-headed man sitting behind the other side of the desk. Lowering his chin, he stares at me over the top of his black-rimmed spectacles. Perched on the tip of his rather pointy nose, his glasses are the outdated sort you expect to see on old-fashioned solicitor types.

"I can assure you, Ms. Donovan, that Hayes, Ryan, Barrett, and Company Solicitors do not joke about such matters." His lips pinch into a disapproving line as he eyeballs me. There isn't a shred of compassion in his tone or his look. His eyes have a dead, empty quality to them. *Like his conscience, no doubt.*

He oozes indifference.

And, sure, what does he care? He's already been paid and the clients who hired him can hardly take him to task over his lack of empathy.

"Why haven't I heard of this"—I swirl my hands in the air—"Kennedy dude before?"

He huffs out a sigh. "Only your parents can answer that question."

"Well," I say, narrowing my eyes, "unless you've figured out a way to talk to the dead, I'm guessing that's one question I won't ever get an answer to." I slump a little in my chair as the wall of grief hits me like a tsunami. Although my smart-arse remark may suggest apathy, it couldn't be further from the truth.

It's been the same these last three days as the aftermath of the accident finally hits home.

The first four days of what I'm now referring to as my "I wish I was dead too" new life is a blur. I vaguely recall the guard knocking on my door, explaining in a soft, sympathetic manner how both my parents were killed instantly in the head-on collision. Their silver Toyota Corolla never stood a chance against the articulated lorry. According to the Garda report, my parent's car was mangled beyond all recognition.

My eyes shutter as a horrific vision surges to the forefront of my mind. I wrap my arms around my waist, rocking slowly back and forth in the chair. Intense pain twists my stomach into knots, and a messy ball of emotion lodges in the back of my throat. No child should ever have to see their parents like that. As long as I live, I'll never be able to erase the memory of their grotesquely distorted faces. But there had been no choice. There was no other living relative to ID their bodies.

Or so I thought.

Until ten minutes ago when my world tilted on its axis for the second time in a week.

"Ms. Donovan? Can I get you some water?" The solicitor's slightly gentler tone breaks me free from the torturous images bouncing around my brain.

I open my eyes, brushing long, sticky strands of my brunette hair back off my face. The weather has been unseasonably warm this summer, and my hair has not thanked Mother Nature for her generosity. Humidity and thick locks don't mix. I've spent the entire summer sporting a sweaty, frizzy mop atop my head. No wonder I've barely scored any action since Luke and I went our separate ways.

The solicitor coughs, attempting to recapture my attention. "Faye?" He leans forward in his chair. "Are you okay?"

I smother my snort of disbelief. *Am I okay? Is the old fart for real? No, you idiot! I am not okay.* My entire life is about to be upended, and my muddled brain can hardly comprehend the implications. Don't even mention the fact that I've barely slept in days or that my heart is shredded into itty-bitty pieces. Torn asunder at the knowledge I'll never get to see Mum's radiant smile again or feel the comforting weight of Dad's ever-loving gaze, I'm the furthest from okay a person can be.

I want to tell him all that—but I don't. I'm incapable of sharing any part of myself with another human being. I'm like a living, breathing, walking shell of a person. A soulless zombie. I even have the sunken eyes and ghostly pallor to prove it. Maybe I'll audition for a part in *The Walking Dead*. Preferably, *before* this Kennedy dude shows up to whisk me away.

Shaking my head, almost amused at the pitiful meandering of my mind, I force myself to focus on the here and now. "Does he know yet?" I ask, ignoring the solicitor's stupid question.

"We have notified Mr. Kennedy of the contents of your parents' Last Will and Testament. He'll be here at two, tomorrow, to take ownership of you."

"I'm not a dog or a possession or something you take *ownership* of," I snap.

Mr. Hayes sits up straighter in his chair, scrutinizing me with those vacuous eyes of his. "I am merely stating the facts. You are a minor, and your uncle, as your sole living relative, has been named your guardian until you turn eighteen. You are his responsibility until then."

"Can't I contest the will? I'm more than capable of looking after myself for the next few months. And you said the mortgage is now paid on the house, and I have my part-time job, so I can manage on that and the savings my parents left me."

I'd willingly donate a limb to avoid living on the other side of the Atlantic Ocean with a bunch of strangers.

I don't want to leave Ireland.

It's the only home I've ever known.

"Those savings won't get you far, and besides," he says, rustling a stack of papers on his desk, "it was your parents' wish that your uncle take charge of you. They didn't want you to be alone."

So, why did they leave me?

Why force this stranger on me?

Compel me to up sticks and move halfway around the world?

I'll add it to the ever-growing list of futile questions that has accompanied their deaths.

"Isn't there anything I can do to stop this?" I issue one last pleading question.

He shakes his head as he stands up. "It's the law, Ms. Donovan. You have no choice in the matter."

I rise, shoving my hands in the pockets of my jeans. I may not have much of a choice now, but this is only short term.

Roll on, January.

As soon as I hit that magic one-eight number, I'm hightailing it home.

"Bottoms up!" Jill clinks her shot glass against mine before tipping her head back and downing it like a champ. I lick the salt from my hand and swallow the tequila in one well-practiced move. It settles like sour milk in my empty gut. Ugh, that stuff never gets any easier to stomach.

Luke burps, and Jill falls off the sofa laughing.

"Damn, that's some good stuff. Top me up." He holds out his glass, and I duly oblige.

I'm tempted to guzzle straight from the bottle. To drown my sorrows in the hope that when I wake I'll discover this has all been a complete misunderstanding, not the actual embodiment of a living nightmare. But, unfortunately, I'm not the delusional type, and that sort of thinking will only get me so far.

"Maybe it won't be that bad, ya know?" Rachel says, fisting a hand in Jill's shirt and hauling her back up onto the sofa. "How many sons did you say this Kennedy bloke has?"

"Seven." I eye the neck of the tequila with longing just as Luke whips the bottle right out of my hands. "Hey!" I stretch over the arm of the sofa and make a grab for it. He lifts it out of my reach, and I slap his chest. "That's mine. Give it here."

"Only if you promise not to drink out of the bottle. You don't want to be sick on the flight."

"Maybe I want to get so drunk that I'll puke all over my new *guardian* and he'll have second thoughts about taking me in." I lunge for the bottle again, but he holds it out of arm's reach. Scowling, I crawl over the sofa onto his chair, making a last-ditch attempt to snatch back *my* bottle of tequila. My fingers grasp the cold, clear glass the same time Luke's opportunistic hand snakes around my waist. He pulls me down onto his lap so that I'm straddling him. Burying his head in my neck, he murmurs, "You smell divine, Faye."

"Knock it off, Luke. You're not getting in my knickers." I try to wriggle out of his lap, but his grip is tight.

"How about one last night together for old time's sake?" His intense green eyes darken with lust.

There was a time when I thought the sun, moon, and stars shone out of Luke's arse.

But that ship sailed six months ago.

We had two good years together before our relationship ran out of steam. I know he was hurt when I ended things, but it was for the best. The chemistry wasn't there anymore, and there was no point kidding myself otherwise.

I'm not one to hang about once I've made up my mind about something.

Although, that hasn't stopped Luke from chancing his arm with me every so often.

Like right now.

Reaching behind me, I yank his hand off my ass and pin him with a stern look. "Not happening, Luke. Now let go."

Luke lets out a pissed-off sigh, and I send him a pleading look. Irrespective of how we ended, I still care about him, and I don't want to leave the country on bad terms. He was an important part of my life for a while, and he helped me get through some difficult stuff.

I won't ever forget that.

Reluctantly, he releases me, and I scoot back over to my side of the sofa.

"You hava send piczures," Rachel slurs, and I chuckle. That girl can't even look at alcohol without getting pissed, but she doesn't let that stop her. "Of your fit cousssins," she adds when she spots my puzzled frown.

"How do you know they're fit?" I quirk a brow at my best friend.

"'Cause all rich Americans are good-looking."

"That is the stupidest thing that's ever come out of your mouth," Luke scoffs.

She momentarily lifts her head off the sofa to send him a filthy glare. "Izz not! I've watched *Gossip Girl*, and those boys are fit and stinking rich."

"Wow! You've seen it on a tacky TV show, so it must be true." Derision drips off his tongue. "That's even stupider." He rolls his eyes to the ceiling.

"Stupider isn't actually a word," Jill pipes up, sounding remarkably sober for someone who looks like she's on the verge of passing out.

"Is too. Google it." Luke flips her the bird before knocking back another shot. "You'd know that if you hadn't nuked all your brain cells with tequila."

Rachel opens her mouth to retaliate, but I zone out of the conversation. Jumping up, I snatch my mobile phone off the side table and plug it into the docking station. I turn the volume up to the max, drowning out the voices of my friends. Booming music blasts throughout the room, and Jill emits a loud holler. My body sways to the beat of the music as she hops up to join me.

The rest of the night becomes one giant messy blur. I vaguely remember others arriving, packing our small sitting room like sardines. Visions of Rachel and Jill escorting me to the bathroom are hazy.

Even hazier are the events leading up to this moment.

My head throbs painfully as I slowly start to regain consciousness. It's as if someone has taken a jackhammer to my skull and they're pounding to their own rhythm. A moan slips out through my lips. My tongue is plastered to the roof of my mouth, and the rancid taste of tequila and salt coats my mouth in a disgusting layer of slime. I moisten my dry lips as I attempt to open my eyes.

The sheets are stained a bright red color, and I blink profusely in total confusion.

Tangled strands of red hair cover my face as I fight a bout of nausea. *What the ...?*

Pushing up on my elbows is a tremendous feat in itself. On shaky limbs, I brush the knotty red hair back out of my eyes and stare at the abundance of red dye coating the white sheets of my bed.

I grunt. Bloody hell. *What did I do?* Rubbing a lock of my hair between my hands, I groan as it starts to come back to me. At some point during the night, I'd had the bright idea that a makeover was in order, and we'd raided the bathroom press.

The red hair dye was Mum's. She had taken to coloring her hair these last few months because a few strips of gray had made an unwelcome appearance. Her hair was dark—like mine—with rich, lush coppery strands running through it. I can still remember how her hair used to glisten magnificently in the sunlight.

A sharp pain pierces me straight through the heart as I flop back down on the bed.

That's when I become aware of issue number two.

A hand tightens on my breast, and nimble fingers start to brush over the tip of my nipple. I'm still fully clothed, thank the stars, but that's not stopping my bedmate. Panic rears up and slaps me in the face. This can't be good. I rack my brains but I can't recall any of the specifics.

I have no idea who is lying beside me.

Or what we may or may not have done.

I stifle a groan as I twist around to the other side.

Luke's mischievous grin greets me, and I silently curse. His green eyes sparkle with excitement, and I think I might puke.

Please tell me we didn't. Please tell me I had more sense than that. Or that I was too far gone to take anything to the next level. I narrow my eyes as I glower at him. His fingers swipe more feverishly over my nipple, and even though I'm protected by my shirt, his frantic tweaking actually hurts.

I send him my best death glare.

The one I usually reserve for vermin and serial killers. "What do you think you're doing?"

"Funny," a heavily accented male voice says. "I was about to ask the same question."

Chapter Two

I scream, shoving Luke's hand away as I shunt up against the headboard, pulling the covers up under my chin. A tall, handsome man with short dark hair and piercing blue eyes is standing at the edge of the bed, staring at me as if he's just seen a ghost.

Crap.

This cannot be happening.

My eyes dart to the small digital clock resting on top of the bedside locker, and I curse when I spot the time. I hadn't even thought to set the alarm, and now I've slept the morning, and half the afternoon, away.

Luke sits up, dragging a hand through his messy hair. "Who the bleedin' hell are you?"

I roll my eyes. *Seriously, is he thick?* I elbow him in the ribs. "Don't be an idiot, it's obvious who he is, or were you not listening to a word I said last night?"

"I was too busy staring at your tits."

Points for honesty but zilch for intelligence.

He's clearly still drunk.

Mr. Kennedy looks like he's seconds away from throwing Luke out on the street.

I'll save him the hassle. "I think that's your cue to leave." I shove him gently. "Go on, go."

He pins me with a contemptible look. "That's not what you were saying last night."

I thrust my hands in the air. Pressing my mouth to his ear, I hiss, "Whatever! You know I was drunk!" I glower at him again.

"I sincerely hope you didn't take advantage of my niece," my uncle says, in a weird half-Irish, half-American accent. He levels a stinging look at Luke. They face off for a couple of seconds, and my uncle's look darkens in a nanosecond. It's a pretty impressive look.

Once I'm not on the receiving end of it.

I take the opportunity to slyly study him. He's tall and lean with an unassuming muscular look that indicates he works out but doesn't take it to extremes. Wearing a navy and red long-sleeved polo shirt and dark denims, he's stylishly dressed for an old dude. The polo is slim-fit and it hugs his defined chest like a second skin. His dark hair is slicked back off his forehead in a feigned effortless manner. My nostrils twitch as I pick up the musky scent of his aftershave.

He gives off an air of understated wealth that is disconcerting. I'm beginning to suspect that Rachel hit the nail on the head with her assessment.

If this is what my uncle looks like, I have a feeling my cousins are going to easily meet the fit-rich barometer she's set.

Luke flips the covers off and stands. He gestures at his clothes. "Relax, I didn't take advantage of her. I'd never hurt Faye—I love her." He starts scanning the floor for his runners, conspicuously avoiding my gaze.

My uncle's chin jerks up. "He's your boyfriend?" He looks skeptical.

"Ex."

Now he looks relieved.

Luke scowls as he sits on the edge of the bed, slipping his feet into his runners. He turns around to face me. "I guess this is goodbye?"

"Eh." I rub my hand across the back of my head as I look to my uncle for confirmation. I have no idea what the plans are—whether he intends to hang around for a few days, or if we'll be leaving immediately. Mr. Kennedy nods, and I turn to face Luke. "Yep. See ya, Luke."

He leans over to kiss my cheek, and I pull him into a quick hug. A sad look briefly flitters across his eyes. "Take care, Faye. I'll miss you." He strolls out of the room with his shoulders hunched over.

A layer of tension immediately fills the empty space. My uncle looks at me, and I look back at him, and we just kinda stare at each other, neither one of us knowing what to say or do. His surprisingly familiar blue eyes are glued to mine, and a whole host of emotions skitters over his face. A muscle clenches in his jaw as he continues scrutinizing me, and I squirm uncomfortably. It's too intrusive—awkward on so many different levels. I chew on the corner of my lip, but I refuse to divert my eyes, meeting his penetrating gaze dead-on.

After a couple of minutes, irritation starts to build. I feel like a monkey in a cage at Dublin Zoo. My patience snaps. "Weren't you ever told it's rude to stare?"

That breaks him out of his trance-like state. He rocks back on his heels, glancing sheepishly at me. "I apologize, Faye. And for turning up like this, but you missed the appointment at the attorneys, ah, solicitors"—he corrects himself when he sees my puzzled expression—"and I was worried."

He slips his hands in his pockets, as I level him with a guarded look. "I didn't mean to offend you. It's just ... you look so much like ... Saoirse." He almost whispers her name. "You're the spitting image of your mom at the same age." As he places a hand across his chest, tears well in his eyes, he drops onto the corner of the bed, and hangs his head. His solid frame heaves as strong emotion rattles through him.

Unless this is an act, he genuinely seems to have cared for my mum.

Their relationship, or lack of one, is a mystery I wouldn't mind unraveling sometime.

I don't know what to do, whether I should reach out to comfort him or not, but he's a stranger to me, and it doesn't feel right, so I do nothing, letting him deal with whatever is going through his head in his own time.

A short while later, he looks up, and I'm startled to see so much devastation in his eyes. In this moment, he appears to have aged twenty years. Raw pain radiates from his eyes, and he doesn't do a thing to shade it from me. I kinda like that. There's an honest quality to it that endears him to me.

Slowly, I release my grip on the covers and slide out the side of the bed. I sit down beside him. "It's true? You really are my mum's brother?"

Not that I need verification. He has the same color eyes, the same complexion, and similar little strips of fiery red trace a path through his dark hair. He's like the male version of my mum. Tears gather in my eyes as her image surges to the forefront of my mind. I blink them away, but not before a sneaky beggar slips out, cascading down my cheek.

"Yes, and I'm James, by the way." He extends his hand and I reluctantly shake it, feeling terribly awkward. "I'm so sorry for your loss, Faye. I've been distraught since I heard the news." He scrubs a hand over his prickly jaw, and at this proximity, it's easy to confirm that truth. Bruising purple shadows hang underneath his bloodshot eyes, and his skin has an unhealthy tinge to it. It's clear he hasn't slept in days.

"Why didn't she tell me about you?"

His Adam's apple bobs in his throat. "We had a complicated relationship." He says it with a real drawn-out American twang that's kinda funny. His accent is a bit messed up. "I didn't realize she had a daughter," he continues, eyeing me earnestly. "I didn't know you existed until a few days ago. I'm sorry you had to go through the funeral by yourself. I should've been here with you, but the solicitor said his instructions were very clear. He was only to contact me *after* the funeral."

"It's okay." I toss him a feeble smile. "I survived the ordeal." Barely, but he doesn't need to know that. I close my eyes, forcing the horrific memories away.

Another layer of uncomfortable silence descends. I smile weakly at him.

"I thought I was going to have to avenge your death," he murmurs a few minutes later, motioning toward the red-stained bed linen.

I can't bring myself to laugh even though I understand he's trying to lighten the mood. "Apparently, I thought it was a good idea to undergo a makeover last night." I grimace as I inspect strands of my now garishly red hair.

"I'm surprised that you would drink yourself into such a state, especially after what happened to your pare ..." He trails off when he spots the expression on my face.

Undisguised misery fills every part of me, and I can't deal. My breathing becomes labored, and that awful fluttery feeling is back in my chest. I need to shut it down before it destroys me. I can't go there. It's still far too painful to think about the specifics of the accident. And who the hell does he think he is? Swanning in here like he knows everything?

He knows nothing.

"You don't get to lecture me," I grit out. "You're not my dad."

If he thinks he can replace my dad, he has another thing coming. He's my uncle, not a substitute dad, and the sooner he understands that the better. I'm only agreeing to this farce of a move because I've no choice. At least not until January.

All bets are off once I turn eighteen.

However, he's also right in his insinuation, and I loathe myself in this moment. My parents were killed by a drunk driver, and drinking myself into oblivion isn't the best way of honoring their memory. Mum hated me drinking, although she was realistic enough to know that she couldn't stop me. She'd be so disappointed in my behavior, and I hate feeling as if I've let her down, which is mad, because she's let me down in a much worse way.

She promised she'd always be here for me.

But she lied.

Because she's gone, and I have to try to find some way of living the rest of my life without her in it.

A painful lump jams my throat as tears gather in earnest. A wayward sob escapes before I can stop it.

"Shoot," James says. "I'm making a right mess of this. I'm not used to girls ... not since ..."

He doesn't need to say it.

Not since my mum.

I look into his sincere eyes, and my sudden burst of rage-fueled grief disappears. I can tell he means well and that this is as hard for him as it is for me. "Well," I say, deciding to be charitable, "I'm not used to having an uncle, or cousins, and I've never even been outside of Ireland, so I think my level of unease totally trumps yours." My fingers pick at a loose thread on the hem of my shirt. "Not that it's a competition or anything. I'm just saying." I shrug.

A huge grin transforms his face, and he looks so young when he smiles. "I have a feeling you're going to fit right in, Faye."

He stands up, offering his hand. "Come on. Let's go home."

Chapter Three

My eyes are out on stalks as we arrive at a small, private terminal at Dublin Airport a little while later. I've been glum the entire half hour of the journey. James didn't waste much time hanging about. I was showered and packed in record time. Locking the door to my house was a heart-wrenching moment. Everything is happening so fast. Too fast. My life is about to flip right over, and I'm ill prepared.

The sight of the private jet awaiting us only adds to the surreal feeling. A narrow red strip stretches along the side of the whitewashed plane, broken in half by a striking, red, circular logo with a distinctive "K" in the center that immediately captures my interest.

I know that brand!

Everyone at school has been raving about their new teen clothing range. It doesn't take a genius to join the dots.

No way!

"Are you kidding me?" I stride purposefully across the tarmac. "This plane belongs to Kennedy Apparel? That company is yours?" I know the stuffy solicitor dude said my uncle was wealthy, but I didn't think he meant the filthy, obnoxiously rich type of wealthy. The enormity of the situation presses down on me like a heavy weight. I'm suddenly feeling a little green around the gills, and the prospect of flying isn't responsible. I'm even more apprehensive over what lies ahead. *What am I getting myself into?*

James chuckles. "This is actually my own personal jet, but it's technically owned by Kennedy Apparel. That's my wife's business. It's been in her family for years, although she rebranded when she took the helm after we were married and she started using my name." He ushers me up the steps, and I walk into the compact cabin.

Plush, white leather recliners engraved with the signature K logo line the spacious cabin on both sides. Chairs face one another, sandwiched between small, glossy, walnut-topped tables. Four pairs of two in total. James leads me past the main area and out beyond a small bathroom, stopping in front of a narrow space passing as a kitchen of sorts. "Would you like a drink?"

Even the thought of alcohol makes my stomach flip one-eighty. Nausea rises up my throat, and I clamp my mouth shut. I'd rather not hurl in front of him. "Water, thanks."

He hands me a cold bottle and two tablets. "They'll help with the hangover." I accept them gratefully, popping the pills in my mouth as I take a healthy glug of water.

"Come on through to the cockpit," he offers.

I follow him into the small space with a frown. "Where's the pilot?"

His lips curve into a smile. "That'd be me." My jaw falls open, and he laughs. "Michael is on hand as co-pilot if I need him." He gestures behind, and I glance over my shoulder at the tall, gray-haired man who has just stepped into the cabin. I smile as he lifts a hand in greeting.

"Strap yourself in," James instructs, dropping into his seat as he gestures at the one alongside him.

A mad swarm of butterflies floods my belly. I never imagined my first time in the air would be in a glamorous private plane and that I'd be sitting in the actual cockpit. Nervous adrenaline floods my system as I lock my harness in place.

James flips a ton of switches on the control panel, verifies info with some dude on the end of his radio, and then pushes a few levers. I settle back in my seat as the thrum of the engine starts up and the plane starts moving.

I've had my nose glued to the window the last half hour, even though all I can see are big, chunky clouds. I still can't believe I'm airborne. I'd presumed my first time would be with my parents, so my euphoria has a bittersweet edge to it.

James taps my elbow, claiming my attention. His smile is expansive as he takes in my awestruck expression. "First time?"

"Yeah. It's every bit as incredible as I thought it would be," I volunteer.

"Let me show you something. Hold on." His grin has turned mischievous.

The plane starts tilting right, and my heart jumps into my throat. I grab onto my harness as the plane continues to veer right, and all the blood rushes to my face. I scream my head off as we roll over, turning completely upside down, and my breath huffs out in panicked spurts. My hair covers my face like a blanket.

My breathing only starts to recalibrate when the plane has right-sided and we're back on track. Pushing clumped locks of hair out of my face, I stare at my uncle with wide-eyed alarm. "Oh my God!" I shriek, when I finally find my voice. "Some warning would've been nice!"

"And miss hearing you scream and seeing the look on your face right now? No way!"

He chuckles, and I find myself laughing with him. "You're insane!"

"What good is having your own plane if you can't have a little fun every now and then?" His face lights up excitedly, and in this moment, he's like a little boy on Christmas morning.

He's into planes.

My dad was obsessed with cars.

What is it with boys and their toys?

"That said," he adds, with a cheeky grin, "it might be best not to tell Alex."

"Alex?"

"My wife."

I twirl a lock of hair around my finger. "I assume she knows about me?"

"Of course. I told Alex and the boys as soon as I found out. Don't worry." He pats my hand. "They are expecting your arrival."

"And how did they take the news?" I watch him like a hawk as he prepares to answer.

"They were shocked, like I was, but they'll come around. The triplets are extremely excited to make your acquaintance."

My eyes pop wide. "Triplets?"

He smiles, obviously used to this reaction. "Our youngest sons are triplets. It was one hell of a surprise, I can tell you." His lips expand wider. "Keanu, Kent, and Keaton will be sixteen in December. They'll be sophomores this year."

An unpleasant sensation forms in my gut. American high school. A bristling shiver travels up and down my spine. I've no clue what I'm in for, but I refuse to allow anxiety to tie me into knots. My brain—unhelpfully— conjures up images from a succession of American movies and shows I've seen, and I have a sneaky feeling that it's not pure fiction. Hopefully, I'm wrong, but if I'm not, I'll deal. I've gotten through worse.

Pushing my concern aside, I focus on getting more info out of Uncle James while he seems to be in a sharing-and-caring type mood. "How old are your other sons? Will any of them be in my year?"

"Kaden and Keven are at Harvard." He graces me with a proud smile. "They live on campus, but they'll be at the house to welcome you. Kaden is twenty and Keven turned nineteen recently."

"All their names start with K?" How cheesy.

He fails to hide his amusement. "Yes. That was my wife's idea. She's rather obsessed with her brand."

I'll say.

"So, um, what about the rest of your sons?"

"Kalvin is sixteen and he'll be a junior this year. Kyler is a senior like you. He's seventeen, too, although you're older by a few months." He glances briefly out the side window.

"Oh." I hadn't considered that any of my cousins could be the same age as me. I hope Kyler isn't one of those do-gooder preppy-male types. Or worse, one of those obnoxious all-American jocks.

"They are all so close in age. Do they get along?"

James snorts. "Well, that's a loaded question if ever I heard one!" A nostalgic look crosses over his face. "They have their moments, but, yeah, they're close. Having the triplets so soon after Kyler and Kalvin came along was a challenging time. Imagine having six kids all under the age of five? I don't know how we survived!" He chuckles, as I shudder at the mere thought.

"And how does Alex feel about the situation with me?"

He opens the top two buttons of his shirt and leans back in his seat. "Alex is ecstatic. She can't wait to meet you."

I examine his pupils carefully, and they don't dilate. I detect no hint of a lie. He's looking at me expectantly, waiting for a response. I shoot for textbook-polite, which always goes down well with the oldies. "That's very nice of her, and I look forward to meeting everyone."

The rest of the plane ride passes by in uneventful silence. Every so often, I catch him sneaking sly looks at me. It's a little unnerving, but I guess it's as strange for him as it is for me.

I'm still finding it difficult to understand how my mother kept our relatives hidden all these years. Or why. I inwardly laugh at the irony of the situation. For years, I yearned for relations, for siblings, for anyone other than Mum, Dad, and me. Don't get me wrong, I loved my parents fiercely, and we had a super-close relationship, but there were times when it felt like I was living in a goldfish bowl.

A dusky skyline greets us when we finally land on the private airstrip attached to Boston's Logan International Airport. James whisks me into a waiting chauffeur-driven car the minute we step off the plane.

I've barely time to breathe before we set out into the heavy urban traffic. The interior of the car is an ode to Kennedy Apparel—the K logo is splashed everywhere—and I'm beginning to sense a theme. I can only imagine what the house is going to be like.

My gaze barely strays from the window the entire journey, and I'm mesmerized by my first glimpse of the United States. As I soak it all up, I allow a tiny glimmer of excitement to take root inside me. I imagine Mum whispering in my ear. *"You're on the adventure of a lifetime, love. Embrace it!"* A familiar stomach-clenching pang sears through me, and I squeeze my eyes shut.

I wonder if the pain will ever go away. Or if I'll feel gutted every time I remember her.

"Faye? Are you okay?" James' voice is soft as he leans forward in his seat. His eyes are kind.

"I'm fine," I say, a little harshly. "Just trying to absorb everything."

He looks shrewdly at me. "Of course. I, ah"—he scratches the back of his head—"if you need to talk to anyone about your parents, I can arrange that for you. I can't even begin to imagine how you must feel."

I grind my teeth down to the molars. "Thank you for the offer, but I'm grand."

"If you change your mind, come talk to me."

I know he's only showing concern, but any mention of psychologists reminds me of a part of my past that I've buried. I also hate to be pitied, and I refuse to be treated like the walking wounded. My parents died tragically. It was—is—awful, and I will miss them every single day, but I have to stay strong. I know that's what they would want.

And I'm more than capable of coping on my own. My parents equipped me well. Independence was something they admired greatly, and I was encouraged to make my own choices. If it were up to me, I'd have stayed at home, finished school, and applied to Trinity College as I intended to. None of this is my choice, but I'm trying to make the best of it.

Can't he see that?

I try to keep my voice respectful but firm. "I don't need a shrink. Not now. Not ever."

He holds up his hands in a conciliatory gesture. "No problem."

Gradually, we move out of the city, zipping along a vast highway with numerous lanes. Everything is bigger and bolder here. Dublin seems so minuscule and mundane in comparison. The farther we travel, the darker it gets. A smattering of twinkling stars emerges in the nighttime sky. We move off the highway onto less crowded roads bordered by statuesque trees wearing varying shades of green, yellow, and amber hues.

The car glides by a sign stating "Entering Wellesley. Norfolk County. Inc 1881." At this hour, the streets are unnaturally quiet. We bypass the main town and head along roads thick with foliage. Houses are ginormous around here, fronted by well-maintained lawns. The farther we travel, the grander they get. There's an eclectic mix of styles and types, but it works. It couldn't be further removed from the typical residential estates back home.

I stiffen in my seat as the vehicle detours into a wide well-lit road. Elaborate mansions extend on either side, barely visible behind huge red-bricked walls. Some peek out behind imposing iron gates.

My heart starts pounding erratically, slamming against my ribcage, and my palms are sweaty. I know we're close, and a layer of anxiety is hovering in the wings, waiting for its cue. The car slows in front of an imposing wrought iron gate bearing the signature K logo.

I rub my hands up and down my jeans as the gates sweep open. The car eases smoothly forward and up a broad tree-lined driveway. A massive flowerbed rests majestically on either side of the lawn, lit up by a multitude of night-lights. The flowerbed is a circular shape, with a precise K-shaped arrangement in the center. White buds rim the border, while vibrant red flowers fill the K, replicating the logo that I feel will be indelibly imprinted on my brain. Honestly, it's getting a little ridiculous at this point.

The driver pulls the car around the bend, and my jaw slackens as I take in my new home. It's not at all what I was expecting.

Oh, it's massive—as in White-House-sized proportions—but it's a sleek, modern, one-story structure made of glass and wood, with differing angled roofs. It screams sophistication and glamour, and the only time I've seen anything like it is while watching *MTV Cribs* or in glossy magazines that showcase celebrity homes. I'm gobsmacked, but I compose my features and hide the whole "deer in the headlights" look I am no doubt sporting.

The house faces onto an expansive well-manicured lawn. Huge trees border the property at the rear. "We have our own private woods, along with a basketball court, putting green, and an indoor and outdoor swimming pool," James says. I perk up at the mention of the pools and he notices. "You like to swim?"

I tuck my hair behind my ears. "Yeah. I was on the county swim team back home."

"There's a swim team at the school. You should try out."

The car pulls into an empty spot in the massive garage, beside a souped-up flashy red sports car. James notices my interest. "That's my baby. Isn't she a beauty?"

It looks like something a teenage joyrider would steal back home, but I keep that opinion to myself. "Absolutely."

I'm such a lick arse.

Several black SUVs line up in a row, and I'm guessing those belong to his sons.

The driver stops the car, and I wrap my arms around my waist to stave off the violent trembling that's taken hold of me.

Their obscene wealth intimidates me.

Not the people.

The money.

The driver opens my uncle's door first before attending to mine. James doesn't make any move to exit. He looks contemplative. "I hope you'll be happy here, Faye. Truly, I do."

"Thank you. Me, too." I hop out of the car as the driver retrieves my suitcase from the boot.

A splash of color in the corner of the garage captures my attention. Three racing motorbikes rest on an elevated platform. One is orange and blue and there is a multitude of brand logos on the side. The other two bikes are no less impressive. One is painted in a dark shade of green, the other bright yellow. A myriad of similar stickers decorates the side panels. I'm inexplicably drawn to them, and my feet move of their own accord.

Reaching out, I run the tip of my finger along the bodywork and up and down the wheels, my fingers dipping into the grooves in the tires. I can almost feel the enhanced adrenaline in the air. Motorbikes have always excited me, and the pure rush I'm getting is sending tingles of anticipation ricocheting all over my body.

I'm so entranced that I barely register the sound of approaching footsteps.

"Get your hands off my bike." The deep male cadence verges on a predatory growl. The possessive quality to his voice isn't lost on me either.

Giant goose bumps sprout on my arms, but I smother my fear and lift my head up in a confident manner. A red flush creeps up my chest and over my neck as a devastatingly good-looking boy reaches my side.

I'm tall—for a girl—and I'm usually pretty much on the level with most guys, but the top of my head barely reaches this dude's chin, so he's got to be at least six-two to my five-nine.

His body exudes warmth like a weapon. It crashes into me, almost knocking me off my feet. Slowly, my eyes travel up his body, taking in every ripped, lean, taut inch of him. He's wearing dark navy jeans and a plain white shirt that's molded to his perfectly chiseled abs like it's painted on. I gulp.

They sure don't grow them like this in Ireland.

My eyes continue their journey, up beyond the inviting, exposed strip of skin at the top of his shirt, and note voluptuous lips that are pinched tight, the light layer of dark stubble on his sculpted chin and cheeks, and the tan, smooth lines of his handsome face. I brace myself, rocking back on my heels, as I stare into stunning pale blue eyes. Framed by a thick layer of inky-black lashes most girls would kill for, his eyes are vast pools that I could easily drown in.

This guy is seriously good-looking, and he knows it, too. Crossing his arms over his chest, he pins me with a venomous look, and I shrink back from the dangerous vibes he's emitting.

"Are you done drooling yet?"

Chapter Four

Poison drips from his words, and everything locks up tight inside me. No matter that he's right—I *was* ogling him like he's my favorite Belgian chocolate ice cream—there's no way I'm admitting to that. I spread a sneer over my lips and level him with one of my extra-special looks. The ones I usually deploy for cocky, arrogant dickheads. "Don't flatter yourself. You're the first specimen of prime American A-hole I've seen. I wanted to memorize the form so I know what to avoid the next time."

He smirks, tilting his head to the side, and waves of smooth, sleek hair hover over his forehead. His hair is shorn real close at the sides but longer on top, styled back off his face. At home, all the guys are into skin fades with slick backs. This dude has a more stylish upper-class version of that.

Figures.

I deliberately force my eyes to stare blankly at him. There's no way I'm letting him see how much I'm affected. I've never met anyone like him before. He oozes raw sex appeal and danger by the bucket load.

It both thrills and terrifies me.

My fingers twitch at my side with an almost compulsive need to touch him. His smirk grows, and my lips curl into a snarl of their own volition. Now, the scumbag is truly starting to irritate me.

Behind me, James is issuing instructions to someone. A-hole leans down, pressing his delectable mouth against my ear. "I don't know how they do things in Ireland, sweetheart, but you're in my house—in my domain. And you don't get to talk shit to me. Keep out of my way, and I'll keep out of yours. Same goes for my brothers."

Wow. He's friendly. Not.

A fiery shiver rips up and down my spine as his warm breath trickles over me like some form of magical mist. He steps back, leering as he spots all the giveaway signs on my face.

Any hint of blossoming desire evaporates.

Smug, good-looking bastard. What an arrogant ass.

Well, good. I'm glad he's ugly on the inside because I should have no trouble repelling him. I've never been attracted to obnoxious boys, no matter how tempting they are on the outside.

"This family is fucked up enough without additional complications. You shouldn't have come. You're not wanted," he adds in a much louder tone, glancing briefly over his shoulder.

"Kyler! That's enough!" James walks toward us with a fierce look on his face.

"Screw you." Kyler glowers at his dad and they face off.

Well then.

I watch father and son as they enter into some form of silent confrontation. After a few minutes, Kyler drops back, laughing. Deliberately eyeing me, he runs the tip of his tongue slowly over his upper lip, and it takes considerable effort not to track the movement. Good God, this guy has all the moves down pat. Is this what I'm up against with every American boy? Rachel and Jill are going to flip out when I tell them about this.

Quick as a flash, Kyler moves in front of me until there's barely any space separating us.

Time seems to stand still.

I hold my posture erect and stare right back at him. James is shouting at him and tugging on his arm, but he doesn't budge. There is scarcely an inch between us, and I can sense the powerful thudding of his heart. My heart races at the naked threat in his eyes. He stares deep into my eyes, pushing and searching, scanning me with his scorching gaze. I'm rooted to the spot, unable to move, hardly capable of breathing. As he probes me with his determined eyes, I lose control for a second, and my shield drops. A spark flares in his eyes the moment he sees me. Truly sees me.

Scrambling to put my invisible wall back up, I quiver all over, and my limbs turn to jelly. I don't think I'd feel any more violated if he'd stripped me bare. I might as well have lain down before him openly exposing all my flaws and my fears, inviting him to psychoanalyze me.

Steadfast resolution seizes me. It's taken years to put my past behind me. It's a part of me I don't share with anyone—a part I can't even bear to acknowledge for fear of what'll happen. No one has penetrated that wall in years, and I'll be damned if this arrogant fucker is going to invade that most private, most abhorred part of me.

I guess it takes one to know one, and two can play that game.

Spearing him with a determined look, I reverse the intrusive lens—turning it on him. My eyes explore hidden, dark depths filled with loathing and self-hate. It's a melting pot of wild, out-of-control emotions. Heartfelt pain has a vice grip on his heart. As I continue looking at him, I see it, churning and snarling and closing him off to the world. His face pales, and our eyes meet in a moment of shared understanding.

We both jerk back at the same time, and whatever bubble we were in bursts, leaving us both vulnerable. My back hits against the handlebars of a bike, and a sharp ache rips across my upper back, but I barely feel the impact.

James is yelling at Kyler, but I can't make out the words over the blood rushing to my brain and the alarm bells flaring like warning beacons in my ears.

The shouting stops and I look up. James prods his son in the side. Kyler pierces me with another inquisitive look, but this one is loaded with caution. Blood turns to ice in my veins as a deathly cold chill rockets through me.

He knows I've seen something in him. Something I recognize, only because it exists in me too. He's issuing a clear, silent warning.

I'm not a fool. I don't need to make any enemies at home because I'm sure I'll have plenty of those once I rock on up to the high school. Yes, he's in pain, and a part of me empathizes, but my bet is he lashes out at the world in a misguided attempt to feel better.

I'm not about to become his new punching bag.

A smart antagonist always knows when to back down.

I arch my back, standing tall. I'll make it clear that I understand, but there's no way I'm letting him think he's intimidated me. Kyler is not going to walk all over me. I promised myself years ago that I wouldn't be a pushover any more. It's a mantra I've clung to, and I'm not about to regress. Especially not for a wanker like him.

So, I'll stand down. For now.

"No touching the bikes. Got it." My eyes widen automatically as I move aside, palms raised in a token gesture.

His lips pinch tightly as he nods, and the smug, smirking look from earlier is gone.

We have an understanding, of sorts.

I'll pretend that I didn't see that hidden dark void inside him, and he'll keep quiet about the empty shell that exists in place of my heart.

Seems like a fair trade-off.

As Kyler strides out a side door, I twist my neck from side to side, trying to get my head on straight for the next meet-and-greet. James plants a gentle hand on my lower back and urges me forward. "I'm sorry about Kyler. That was rude, but he doesn't mean it. He's going through some stuff, so don't take it personally."

I'll say, if that teeny glimpse is any indication. But I seal my lips as James leads me through a large utility room out into a narrow corridor. The sound of several voices chatting grows louder as we advance. I'm surprised, and a little uncomfortable, when James takes my hand and leads me into a vast open-plan kitchen and dining area. Floor-to-ceiling windows frame the room at the front, facing out onto the magnificent gardens.

All conversation mutes instantly, and eight heads fixate on me. I clasp James's hand more firmly, previous discomfort forgotten. "Everyone," he says, smiling warmly, "This is Faye."

I do a quick scan of the room, and my eyes almost bug out at the sight of so much male hotness. Three near-identical-looking boys are seated on benches surrounding a long narrow table at one end of the room. They have the same dark hair and blue eyes as Kyler, but their faces are rounder and still a little babyish. The triplets, I'm guessing.

Two older boys are propped against one side of a long, wide island unit, eyeing me intensely. One of the boys straightens up, crossing his arms around his chest as he blatantly stares at me through almond-shaped blue eyes. Biceps bulge under the short sleeves of his shirt, and my eyes gravitate to the edge of the tattoo peeking out. His hair is longer than the others, but that messy bed-head look suits him.

Kyler is leaning back against a marble countertop, sporting an impressively blank expression. Another boy is at his side, blatantly checking me out. He's a couple of inches shorter than Kyler and every bit as obnoxiously good-looking. He is wearing an unbuttoned black shirt and khaki shorts. Wide blue eyes lock on mine, and he winks. I lift a brow and his grin expands.

This gene pool is completely unfair to the rest of us mere mortals.

Add the obvious obscene wealth to the mix, and you have quite a heady combination. Girls must be crawling all over these dudes.

James squeezes my hand, and I refocus. Clearing my throat, I offer up a semi-confident smile. "Hi."

A stunning blonde-haired woman steps forward to greet me. Wearing a figure-hugging black pants suit with a cream silk blouse and a string of pearls at her neck, she is the epitome of classic chic. Her short hair is styled into an edgy bob that works well with her heart-shaped face. Her pale blue eyes are carbon copies of Kyler's.

"Oh my gosh, honey," she says, smiling as she reels me in for a hug. "It's so wonderful to meet you. I'm Alexandra Kennedy, but you can call me Alex." I stand awkwardly in her embrace, conscious of the focused stares of her seven sons.

All eyes are on us.

She steps back, holding me at arm's length. "Wow, I see my husband wasn't exaggerating. You are stunning. Totally gorgeous." Unease prickles my skin as she peruses my body. "Could you remove your sweater?"

Hello? WTF?

This family is so weird. With a capital W.

My eyes dart to hers as someone shouts out, "Now we're talking."

"Kalvin!" James reprimands his son, and a low chuckle rings out in the room.

"What?" I staple my arms over my chest, making my intent clear.

"Alex." James' tone is exasperated. "Leave the poor girl, alone. She only just got here!"

"Relax, sweetheart." She pats my arm. "I'm only trying to gauge your dimensions so Courtney can organize your closet."

"You could just ask," I suggest. "And Courtney is ...?"

"My personal assistant," Alex confirms. "She'll organize some things for you. Here's her business card." She thrusts a white, black, and red embossed card into my hand. "Email her your sizes and requirements tomorrow. I already have a few items in mind. With your figure, and your height, you can carry off most any look." She taps a finger against her lips as she ponders something. "Have you ever considered modeling, honey?"

A chorus of groans echoes in the room. "Mom! Seriously?" One of the triplets climbs out of his seat and crosses the floor. "Do you have to ask every person you come into contact with?" He stops in front of me, mock-bowing at the waist. Lifting my hand to his lips, he deposits a light kiss on my skin. "I'm Keaton." He straightens up. "And you're hot." He flashes a cheeky grin, and I can't help but reciprocate.

"Um, thanks?"

"And that's Kent and Keanu," he adds, pointing at the other two triplets who have yet to make a move. The stylishly groomed one gives me a quick wave while the sullen-faced boy barely tips his head in my direction. "Don't take their lack of enthusiasm too personally," Keaton explains. "Keanu, a.k.a. 'The Poser' is far too obsessed with himself and 'The Delinquent'— that's Kent—is probably too busy plotting his next criminal activity." Kent scowls at his brother with barely contained annoyance.

I'm trying to figure out if Keaton is joking or serious when the boy lounging beside Kyler pushes off the counter and saunters toward me. I notice a faint purplish mark on the side of his neck as he stands directly in front of me. Reaching out, he rubs locks of my hair between his fingers. I jerk back out of his reach. "What's with the hair?"

"What's with the hickey?" I retort, flicking my fingers in the direction of his marked skin. He tosses me a lazy smirk, as Keaton chuckles.

"Kalvin! Stop," Alex says, staging an intervention. "You're being very rude."

"We weren't the one asking for her bra size." Kalvin sends me a wolfish grin as he zones in on my chest. "C cup, if I had to guess. Of course"—he gives me a flirtatious wink—"I'd be more accurate if you let me feel." He cups his hands suggestively. Keaton shakes his head and rolls his eyes.

I moisten my dry lips. "In your dreams, sunshine."

"Don't worry, sweetheart"— he strokes my arm in a languid manner—"you'll definitely be featuring in a few wet dreams."

Ugh. TMI.

James wrestles Kalvin away from me. "That's enough! I will not listen to any more of that disgusting talk. Sit down, and don't even attempt to speak to your cousin until you regain a civil tongue."

Kalvin flips up his middle finger as he takes a seat at the table. "Love you too, Dad."

These boys are crazy. Certifiable.

One of the older boys—the scary well-built one—pushes off the island and strolls toward me. "I'm Keven."

Saliva pools in my mouth. "Hi."

He gives me a curt nod. "Not that this wasn't entertaining, but we've got to head back to Harvard."

"Okay." I don't know what else to say, and this boy kind of intimidates me.

The other boy appears behind him, leveling a vicious look at his dad. "If we'd known you were delayed, we could've arranged to spend the night, but you seem to have a habit of waiting far too long to inform us of important things." He doesn't attempt to disguise his embittered tone.

James shares a loaded look with Alex. "Kaden—"

He thrusts his palm in his dad's face. "I don't want to hear it. We're out of here." He tosses me a quick nod before clicking his fingers at his brother. Keven saunters out of the kitchen with him.

Okey-dokey, then.

Kyler's "fucked up" comment from earlier isn't so remiss now.

"I apologize for my sons, Faye," Alex says, knotting her hands in front of her chest. "Are you hungry? Greta put some leftovers in the refrigerator."

I shake my head. "Not really. I wouldn't mind heading to bed, if that's okay. It's been a long day." I'm still feeling nauseated, and I doubt I could stomach any food. Tiredness envelops me in a heavy blanket of exhaustion, and I yawn.

"Of course, sweetie." She drapes her arm around my shoulder. "I'll show you to your room."

We pass through a succession of generous-sized rooms before landing in a resplendent porcelain-tiled lobby. I notice the K logo everywhere as we pass, and I have to make a conscious effort not to roll my eyes. It's a tad over the top.

In the lobby, a decadent crystal chandelier hangs overhead, sending shards of glistening light raining down on us. An elegant glass display cabinet rests against one wall, filled with trophies and medals. Several black-framed photos and certificates reside on the other side of the wall, surrounding an old-fashioning-looking plaque that appears to be a coat of arms. A huge circular K logo is engraved into the center of the glossy floor. A narrow set of stairs resides at the back of the room, ascending toward a mezzanine level above.

We pass by the entrance door out into a corridor on the other side of the building. This part of the house seems more contained. Wooden doors line the passageway on both sides. Obviously, these are the bedrooms. Alex asks me random questions about school and my grades as we walk.

My room is more of a suite and almost bigger than my entire house back in Dublin. A gigantic bed occupies prime position along the rear wall. A massive walk-in wardrobe extends to the left with an en suite bathroom on my right. Light gossamer-type curtains drape across the wide window. I have a front row seat to the pool area outside. It's lit up and the water looks so inviting. Various soft couches and eating areas offer plenty of ways to maximize the outdoor space.

A small path snakes from the pool area out toward the woods at the rear of the property.

"I hope you'll be comfortable here," Alex says.

I turn to face her. "It's beautiful. Thank you for letting me live here. I promise I won't be any trouble."

She perches on the edge of the bed and pats the spot beside her. I sit down. "I already know that, sweetie. You're family, Faye. You belong with us, and we hope one day soon to make that official."

A layer of ice hardens my heart as I tilt my chin up. "What do you mean?"

"James and I would like to adopt you, Faye."

Chapter Five

All the blood leaves my body at once. A sharp, twisty pain lodges in the pit of my stomach, and the icy layer around my heart shatters, driving imaginary splinters deep into the very center of me. "Oh, sweetie, I didn't mean to upset you," Alex rushes to reassure me. "I just want you to know that James and I will love you as if you are our own flesh and blood. We want you to be on an even footing with the boys. For them to be your brothers."

"Don't I get a say?" My voice quakes.

Gently, she grasps my hands. "Of course, you do. I'm sorry. I shouldn't have said anything. It's too soon. I only want you to feel like a proper part of the family. To know you aren't alone."

One part of me gets that and is grateful, but another part of me wants to run as far away from this madhouse as possible.

I don't know if I want a new ready-made family.

I still haven't come to terms with losing the one I had.

Tears well in my eyes, but I blink them away. I scoot down the bed, propping against the headrest as I tuck my knees into my chest.

This is too much. I can't deal.

"I appreciate the gesture, but I can't even contemplate that right now. I have a plan for my future, and I don't know where, or if, all this"—I wave my hands around the room—"fits into the overall scheme of things. And it's way too soon to be even considering something like that." The "adoption" word is stuck in my throat, refusing articulation.

I don't want a new mum and dad.

I want my old ones back.

Her eyes are kind as she looks at me. "I'm sorry, Faye. That was insensitive of me. You're still grieving. Take whatever time you need. We've no intention of doing anything without your approval, so don't worry. Forget about it for now."

I can only nod.

She stands. "Try and get some sleep. I'll be away on a business trip for the next few days, but I'll call you tomorrow. Courtney will be here, and she'll get you anything you need. We'll talk more when I'm back."

She halts at the door, her fingers curling around the handle. "I'd prefer if we kept this conversation between us. We haven't spoken to the boys yet, and I'd rather they hear it from us."

"Sure." Yeah, I've zero desire to drop that bomb on my cousins. They don't need additional reasons to be wary of me.

The door snicks shut, and I flop down on the bed, staring at the stark white ceiling. Everything is foreign, and I can't remember ever feeling this alone.

Stripping off my clothes, I take a long, hot shower.

Re-dressing in a pair of sleep shorts and my white lacy bra, I sit cross-legged on the bed and retrieve my phone from my bag. Quickly computing the time difference, I FaceTime Jill, hoping Rachel is with her and that they are still up. A comforting sensation spreads over me as Jill's familiar face fills the screen. Rachel's head materializes in the frame, and I grin. "How's it going?" she asks.

"It is *so* good to see you. I miss you guys so much already."

"Ditto. We can't believe you are actually gone, *gone*." There's a pregnant pause before Jill forces a smile on her face. "So, what's it like there?"

"Honestly, it's pretty insane." I proceed to give them a blow-by-blow account of everything from the plane to the car journey to the house and meeting the boys.

"Ohmigawd!" Rachel shrieks. "I love Kennedy Apparel! Do you think you can get them to send me some clothes? I had my eye on this amazing dress from the autumn collection, but it'd bankrupt me to buy it."

I roll my eyes. "Seriously, Rach? My whole world's been turned upside down, and you want me to score you some freebies?"

She looks instantly chastised. "I know that, and I'm sorry. I'm just super excited. This is big!"

I get up and pace the floor. "I wish you guys could be here to see it with your own eyes. It's ... I can't even find the words." It's fucking overwhelming, and I still can't work out how I feel about it. "That K brand is everywhere, and all my cousin's names start with K. I mean, it's like no other letter exists in the feckin' alphabet. It's the biggest load of pretentious bullshit I've ever come across. How am I going to live with these people? My aunt and uncle seem decent enough, but my cousins are either downright hostile or cagey or ripping the piss out of me. I..." I rub a hand low on my belly in an attempt to calm my churning stomach.

A low whistle pricks my ears, and I jump in fright, almost dropping the phone. Kalvin is lounging against the doorframe, wearing only khaki shorts, which hang low on his hips, giving me a full view of his ripped abs. His eyes unashamedly rake me up and down, and anger ignites my insides. "What the hell are you doing?"

"Hey, hot stuff." He pushes off the door and saunters toward me. "Who you talking to?"

Before I have a chance to answer, he's whipped the phone from my hands and he's introducing himself to my friends.

"I think I'll have to immigrate to Ireland when I graduate. You *lay-dees* are mighty fine."

Jill and Rachel practically drool at the mouth, and I shake my head. "You're like a walking American cliché. Do girls here actually fall for that cheesy crap?"

He messes up my hair, smirking at my scowl. "Works every time."

A snort escapes me, and he laughs. "The guys in school are going to go crazy for you. Hot and sassy is the ideal catch." He lets out another low whistle as he circles me, his eyes inspecting every inch of me. Jill and Rachel titter like three-year-olds. Fat lot of use they are. "They'll be walking around with permanent boners," Kalvin adds.

I cross my arms protectively over my chest. "I'm not interested in boys."

"You're batting for the other team? Man, that's totally hot."

Another round of giggles emits from the phone, and I'm starting to get really irritated with my friends. Kalvin doesn't seem to need much encouragement, and their juvenile behavior isn't helping.

"I'm not gay."

He winks. "Prove it then." Puckering his lips, he makes a kissing sound as he steps in front of me with a devilish grin.

"Knock it off." I shove a hand in his chest, keeping him at bay.

I ignore my friends who are currently acting like brainless dimwits, hollering at me to kiss him.

He leans in, sniffing my neck, and I jerk back in alarm. He cranks out a laugh. "Relax, cuz. I'm only messing about." I narrow my eyes, and he laughs again. "Or maybe not." He nuzzles my neck with his nose. "Maybe I'm into the whole kissing cousins mentality."

Jill and Rachel start yelling demands at me again, and I snatch the phone out of Kalvin's hands while he's distracted. I press the button to disconnect the feed as he dips his head and presses his mouth to my collarbone. I nearly jump out of my skin.

"What the hell is going on here?" Caught off guard, I emit a screech, and the phone flies out of my hand, spinning across the room.

Kyler stalks into the room, his eyes moving from the stubborn set of my eyes to my mouth and onto my semi-exposed chest. I stare back at him, and we face off for a few seconds. My mouth is suddenly desert-dry, and the air is charged with ... something indecipherable.

"Do yourself a favor, Ky," Kalvin says, chuckling. "Don't let Addison see you looking at her like that, or there'll be hell to pay."

Kyler grasps him by the shoulders, pulling him upright. "Don't talk crap, and stay out of her room, Kal. I told you already. No sleazing. She's our cousin, you sicko. Don't think I won't beat your ass."

Kalvin snorts. "As if. I can easily take you."

He's clearing bluffing. While Kalvin is tall and broad and looks like he can take care of himself, he isn't an even match for Kyler.

"Besides, we both know you can't risk injury right now." Kalvin sends him a smug smile.

"Out. Now." Kyler drags him toward the door, and they both leave without even acknowledging me.

I gulp as I stand rooted to the spot. I'm not sure if I'm wanted here. At least not by my cousins. James said the triplets were excited, but that wasn't the impression they gave off in the kitchen. With the exception of Keaton, and possibly Kalvin, the rest of my cousins didn't exude overly welcoming vibes.

They don't want me here.

I don't want to be here.

At least we have that much in common.

Air whooshes out of my mouth as I claw my fingers through my damp hair. Remembering my phone, I scramble toward it, dropping to my knees. Flipping it over, I feel like crying when I see the smashed screen, and not just because I no longer have a way of staying in touch with my friends. This phone represents the last birthday gift I received from my parents. I wonder if it's repairable.

I plop onto my bum, crossing my legs in front of me. Tears linger at the base of my eyes, waiting for instruction, ready to break free. And it's tempting. Oh, so tempting. How I'd love to let loose, to let it gush forth like the Nile. But I'm afraid that once I open the floodgates, I won't be able to shut them again.

A subtle movement at the door causes my heart rate to kick off again, and I lift my head. Kyler blocks the doorframe with his powerful body. Smoldering eyes lock on mine as he sticks me with an intense gaze. I wonder how long he's been watching me and what insight he's gleaned this time. I can't show vulnerability around a guy like him. He'll most likely latch onto that and try to use it against me. If he's anything like me, he won't be happy that I saw inside him, that I glimpsed a sliver of the inner turmoil he's in.

I need to regain control.

Clutching the broken phone to my chest, I climb to my feet and glare at him. Throwing his words back at him, I snap, "Are you done drooling yet?"

A slight twitch of his lips—barely perceptible—is the only clue to his response. Stepping back into the corridor, he pulls the door shut without a word.

I crawl into bed, wishing I could fast forward the next few months.

I wake a few hours later in desperate need of the bathroom. I'm creeping back into bed when I spy a lonesome figure trekking across the lawn toward the entrance to the woods. It's too dark to tell who it is. Glancing at the clock on my wall, I note it's past one a.m. *What on earth are they doing outside at this time of night?* If I wasn't so wrecked, I might be tempted to follow, but I can barely lift a muscle. I watch the retreating form until it's swallowed up by the forest.

I sleep fitfully the rest of the night, tossing and turning relentlessly. Jet lag and anxiety clearly don't sit well together. At five a.m., I give up the fight and change into my swimsuit. Grabbing a towel from the en suite press, I head out in search of the pool.

The house is unearthly quiet as I pad through the empty corridors. After about ten minutes of trying different passageways, I finally find the exit leading outside.

The air is already balmy, even at this early hour. Lilting little chirps emanate from the vicinity of the forest as I slip into the heated pool. My limbs relax as I dive in and out of the water. Limbering up, I swim countless laps of the pool as day breaks, only getting out when I feel an achy exhaustion seeping bone deep. Wrapping the towel around my body, I head inside.

Faint sounds of music reach my ears as I walk the corridor leading to my bedroom. Curious, I keep walking beyond my door, beyond the corridor, and out into a wide recreational room. Huge black leather couches surround the biggest wall-mounted screen I've ever seen. Tons of Xbox paraphernalia litter the top of the low coffee table. A foosball table rests beside a pool table on the other side of the room, alongside a snazzy-looking stereo system.

A bunch of framed photos occupies one wall, and I move closer to inspect them. I spot Kalvin and at least one of the triplets captured in action on the football field. Others show a helmeted figure atop a dirt bike on a mucky track. Kyler, I'd guess, judging by the covetous display in the garage last night. There are photos of a younger Keven shooting hoops on the basketball court and ones of Kaden playing baseball. Professional modeling shots of one of the triplets look out of place, but there's no denying the boy was born to be in front of a camera. He has that moody pout down to an art form.

I keep walking along another corridor lined with doors on either side. I sneak a peek into some of the rooms as I pass. One houses a private cinema complete with popcorn station and reclining chairs, and another grants entry to the indoor pool.

The music grows louder as I approach the very last room. I open the door slowly and quietly and peer in. It's a reasonably sized gym with a multitude of different equipment. Kyler's back is facing me from his position on a cycling machine. His well-defined legs are thrusting so fast I can't even follow the movement. His upper torso is bare, and every inch of his muscled back glistens with sweat. Well-developed arms grip the handlebars as he lifts his ass off the chair and cycles half-standing. My eyes are glued to his firm ass cheeks, and my face flares up. He is sex on legs, and it's doing funny things to my insides.

I may have only just met him, but I know his type.

Kyler is trouble.

Major trouble.

So why the hell does that excite me so much?

Why do I feel drawn to him instead of wanting to run a million miles away?

I don't need to answer my own question. I already know, but I'm not willing to face facts yet; to acknowledge that I'm in way more danger here than I imagined.

Suppressing my concern, I quietly shut the door before he notices my presence.

Chapter Six

Back in my room, I get dressed and carefully blow-dry my hair, wondering what Mum would make of my new, bold style. It seems appropriate that I no longer look the same, because, on the inside, I can scarcely remember who I am anymore.

Two of the triplets are already sitting at the table eating breakfast when I arrive in the kitchen. "Morning."

"Yo," Keaton—I think—says, giving me a thumbs-up. The other one, whose name I can't remember, mumbles a measly hello under his breath.

The island unit is full to the brim with a variety of different foods. Taking a plate, I load up with scrambled eggs and bacon and pour myself a glass of cranberry juice.

I slide onto the bench beside Keaton and tuck in. In between mouthfuls, I try to draw the boys into conversation. "So, is there some trick for telling you guys apart?"

"He's the one with the poisoned dick and the affliction for taking things that don't belong to him," Keaton supplies, jabbing his spoon pointedly in his brother's direction.

I almost choke on my eggs.

"And he's the one with his V-card still intact," his brother retorts. His smirk is nasty as he points his finger at a rapidly reddening Keaton.

I feel instantly defensive of him. "Wow, thanks for clarifying that. Super helpful. Maybe I'll just buy name badges." A tinge of sarcasm laces my tone.

Keaton recovers, nudging me gently. "That's Kent. He's the shortest of the three of us."

"Dude!" Kent protests. "By one-freaking-half inch."

"It still counts. She's looking for some way to tell us apart, and I'm explaining the most obvious way."

Kent pushes his empty plate away, leaning his elbows on the table. "Keaton is the joker around here, and Keanu is the tallest and the vainest. Exactly the way Mom likes it."

Both boys scowl.

"What?" I glance from one to the other.

"Keanu models for Mom." Now I know which triplet was in the framed shots back in the games room. "That's where he is now. At *work*." Kent spits the word out like venom. "He thinks he's this major celebrity 'cause his face has hit the billboard in Times Square."

"She didn't want you guys?" I'm incredulous, because all three of them are totally gorgeous and definitely model-worthy. Hell, the whole family is. Alex could probably save a fortune by lining her family up for photo shoots instead of hiring the latest supermodels.

Kent drums his fingers off the table. "Oh, she did. But there's no way I'm doing that pompous shit. Modeling's for pussies."

"And there you have it." Keaton drains his juice and slams the glass down on the table.

"Keanu does what Keanu wants. Always has." Kent shrugs indifferently. "We're too far beneath him now." He stands up. "I hate thinking of this shit. Puts me in a bad mood. Later, bitches." He strides out of the room, leaving a sour note in his wake.

"Don't pay any attention to him. Kent's angry at the entire universe."

I twist to face him, swinging one leg over the other side of the bench. "I thought triplets would have this amazing bond. You guys aren't close?"

"Nah, we are." He looks reflective as he stares blankly out the window. "Not as much as we used to be." He shrugs. "Guess we can't stay joined at the hip forever."

"True, dat."

He grins. "I've always wanted to visit Ireland, and Dad has promised us so many times, but for one reason or another, it's never happened. What's it like?"

"It's great." I pull my knees up to my chest, resting my feet on the bench. "It's so beautiful and the people are so friendly and"—a raw lump sticks in my throat—"actually, could we talk about something else? Anything else?"

His look softens. "You miss home." I bob my head. "You don't want to be here, do you?"

"I ..." I sigh. "It's not that. It all happened so fast, and I'm still trying to get used to the idea. Plus, your brothers don't seem overly enamored at my presence."

He leans in. "Try not to take it to heart. We don't have an issue with you here per se; it's just that Mom and Dad have been fussing over your arrival, and Mom even took a day off work. They don't tend to do stuff like that." A dark cloud passes over his face.

"I'm sure that's not true." I remember how James' face lit up when he was talking about his sons.

Keaton shakes his head and a teasing smirk surfaces. "Look at me, hitting you with the heavy stuff already. We should go out and have some fun. There's only two weeks left until school starts back so we should make the most of it. If you like?"

Considering Keaton seems like the only one who actually *wants* to spend time with me, I'd be a fool to turn him down. "'Kay. What did you have in mind?"

He opens his mouth to answer when we're distracted by a new arrival. Kyler strolls into the room, wearing black jeans, heavy-style boots, a plain black T-shirt, and an open black leather jacket. Add his attire to his unshaven face, and the dangerous glint in his eyes, and he looks like a total badass. Aaaannnddd ... it's like a shot of pure adrenaline straight to my hormones. An unfamiliar coil twists low as fire explodes in my lower belly.

I was wrong last night. Kyler isn't just trouble. He's an apocalypse-level disaster waiting to happen. I need to find some fallout shelter to hide in. And quick.

45

Kyler plonks a heavy-looking helmet on the island, and it lands with a loud thud. "Joker." He nods his head at Keaton as he grabs a covered bowl of pasta from the fridge.

I must be invisible.

"You eat pasta for breakfast?" The words fly out of my mouth unfiltered.

Kyler places the bowl in the microwave and switches it on. Slowly, he turns and faces me. He replies without even looking at me. "I'm in training." The words sound begrudging as they leave his mouth, and that's obviously all I'm getting.

"Training for what?"

Pouring a large glass of juice, he knocks it back in one go. His throat works hard as he swallows, and even that is sexy. He eyeballs me without replying. After a couple of seconds, I force myself to look away, pulling my legs back in under the table.

The guy is an ignorant ass.

"You heading to the track?" Keaton asks him.

"Yep," is Kyler's succinct response.

My brows knit together. Keaton notices, and he takes pity on me. "Ky is a serious dirt bike rider. He almost made pro last season. You'll notice how dedicated he is when it comes to exercise and nutrition."

Kyler slams his bowl down on the table as he slides into place beside his brother. "Keaton." With that one word, he silences his little bro.

"Dad says you're into swimming?" Keaton asks, deliberately changing the subject.

Kyler keeps his head down, wolfing his pasta, as he deliberately avoids engaging in our conversation.

"Yeah. At one point, I was serious about it as a sport, but"—I stop, well aware of the reasons why I gave up that ambition—"I guess I outgrew it," I lie.

Kyler lifts his chin and stares at me. I plant my poker face on and wait it out. Sure enough, he relinquishes his interest when he sees I'm giving nothing away. When he's finished eating, he gets up, snatching a bottle of water before he leaves.

I release the breath I'd been holding.

"Friendly, isn't he?" Keaton jokes.

I only contemplate responding after his footsteps fade. "Is he always that intimidating?"

He releases an amused laugh. "For as long as I can remember, he's rocked that mean and moody vibe but not to the same extent. Addison did a real number on him. He's shut himself off from pretty much everyone. Now he lives for motocross and that's about it."

That's the second time that girl has been mentioned. Judging by the comments, I'm guessing she's an ex.

As if on cue, the roar of an engine tickles my eardrums, and I watch as Kyler emerges from the garage at high speed. The bike swerves from side to side as he expertly maneuvers it down the driveway and out of sight.

"Wanna head into town for a tour?" Keaton asks, his eyes lighting up.

"Sure. That sounds great."

He jumps up, grinning. "I'll meet you in the lobby in ten."

I start loading our dishes into the dishwasher as a petite woman with neat gray hair enters the kitchen. "You must be Faye?" She smiles warmly.

"Yes."

"I'm Greta. I work for the Kennedys. It's very nice to meet you."

"Same here."

"Go on." She shoos me away. "Unless you want my job?" Her teasing tone is kind.

I'm walking through the lobby when the doorbell rings. I open the door without hesitation and clock the stunner standing on the doorstep. She perfectly represents my vision of the all-American sweetheart. Her golden locks cascade down her back in flawless straight lines. Her slim figure is clothed in a short white mini-dress that displays her tan skin to perfection. Although she's slender, curves flow in and out of her body in all the right places. Her lips are plump as they pull back in a sweet smile. Brilliant white teeth beam at me.

I hate her instantly.

I can't quite explain it.

I can count on one hand the number of people I've taken an instant dislike to, and this girl is one of them.

And it's not because she's my polar opposite—I don't like the vibes she's emitting. Oh, she might look like butter wouldn't melt, but there's a viper hidden underneath the surface, waiting for the right moment to strike.

My guard goes up immediately.

"Oh, you're new," she says flippantly. "I'm here for Kyler."

"He's not here, Addison." Keaton shows up, placing a protective arm around my shoulders. "And even if he was, you know he'd tell you to get lost." Malice is evident in his tone.

Addison's alert green eyes assess the situation. "Getting it on with the help now, Keaton? That's low. Even for you."

Keaton drills her with a contemptuous look. "This is our Irish cousin. She's living with us now. Better get used to her face because she's all anyone's going to be talking about at Old Colonial."

Addison's eyes narrow suspiciously, as she takes in my outfit. The viper starts to raise its ugly head. Internally, I bristle at the obvious look of disgust on her face, but outwardly, I'm Switzerland.

"My bad. It's unusual to see a Kennedy so"—she taps a manicured finger off her bottom lip—"casually dressed."

What a nasty bitch.

"And it's unusual to see you with your clothes on," Keaton bites back. "So I guess that makes you even. Was there anything else?" He moves to close the door.

"Tell Kyler I called."

"Bye, Addison." Keaton slams the door in her face, and I laugh.

"Holy crap." I lean against the side of the door. "They're all going to be like that, aren't they?"

His look is apologetic again. "Pretty much."

"Oh, joy. I can hardly wait."

"Watch out for that one—she's lethal. Every pretty girl is competition, and judging by that reaction, you're most definitely on her hit list."

"Who is she exactly?" I ask, as we walk the corridor toward the bedrooms.

"She was the love of Ky's life, until she ruined him."

Chapter Seven

Max, the Kennedy's chauffeur—*yes, they have a full-time chauffeur*—drives us into town. "So what exactly went down with Kyler and Addison?" I ask, as we sit side by side in the backseat. Purposely inspecting my nails, I'm trying my best to appear innocent.

Keaton splutters. "No way." He holds up his hands. "I'm not touching that."

I try a different approach. "It's no biggie. I'm only trying to understand your brothers. Apart from you and Kalvin, the rest of them seem pretty closed off. Maybe if I knew what was going on with them ..."

"You'll find out soon enough, and then you'll wish you'd left well enough alone," he replies cryptically.

"What did ... Kaden mean last night? He has some issue with your parents?" All the K names are confusing me, so I hope I've referenced the right cousin.

"You caught that, huh?"

"He wasn't exactly subtle."

He angles his body and his knees brush against mine. "He's been acting like that ever since he turned eighteen. Keven too. I swear, for a while, I actually thought they were in some secret 'coming of age' club"—he gestures with his fingers—"you know, like Jacob and Co. in *Twilight* when they became members of the wolf pack and they couldn't talk about it?"

I burst out laughing. "You think your brothers are shape shifters?"

He grins. "It'd be cool, right?"

"Totally." I laugh. Keaton is so easy to like. "But I doubt that's in the realm of possibility, so what do you think it could be?"

His smile withers up and dies. "I don't know. Only that it's nothing good. Things have been strained between them ever since. If the same thing happens when Ky turns eighteen next year, then I'm definitely reevaluating my wolf pack theories."

He loops his arm in mine as Max slows the car down. "Anyway, enough of my idiot brothers," Keaton says. "Ready for your guided tour?"

"Can't wait." A genuine smile plays across my lips as I beam at my cousin. I'm glad I'm developing a rapport with at least one of them.

We get out in the middle of a busy town. It's modern but quaint. Keaton is animated as he points places out to me. We walk around for hours, peppering each other with questions. Keaton knows everything about everyone, it seems, and he introduces me to people left and right. The names fly over my head. Some are friendly, others less so. The boys seem more enthusiastic than the girls, and that isn't in anyway reassuring. Most of them go to Wellesley Old Colonial, the private school my cousins go to and the one I'll also be attending.

Spotting a bench, I plop down, and my aching legs offer up silent thanks. "I'm knackered," I tell him as he drops down beside me.

He laughs. "You're what?"

"Worn out, tired." I grin back at him. "That's a new one, huh?"

"Yeah, and I'm most definitely storing it for future use." He gives me a cheeky wink. "How about I treat you to lunch, and then we can head back?"

"Sounds like a plan."

He opens the door to Legend's Diner and Family Restaurant, stepping sideways to allow me to enter first. A pretty girl with shocking pink hair and warm brown eyes shows us to a booth by the window. Keaton says hi to a few school friends before sliding in beside me. I order a Cobb salad and iced tea and settle back in my seat.

My eyes rove over the diner, and it's like stepping back to the 1960s. The black-and-white checkered, tiled floor contrasts perfectly with the red-and-white themed booths. Quirky signs dot the walls at odd angles in a strangely stylistic fashion. Black, white, and red drapes frame the windows. It's contemporary *and* old-fashioned, mirroring my first impression of the town.

People sit on high stools in front of a long counter at the top of the restaurant. An old-fashioned jukebox throws out tunes from another era, and my foot taps idly off the floor. A shadow darkens the tabletop and I look up at the musclehead clearly checking me out.

His shoulders are so broad it's a wonder he squeezed through the door. Bulging arms stretch over a fitted green shirt, and he wears black cargo shorts and black-and-white runners. His sandy hair is half-hidden under a branded cap. "It appears the rumors are true." He's blatantly undressing me with his eyes. "Nice." He whistles appreciatively.

"Fuck off, Jeremy," Keaton says. "And stay away from her."

"Now, now, little Kennedy." Jeremy tousles Keaton's hair in a condescending manner. "That's no way to speak to your elders."

"Speak to this." Keaton gives him the middle finger, and I almost choke on my laugh.

"Don't mind this douche." Jeremy reaches out and takes my hand uninvited. "He is utterly clueless when it comes to the opposite sex." Keaton's face turns puce as Jeremy winks, then lifts my hand, and presses his mouth to my knuckles.

I wrench my hand back and pin him with a ferocious glare. "On the contrary." I lean forward on my elbows. "Keaton has been perfect company all morning."

"Damn." He rubs a hand over his stomach. "You are too fucking cute. You're killing me with that accent." Lifting a hand to the side of his mouth, he hollers, "Yo, guys! Get over here already!"

There's a virtual stampede to our booth, and I squirm in my seat. Keaton groans and rolls his eyes. At least seven or eight boys loom over the table, taking their fill of me.

They are all giants. Like, at least six foot three or more. Most of them are examining me as if I'm a Big Mac with fries, and it's creeping me out. But I won't give them the satisfaction of knowing they are getting to me. Schooling my features into a disinterested line, I stare impassively at them.

One of the guys hangs back. He's very good-looking with blond hair and crystal-clear blue eyes. He shoots me a sympathetic look, and I smile. The boys in front of me go wild, and some jackass starts spouting crap about pretty Irish eyes and smiles. I tune them out as I wonder what kind of stuff is in the water around here.

"Clear out! Coming through," a confident female voice shouts out, and the hot crowd dispels. I slump in relief. The pretty waitress with the pink hair slides a plate in front of me, nudging the remaining guys out of the way with her hip. "Get lost, Jeremy, or I'll have you thrown out."

"You wouldn't dare, Rosie," he retorts.

Fixing her hands on her slim hips, she glares at him. "For the millionth time, my name is Rose. R.O.S.E with no I. And I would, and you know it."

He backs up, palms raised. "'Kay. You win. I'm going. Lovely to meet you, Ireland." He winks, blowing me a kiss before he reclaims his seat.

Ugh. I shiver all over.

I look up at Rose. "Thanks."

"No problem. He's a total jerk, and he's riddled. You should steer clear." She winks as she moves on to the next booth.

"Does everyone from your school come here then?"

"It's a popular hangout," Keaton confirms, before taking a huge bite of his burger.

After we've finished eating, Keaton heads to the bathroom while I studiously avoid looking in Jeremy's direction. He has barely taken his eyes off me the entire time.

A sign on the far wall summons me, and my feet move of their own accord. Leaning over the counter, I gesture for Rose's attention, pointing at the notice. "Are you still looking for a waitress?"

"Yeah. You interested?"

"Definitely."

Something flickers in her eyes. "Any experience?"

"I worked part time in a restaurant back home in Dublin, and I'm a quick learner."

"You can handle yourself?" She gives me a brief once-over.

"Yep." My eyes drill into hers, daring her to challenge me.

She ponders for a minute or two. "Yeah, I think you can. Hang tight." She darts into the back, returning a moment later with an older man with dark hair and hard hazel eyes. His skin is heavily tanned and lined, and it's hard to gauge his age. He is tall and broad with a flabby stomach that hangs over the band of his trousers. "I'm David." He offers me his hand, and I shake it, trying not to grimace at his clammy grip. "I own this joint."

We talk for a few minutes, and I notice Keaton hovering beside me with an amused expression on his face. David asks me to come back on Friday for a working trial, and I leave the diner with a massive smile on my face.

"Why the hell did you do that?" Keaton asks once we're securely tucked in the back of the car.

"I need a job."

He almost gags. "For what?"

"For money. What else?" I pin him with a skeptical look. "Haven't you ever had a job?"

"Nope, and I plan to stave that off for as long as possible." He leans back in his seat, holding his hands behind his head.

"I like working. It's good to feel independent. And I like having something else besides school and swimming."

"You don't need to. You'll get an allowance like the rest of us. Dad's going to blow a gasket."

"He's not my dad, and I don't get why it's such a big deal." I cross my arms, as a surge of irritation surfaces. I agreed to come and live with them, and I will be respectful of their rules, but they're not going to cage me, or turn me into something I'm not. I'm no sponger, and I like to be financially independent. I refuse to take their money.

The car drops us off at the front entrance, and the door opens immediately. A gorgeous blonde-haired girl waits to greet us, and I blink profusely. For a minute there, I thought it was Alex. Or a green-eyed younger version of Alex. This girl sports the same edgy haircut, the same type of stylish clothing, and an equally warming smile, except hers doesn't quite meet her eyes.

"Courtney," Keaton greets the woman. "You're early."

"No," she chastises, pinching his cheek in an affectionate manner. "You're late!"

I stand awkwardly in front of them, feeling like an intruder. "You must be Faye. I'm delighted to meet you." If her grin was any wider, it'd split her face.

"Nice to meet you too."

"Come on through," she says, motioning me forward. "We have lots to get sorted." She steers me to my bedroom, locking the door firmly behind us. "You didn't email me your sizes, so I had to improvise." She looks me up and down with a contemplative expression.

"My phone is broken. Sorry."

"Oh, yes. Of course. Here you go." She extracts a shiny, silver phone and hands it to me. "I switched your old sim over and transferred all your data so you should be good to go." My mouth hangs open. This is the latest model and so hard to get back home. Plus, I have a custom Kennedy Apparel phone cover.

"How did you kn—"

She ushers me into the walk-in wardrobe. "It's my job to know these things. Come, let me show you how to coordinate your outfits."

I don't know how long we stay in there, but it feels like centuries before we emerge into the fading daylight. Who knew trying on clothes could be so exhausting? I feel like I've just swum one hundred lengths of the pool with a ten-ton weight strapped to my back. I have never seen so many expensive clothes in my life. Thank God, none of them had any labels on. I'd probably collapse if I knew exactly how much my entire wardrobe cost.

All those clothes and not a single pair of jeans in sight. None of them is anything I'd ever pick for myself. Cute dresses, skirts, and tops are not my usual style. I'm much more of a jeans and tee type of girl.

"Faye?" Courtney drags me back into the moment. "Did you hear me?" A note of frustration enters her tone.

"Sorry, Courtney. I was a million miles away."

She gives me a stiff smile. "I said do you need anything else?"

"No, I'm good." I tuck my hair behind my ears. I'm not going to appear ungrateful. I brought enough jeans to see me through the next few months, so I'll manage. "Thanks so much. I appreciate you doing all that for me."

"It's my job." She's decidedly snippy all of a sudden, and I detect a trace of bitterness. It's almost imperceptible, and most would probably miss it, but I have an uncanny ability to pick up on stuff like that.

Mom used to say I was a shrewd people watcher, a good judge of character.

There was a time when I might've agreed, but after what happened, I realized the brutal truth: I was actually a *terrible* judge of character.

Chapter Eight

Dinner is a pretty awkward affair. James must've decided to invent his own version of twenty questions as he launches into a lengthy interrogation, asking me all about my school and my friends back home. I notice he steers clear of any topic involving my parents. I'm not sure if that's for my benefit or his. Kalvin smirks every time I speak. Kyler studiously ignores me, and Kent looks bored to tears. Keaton is the only one who engages in conversation with us.

I offer to serve dessert purely to take a break from the tension at the table. I'm instantly suspicious when Kalvin hops up to help. I'm slicing the cake when I feel a slight pressure against my leg. Kalvin leans around me to slide plates onto the counter. His body pins me from behind, and his hand lands heavily on my upper thigh. I shriek and every head at the table turns in my direction. Kalvin's hand rubs up and down my thigh as he laughs quietly.

Is this his idea of a joke?

I decide to call his bluff. "I think it's rather foolish to feel me up while I'm in possession of such a big knife." I speak clearly, brandishing the sharp utensil in the air. "And you should know I'm not opposed to using it."

The bench screeches as James shoves it back, stalking around the island unit toward his son. There's a thunderous look on his face. Kalvin steps back, holding up his hands in defeat. "Chill, Dad. It's hardly

SIOBHAN DAVIS

my fault if Faye has no sense of humor." I whip around and glare at him. "You know I was only kidding."

"Try that again and I'll cut it off." I slice the knife through the air to drive my point home.

James gently takes my wrist and removes the knife from my grip.

"My hand or my dick," Kalvin asks, seeming unperturbed.

"That's it. Out now." James stabs a finger in the direction of the door.

Reaching around me, Kalvin grabs a piece of cake and stuffs half of it in his mouth before sidling back over to the table, blatantly ignoring his father. He drops onto the bench beside Kyler, grinning at me through a mouthful of chocolate crumbs. He sticks his middle finger up at James, and he sighs in exasperation.

Shaking my head, I hand the plates around.

I've only taken a couple of spoonsful of cake when something warm brushes against my leg. My eyes dart to Kalvin automatically. His devilish grin tells me all I need to know. I narrow my eyes at him as his foot starts stroking up and down my calf. His gaze is challenging. This guy does not know when to quit.

Let's bring it.

My move.

Under the table, I slip my foot out of my sandal and discreetly angle my body forward. Very slowly, I lick the chocolate cake remnants from the back of my spoon in deliberate, seductive strokes. At the same time, I stretch my leg out and begin a journey up the inside of his leg. Kalvin's eyes pop wide and he jumps a little, but his eyes stay locked on my tongue. Kyler glances sideway at him, following his gaze to mine. He surveys us intensely. Keaton and James are chatting away, and Kent is staring off into space, totally oblivious to anything around him.

I move my foot higher and higher, and a dark glint flashes in Kalvin's eyes. His smile is mocking. He doesn't think I'll follow through. He's about to find out that I don't back down from a challenge. My foot hits that sensitive area between his legs and he gasps. I can't hide my smile. I curl my toes as my foot makes a circular motion back and forth across his hardening length. A teasing smirk plays across my lips as I quicken the pace. The mocking quality is missing from Kalvin's stare now, replaced by something much darker. I move my foot even faster, and he squirms in his seat. Kyler's eyes drop to Kalvin's lap, and I know he can see what's going on, but his expression doesn't falter. Kalvin jumps in his seat, rattling the table, and James levels a perplexed look at his son.

"You okay over there, Kalvin? You seem awfully jumpy tonight." I don't know how I manage to say it with a straight face.

He looks almost pained as he grits out, "Peachy."

When it's obvious he's almost at the point of no return, I pull my leg back and sit up straighter in my chair.

Now, that'll teach him.

The look in his eyes shifts, and he scrambles out of his seat as if there's a nuclear-charged rocket up his ass. "Uh, bathroom." He dashes from the room as I clamp a hand over my mouth to stop myself from exploding.

Kyler faces away but not before I see a slight smile tug up the corners of his mouth.

Kalvin may have won round one, but I've nailed this one.

"Can I talk to you?" I ask James the next morning after we've all finished eating breakfast.

"Of course. Join me in my study."

His study is located on the mezzanine level accessed by the staircase in the lobby. The master suite, which he shares with Alex, is also up here along with their private living area. He steers me into the study, and my jaw hangs open. It's exactly like one of those libraries you see in old stately homes in the movies but without the high ceilings. It's all dark wood and dim lighting. Row upon row of shelves is filled with thousands of books. An elegant mahogany desk and chair lies to one side while two huge grandfather chairs, covered in red velvet cushioning, rest in front of an old-fashioned open fireplace. It's a million miles away from the modern interiors of the rest of the property. There's a certain old-world charm about the room that is instantly inviting.

"Take a seat," he says, and I plop down. He walks to his desk and retrieves two large leather-bound photo albums. "I presume you want to ask me about your mum?"

"Yeah." It's barely been out of my thoughts since I found out about my secret relatives in America. "Why were you two no longer in contact?"

He sighs deeply as he pours himself a drink from a crystal decanter. Noticing my skeptical look, he says, "I know it's early in the day, but I need a drink for this."

Sitting in the chair beside me, he looks lost in thought. His chin lifts and his piercing blue eyes stare into mine. He looks far too young to be a father to so many children. I guess it must be all the good living.

"I was nineteen when your mum ran away," he starts explaining, swirling the amber liquid in his glass. "We were as close as any two siblings could be. Closer, perhaps." He looks away as the ghosts of the past resurrect to taunt him. His Adam's apple jumps in his throat. "Our parents died when she was fourteen and I was sixteen. Did she even mention that?"

"She told me her parents died in a house fire and that she had to fend for herself after that."

He shakes his head sadly. "She wasn't alone. She had me. In a lot of ways, we were better off. Our parents were … neglectful at the best of times. Saoirse and me were always close but never more so than when we were on our own. I got a job in the local factory so I could take care of her. I insisted she stayed in school so she could complete her education."

He clamps his hands around his nose and mouth. When he speaks again, he's all choked up. "I was happy to do it. I loved her, and I only wanted the very best for her."

James genuinely loved my mum. That is as obvious as the nose on my face. So what happened that Mum relegated him to the back of her mind? So much so that she acted as if he didn't even exist? "Why did she run away? She must've been young."

"She had only turned seventeen three months previously." He averts his eyes. "We'd had a terrible argument, and she hadn't spoken to me in days. I came home from work one day, and she was gone. All her stuff was gone." He lifts the glass and takes a drink while I wait patiently for him to continue. My nerves are hanging by a thread. I chew on the corner of my fingernail, and my heart is thudding in my chest.

"I'd no idea where she went, and no one had seen anything. I was working a full-time job, so I couldn't just take off to find her. And at first, I thought she'd come back. When she didn't, I spent every weekend searching for her. I trailed the length and breadth of Ireland. I posted notices in all the main papers. I canvassed her friends continuously. But no one had heard from her. It was as if she'd vanished into thin air."

I lean forward in my seat. "So, that was it? You never saw her again?"

He tilts his head back and drains the remainder of his drink in one go. Briefly, he closes his eyes. "Oh, I found her all right. Years later, when you were living in County Waterford."

My spine goes rigid at the mere mention of our former home, but James doesn't notice.

His eyes glisten with unshed emotion. "She gave me no explanation. She barely gave me five minutes of her time. God, she was so cold." He shakes his head at the memory, and his breath rattles in his chest. "She told me, in no uncertain terms, to stay away from her. That she never wanted to see me again."

"Why? Why would she say that? It makes no sense." I implore him with my eyes. He must know the reason. Your only sibling, your only family, doesn't cut you out of her life without justifiable cause.

"I don't know what you want me to say, Faye. She never explained herself. All she told me was that she was happily married, and she had put her past behind her. She never even mentioned you." He stares at the empty fireplace as he speaks.

I slouch in my chair as a wave of rejection washes over me.

James leans forward and touches my knee. "It's not what you are thinking. She was protecting you." I click my tongue. "From me." My forehead furrows in confusion. "I told her I'd a wife and children, and she could see how devoted I was to my family. The triplets hadn't been born yet, and Alex had only returned to work after Kalvin's birth—the business had taken off by then—and I was a stay-at-home dad. We had more room here than we knew what to do with. I offered her the chance to move here, to be a family again, but she turned me down flat."

He clamps a hand over his mouth again and hangs his head. I'm sensing how difficult it is for him to relive this, but my thirst for information outweighs any guilt. James regains his composure after a bit. "Alex is an only child, and although she has plenty of distant relatives, you were my boys' only real cousin. Saoirse knew I wouldn't let it drop if I was aware of your existence, and I think that's why she didn't tell me."

He gets up and pours himself another drink.

"Yet she requested you as my guardian?" Something about this whole scenario doesn't add up.

"I'm guessing she felt I was the lesser of two evils."

I jerk my head up at him.

"She knew I wouldn't turn you away, and she didn't want you to be alone."

I knot and unknot my hands in my lap. A messy ball of emotion sits like a heavy load in my stomach. Subconsciously, I twirl a lock of hair around my finger as I grapple with my feelings.

"You remind me of her so much. She used to do that, too." He gestures at my finger, and I instantly cease twirling. He chugs his drink. The air is supercharged with heightened emotions, and I'm regretting ever asking.

I've more questions now than I started with.

Placing his empty glass on the table beside him, he opens one of the leather-bound albums, flipping through a few pages. "This is the last photo of us together," he explains, pointing at a dog-eared creased photo. I gasp. It's as he said—it's like looking in the mirror. Her hair is bright red, and I instinctually touch my head. "She loved experimenting with her hair, and I was always handing over my hard-earned money so she could try out something new." A wistful smile softens his features.

We flick through the rest of the album in relative silence. At first, he is explaining the circumstances and regaling me with the stories behind the images, but after a while, his voice gets more strangled until gradually he stops talking altogether.

A tidal wave of sorrow sweeps over me. Mum's loss weighs heavy on James' soul, and he's been grieving for far longer than I have.

I always thought Mum was an open book. Yes, she was cagey whenever I asked her about my grandparents, but I thought that was because it was too painful for her to recall details of the house fire they both perished in. She led me to believe she was all alone after that, but she wasn't. James cared for her. Looked after her. Made sure she didn't go without. *Why would she hide that from me? Was my father even aware?* With all I've learned this past week, I'm now questioning everything.

On top of my grief is the sense that I didn't know Mum at all. Because the mother who loved me with so much intensity and passion wouldn't have lied to me about such important things.

But the awful truth is that she did.

And I want to know why.

Chapter Nine

A loud commotion from downstairs distracts us. James is up on his feet in a jiffy, dashing out of the study to investigate. I follow behind him at a more leisurely pace, gawping when I spot the scene at the entrance.

"We need to speak to your father," a well-built policeman in a black uniform is telling Kyler at the front door. His meaty hand rests solidly on Kent's shoulder, and Kent's arms are securely restrained behind his back. Keaton is shaking his head at his brother. Kalvin is lounging against the wall, failing to contain his laughter.

James bounds down the stairs two at a time. "What have you done this time?" he fumes as he approaches his son.

Kent's swagger doesn't fade as he shoots his father a knowing look. "Ah, the usual. You know."

"Mr. Kennedy, sir," the officer interjects. "Your son has been caught shoplifting again. This time the store is insisting on pressing charges, so we need to take Kent down to the station for formal processing."

"I appreciate you swinging by, Officer Hanks. I'll follow you in my car." James grabs his keys as he turns to Kyler. "Inform your mother, please." He leaves, slamming the door shut behind him.

My three cousins turn and face me.

I prop myself up against the balustrade. "Shoplifting? Really?"

"Don't sweat it, cuz," Kalvin says, sauntering toward me. "This is a regular occurrence. Dad will write a check, and the situation will be brushed under the carpet. Mom will have a few choice words for Kent when she gets home, and then it'll be forgotten about, until next month, when the cops arrive on our doorstep again."

"Why on earth would he shoplift? You guys are totally loaded, and it's not like he wants for anything. I don't get it."

"It's never about the stuff he steals," Keaton says. "He never even attempts to conceal what he's taking—he *wants* to get caught."

Kyler folds his arms over his chest, observing but not contributing to the conversation.

"That's a rather drastic way of ensuring attention."

"Kent's all about the drama," Keaton confirms.

"And it's a pointless exercise anyway," Kalvin says, walking in front of me. "Mom's engrossed in work, and Dad's working on his handicap, so all he's doing is pissing them off. Wait 'til you see—they won't pay him a blind bit of notice once this has blown over."

Sure enough, when James returns from the police station with Kent, I hear him tearing a few strips off him before telling him to get out of his sight. Later that night, Kent strolls out the door to meet his friends as if he hasn't a care in the world. Kyler tries to stop him, but James refuses to intervene, and Kent leaves looking like an earthquake is about to erupt inside him.

I actually feel sorry for him.

He must be feeling pretty lousy to resort to petty crime to garner attention. All the money in the world is no substitute for parental love. My parents weren't well off, and I can remember plenty of times when penny-pinching was the order of the day, but I never wanted for anything, especially not love and affection.

I haven't lived here long, but James and Alex love their kids. I've seen enough to know that, but they aren't around much, and that appears to be at the root cause of Kent's issues. However, I'm curious to know if it's more than what's on the surface. *How much have Alex and James invested in trying to uncover the truth behind their son's behavior?* Whatever Kent is trying to achieve, it's clearly not working, and I wonder how long it'll take him to bring things to the next level.

I stand beside Kyler at the door, tracking Kent until he is gone from sight. "You're worried about him," I remark, not expecting him to reply.

He sighs. "Yeah. Someone has to." He casts a scathing look over his shoulder at his dad.

"I'm sure your parents are worried about him, too. They probably just don't know how to deal with it."

"Well, they should know. They're supposed to be the grownups."

"That doesn't mean it's any easier to be them than it is to be us. I think it's hard for the older generation to truly understand what we're going through, especially when we resort to desperate measures to show them how we're feeling because we're incapable of using our words."

His face turns a sickly green color, and I wonder what I said that apparently upset him. His eyes stare through me, as if I'm not even here. I lightly touch his arm. "Are you okay?"

He emerges from that lost place in his head, with a familiar-looking snarl plastered across his face. "Well, Dr. Faye, considering you seem to know everything, why don't you tell me?" His harsh glare is challenging, but it'll take more than that to push me away.

"You're hurting."

"Give the girl a gold fucking medal," he sneers.

Ignoring his snippy tone and snide comment, I push on. "I'm a good listener, and I might understand more than you realize."

He leans into my face in a deliberately intimidating move. His closeness does twisty things to my stomach that aren't in any way unpleasant. My breath hitches as he stares deep into my eyes. I'm not sure that was the desired effect. "You know jack shit about me, and that's exactly the way it'll stay. Stop prying into stuff that doesn't concern you. We may have no choice when it comes to you living here, but that doesn't mean we're all going to join hands around the campfire and sing Kumbaya. Butt out, Faye, or you'll be sorry."

Before I've even had a chance to respond, he pushes past me out the door like a tornado hell-bent on inflicting the worst possible destruction. I'm left standing there in his wake, wondering what the hell I said that was so wrong.

67

James' history lesson and that awful conversation with Kyler sends me into a depression of sorts, and I spend the next few days skulking around the house like I have the weight of the world on my shoulders. Everything is still so alien, and I feel like a stranger in my own skin. I don't know if I'll ever settle here or if I'll always feel like an outsider.

Alex and Keanu are still MIA, and Kent and Kyler barely acknowledge my existence. Kalvin has been conspicuous by his absence. I've no idea what he's up to, but I've hardly seen him since our little "show" in the kitchen.

James drags me out to lunch one of the days and tries to get me to open up, but I deflect all his efforts. My head isn't a groovy place right now, and I just want to be left alone to work through my crap in my own time.

I meet with the principal of Wellesley Old Colonial High School, and I guess I must meet his approval because he sanctions my enrollment before I leave. Not that I can summon much enthusiasm. The school has the best of facilities, and I'll want for nothing here, but a stuffy, snobby, off-putting aura in the air seems to linger on my skin, aggravating me. Maybe it's true what some people say. That buildings do emit vibes, because this place doesn't give me a warm and cozy feeling. I console myself with the fact that I'll only have to stomach it until January.

Keaton manages to coax me from my room to the pool most days, but I'm quiet and withdrawn, and after a while, even he gives up trying to tempt me out of my vegetative state.

It's Thursday, and I'm lying on a lounger attempting to read a book when Kyler steps out onto the patio. Wearing a towel over one shoulder and black swim shorts that rest above his knee, he looks like he's just stepped off the pages of a sports magazine. I try not to look, but my eyes have a plan of their own. To be honest, he's the first thing to spark any modicum of interest in days, and I welcome the distraction, even if I am still pissy at him over the way he spoke to me the last time.

Dropping the towel on a lounger across from me, he casually looks me up and down, his gaze lingering briefly on my bikini top. Little fluttery sensations twist in my stomach, and my mouth feels unnaturally dry. I shift around on my chair, but I don't avert my gaze. It's as if someone's cast a spell over me.

It's been the same with us all week.

No words are spoken, but I intercept his heated glances, as he no doubt catches mine. And it's much more than his blatant warning to stay out of his way. There's no denying there's some weird attraction between us even though we are consciously avoiding one another.

Kyler dives into the pool in one skillful movement, and I'm mesmerized by the sight. He cuts through the water with precise, measured strokes. Muscles flex in his back and bulge in his arms as he glides up and down the length of the pool.

Watching him is turning me on, and I'm feeling hot and bothered—I need to cool down. Without overthinking it, I shuck out of my shorts and pad toward the other side of the pool and dive in. The water soothes my skin, but my body still burns hot for him. Wishing he didn't affect me so potently, I deliberately avoid looking at him. I stick to my side of the pool, but I'm hyperaware of his attention. His eyes trail a scorching path along my body as I push myself to my limits. I swim harder than I've swum in ages, and the agonizing ache in my limbs is like a balm to my fragile state of mind. I'd almost forgotten how exhilarating being in the water can be. How much it strengthens body and mind.

The pitter-patter of wet feet on asphalt brings me back into the moment. I glance up in time to see a dripping wet Kyler walk into the house. My body sags in relief and a tinge of disappointment. I stretch my arms out on the edge of the pool, lean my head back, and close my eyes. Extending my body in the water, so I'm stretched out in one even length, I lift my legs slowly up and down, stretching my tired muscles. The water laps at my body like a gentle caress.

Fingers brush against my collarbone, and my eyes snap open. Kyler is crouched over me, his wet hair pushed back off his face and his eyes piercing me with dark intensity. I stare back at him, feeling the warmth of his breath as it fans over my face. Tiny beads of water cling to his skin, and I eye them jealously. My fingers itch to roam all over him, and I'm shocked at the depth of my longing.

My nipples harden under his keen gaze, and a throbbing sensation pulses low in my belly. The air is fraught with sexual tension, and there's no way he's not feeling this too.

Wordlessly, he holds out a bottle of water. I accept it, and our fingers collide. That simple touch detonates fireworks inside me. My cheeks stain a delicate shade of red. "Thanks," I croak, barely able to form a coherent word.

His fingers still linger against my skin, burning through me, and my eyes alternate from his hand to his unreadable face. His fingers press into my shoulder more firmly, and my pulse throbs wildly in my neck. Tiny shivers rocket all over me, and I visibly shudder.

Kyler jerks back, as if electrocuted. Turmoil mixes with fury in his expression as he runs his hands through his hair. Shooting me one last meaningful look, he grabs his towel and darts into the house.

I release a shaky breath. Reaching up, I rest my palm against my collarbone, still feeling the searing heat from his hand.

Bloody hell.

What in God's name was that?

I'm lying on my bed a couple of hours later when there's a loud rap on my door. "Faye?" Keaton calls out. "You decent?"

I'm not in the mood for company, but I don't want to ostracize my only real friend in the house. Besides, I've come to the conclusion that I can't hide myself away forever. Wallowing in a pit of grief and despair is the last thing my parents would want for me. "Come in."

He swans into the room looking sharp. "It's time to *par-tay*," he exclaims. "You up for some fun?"

I prop up on my elbows. "Whose party is it?"

"Ours," he mumbles, heading for my closet. "You need to wear something that makes a statement."

"Your dad's letting you have a party here?" Disbelief resonates in my voice. He snickers.

"Hell, no. We always use the guest house in the woods, and the oldies are none the wiser." He flings some clothes at me. "Put these on and I'll meet you out by the pool."

Deciding against the little black dress Keaton picked out, I settle on my favorite skinny black jeans and a tight-fitting black leather paneled vest top. The back of the top is some kind of sheer mesh material and the straps of my bra are clearly visible through it. I'm trusting that's enough of a statement for Keaton. Tipping my hair upside down, I coax it into an artfully messy style and spray a shit-ton of hairspray all over it. A slick of red lipstick, a dab of blush, and a thick coating of mascara complete my nighttime look. A light squirt of perfume and I'm out the door.

Keaton lets out a low whistle when I emerge by the pool. He's comfortably seated in a lounge chair, sipping from a bottle of beer.

We trek across the lawn, following the cream-colored stone path to the edge of the woods. Keaton chatters non-stop as we walk through the forest. He's such a sweetheart, and he already feels like the little brother I've never had.

Fresh, earthy smells linger in the air. The path is clear and well lit. After a few meters, we approach a decent-sized bungalow nestled off to one side of the forest. A trail of smoke flitters out of the chimney, and though all the windows are draped, the house gives off a welcome, homely feel. "That's Greta and John's house," he offers up when he notices me looking. "John is Greta's husband, and he maintains the grounds," he adds before I've even had time to pose the question.

As we walk past the edge of the house, I spy a dark-haired girl peering out at us from the side window. I lift my hand and wave. She waves back. "Who's that?"

Keaton looks over. "That's Lana. Their daughter. She goes to Wellesley Memorial High School. That's the public school," he adds for my benefit.

She looks nice, normal, not all blonde hair, sleek curves, and fake smiles like some of the girls we encountered in town. My feet stall. "Should we invite her to come with us?"

"She mainly keeps to herself, and that's the way Mother likes it. She doesn't want us associating with the staff." He loops his arm through mine and pulls me forward.

"Your mum didn't strike me as a snob."

Keaton tips back his head and roars laughing. "Are you kidding? My mom is the Queen Bee of Snobs. You'll see. Come on, we don't want to miss all the action."

We walk deeper into the woods, and faint sounds of music reach my ears. After a mile or so, my feet start protesting, and I whip off my heels, content to walk barefoot the rest of the way. The music gets louder and louder, mingling with the chatter of several voices as we approach.

Rounding the next bend, we arrive in front of a split-level log-cabin-style house with a massive, wide wraparound deck. Copious deck chairs and love seats are occupied with girls dressed in a variety of skimpy clothing and guys dressed more casually but nonetheless stylishly. Large buckets filled with ice and beer rest on a makeshift counter that's been set up on the opposite side of the deck. Bowls of chips and dips are half-eaten. I slip on my heels. "How the hell do your parents not cop on to all this?"

"Mom's traveling most of the time, and Dad's out late most nights. Everyone sneaks in through an old, unused gate at the back of the woods so there's little evidence of what we're up to. It's the perfect foil." Beats pump out, merging with flashing strobe lights as Keaton escorts me up the steps and into the large open-plan room. Several hands go up as we pass, and Keaton high-fives a few guys. I catch more than my fair share of inquisitive looks, but he doesn't waste long on introductions, guiding me swiftly through the house. We maneuver our way past the crowd dancing in the main living area. A few couples are making out in the shadows under the stairs, and sounds of heavy panting accost my ears.

A bunch of boys and girls are lining up shots in the kitchen. "What'd you want to drink?" Keaton asks, waving his hand at the counter where every type of alcoholic beverage imaginable is stacked. My cousins sure know how to throw a party. Rachel would be in her element here. "There are wine coolers in the refrigerator."

James' comment about the cause of my parent's demise has been weighing on my mind. I don't know if I'll ever look at alcohol in the same way again. If I'll ever have the stomach for it, or if I'll always associate it with the drunk driver who killed them. "I'll have a water, thanks."

His eyebrows shoot up. "You don't drink?"

"Sure she does," Kent says, coming into the room from outside. "Didn't you notice how hungover she was the day she arrived?"

I narrow my eyes at him. *My parents just died, asshole.* I think it, but I don't say it. The words still hurt too much to speak them out loud. And I get that he's pissed at the world and lashing out. He doesn't mean it.

"That's when you did this too? Right?" Kent runs his hand through my hair.

"What?" Keaton looks perplexed.

"She was brunette in those pictures Dad showed us." He swigs from a bottle of beer.

"What's it to you?"

"Nothing. It was only an observation." He pushes past me into the heaving crowd out front.

"How are you the only one with normal social skills in this family?" I ask Keaton, accepting the bottle of water he offers me.

A hand snakes around my waist and I'm hauled back against a solid male chest. "I'll try not to take that as an insult."

Chapter Ten

"Where have you been all week?" I ask, attempting to wriggle out of Kalvin's arms.

He snickers. "Ah, did you miss me?"

"Like a hole in the head."

Burying his nose in my neck, he sniffs appreciatively. "You smell gorgeous. Want to finish what we started the other day?"

"What's he talking about?" Keaton asks, frowning.

Removing Kalvin's arm, I turn around to face him. Damn, he looks good. He's wearing jeans and a light blue shirt that brings out the color in his eyes. His shirt is unbuttoned and rolled up to the elbows, highlighting his strong arms and impressive six-pack. His hair is falling in lazy waves over his forehead, giving off an air of calculated indifference.

He smirks as he notices my approving gaze, and I stick my tongue out at him. "I believe I won that round." I unscrew the cap off my water and lift it to my lips.

"I'll allow it." He yanks the bottle out of my hands and takes a quick glug. "But you still owe me."

"In your dreams, cuz." I push the bottle back at him when he tries to return it. "I'm not drinking that now. God knows what I'll catch."

Keaton laughs as he tosses another bottle of water my way. "She catches on quick." He winks at me.

Kalvin smiles. "You're all right, Faye."

75

I send him a derogatory look. "High praise indeed," I mutter.

He laughs. "Don't push it."

"Does that mean you'll lay off all the pretend sleazy stuff?"

"Not a chance in hell." He playfully tweaks my nose, and I swat his hand away. "And who says I'm pretending?" He leans down, pinning me with mischievous eyes. "It's too much fun, and I'm only warming up." He winks, as two small hands creep under his shirt, wrapping around his bare chest.

"I was looking everywhere for you." I hear the phony pout in the girl's voice.

Kalvin slaps his arm around the petite brunette, hauling her into his side. "I came to say hi to my cuz, but I'm all yours now, babe." The girl eyes me suspiciously, as she runs her hand dangerously low over Kalvin's abs. He bends down and sets a searing kiss on her lips. The girl curls into him, all but crawling up his body. His fingers dip into the band of her skirt, and she moans her approval. Reaching down, she cups the front of his trousers and starts fondling his crotch.

Okay then.

"Don't mind us," I murmur.

Kalvin emits a low, primitive growl, and without breaking the kiss, he maneuvers them out of the room.

"Damn," I say, fanning myself. "I think I got pregnant just watching."

Keaton snickers. "I wouldn't be surprised if that was part of his repertoire."

An intoxicating haze sweeps over me, causing all the tiny hairs on my arms to stand firmly to attention.

Instinctively, I scan the room for him.

Kyler is watching, through the window, from his place on the deck. Leaning back against the railing, he stares at me through dark, clouded eyes. My heart starts pounding in my chest as I level him with a similar stare. He inserts a finger in his mouth, sucking suggestively as he moves it slowly in and out. Saliva pools in my mouth, and that one tiny gesture sends warmth flooding to my core. His lips curve into a cocky grin, and I'm pretty sure he's well aware of the effect he has on girls.

On *this* girl.

Even though he's outside, electricity sizzles in the air. I've never felt such an instant, heady attraction to a guy before. With Luke, it was a steady, innocent build-up over time and more of a sweet-butterfly-type feeling in the pit of my stomach.

This is the complete opposite of that.

Kyler emits dangerous, seductive vibes that speak directly to that secret chamber inside me. It's like he possesses a silent calling card that resurrects a hidden wild part of me. One heated look from him, and my body ignites with lust.

I still can't decide whether I want to run *toward* it or *from* it.

His mixed signals aren't helping either. It's almost as if he's punishing me for this attraction between us.

And is it right to have these kinds of feelings and thoughts about my cousin? It's kind of weird to refer to him as that, because he's still a complete stranger to me, and the way I react to him is the same way I'd react to any boy I'm attracted to. Does it really matter if, technically, we're related? In Ireland, there's no legal impediment to being with your cousin, but I'm sure it's forbidden in plenty of places. Considering I grew up thinking I had no cousins, this isn't something I've ever given much thought to. I'm not sure whether it matters either way.

I probably *shouldn't* be having these thoughts about Kyler, but I'm powerless to resist the insistent pull between us.

He hasn't looked away this whole time. His eyes sear me, spear me, and I'm seconds away from storming outside—to do what, I'm not sure—when a familiar blonde surfaces at his side, tugging on his arm and smiling sweetly up at him. Addison spots the look in his eye and the focus of his attention. Her eyes narrow to slits as she sizes me up.

Someone steps in front of me, blocking my view and snapping me out of my hormonally charged trance. "Hey, it's Faye, right?" the girl with the pink hair from the diner asks.

"Yeah. Hi, Rose." I give her a grateful smile.

She moves beside me, taking a sip from her wine cooler. Kyler has his back to me now, and Addison is draped around him, running the tip of her finger up and down his arm.

"You want to watch yourself with that one. She has claws and she ain't afraid to use them."

"You intervened on purpose?"

"I was trying to do you a favor." She sounds a tad prickly.

"I'm grateful," I rush to assure her, in case I've inadvertently offended her. "Thanks."

Her shoulders relax. "Addison is a complete bitch, and she scares every girl away from Kyler. You don't want to get mixed up in that shit."

I frown. "What happened between them?"

"You don't know?"

"My cousin has thrown out a few random comments, but I'm not aware of their exact history."

She cocks her head. "Not here, follow me."

We head across the house, plowing our way through the boisterous crowd writhing on the dance floor. I spot a few of the guys from that day in the diner scanning my every move. Jeremy taps his finger off his forehead in a form of salute, but I ignore him and the gesture.

Rose takes my hand firmly and leads me outside, away from the party. We sit down against the trunk of a wide tree. I kick off my shoes and curl my feet up underneath me.

"Even the walls have ears in there. What I'm about to tell you, you can't repeat to your cousins. They don't like idle gossip."

"I won't breathe a word. Promise."

She reviews me with intelligent eyes. "I'm only telling you this because I saw the way you two were looking at each other, and if you decide to go there, you should know what you're getting yourself into."

"I don't know what you think you saw, but Kyler can barely tolerate me, and he has hardly spoken to me since I arrived."

Liar, a taunting inner voice throws out. I wipe my sweaty palms down the front of my jeans. "Besides, he's my cousin."

She picks at the label on her beer bottle. "True, and if you decide to get with him, you can expect a ton of hostility. Personally speaking, I don't think it makes any difference. You can't help who you fall for, and love comes in many different guises, but most don't share my view."

"I'm not in love with him." The words fly out of my mouth with urgency. *Let's not get carried away here.*

"Not yet," she teases. "But I know a horny look when I see one. You two are definitely hot for each other." I open my mouth to protest, but she waves me away. "Stay in denial, if you like. That's totally your business. I'll tell you what you need to know so at least you aren't walking into anything blind. Addison doesn't miss a thing, and you can bet she's already picking up on the attraction between you two."

"Why are you looking out for me?"

She sighs. "Anyone would swear you didn't want my help." She pins me with a slightly irritated look.

"That's not it. I ..." I pull my knees into my chest. "I guess I'm just a naturally suspicious person."

"That skill will stand to you around here."

"So, what *is* the score with the two of them?"

"I don't know the specifics, but Kyler and Addison were going steady for a couple of years. Ky was really into her, or at least that's the way it always seemed to me. But she started hooking up behind his back, and it was months before he found out. I heard he was devastated, though he didn't hesitate to dump her cheating ass the minute he found out. He's always been a moody son-of-a-bitch, but he turned even moodier and more reclusive. He's hooked up with a few random girls, here and there, but I haven't seen him show interest in anyone." She fixes me with a straight-up look. "Until now."

A tiny sliver of excitement blasts through me.

"Lately, Addison has been all up in his face, like a nasty dose of the clap. She's trying to sink her teeth into him again."

"So he's a man-whore, too? Is that like the new American pastime?"

She sniggers. "Nothing new about it, and no, Kyler isn't on Kalvin's level if that's what you're asking." She shakes her head. "Addison messed him up bad."

"I knew there was a reason I didn't like her the minute I met her," I admit.

"I presume you're going to Old Colonial too?"

"That's the plan, apparently. Do you go there?"

That incites a laugh. "Me?" Her eyes grow wide as she gestures toward herself. "Nuh-uh. I'm from the wrong side of town, and my parents don't have that kind of money. I go to Wellesley Memorial High School. We've got our fair share of dicks there too, but at least they don't try and hide what they are. You'll need to keep your wits about you in O.C. They'll eat you for breakfast otherwise."

"Noted, thanks. I've seen enough American TV shows to have a fairly accurate idea of what to expect."

"Girl, if that's what you're basing it on, you're in for a shock. Imagine the very worst and multiple it a hundredfold, no, a thousandfold, and then maybe you'll have some idea of what's lying in wait. They devour regular ole newcomers but they'll be out to *annihilate* you."

"Why?"

She twists around so she's facing me, hugging her bottle between her legs. "So many reasons. One, you're totally hot. Two, you're from Ireland, and you have that whole cute accent thing down pat. Three, Addison commands the girls in that school like a commander in chief, and given what I've witnessed, you are now top of her hit list. Plus, you're living with the Kennedy boys, and the girls will want to rip you from limb to limb for that fact alone. I could keep going, but I think you get the gist."

"Great. Something else to look forward to." I massage my temples.

"Expect the unexpected, and don't let them bully you, and they'll eventually go away." She doesn't sound too reassuring or look too hopeful.

"Pity you don't go there. It'd be nice to have at least one friend."

"I know. I moved here three years ago from Colorado, so I understand how hard it can be to fit in, but I think you'll be fine." She climbs to her feet. "I'm going to call it a night. Early start tomorrow."

I slip my shoes back on. "I'd better go find Keaton. I'll see you at work?"

"Definitely." She waves as she makes her exit.

I'm walking back toward the house when the sound of voices reaches me. "Come on, Ky. You know I'm sorry. If you let me, I'll show you just how sorry I am." The girl's tone is husky and suggestive.

"You don't deserve a second chance, Addison. You blew it with me."

Kyler's deep cadence sends chills all over me. I lean against the nearest tree and cautiously peek around it. Kyler and Addison are on a deserted part of the deck, by themselves. He's leaning against the wall with his arms folded in a protective stance across his body.

Addison is pressing into him with her arms slung low around his waist. An inexplicable surge of jealousy waylays me. "Baby. You know you miss me. I know what you need, and I'm prepared to give it to you, but I'm not going to keep offering. Addison Sinclair doesn't beg. She doesn't have to. Guys are falling over themselves to date me."

What a conceited stuck-up bitch! And I despise girls who refer to themselves in third person. *What an idiot.* A disgusted snort escapes my mouth before I can apply a filter. I clamp a hand over my lips as I flatten my back to the tree. My blood pressure skyrockets. *Crap!* They can't find me spying on them! But I'm stuck here, because if I try to flee, they'll see me. My pulse picks up, and I swallow the panicked lump in my throat.

"What was that?" Addison asks.

"Nothing, babe." Kyler's attitude isn't as cold as before. "Maybe you're right."

"I knew you would come around to my way of thinking eventually," she purrs.

There is silence for a minute, and all I can hear is the panicked beating of my heart. A nasty taste floods my mouth.

"Oh, that feels so good." She's breathless as she emits a little whimper.

I feel a sudden, compelling urge to puke. I risk another quick look. My eyes spring wide, and I stumble slightly when Kyler's shrewd eyes lock instantly on mine. I gulp. *He knew someone was watching!*

"I know what you need too, baby. Let me take care of you." He presses his mouth to a spot below her ear and starts trailing a line of kisses up and down her neck. He pulls her body in flush to his, and his hands roam along her spine. Dramatically throwing back her head, she offers him more access, and he takes it. His mouth moves lower, his eyes never once straying from mine. We're caged in that silent place again. His hand inches down to cup her ass, and he squeezes. She moans again, and my cheeks flare up.

Holy shitballs for dinner, how did I get myself into this mess? I should look away. I want to, because the sight of them together makes me want to hurl. But I can't tear my eyes away. Not when he has me locked under that enchanting glare of his.

His fingers creep under her dress, and she gasps. "Touch me, Ky. Do it, now." That's less of a request and more of an order. Kyler obeys without argument, and her moaning picks up pace.

My clothes are welded to my skin, and my breathing is labored as I continue to watch. It's wrong on so many different levels, but it's as if I'm under some kind of perverted spell. His hypnotic eyes have entrapped me, and I can't find the key to release myself.

His hand moves faster under her dress, while his eyes stay fixated on me. This whole scenario is sick, depraved, but also grossly fascinating.

I've become a Peeping Tom.

And. It's. Turning. Me. On.

She's pleading with him now.

Oh, dear God. What is wrong with me? What has Kyler turned me into? Bile travels up my throat, and a line of sweat drips down the gap in between my breasts. I ache down below.

Kyler's eyes haven't left mine. Not once. And he hasn't kissed her on the lips either. I find that a bit strange.

"I know you want me. Tell me you want me."

He eyeballs me as the words leave his mouth.

A layer of ice smothers me, extinguishing the fire.

He isn't speaking to her.

Looking directly at me, he smirks knowingly.

No, that sentiment most definitely isn't directed at Addison.

Those words are meant for me.

Chapter Eleven

The fog immediately clears in my head, and I stagger away, stumbling all over the place as if I've downed a hundred vodka shots. I need to get out of here, and pronto.

Kicking off my shoes, I take off in a sprint, running back down the path, away from this insanity. My whole body is trembling and crying out in need.

A shrill snap to my left grabs my attention. The dark-haired girl—the housekeeper and gardener's daughter—is cowering behind a tree. What did Keaton say her name was again? I rack my fuzzy brain until it comes to me. "Lana?" I call out.

Startled eyes meet mine before she turns on her heel and takes off. "Wait!" I run after her, bristling as my feet move off the smooth stone path and hit the rougher terrain of the forest. Ignoring the prickling, stabbing pain underfoot, I give chase. But she's damn fast, and I lose her almost straightaway. Cursing, I turn back around and start backtracking. It'd be just my luck to get lost out here. Spying the lit path up ahead, I charge toward it with purpose, not looking where I'm going. Tripping over a fallen log, I groan as I face plant the ground. A stinging pain tears at my foot, and I release a string of obscenities. Pushing off the ground, I sit up and inspect my injured foot. There's a shallow gash across the bridge of my foot, clustered with dirt and debris.

"Super," I mutter to myself as I spot the rip in one knee. Not only have I made a total ass of myself in front of my dickhead cousin, but now I've injured myself *and* ruined my favorite jeans. *Way to go, Faye.*

I'm limping down the path when a bulky, dark form steps out from behind the trees directly in front of me. Shock skitters through me. With my heart crashing against my ribcage, I emit a loud scream. Jeremy places a hand over my mouth. "Relax, Ireland. You'll wake up half the neighborhood. Either that or give yourself a coronary." He grins.

I slap his hand away. "Jayzus! You scared the hell out of me. Didn't your mum ever tell you not to jump out in front of girls in the middle of the night?"

"My *mom* always told me to be a gentleman. I saw you wandering off by yourself, so I came to offer my services." He holds out a beefy arm.

I try to quell the rampant pounding of my heart. "Thank you, but I'm grand."

He chuckles. "You're too cute." I narrow my eyes. "Although," he adds, pressing his mouth close to my ear. "There's nothing cute about how you look right now." He steps back, drawing his gaze up and down my body. A prickly sensation crawls over my skin. And I'm not talking about the good kind. "That's all sex kitten," he murmurs, gesticulating with his hands. "We should go out."

I stare at him, slack-jawed, and he chuckles again.

"On a date," he adds, mistaking my expression for confusion. "You do have dates in Ireland, don't you?" He says Ireland in a real nasally tone of voice which grates on my nerves.

"I know what a date is, and thanks, but no thanks." I move to sidestep him, but he blocks my path.

His smile loses its sheen. "No need to be hasty. Sleep on it." When he moves aside, I release the breath I'd been holding. "I'll call you." Taking my hand without permission, he presses it to his lips. "Sweet dreams, hot stuff." He winks as he retreats, heading back in the direction of the party.

Sleazy wanker.

I hobble back to the house, chastising myself for my stupidity the entire time.

When I reach my room, I tap out a quick text to Keaton in case he's looking for me. I fill the bath and soak for ages, only getting out when the water has turned completely cold and my skin has started to resemble an eighty-year-old woman's.

After dressing in the silky sleep shorts and camisole-type top Courtney provided, I turn on my lamp and prop up on the bed to properly inspect the damage to my foot. The gash is clean now but still sore to the touch.

Hushed voices trickle in through the open window, and I immediately perk up. Scooting off the bed, I crouch down and tentatively peek under the lip of the curtain. Kyler and Kalvin are out by the pool, and judging by their stance, they are arguing over something. I strain my ears to pick up their conversation.

"What the hell do you think you're playing at?" Kalvin hisses, grabbing Kyler by the elbow.

"Butt out. It's nothing to do with you" is the snarky retort. Kyler shoves Kalvin's arm away.

"You're seriously fucked in the head."

"That's rich, coming from you. You bone any female with a pulse," Kyler growls.

"This isn't about me. Man, she's going to stomp all over your heart a second time. And you'll be a fucking demon to live with again."

I'm unsure how that would be any different from now.

"I know what I'm doing, and it's not what it seems," Kyler protests.

"I understand the need for vengeance, I do, but she destroyed you last time. Don't give her that power again."

"It's not the same now," Kyler snaps. "She means nothing to me. Less than nothing." He batters his forearms.

Huh, could've fooled me. I'm presuming they're discussing Addison— you know, the same girl he was pleasuring in the woods not even an hour ago.

Kalvin exhales heavily. "I hope you know what you're getting yourself into. She's got to be playing some angle. If it turns sour, the fallout won't impact you alone, either."

"She wouldn't dream of going after any of my brothers."

Kalvin stiffens imperceptibly. "I'm not talking about us. I saw *him* watching Faye all night. Oh, he was clever about it, but I know that look. He's set his sights on her. If you do this, you'll only encourage him."

The hair on the back of my neck prickles. *What the heck? Is he talking about Jeremy?*

Kyler rubs his chin, deep in thought. "Are you sure?"

Kalvin nods.

Kyler curses. "I won't let that happen. Thanks for the heads-up."

Kalvin scrutinizes his face. "You like her, Faye, don't you?"

My breath hitches in my throat as I wait for his reply.

He shrugs. "Not in the way you're insinuating. She's part of this family now, or at least that's the perception we need to portray. To the outside world, she's one of us."

That's hardly a ringing endorsement. *Well, don't go doing me any favors, buddy.*

Kalvin leans against the side of a deck chair. "Uh-huh."

"What's that supposed to mean?" Kyler growls.

"I've seen you. You're hot for her. Admit your weakness." A smug grin settles on his face.

Kyler runs his hands through his hair, and my breath snakes out in noisy, cloudy puffs. "You're an ass. She's our cousin."

It's not exactly a denial.

"What the fuck has that got to do with anything?" Kalvin is incredulous.

"We're family, butthead. That's what."

"There's no law against it, and it's not like we all grew up together. If you met in a club and you were attracted to her, you wouldn't think twice about going for it. Why should this be any different?"

"Not everyone would share your liberal view," Ky says, rubbing the side of his face.

"Hey, if you're worried what others would think, you could always keep her as your dirty little secret. Man, that'd be superhot!"

"Go for it then." Kyler's gaze gravitates to my window, and his eyes narrow slightly. I duck down, silently cursing. Please let him *not* have seen me spying on him for a second time tonight. The earlier incident was bad enough. My heart is thundering in my chest, growing in intensity the longer the silence outside extends.

"What?" Kalvin asks.

Shit. Shit, shit, shit, shit! I slam my palm into my forehead as I slump to the ground.

"Nothing," Kyler mumbles before adding, "Are you interested in her?"

"I'm not."

"So that wasn't you playing footsie with her under the table the other day?"

"Ha!" Kalvin straightens up. "I knew it! You're jealous!"

"Don't be stupid. Of course, I'm not. I told you, I'm not interested in Faye or any girl for that matter. Girls fuck with your head. I'm done with relationships and all that shit."

"Sure. That's why you're sharing all those hot and heavy looks with her. Because you're *not* interested." Kalvin's mocking attitude is obvious in the extreme.

So, it wasn't my imagination, or one-sided, from the sounds of it. That shouldn't cause my heart to spike into coronary-inducing territory, but it does. A quiver of excitement races through me, and I shudder.

"Shut the fuck up." Annoyance slips into Kyler's tone.

I hear a loud slap. "She's hot, smart, snarky, *and* funny. She's perfect for you. You should totally tap that."

"Cut it out, Kal," Kyler growls. "You're making something out of nothing, and you heard what Dad said. Faye's off limits, so don't go getting any ideas."

James has warned them to stay away from me? Was that really necessary?

"All the more reason to go there," he retorts.

I roll my eyes as I stretch up slowly and peek at them again. They both have their backs to my window now.

Kyler grabs Kalvin into a headlock, mussing up his hair. "So, that's why you're doing it? Dad should've known better than to bait you."

"Asshat!" Kalvin extracts himself and hammers his fist into Kyler's arm. Laughing and pushing one another, they wander out of sight.

I'm padding quietly to the kitchen, lost in thought, pondering all I've heard. Kyler didn't confirm or deny Kalvin's statement, and I hate the well of hope that springs up inside me. This thing with Kyler is ridiculous, and he's right about the cousin aspect. I've plenty of other stuff to sort through, so guys should be the last thing on my mind.

The problem is, I've struggled to evict Kyler from my head since that first meeting.

It is like he hypnotized me the minute we met.

Or maybe it's the American air turning my brain doolally.

I'm in the dark, foraging in the kitchen presses when that same intense sensation washes over me.

"You'd make a lousy spy."

I slap a hand over my chest as I shriek for the second time tonight.

Kyler lounges against the counter with a customary blank expression on his face.

"You scared the crap out of me."

"What are you doing sneaking around in the dark?"

"I'm looking for a first aid kit. I need a plaster."

His brow furrows. "A what?"

"A plaster." I shoot him an "Are ya dumb look."

He still looks confused.

"For my foot. I hurt it on the way home." I point at the aforementioned injury.

The corners of his mouth kick up. "You mean a Band-Aid?"

"Whatever. We call them plasters," I mumble as he stalks toward me. My pulse, predictably, kicks into high alert. He stretches over me, and his body presses in closer with the movement. I close my eyes as I breathe in the musky, woodsy scent of him. Heat rolls off his sculpted body in hypnotic waves. I press my hands behind my back to quell the urge to touch him.

"Hop up."

I blink my eyes open, staring up at him. "Wh ... what?"

His hands land briefly on my hips, scorching my skin through my thin pajamas. Quick as a flash, he lifts me up, placing my arse on the counter. "May I?"

Mad, jumbled thoughts rush through my head, and a splash of color paints my cheeks.

His brows nudge up, and he looks like he's fighting a smile. "Let me see your foot," he clarifies, and I relax a smidge. I stretch my leg out, and he dips his head. I flinch when his warm fingers gently prod the damaged area on my foot. Ripping a Band-Aid open with his teeth, he carefully seals it over one side of the wound. He adds two more and presses down softly to ensure they have adhered to my skin. A flurry of tingles zips up and down my legs, sending a deluge of heat flooding between my legs. I discreetly press my thighs together.

Kyler traces the curve of my foot with the pad of his thumb, creating delicious tremors all over. An electric current charges the space between us as his hand clasps around my ankle, and he starts moving firmly up my leg. His skin is callused but not unpleasant to the touch. My breath hitches, and I can scarcely hear over the blood thrumming in my ears. My chest heaves up and down, and my nipples jut out through the flimsy camisole. His fingers sweep over my skin, and I bite down hard on my lip to cage my whimpering sigh of approval. Reaching the hem of my shorts, he stops, his fingers hovering so close to where I'd like them.

Gradually, he lifts his head, looking at me through glazed, hooded eyes. His gaze tracks languidly over my body, and he notices my obvious arousal. I gulp, and blood rushes to the surface of my skin, heating me all over.

A flare of desire sparks in his eyes, and he pushes my thighs apart. Stepping between my legs, he presses the length of his body against mine. I'm rooted to the spot, unable to move or even breathe as every inch of his hard, solid body brushes against mine. His breath is labored as he lowers his head toward mine. His eyes land on my lips with undisguised hunger.

I'm parched, and he's the only drink I need. I lick my dry lips, and his eyes follow the movement with possessive intensity. My heart is barely contained in my chest, and I'm half-expecting it to take flight any second now.

Angling his head farther, he tilts downward, moving steadily in the direction of my mouth. My heart starts galloping in my chest.

At the last second, he changes course, putting his lips against my ear. "You were turned on earlier watching me and Addison."

It's not a question. More a statement of fact. One I'm not going to acknowledge in any shape or form.

"You're turned on now," he adds in a sultry voice. A tiny whimper escapes my mouth as his warm breath turns me into a pile of liquefied goo.

So are you. I think it but I can't say it. I'm incapable of forming words right now.

He skims a hand across my cheek, leaving a fiery trail in his path. I squirm on the counter, more aroused than I've ever been in my life, and he's barely even touching me.

Kyler has seduction down to an art form, if this is any indication.

He aims for my mouth again, and I stop breathing for a second. His eyes are blazing with need as he pins me in place. He runs the tip of his finger across my lips and I part for him. As his mouth lines up with mine, there's only a minuscule gap between us. He peers deep into my eyes, and his lust-fueled glazed look no doubt mirrors my own.

Anticipation has my body locked up tight.

Suddenly, his lips curl into a sneer and he snickers.

The moment is gone. The heat in my veins extinguishes.

He steps back, creating space between us.

Disappointment wars with rage and humiliation inside me.

"You and me," he says, gesturing between us. "I know you want it. You're practically begging for it, but hell will freeze over before I touch you like that."

Chapter Twelve

The urge to flee is riding me hard. Humiliation scalds my skin, but I'm not letting him see he's gotten to me. "Actually, we're on the same page." I slither down the counter away from him. "Because I don't touch wankers with shit for brains." I push off the counter, plastering the most venomous look on my face as I give him a derisory once-over. "I wouldn't lower myself."

"We both know that's bullshit, but you continue lying to yourself, baby. Whatever makes you feel better."

"Fuck you."

"Wouldn't you love to?" He casts a final derogatory look over his shoulder as he saunters out of the room.

Tears prick my eyes but I blink them away. I will not be reduced to tears by that fuckwit. The other day, I thought I saw a more tender side to him, but I was clearly mistaken. He *is* the sum of how he appears, and that's not a compliment. My tears quickly transform, and I'm seething now. Beyond angry. *Who does he think he is to treat me like this?* Pumped full of self-righteous indignation, I storm after him, prepared to give him a piece of my mind.

Charging into the lobby, I slam face-first into someone and stumble back, crashing to the ground for the second time tonight. *Jeez, can this day please be over with?*

James curses. He crouches down on his heels, swaying slightly as he inspects me. "I'm so sorry, Faye. Didn't see you there. Are you okay?" I instinctively shrink back from his stinking whiskey breath.

"What di ..." Kyler marches into the lobby, his speech trailing off as he spots his dad and me.

James struggles to get to his feet, and Kyler's face contorts sourly. He extends his hand to help me up, but I ignore it, and him, scrambling to my feet by myself.

"Get to bed, both of you, it's late." James voice is slurred, and Kyler's face twists into an ugly sneer.

"You're an asshole." His acidic tone cuts right through me.

"I am your father," James grits out between clenched teeth. "And you will RESPECT me!" He roars the last part, and I flinch a little.

I start to maneuver around them, not wanting to get caught in the middle of whatever's going on here. James sways again as he tries to straighten up. He is steaming drunk. My eyes roam over him in amazement. He's wearing a slim-fit black shirt with the sleeves rolled up to his elbows, trendy slim-fitting jeans, and black sneakers. All his clothing bears the signature K symbol—of course—but that's not what's surprising. He's dressed exactly like his sons, and, to be honest, he looks absurd. That old chestnut, *Mutton dressed as lamb*, springs to mind. I briefly wonder if he's going through some type of mid-life crisis.

"I will respect you," Kyler says through gritted teeth, "when you have earned that right."

James jabs his finger into Kyler's chest. "I have sacrificed everything for you! For this family! And this is the thanks I get?!"

"What have you ever given me?" Kyler pushes his angry face into James'.

"I gave up my life, and none of you give a shit."

"You are frigging pathetic. A sorry excuse for a father. A husband. Maybe it's time Mom knew what a whoring, cheating slime ball she's married to."

My eyes bounce from Kyler to James as aggression and hostility drives a further wedge between them.

"Where were you tonight?"

"That's none of your business, Kyler." Kyler squares up to him. "Go on, I dare you." James rather stupidly challenges his son. Kyler's jaw clenches and unclenches, and James barks out a laugh. "Yeah. Didn't think so. Maybe the apple didn't fall too far from the tree?"

"I am nothing like you! NOTHING!" Kyler shoves his dad as he yells at him, and I gasp, drawing both their attention. I think they had forgotten I was here.

James takes a step back, dragging his hands through his hair as he curses again. "Go to bed, both of you. We'll discuss this in the morning." Ignoring us, he stumbles toward the kitchen.

Kyler is pumped to explode. I see it in the rigid way he holds his body and the barely restrained expression on his face. An unbidden urge to comfort him accosts me, but I push it away. Much like he did to me minutes earlier. Humiliation regurgitates in the pit of my stomach, and I welcome it, using it to swat my empathy away.

I push off the wall and start walking toward my bedroom. Kyler's quiet footsteps follow me, and a dangerous aura bleeds into the air. My hand is clasped around the door handle, when Kyler grips my elbow, swinging me around to face him. His rage is still boiling away underneath the surface, and the look in his eyes scares me a little. I'm not sure what he notices on my face, but his look softens. "Don't try to fit in here," he says quietly, "because you don't belong. You shouldn't belong. You should leave." He stares at me, letting his words settle. Perhaps he's waiting for a hostile reaction, but he can wait until the cows come home for all I care. I'm too tired and upset to enter into another battle with him. He strokes my cheek once and then walks away.

He's a mass of contradictions. Unfortunately, that only seems to enhance his appeal.

I'm one sick bitch, that's for sure.

Shuffling into my room, I climb into bed as if on autopilot. Even though the covers are tucked right up under my chin, I can't stave off the violent trembling that has taken hold of me. Everything that's transpired today plays on a continual loop in my head until, eventually, exhaustion consumes me and I conk out.

Both James and Kyler lay low the next day, obviously licking their wounds, and I'm glad. I still haven't figured out what the hell is going on between Kyler and me and Kyler and his dad, and I don't want or need any more drama. If what Kyler insinuated is true, James has gone downhill in my estimation. So far, he has been an absolute gentleman—but last night I witnessed a different side to him.

A side that I don't much care for.

Not for the first time, I question why I didn't do a bunk before he even showed up to claim me. Perhaps I should've sought a second legal opinion, and contested my parents' will. Maybe I accepted this guardianship far too easily.

I hope I won't regret the decision to come and live here.

Already, it feels like I've bitten off more than I can chew.

I take a lengthy swim, allow Keaton to teach me how to play NBA on Xbox, and concoct a pasta bake and salad for lunch. Cooking has always helped calm me down, and I desperately need that today.

At four p.m., I am leaving the house for my trial shift at the diner when Alex's assistant, Courtney, arrives. I stop in my tracks, assuming she's here for me. Her features are pinched, and her face looks glum as she steps into the lobby. "What?" she hisses, noticing my gaze.

"Do you need me for something?"

"The world doesn't revolve around you," she snaps, and I'm taken aback at the resentment in her tone. *Surely, that can't be directed at me?* I'm struck by the sense that she's doing this job out of necessity rather than any genuine love for it.

As Max drives me to work, I'm nervous but excited. I'm actually delighted to be getting out of the stifling atmosphere in the house. Alex and Keanu are returning tonight, and I'm hoping that the ambience will have improved by the time I get back.

But it's more than that. It feels great to have a job again. To have a purpose and something productive to occupy my time. I've worked, in some capacity, since I was fourteen, and I like it—the freedom and the empowerment that comes from earning my own cash.

Rose greets me with a big smile when I arrive. "I thought you might chicken out." She hands me a uniform.

"Why on earth would you think that?" I ask, hugging the clothes to my chest.

"I'm wondering why you're doing this. It can't be that you need the money."

I'm thinking that's a little too nosy from someone who's still pretty much a stranger. She was affable last night, and she seems like the type I could become friends with, but I don't know her from Adam. "I have my reasons," is all I offer up.

"'Kay," she says pleasantly, not put out by my obvious evasion.

I change in the small locker room out back. The red-and-white striped knee-length dress and matching apron is not the height of fashion, but it's comfortable and practical, and I can live with it.

Rose shows me the ropes, explaining how things work and showing me where everything is. In between training, she serves customers at the counter while the other waitress on duty attends to the customers seated at tables. After a half hour, she sends me out on the floor, and I get to it.

Time flies by, especially as the tables start to fill up. Friday and Saturday nights are their busiest times. Nothing like throwing the newbie into the deep end. But I'm enjoying it, and I think I'm going to like working here, if I get through this trial.

"Hey, you. Servant girl," a sharp female voice says, and my head whips up. Addison is seated with three other girls at a booth in my section, holding her hand aloft in the air. "Oh, silly me. What was I thinking?" She looks to her friends, and they all feign apologetic looks. "I meant to say waitress," she adds, keeping up whatever charade she's playing. "That just slipped out. I hope you'll accept my apology."

I might if she'd offered up a genuine one. All manner of catty remarks lie impatiently on my tongue, but I won't do anything to jeopardize this job, so I swallow my bitchy retorts and smile sweetly at her instead. "No problem. What can I get you?"

"We'll all have The Works Burger with fries and extra onions and cheese," Addison confirms, and my brows lift in surprise. Judging by the minuscule amount of clothing they are wearing, and the abundance of skinny limbs on display, I was expecting them to order water and fresh air. "Is there some problem with that?" She dares me to challenge her.

"Nope. I got it."

"Thank you, Faye." She smiles sweetly, and I bristle at her use of my name. Keaton never divulged that information, and I'm fairly certain Kyler didn't bring me up in conversation. Gauging her intent, I can tell she wants me to know she's been asking around about me. That doesn't bode well. But hell, I knew this was coming. At least I know now that Rose was solid in her advice.

"No problem, Addison."

"Is she hassling you?" Rose asks, when I duck under the counter.

"It's nothing I can't handle."

"Cool." Rose gives me an approving smile as I head to the register to input the order into the system.

Twenty minutes later, I slide two burgers in front of Addison and the redhead seated beside her while Rose carefully places plates in front of the other two girls.

"What is *that*?" Addison inspects the food with a look of sheer revulsion on her face. You'd swear I just handed her a plate full of arsenic.

"The Works Burger with fries and extra onions and cheese, exactly as you ordered." I keep my voice level.

She sends me a scathing look. "Do I look like I'd ever consume that amount of saturated fat?" She gestures toward herself while the other girls push their plates away in disgust.

Damn it! I knew she was up to something. I should've trusted my gut.

I know I should act professionally, but screw it; she has probably cost me my job. I have no cash to pay for this wasted food, and there's no way I'm tapping James to come bail me out. He doesn't want me working here, so I doubt he'd cough up, preferring if I got my ass fired.

"I figured you'd puke it up later." An outraged look washes over Addison's face. "Isn't that usually what you do?" I say, angling my head to the side.

"I wouldn't subject *this* body to that sort of abuse, and shame on you for suggesting it." The other girls all tut-tut their disapproval. "Not that I expect someone like you to understand." She skims my body in obvious disdain.

"Oh, I understand all right. I know exactly what's going on here." I cross my arms over my chest as I let her see my game face.

Her eyes glimmer maliciously. "Oh, goodie. I'm really going to enjoy this year."

The challenge is set.

Let the games begin.

Chapter Thirteen

I send her a malicious smile. "You know what, I think I will, too. I can't wait to see you get what's coming to you."

Throwing back her head, she cranks out an exaggerated laugh. "You have no idea what I'm capable of." An evil glint darkens the green hue of her eyes.

I bend over the table, putting my face right in hers. "Right back at ya. Do your worst, bitch. I've faced bigger threats than you."

"Yeah, I'm definitely going to enjoy this," she rasps, smiling as if all her Sundays have come at once. Extending her neck like a giraffe, she wiggles her fingers in the air, attracting my boss's attention. "David. A word, please." She clicks her fingers as if he's at her sole beck and call. "I'd like to make a complaint."

David approaches, looking from Rose and me to Addison and her friends. "What exactly is the problem, Ms. Sinclair?"

She pats his arm and her fingers linger on his skin. "How many times, David." She emits a girlish giggle, and a sudden violent urge sweeps over me. How I'd love to wipe that sickly sweet smile off her face. "Call me Addison. All my friends do."

I roll my eyes the same time Rose does, and we share a conspiratorial smile. Shame I'm going to lose this job. I would've enjoyed working with her.

"I know your waitress is new, and clearly struggling to grasp the concept of the job, but how anyone is dumb enough to mix salads with burgers is actually quite shocking," she tells him. "Don't your staff have to pass some form of basic intelligence testing before you inflict them on unsuspecting customers?"

You'd swear I was working for NASA, not the bloody local diner, for flip's sake. Addison is testing every last one of my nerves. And we haven't even started the fun and games in school yet.

I swallow the bile in my throat as David fusses over her, apologizing profusely and gesturing at Rose and me to clear the table.

I hold my head up high as I walk away with the offending plates.

"We'll take those off your hands," a husky masculine voice says. I look up into gorgeous blue eyes I've seen before. It's the same guy I saw the first day in the diner, the blond jock who was hanging back from the crowd. I think he was at the party last night too, although I can't be one hundred percent sure on that.

"You will?"

"Sure," one of the guys behind him says. "We're totally famished. Hand 'em over."

Rose winks at me, and I grin. Problem somewhat solved.

The blond guy slides into the booth beside his buddy, and I set the plates down in front of them. I grace him with a massive smile. At this moment, he's the equivalent of my own personal knight in shining armor. "Thank you."

"You're welcome." He smiles back at me, a real genuine smile without any hidden depth or meaning. It's kind of refreshing. *He's* kind of refreshing. "By the way, I'm Brad."

"Faye."

"What the hell, Brad?" Addison's heels tap noisily off the tiled floor as she stomps toward the booth. "What are you doing?"

He motions toward the table. "Eating. What does it look like I'm doing?"

"That's not your order!" she fumes.

"No, you're right. It's yours."

"So you did order this?" David asks, also approaching. "What's going on, Addison?"

"Nothing, David." She grabs his arm, bamboozling him with that faux sugary smile of hers. "I guess it's lucky for your waitress that she managed to resolve her fuck-up."

I ignore the dig, happy to take this win.

I give Brad one last smile before heading to join Rose at the counter. "That was awesome," she says.

"I know. Although, she's only going to have it in for me worse now, right?"

"I doubt it'll make much of a difference. I wonder why Brad did that." She looks reflective.

"You know him?"

"Yeah, he's t—"

"A word, please, Faye," David says, officially ending our convo.

Rose gives my hand a reassuring squeeze before I follow him into his office. "Sit down," he barks. I drop into the seat, preparing myself to be fired. "I don't know what went on out there, but if you have some issue with Addison Sinclair, you need to keep that out of my restaurant."

"I don't have any issue with her. I arrived in this country a week ago, and I've only met her briefly a couple of times. She's the one who seems to have an issue with me."

Leaning back in his chair, he scrutinizes me, and I hold my breath waiting for his decision. "Very well, but I can't have a repeat of that."

"I understand, and there won't be."

"Apart from that incident, I think things have gone very well. If you are still interested in the job, it's yours."

I sit forward in my seat, my eyes lighting up. "I am, and that's great. Thank you so much."

"I'll need you Friday and Saturday nights and short shifts on Tuesdays and Wednesdays. Give your details to Rose before you leave tonight. Provided everything is in order, you can start straightaway."

I'm so glad Alex had the wherewithal to rush through my paperwork and that there's no impediment to commencing work immediately. I stand up. "Thank you, David. I won't let you down."

I give Rose a thumbs-up when I return, and she high-fives me.

The rest of the shift passes by without incident. I didn't get to see Brad leaving, to thank him again for helping me out of a hole.

Thankfully, Addison and her group of bitches had left by the time I exited David's office.

It's after eleven when I get back to the house, and I'm bone-weary from being on my feet for hours, but it's a happy weary. Despite the incident with Addison, for the first time since I got here, I feel like I might adjust. Like I could fit in.

James is pacing the corridor when I step through the door. "Can we talk?"

I drop my bag on the ground. "Sure."

He guides me into his study. "I wanted to apologize for last night and for not seeking you out this morning." I figured he was managing the mother of all hangovers. Either that or hiding from me. I sink into a seat while he props his ass against the edge of the desk. He knots his hands in front of him, and I try to smother my laugh at the get-up he's wearing today. You would think the man married to the CEO of Kennedy Apparel would dress more age-appropriate. "You shouldn't have seen me like that or borne witness to that argument. That wasn't fair on you," he says, and I drag my eyes away from his skinny jeans and form-fitting T-shirt combo.

"If I'm going to be a part of this family, you won't be able to shelter me from normal family stuff."

He crosses his feet at the ankles. "No, I suppose I won't, but I doubt it's what you're used to."

It isn't. My parents rarely argued, and we had a good relationship. It wasn't often that I raised my voice or gave them reason to raise theirs with me. I shrug. "It's not comparable. There was only three of us."

"I don't want you to feel uncomfortable here. To feel uncomfortable around me."

I didn't. Not until last night. Kyler's words are on the tip of my tongue. I want to ask James if the accusation is true, but I don't think it's my place.

"I don't. Everything's happy out. Honestly. I'm fine."

He smiles but it doesn't quite reach his eyes. "Good. That's good." He scrunches up his face. "I'd, ah, prefer if we didn't mention this to Alex. I don't like her worrying about anything while she's attending to business. She has a huge amount of stress on her shoulders as it is."

I don't dispute that. You can't be CEO of one of the largest retail brands in the world without a shit-ton of pressure. But I wonder how much his request has to do with genuine concern for his wife and how much is about keeping Kyler's accusation contained. I won't lie for him. But right now it's all speculation, and given my feelings toward Kyler aren't all that charitable, I'm going to give James the benefit of the doubt over him.

"She won't hear about it from me."

The relief is evident on his face. "Thank you, Faye."

I hope I won't come to regret it.

"Sweetheart, there you are!" Alex says, enveloping me in her arms the instant I walk into the living area. "James tells me you found yourself a job?"

"I have. I'll be working at The Legend's Diner from now on." I shuck out of her embrace, slightly uncomfortable with her over-familiarity.

"That's fantastic. You could teach my boys a thing or two about the importance of goals and values."

James crosses to the bar and pours two glasses of wine. He hands one to Alex, and she smiles up at him, but it seems a little brittle. "I worked in the family business from the time I was thirteen. Of course, I've tried to get the boys involved, but the only one who has shown any interest is Keanu. It's one of the reasons why I introduced an allowance. I don't want my kids thinking they can have everything on a whim. If they work for it, fine. But other than that, they have to budget for what they want."

I don't see any of the boys wanting for anything. Clearly, we have different interpretations.

She presses a bankcard into my hand. "Courtney should've given you this the other day." A brief look of consternation flickers over her face. "Your allowance will be paid into that account every week. It is yours to do with as you please. If you have any extraordinary financial needs, please speak to myself or James, and we will discuss it on individual basis."

I push the card back into her hand. "Thank you for the gesture, but you don't need to do that. I have savings my parents left me and income from my job."

She holds the card out to me. "Nonsense. You're a part of this family now, Faye, and you will be treated the same way as the boys."

She's preparing to dig her heels in. Mum's mantra flits into my head. *Pick your battles, Faye.* I decide to let it go. "Okay, if you insist. Thank you."

"You're welcome. I hope the boys are looking after you?"

I suppose it depends on the definition. I don't want to land any of them in trouble, not even asshole Kyler, but I don't want to lie to Alex either. "I've been spending lots of time with Keaton. He's great."

"I'm glad to hear it. He's such a good boy." She puts her arm around my shoulder and steers me into the kitchen.

Keanu shows me shots from his latest photo shoot while Alex heats up the soup Greta left for us. She places bowls on the table, leaning over to admire the frames. "Keanu is a natural in front of the camera."

"I can tell," I admit. "Who's the girl?" I point at an absolutely breathtaking girl with midnight-black hair. Her sultry brown eyes are locked on Keanu, and their chemistry pops off the page.

"That's Selena. She's no one." Keanu's tone is clipped.

Alex musses up his hair, and he scowls, instantly whipping his hand up to smooth it back in place. "That's not very nice."

"She's a work colleague," he supplies, before turning his head to his mother. "Is that better?"

"Keanu, please." Alex sounds tired.

"You started it," he huffs immaturely, gathering the photos into a neat pile. "I'm going to hang with Keaton and Kent for a while before bed."

Alex and I eat our soup in silence after that.

After I've rinsed my bowl, I make my goodbyes, grateful to escape to the sanctity of my bedroom.

I'm dressed in pajamas, sitting up cross-legged on my bed, chatting with Jill and Rachel when Kalvin comes barging into my room. I place the phone on top of my bedside locker, and sigh. Sliding off the bed, I hop up and take his hand. "I want to show you something." I drag him out of the room and pull the door shut behind me.

"You see this wooden thingy here?" I point at the door. "It's called a door. If it's closed, it means the person inside wants privacy. In polite societies, people do this thing called knocking. It goes like this"—I rap my knuckles against the door—"and you only open the door when the person inside says you can come in. Comprende?"

Kalvin laughs. "You're too funny."

"Did I make my point?"

"Loud and clear." He grins, giving me a two-fingered salute.

I open the door, but he grabs my wrist and pulls me back. "What now?"

"No one said 'come in.'"

"Oh my God! You're infuriating!" I slap him about the head, and he laughs again.

We walk into my room, and he flings himself on the bed, sprawling spread-eagled across the length of it. "Make yourself at home, why don't ya."

"Happy to," he says with a saucy wink.

I throw the pillow at him. "Was there a reason for your visit?"

He slaps a hand across his bare chest. "Ouch. That hurt. Here I am trying to be a good cousin, and you shoot me down the minute I walk in." He's teasing, but there's something serious at the back of it too.

"Spill. What's going on?" I perch on the edge of the bed.

"Hey. Stop robbing all my lines!"

"You do know it's virtually impossible to have any kind of normal conversation with you?"

"Normal is boring."

I shove his legs aside. "You are the furthest from boring that I know."

"Now I feel much better. You have redeemed yourself in spectacular fashion." He leans back a little, giving me some space. "I did want to ask you something." An earnest expression emerges on his face.

"Okay."

"Did something go down at the diner tonight?"

I groan. "What did you hear?"

"That Addison was giving you a hard time."

Damn, the grapevine is thriving in Wellesley, something it has in common with my hometown. I doubt there is much that'll get past my cousins.

I pick at a loose thread on the duvet. "She was, but I handled it."

"She's a total bitch, and you won't be able to handle her on your own."

"I've dealt with her sort before." My nostrils flare. "I can manage Addison."

"That's cool. But I want you to come to me if you need help with her. Don't go to Ky. He's in way over his head."

The conversation I overheard last night comes to the forefront of my mind. "Okay. If she gets too much, I'll let you know, but you're not to involve yourself deliberately. I can fight my own battles, and if she thinks you are running around protecting me, she'll only dig in her heels. I know her type. Let me manage this my way."

He smacks a quick kiss on my cheek. "I can respect that."

A pleasant warmth sinks bone-deep. While I like being independent, I can't deny it's nice to have someone looking out for me and comforting to know I have someone I can call on if I need help.

He springs off the bed like a panther in heat. He's at the door when I call out to him. "Kalvin?"

He grips the top of the doorframe as he spins around to face me, showcasing his sculpted chest and abs.

"You are totally checking me out." His grin is smug.

"What do you expect when you parade around half-naked all the time?"

"It's too hot for clothes." He sends me his best innocent expression.

"A likely excuse." Something tells me Kalvin knows exactly the effect he has on girls and that he enjoys feeding off that. "Stop distracting me. I want to ask you something, and don't read anything into this."

He lowers his arms and leans against the side of the door. "Okay. Dying of curiosity here."

"Do you know a guy called Brad?"

Kalvin has barely opened his mouth to speak when he's shoved aside as Kyler motors into the room. Placing his hands on my shoulders, he pins me with a furious look. "Stay the hell away from Brad. And I'm not asking. That's an order."

Chapter Fourteen

"Screw you and the ship you rowed in on. And get your filthy hands off me." I pull at his wrists, but his hold doesn't budge.

"Ky." Kalvin walks across the room. "Let go. You're hurting her."

He's right. He is. His fingers are digging painfully into my skin, but I don't think it's intentional. He seems lost in an angry haze. "Who the hell do you think you are ordering me around like that?" I bellow.

Releasing me, he steps back, locking his hands behind his head. The look on his face is downright scary, and I step around the bed, standing alongside Kalvin.

"It's for your own good."

I harrumph. "Yeah, right. Like last night was for my own good?"

Kalvin's gaze jumps between us. "What happened last night?"

"Nothing," Kyler and I answer in unison.

"You should tell her," Kalvin says to Kyler. "Then she'll understand."

"I don't have to explain myself." He shoots Kalvin a filthy look.

"The hell you don't." I plant my hands on my hips and lance him with my fiercest expression.

"Just do what you're told. Brad isn't a good guy. Stay away from him."

I stare him down with a furious look of my own.

"Please."

I shoot him an incredulous look. As if a little 'please' excuses his caveman-like behavior.

He rams his fist into the wall in a temper, making a noticeable dent in the plaster. "To hell with this." With that parting sentiment lingering in the air, he storms out of the room, leaving a maelstrom of confusion in his wake.

"What is that dude's problem?"

Kalvin exhales loudly. "How long have you got?"

"Know what? I don't want to hear it. I don't care. Nothing that comes out of that asshole's mouth will make a blind bit of difference anyway. Brad is a million times nicer than Kyler."

"Oh, fuck me," Kalvin exclaims. "This is a mess." He shuts the door with his foot and then joins me on the bed. "I can't tell you everything because it's not my story to share, but you need to understand that Brad isn't the guy you think he is."

"Enlighten me."

He tucks my hair behind my ears, surveying me with keen eyes. "You're very pretty."

"Oh, for fuck's sake. Get on with it." My patience is resting somewhere between fleeting and nonexistent.

"Addison was Ky's first serious girlfriend, and he was craaaazy about her."

"I guess there's no accounting for taste," I spit out cynically.

Kalvin continues, ignoring my little burst of jealousy. "They were an item for two years, and they were even talking about going to Harvard together. Brad was Ky's best friend since kindergarten. He's on the football team, and he's into motocross too."

I have an inkling of where this is going.

"Brad and Ky were as close as two dudes get, without coming out of the closet, if you catch my drift."

I roll my eyes and urge him to go on.

"Brad was hooking up with Addison behind Ky's back. It was going on for months before he found out. It shattered him. Overnight he lost his girl and his best friend. It's been more than six months, and he's still not himself." He gets up. "Brad is bad news, and Ky is only looking out for you. We both are."

I nod. "I get it. Thanks for telling me."

After Kalvin has closed the door, a shrill squeal rips through the room. I pick up my phone, and Jill and Rachel are talking at ninety miles an hour, chattering over one another, and I can't make any sense of their rambling. I'd completely forgotten they were still on the line—they heard everything.

Rachel is audibly palpitating. "You should totally shag Kyler. He is seriously fit, and I'm not talking about Luke-level fit. We're talking Zac Efron and Liam Hemsworth level of supreme deliciousness. He's a total ride."

"He's a total asshole, Rach."

"You don't need to actually like him to screw him."

"Who are you and what have you done with my best friend?"

Jill, always the more diplomatic of the two, interjects. "What Rach means is you need to get back on that horse, and Kyler is the perfect steed to ride into a state of orgasmic bliss."

I flop back on the bed. "Not you, too! I'm not sleeping with Kyler. I'd rather sign up for invasive genital surgery than have sex with that tool. And have you forgotten? He's my *cousin.*"

Rachel splutters. "Cousin smousin! Who cares!"

"I think it's majorly frowned on over here. Trust me, there would be plenty of people with things to say if I got with him."

"Tell them to get lost!" Jill snarls. "We looked it up and it's not illegal to date, or even marry, your cousin in the state of Massachusetts. So go for it girl!"

"You did what?!" I shriek.

"Take a chill pill, Faye. It took all of five seconds to find the info on my phone. And, you're welcome." She gives me a smug grin, and I wish I could reach into my phone and wipe it clear off her face.

"Doesn't matter anyway," I mumble. "He hates my guts."

"Get over yourself," Rach throws out. "He so doesn't. We weren't even in the room and I could sniff the sexual tension in the air."

"You got all that over the phone?" I'm skeptical even if my heart is ridiculously hopeful.

"Yep," they chime in unison.

Stop! I implore them in my head. I don't need to be given any green light where Kyler is concerned. I'm already obsessing over him far more than I should. And he's a jerk.

I. Don't. Like. Jerks. No matter how good-looking they are.

Hanging onto the cousin argument was one way of convincing myself not to go there. But now my friends have me considering all kinds of options.

"I'm not discussing this anymore," I huff, my finger hovering over the end call button. "Not until you two come to your senses and can actually offer constructive advice."

I say it but I don't mean it.

The fact is, I think they just have.

I rise early the next morning and head to the indoor pool to do a few laps. I'm full of pent-up stress, thanks to Kyler and this mess that I've been unwittingly drawn into. My thoughts churn as I slice through the water. Addison has clearly put a target on my head, and I need to stay sharp if I'm to stand any chance of playing her at her own game.

But it's Kyler keeping me awake at night.

I know he's attracted to me, too; the evidence was pressing against me two nights ago. I also know that he's toying with Addison as some form of payback. What I don't understand is where all the cruel comments and mean behavior is coming from? If my only sin is feeling an inexplicable draw to him, then how has that invoked such wrath?

A part of me would like to believe he's warning me off Brad out of some hidden protective nature. But it's most likely his way of getting back at Brad for his betrayal. I'm a means to an end to Kyler. Nothing more.

A light breeze raises goose bumps on my arms, and I stop swimming, looking over my shoulder at the door noticing it's slightly ajar. Strange. Could've sworn I closed it when I came in.

A small sound in the top corner of the room causes my heart rate to kick up exponentially. Daylight is only breaking outside and the lighting is dim in the room. I spot a shadowy figure sitting on the bench, quietly watching me. My heart rate accelerates to life-threatening proportions. I swim across the width of the pool, propping my arms up on the cool tiled floor.

Kyler is resting his arms on his knees, and his hands are clasped together. His gaze slams into me, and sudden unease trickles down my spine.

"What do you want?" I push wet, straggly bits of hair off my face as he continues to stare wordlessly at me. Every instinct roars at me to ignore him, to treat him in the same dismissive vein, but I refuse to sink to his level. I swim toward the ladder, conscious of his eyes following my every move. Drawing a brave breath, I pull myself up the steps and walk toward him with my chin held high. Water cascades down my body, soaking the ground underneath me.

His darkening eyes latch onto me as I advance, and I may as well be naked. My nipples harden under the intensity of his attentive gaze, but I resist the urge to fold my arms over my chest. I stop in front of him, towering over him for a change. Sweat plasters his hair to his forehead, and judging by his attire, he must've just come from the gym. "Why are you here?"

His eyes start at my feet and slowly cover every inch of my body as he takes his time checking me out. Although I'm outwardly shivering, I don't feel even the tiniest bit cold. The look on his face sends hot tingles of desire all over my body, and I'm having a hard time disguising that fact. Fixing a knowing smirk on his face, he rises, stepping close to me until there's barely any space separating us. Blood pumps ferociously through my veins, and my head is a cluttered, swirling ball of hormonal-induced confusion.

I step back, needing space to unclog my brain. In a matter of seconds, he has me pinned flat to the wall, his arms forming a loose cage around me. His lower body presses against mine, and I bite my lip to confine my needy whimper. Flippin' hell. *Why am I so attracted to this tool?* Even the mere thought of any of my other cousins getting this close to me makes me feel ill, so why do I feel completely differently around Kyler? *Why does this turn me on when it should gross me out?*

He grazes his nose along the length of my neck, and a tiny moan escapes my lips. His tongue darts out, tasting my flesh, and I clench my fists tight at my side to curb the inane urge to touch him. My body is shuddering all over. "Brad is only trying to get close to you to get back at me," he murmurs, running the tip of one finger across my collarbone. His gaze latches on to the swell of my breasts under my swimsuit, and his dark stare turns even darker.

Pressing into me again, he licks his lips, as the bulge in his shorts grows harder. My chest swells and deflates in demonstrative fashion, and my nipples are tight to the point of soreness. "Although I'm sure he's happy to take it there. You're definitely his type." His fingers brush the side of my breast in a barely-there caress, but I still feel the pleasurable sensation all the way to the tips of my toes.

A bead of water runs down my face and over my neck, heading for the gap between my breasts. His tongue darts out and laps it up, all the while his eyes stay locked on mine.

It's the singular most erotic moment of my life.

My core pulses with painful need as his hand sweeps over my hip and he moves his face over mine. His warm breath is intoxicating as he kisses the very edge of my mouth. I turn my head toward him, desperately craving his taste, when he jerks back with urgency. His fingers dig into my hips, and I cry out. "Stay away from Brad. This is your final warning."

Stepping back, he treats me to one of his trademark smug smiles before blowing me a mocking kiss. Then he exits the room without a second glance.

I press a hand to my stomach, rooted to the spot, watching the door swinging in and out after him. Conflicting emotions are running riot inside me as I snatch up my towel and stagger from the room like a drunk after a rowdy all-nighter.

Chapter Fifteen

After showering and dressing, and trying my best to shake all thoughts of Kyler from my head and my heart, I walk to the kitchen for breakfast. It's empty. Guess everyone sleeps in on the weekend. I make a healthy fruit salad and eat it with some yogurt, before deciding to take a walk on the grounds.

As I step outside, Kyler shoots past me on a mountain bike, almost taking the knees out from under me. His feet cycle unbelievably fast. His focus and dedication is clearly keeping him in tiptop shape, I begrudgingly acknowledge. Still doesn't excuse his behavior.

Less than an hour ago, he was all up in my personal space, and now he doesn't care if he runs me over?

Jerk-face.

I flip my finger up at his retreating form even though he can't see me—makes me feel heaps better, though.

Strips of buttery sunshine heat my bones as I stride across the lawn toward the woods. My book is tucked in the back pocket of my shorts, and I intend to find a comfy spot to read. Fresh, minty scents invade my nostrils as I make my way through the forest.

A sorrowful pang assaults me as memories of family walks in Djouce Woods soar to the front of my mind. Heartfelt misery twists my stomach into knots, and I bend over, clutching my torso as if I'm winded. Unimaginable pain rips through me, shredding vital organs in its wake. I sink to my knees, hugging my arms around my torso, desperately trying to hold myself together.

"Are you okay?" a soft lilting voice asks, and I stiffen. Glancing over my shoulder, I spy Lana looking at me with obvious concern etched across her face.

"You ran off on me," I say, climbing to my feet. "At the party."

Her cheeks flush red. "Yeah, sorry about that. I didn't mean to be rude. I was a little upset over something."

"Anything I can help with?"

She shakes her head. "I'm over it now, but thanks."

I walk toward her and extend my hand, super grateful for her distraction. I was starting to fall into a hole that wouldn't have been easy to get out of. "I'm Faye."

"I know. My mom told me about you." She looks down at the ground as her cheeks stain darker.

"Greta's nice, although I don't think she's happy that I want to actually *use* the kitchen."

"You figured that out already, huh?"

"It's no biggie." I shrug. "I'll work on her."

She shifts awkwardly from foot to foot. "Do you have plans right now, or would you like to hang out? My parents are both working, so the house is empty."

"I've no plans. That sounds great."

I follow Lana as she guides us through the forest. "Mom is quite set in her ways, but she's a big softie. She's worked for the Kennedys for years, and the job means a lot to her. She likes to feel indispensable."

"I can understand that, and it's admirable that she's so dedicated to her job. Trust me, she's nothing to fear from me. I like to let off steam in the kitchen, that's all. My mum was a fantastic cook, and I was essentially raised in front of a cooker."

"You must miss her."

"I do. So much."

Lana steers me along the side of the bungalow and out around the back to a small well-worn decked area. Tasteful wicker furniture sits atop the raised area, facing out onto an impressive garden. Even though it's not the biggest lawn—certainly not by Kennedy standards—it's beautifully designed with flowers and shrubbery of every size and color. A large apple tree occupies prime position in the center of the garden, holding court like a majestic overlord.

"Wow, your garden is fab."

Lana walks into the house via a side door as I plonk my ass into one of the comfy seats. She returns brandishing a jug with pink liquid and two glasses. "Would you like some lemonade?"

"Cool, thanks."

She sets the lemonade down on the table resting between us and pours me a glass. "Dad maintains all the gardens for the Kennedys, but it's more than a job to him. He's the original green fingers." She smiles and her whole face transforms. A fleck of amber glistens in her hazel eyes, and the smattering of freckles dotting her nose and cheeks sparkle like tiny little stars are embedded in her skin.

She rests back in her chair, taking a sip of her drink.

"How long have you lived here?" I ask as I lift the glass to my lips. The sweet liquid fizzes in my mouth. "Gosh, this is sooo good. Did your mum make it?"

She bobs her head. "We have pink lemonade on tap." She grins. "And I've lived here my whole life."

Now that's an interesting nugget of information. "So you must know the Kennedys well?"

She looks off into space. "I suppose so, though I don't hang around with them anymore."

I take a big slurp of my drink. "How come?"

"It wouldn't be appropriate for them to be seen associating with the help."

I detect no bitterness; she's merely stating the facts. "Is that coming from the boys or their parents?"

"Their mom, mainly. I don't think James is too hung up on social norms, but appearance is the only thing that matters to Alexandra. Especially with their links to the infamous Kennedy dynasty. One mustn't do anything to disgrace the Kennedy name."

I lean forward in my chair, my hair hanging loosely around my shoulders. "What the what?"

She pins me with a disbelieving look. "No one has said anything to you? You don't know about your own heritage?"

Of course, I knew Mum's maiden name was Kennedy, but Kennedy is a popular surname in Ireland, so I would never have assumed any links to *those* Kennedys. And she never mentioned any connection. I shake my head in frustration. "Are you saying they—I—am related to JFK?"

Her brow puckers. "I don't think you're directly related to *that* side of the family. The connection is further back, and more distant. You should ask your uncle. He'll fill you in."

"Don't worry, I intend to. Hhmph." If what Lana is saying is true, it's further evidence of my mum's dishonesty. I don't understand why she didn't want me to know this stuff. I'm left feeling confused and hurt all over again.

We sit in comfortable silence for a bit.

"Keaton says you attend the public school. What's it like?"

"It's okay, I guess." She pushes her bangs back off her forehead. "The teachers are decent."

"What year are you in?"

"I'm a junior, same as Kal."

"Kal? Huh? Someone sounds on friendly terms." She stiffens in her chair, and her cheeks turn strawberry red. I think I may have offended her. "I'm only messing, don't mind me."

A nostalgic look spreads across her face. "He used to be my best friend. When we were kids, I hung out with them most summers. I even went to Nantucket a few times. Kal and I used to build sandcastles together." Her look is wistful.

"What's Nantucket?"

Her eyes ping with curiosity. "They haven't told you about Nantucket either?"

"Nope." I try not to feel insulted.

"Nantucket is an island off The Cape, and it's where a lot of the wealthy Bostonians and New Yorkers have vacation homes. Alex and James purchased their house about ten years ago, and they spend a lot of weekends there. I think Alexandra would prefer a vacation estate in the Kennedy Compound in Hyannis Port, but properties rarely come on the market. Taylor Swift outbid her a few years ago, and I thought Alex was going to blow a gasket."

She snickers, and her face lights up again. As she turns her head, sunlight glints off her hair, highlighting all the fiery red undertones. My smile falters as another reminder of Mum threatens to floor me. Blinking away the memory, I take another glug of my lemonade, hoping the almost sickly sweet liquid will overpower the sour taste in my mouth.

"I'm surprised they haven't mentioned it. I'm sure they'll take you there. It's an awesome place. You'll love it."

"Lana? Where are you?" a man's voice rings out from somewhere in the bungalow.

"It's my dad."

"Will he mind that I'm here?"

Her eyes crinkle at the corners as she thinks about it. "I'm not sure, actually."

"Then I'll go." I drain the rest of my lemonade and hop up. "I don't want to get you into any trouble. I'll see you around?"

"Absolutely."

At the sound of approaching footsteps, I hightail it out of there and jog back to the house.

No one is around when I return although I hear Greta humming gently to herself as she runs the hoover around the living area. I take the stairs to the mezzanine level on the off chance that James is here. I want to probe him about Lana's claims. She was a minefield of information, as well as being a genuinely nice person. I can't help thinking that the only girls I will meet—if I socialize in the Kennedy circle—are bitchy, spiteful types like Addison. It serves to further cement the view that I don't belong in their world.

The sound of an argument greets me when I reach James' study. The door is slightly ajar, and I hesitate outside, wondering if I should knock or go back downstairs and wait it out.

"Come in, Faye," James calls out, removing the decision from my hands.

Smoothing my hair off my face, I step into the room. James is standing in front of the fireplace with his back to the hearth. Kyler faces him, standing rigidly tall, his shoulders knotted into solid, tense blocks of muscle. He's wearing shorts and a sleeveless sports top, both of which are soaked in sweat and plastered to his body. His body odor wafts through the air, stirring my loins.

Again, I should be grossed out instead of turned on.

I'm genuinely starting to worry about myself.

"I need to reflect on it. Let's pick this up later," James tells his son.

"Dad, please. I need to tell them this week. Otherwise, it'll fold. They don't have the funds to stay open much longer. And it's not solely for my benefit, think of all the other kids wh—"

James holds up one hand. "I've taken onboard everything you've said, and I'll discuss it with your mother tonight. I don't need you to repeat yourself."

"Maybe I should have a chat with Mom myself." Kyler lowers his voice, and there's a definite edge to it.

James' shoulders tense. "Are you threatening me?"

"If that's what it takes, then yeah." Kyler squares up to his dad, but his back is to me so I can't make out his expression.

James looks like he's ready to take a swing at his son. Curling his hands into fists, he stretches the skin so tight it blanches white. "Get out before I do something I'll regret."

Ky thumps the top of the desk in fury before stomping past me with a ferocious look on his face.

I start retracing my steps. "This is a bad time. I'll come back."

James sighs. "Don't leave. My frustration isn't directed at you. Come"—he taps the arm of the chair—"sit."

I flop into the chair, crossing my legs. "Is there anything I can help with?"

He pours himself a glass of water and sits down across from me. "Don't suppose you have access to the Tardis? It'd be handy if I could rewrite my own history."

I peer into his eyes, wondering if he's on something.

He chuckles when he spots my confusion. "Your mum never mentioned *Dr. Who* to you? We used to watch it as kids."

"Nope. Guess it's something else I'll add to the list." A flare of anger sparks to life inside me.

James arches a brow. "The list?"

"Of all the things she kept hidden from me."

"We can watch it together sometime. If you like?"

"I've seen episodes of *Dr. Who*! It's not about the damn show!" I snap. Pulling my legs into my chest, I bury my head in my knees.

James perches on the edge of the chair, tentatively circling his arm around my shoulders. "I know, sweetheart."

I lean into him, and it's nice to feel like someone cares.

"Dad?" I jerk my chin up as Kent comes barreling into the study. He takes one look at the two of us and scowls. Before James can even acknowledge him, he legs it out of there without another word.

James squeezes my shoulder before retaking his seat. Deep creases furrow his brow as he stares numbly at the empty door. There's a world-weary defeatist aura around him, and it makes me want to shower him with love. Clearly, he's concerned about Kent. "I still remember the years when my boys thought I was Superman, Batman, *and* Spiderman, all rolled into one." He runs a hand through his hair, and I notice it's lighter than usual. I try not to gawp as I take in his newly acquired blond highlights.

"When all they wanted was to play ball with me. Or try and drown me in the pool," he continues. A huge grin splays across his face. "Those were good years. Great years. When I lived for them and they lived for me."

The grin fades away, replaced by a look of utter despair. He looks so sad and my heart aches for him. One doesn't have to be a genius to see he adores his sons. Or that it's breaking his heart that their relationship is on the skids.

"It'll come full circle. Teenage boys are the worst kind of beast to tame." And don't I know it.

James smiles. "You sound like you're speaking from experience."

"I am. I've been living in the jungle for over a week now."

Chapter Sixteen

A little while later, Alex informs me that she's booked a restaurant near Boston Harbor for a family dinner. I'm not blowing off my shift after only officially getting the job, so I inform her that I'll have to pass. She refuses to have dinner without me, so she leaves to reschedule the meal to Monday night instead.

I hang with Keaton by the pool all afternoon before getting ready for work. He's such easy company, and I could get used to relying on him, but I can't ride his coattails forever. Besides, I suspect he's ditching his friends to hang out with me, and I don't want that either.

When James shows up, beseeching us to play Xbox with him, I use the work excuse to bow out, allowing them some father and son time.

Rose is pulling up to the diner as Max drops me off. She slides off the pillion of a motorbike and waves as a helmeted mystery boy puts his foot on the gas and weaves into the traffic.

"Hey, girlfriend." Rose greets me with a generous smile, fluffing out her hair with her fingers.

"Who was that?"

She pushes the door open. "That was my boyfriend, Theo. He gave me a lift from the pool."

My eyes flit to her damp pink hair. "You swim?"

"Yeah, I'm on the school team. During summer break, I train with a private coach." She ducks her head under the counter, and I follow her into the back. "It's why I need this job. I used to work at the ice cream parlor, but they closed a few months back. I was lucky to find this job pretty much straightaway. I wouldn't be able to afford the swim lessons otherwise."

I'm surprised that she's only worked here a couple of months. It seems as if she's worked here her whole life.

"I've put my name down for the swim team at Old Colonial," I admit, yanking off my jeans and tee. "I'm waiting for my tryout."

"They suck." She casts her eyes over me. "You have a swimmer's body." Her gaze latches on my ample chest. "Well, except for those baby girls. No wonder the guys are all talking about you."

I pull my uniform on and turn to stare at her. "They are?"

She zips up her dress. "Oh, yeah. Fresh meat always attracts attention, but you're not the average newbie. Theo says they're already taking bets on who'll hook up with you first."

My jaw hangs open. "Please tell me you're joking."

She scrapes her hair back off her face, securing it with a hair tie. "No, straight up."

I lean back against my locker and groan. "Who's currently in the lead?"

She snickers. "Jeremy, but that's only because he got in there first. I heard Ky went crazy when he called for you the other day."

That's news to me. "I didn't know that."

"Figures. Expect more of the same." She slams her locker shut as she sits down, bending over to tie her laces. "I'm figuring those cousins of yours will want to pass all potential dates through their rigorous selection process."

I sit on the bench beside her as I attend to my own shoes. "Do I even want to know?"

She snickers. "Look, I think they're decent guys underneath all the arrogance, bravado, and the wealth. But they have a certain rep to uphold. This town treats the whole family like Grecian gods, and the Kennedy boys rule supreme at Old Colonial. Nothing happens without their approval. And even though they don't go to my school, they are still idolized. I really don't get it." She scratches her head. "But that's because I'm a blow-in. Anyone that has grown up around here hero-worships the ground they walk on.

All the guys want to be them, or at least be in their crowd, and most girls would saw off a limb to date them." She shoots me a sympathetic look.

"Meaning, I'm a perfect target."

"Exactly. The guys all want to date you, and the girls hate your guts."

"Don't sugarcoat it or anything," I murmur.

She stands up. "If you want to be babied, go cozy up to Lana."

I brush my hair and pin it into a casual bun on top of my head. "You know Lana?"

"She goes to my school. And living on the grounds of the Kennedy mansion brings its own form of notoriety."

"She seems sweet."

"She *is* sweet but completely naïve too. If you knew the amount of times girls befriended her in the hope that she'd introduce them to the Kennedy boys." She shakes her head. "Once word got out that they have nothing much to do with her anymore, the vultures dispersed. But that doesn't mean she isn't hit for gossip from time to time."

"I don't get it," I jump up and cross my arms. "Why don't they hate on her? I mean, don't get me wrong, I'm glad they don't because she doesn't deserve it, but neither do I."

Rose stands up beside me. "She isn't any competition. You"—she prods me gently in the chest—"are major competition."

"That's utter crap," I huff, feeling pissed off on Lana's behalf. *Lana is pretty and super nice, but she isn't viewed as competition because she's not a Kennedy and she doesn't come from money?* It's total baloney.

"I know, but that's the way it is." She shakes her head. "You could lean on your cousins if you need to defuse some of the heat?"

"I shouldn't have to, and I don't want to." I sigh dramatically. "I knew, coming here, that it would require adjustment, but I'd no idea how much. Or that so many things would be out of my control. I don't want this attention. I'd much rather be left alone."

The shift passes by in a blur. We are crazy out-the-door busy, and I'm grateful, but it doesn't stop my mind from replaying everything Rose has said. I didn't have much choice in coming to this country, and while I don't want to rock the boat, and it would be disrespectful to deliberately challenge my aunt and uncle, it doesn't mean that I have to change into someone I'm not. I need to find a way of retaining who I am as a person while fitting into this new society. A fizz of excitement wells inside me as ideas start turning over in my head.

Sunday comes and goes without incident. On Monday, Rose attends my appointment with me, squealing afterward when I tell her everything is in place. No one questions my absence during the greater part of the day, and I'm grateful. I'd prefer to deliver my news in a carefully controlled manner to avoid unnecessary drama. Although I'm beginning to suspect there's no such avoidance in this household.

"Oh my goodness," Alex exclaims, the minute she walks into my bedroom that night, carrying a sheathed dress bag in her hand.

"You don't like it?" I say, lifting my hand self-consciously to my newly dyed hair.

"I love it!" She beams at me. "It's much more sophisticated than the red."

I smooth my hand over my brunette locks, glad I returned to my natural roots. Between that and the other decision I made today, I'm already feeling more comfortable in my own skin. "This is who I am, and if I'm going to fit in around here, then people need to see the real me."

A slightly nervous look washes over her face. "I brought you something to wear. I hope you don't mind." Her eyes plead for understanding. "It's a dress from our new collection, and from the moment I saw you, I knew this would look perfect on you."

My aunt looks so glamorous in her green and black fitted dress and matching heels. Glistening diamonds sparkle on her wrist, ears, and neck; I realize that I'm significantly underdressed in my jeans and silk shirt combo. "I'm not really a dress person."

"I'm beginning to understand that, but it would mean a lot to me if you would wear this tonight. The restaurant has a strict dress code, and they won't let you in like that."

I draw a long breath. I suppose it's only fair to compromise considering I am living in their home and expected to abide by their rules. If I'm going to demand I do certain things my way, then it's only fair that I bend where I can. *Choose your battles.* Mom's silent coaching echoes in my ear, and I can picture her in my mind's eye with her hands on her hips and a cheeky glint in her eye.

Even though I'll probably feel like a right idiot in some fancy-pants dress, it can't hurt to try to butter Alex up. "I can do that. No problem."

Her shoulders visibly relax as she unzips the bag, removing a delicate black, silken dress. I pull my jeans and shirt off and stand in front of her in my black lace undies.

"It's such a shame you won't model for me."

"I'm too heavy to model, and don't you have to be, like, super tall for the catwalk?" I extend my hands for the dress.

"You're not tall enough for the catwalk, but you'd be perfect for catalogue work." Her eyes skim my body. "You have a toned, curvy figure which is the perfect look for one of our new trial ranges. Are you sure I can't entice you?" Her eyes look hopeful. "One shoot?"

That's one compromise I definitely can't stoop to. "I'd make the worst model, honestly. I'd be all gangly and self-conscious, and I'm sure that's not the type of look you're going for."

She motions for me to hold up my arms as she lifts the dress over my head. "It's fine, Faye. Don't pay me any heed. I know I'm too pushy at times. The boys are always teasing me about it."

"You're passionate about your work. That's a good thing."

Silky-smooth material shimmies over my body like a lover's feather-light touch. Alex fixes the dress in place, securing a black and gold cummerbund around my waist. The dress is structured in wispy, floaty layers with the hem resting above my knee. She pushes the top of the dress down a little so it rests on the edge of my shoulders. She darts into my wardrobe while I stare at my reflection in the mirror. She was right about one thing—this dress could've been custom made for me. It hugs my curves in all the right places, and it's elegant and classy with the right hint of sexiness. My dark hair falls in bouncy waves, lightly brushing my shoulders.

Alex smiles as she returns with the black and gold shoes that I wore the other night and a gold clutch. I slip my feet into the shoes and marvel at how grownup I look.

"You look beautiful." Alex beams at me, and a look of ... pride swims in her eyes. "I love my sons to death, but I always wanted a girl. To have the kind of business I have and not be able to share that with my own daughter ..." A sad look develops on her face.

I'm rooted to the spot, slightly perturbed. I can't be her substitute daughter or a replacement for some long-held yearning.

"I'm not trying to replace your mother." She looks at me sincerely. "No one can ever do that, but I would like to be your friend." She offers me a hopeful smile. "Sometimes all the testosterone around here becomes a little overpowering. I'm in need of some female companionship." She offers me a bigger smile, but there's a litany of sadness behind it that I don't properly understand.

My previous anxiety starts to disappear. I'm getting the sense that Alex genuinely needs a friend, and it's not as if I have friends breaking down the door right now. Of all the potential scenarios for our relationship, that one appeals to me the most. "That would be nice. I'd like that."

Her smile is even wider this time. "I'm glad. You're a sweet girl. Don't let anyone or anything change you."

Alex has gone to round up the others while I put the finishing touches to my outfit. Her parting words have helped to quell my nervousness. I'm hoping she'll still mean it when I share my news.

A loud rap on my door snaps me out of my reverie. "Knock, knock, cuz. Can I come in?" Kalvin asks.

I open the door and usher him in. "You're learning." I send him a cheeky wink. "Can you fasten this for me?" Sweeping my hair to one side, I show him my back. I clutch my gold and emerald Claddagh necklace around my neck as Kalvin fastens the catch.

Letting my hair fall back down, I turn and face him. "Thanks."

He darts in and kisses my cheek. "You look totally fuckable, and I love the hair."

"Gee, great. Because that was definitely the look I was shooting for," I deadpan.

"That's the best compliment a girl can receive." He holds out his arm for me.

"Your morals are seriously skewed. I can see I have much work to do."
I grin as I loop my arm in his, letting him escort me from the room. He's
wearing smart black pants and a fitted blue dress shirt. "Your mu—mom
wasn't joking about the dress code."

"Nope. This place is as pretentious as they come, but the food and
the view is to die for. You'll love it."

The others are congregated in the lobby when we arrive. All the guys
are formally dressed, and it's amazing how different everyone looks. No
wonder these Kennedys make waves wherever they go. This is one seriously attractive family.

Keaton lets out a shrill whistle when he sees me. "Sexy." He high-fives
me, and I can't help grinning.

James glares at his son, and Keaton steps back with his palms raised.
"Faye, you look absolutely stunning." James looks slightly shell-shocked
as he leans in to kiss me on the cheek. He looks smart, and age-appropriate, for once, in his tailored suit.

Keanu winks approvingly while Kent stares at me as if he's already
bored of this conversation. Kyler looks through me, and I may as well be
invisible. I hate the way my heart rate picks up at the mere sight of him.
He's wearing a fitted black shirt that clings to every defined muscle of his
chest. Black trousers and shoes complete the look. His hair is slicked back
off his face, and he's sporting the usual amount of facial hair. No matter
what he does, he exudes badass sexiness that I'm incapable of resisting.
The usual undercurrent fizzes under the surface, and I hope no one else
has picked up on the dangerous attraction between us.

As much as Kyler might wish to ignore our chemistry, he has to be
feeling the same intense connection that I do. Staring out the window,
blatantly ignoring me, won't do jack to change that.

Conversation is kept to a minimum as Max drives us to the restaurant.
It's on the top floor of a posh hotel, overlooking Boston Harbor. Kaden
and Keven are already seated at a table by the window, offering glorious
views over the harbor and the financial district beyond.

Kalvin sits on my left, and Keaton sits on my right. Kyler is sitting on
the other side of the table, which is unfortunate because it means he is
directly across from me, and it's far too easy to cast sneaky glances his

way when he's not looking. I don't want to stare at him like some love-sick puppy, but my eyes have an agenda of their own. Each time my gaze zooms in on his, I silently plead with my body to get with the program.

"What's going on between you and my brother?" Kalvin asks under his breath, as he butters a bread roll.

"Nothing whatsoever." I take a small sip of my water.

"Uh-huh. That's why you're both staring relentlessly at one another when you think no one's watching?" He gives me a cheeky wink.

I press my lips close to his ear. "He's staring at me?"

His eyes spark to life. "I knew it! Admit it—you *lurrvve* him."

"Shut it. I don't even *like* him, and you can quit playing matchmaker, or whatever it is you're trying to do."

"Calling it as I see it, and you'd better be careful. You don't want Mom and Dad figuring out this thing between you. They won't be pleased. Especially not Dad."

It's not as if I don't understand why starting something with my cousin would be frowned upon. Appearance is crucial to the Kennedys. That's becoming more and more obvious. Maintaining a certain image feeds into the brand they've so carefully cultivated, and I understand that it's more than social reputation that's at stake. Any whiff of scandal could significantly damage their brand.

My heart splinters a little at that realization, knowing Kyler and I will never be able to act on our attraction. I wonder if that's the underlying message behind his cruel comments.

James slips into Kalvin's seat when he gets up to use the bathroom. "Are you enjoying your meal?"

"Yes. Thank you. It's yummy."

"We used to come here a lot, but we haven't been in ages. It's nice to have all the family together again."

I put down my knife and fork. "James? Can I ask you a question?"

"Of course."

"Are we really related to those Kennedys? The famous ones."

He dabs a napkin to his mouth. "I assumed you were already aware because the Kennedy Apparel brand has been built on the foundation of that legacy. While we aren't related to the exact same branch of the family as JFK, we can trace our ancestry back to the Kennedys from New Ross. I thought everyone was in the know. It isn't something we try to hide, far from it."

"I was aware of the brand, but it's only becoming popular in Ireland now, and I don't know the background."

Kalvin returns to the table, but James motions for him to take his seat instead. James rests his arm across the back of my chair. "When I first met Alex, she was working in the family business alongside her father. He had built it from scratch, and when she was growing up it was hugely successful. However, the brand was dated, sales were declining, and times were tough. Her parents wouldn't officially sign the company over until she could prove that she could turn it around."

"We met when I was in Ireland on business," Alex intervenes, having overheard our conversation. She leans across the table.

"And it was love at first sight," James adds, his face softening with the memory.

All conversation halts at the table as the boys stop to listen to their parents.

"It was the best two weeks of my life. I knew he was the one for me the minute I laid eyes on him." Alex smiles through glistening eyes. "When it was time to return home, James came with me."

They share a sweet loving look that reminds me so much of the way my parents used to look at one another. Out of the corner of my eye, I notice how Kaden stiffens and Kyler and Keven frown as they exchange guarded expressions.

"It took a bit of time, but I secured her parents' seal of approval," James continues, oblivious to the hostile looks emanating from the other side of the table, "and we were married within six months. We worked closely together in those early days to try and turn things around. When I explained my background to Alex, it felt natural to rebrand the business and use my family name to build it into the billion-dollar enterprise it is today." A pained look flits across his eyes. "Of course, I can't claim any of the credit for that. I was only a stay-at-home dad by that stage. Alex was the breadwinner." An acerbic note has crept into his tone.

Alex's smile falters, and she glances around the room nervously. "That's not true. It was a partnership. You know I couldn't have built the business without your support. Without your name."

James lifts his wine glass and takes a hefty sip. "Yes. My name." He eyeballs his wife. "How fortunate that I had distant links to the infamous Kennedys." A muscle clenches in his jaw, and tension seeps into the air.

Alex stares directly at him, and some unspoken communication flows between them. James' eyes never leave hers as he knocks back his wine. The boys are watching this with transparent wariness, and I can tell this isn't the first time this particular argument has cropped up. I'm sorry I brought the subject up.

By the time he puts his glass back down, James has remembered his environment and regained his composure. "Don't mind me. I get frustrated sometimes that my own career ambitions went unfulfilled, but I don't regret the years I spent looking after the boys."

Keven snorts, and Kaden shoots him some type of warning look. Pushing back his chair, Keven rises and heads for the bathroom. James ignores his sons hostility, adding, "And Alex is right. It worked because we were a team, we had set roles, and we made it work."

"Why didn't Mum tell me about our Kennedy connections?"

James stares off into space. "I don't know, Faye. It seems Saoirse was determined to forget her past completely."

We've come full circle, and I'm adrift at sea again.

Why, Mum? I send the question out into the silent universe. *Why was it so important to hide?*

"You can have your seat back," James says to Kalvin as he stands.

"Um, actually, there was something I wanted to tell you." I look up at him.

All eyes fix on me as James sits back down. Keven is still in the bathroom, but it's not as if I need his permission, or any of their permissions, and I'm even wondering why I've decided to tell them like this. But I can't backtrack now.

I sit up straighter in my chair, clasping my hands in my lap. "I've made a decision. One I hope you will respect." Ignoring the boys, I focus my gaze on Alex and James. "I won't be attending Old Colonial. I've enrolled myself in Wellesley Memorial High School."

Chapter Seventeen

"Why on earth did you do that?" Alex looks genuinely confused. She turns to James, and he gives her a one-shouldered shrug.

"There are a few reasons," I start to explain, crossing my legs at the ankles. "I know I'll feel more comfortable in that environment, for starters. They have the best swim team, and I want to train with the best. And I won't be in my cousins' shadow there. I need to stand on my own two feet, and it's become clear that that would be almost impossible in Old Colonial."

"I don't understand, Faye." Alex presses into the table as she leans forward in her seat. "My family has attended Old Colonial for generations. It's tradition, and unheard of for any of the family to attend the public school."

"With the greatest respect, Alex, I'm not your family. That's not my legacy to uphold."

Kaden and Kyler share an indecipherable look, as Alex visibly pales. I weave my hands through my hair, starting to feel a little anxious. "I don't wish to upset you or insult you. And I'm very grateful for all you are doing for me, but I have to do this for myself. My parents always encouraged me to forge my own path in life, and I had a plan, a goal before they ..." I stop, unable to say it. A panicky, fluttery sensation floods my chest, but I keep it at bay, drawing a brave breath. "I've always known what I wanted to do with my life, but everything has changed now, and I'm trying very hard to adjust my plans accordingly." Alex's lips are set in a grim line, and I can tell she doesn't understand. I look at my uncle, and there's little understanding in his eyes either. "This is important to me. I'd really appreciate your support, but I'm doing this with or without your approval."

"Which one of you put her up to this?" James glares at his sons.

My face contorts. "Why would you think your sons have anything to do with this?"

"Because this is the exact type of emotional blackmail they are so fond of," James snaps.

I look down at my lap. "I'm not trying to blackmail anyone. I just want to be happy."

"And you think you'll be happy at Memorial?" Keanu sounds incredulous.

"Yes. I do."

"If this is because of the Addison thing, I told you—" Kalvin is cut off by a razor-sharp look from Kyler.

"What Addison thing?" Kaden asks, looking directly between Kyler, Kalvin, and me.

"It's nothing to do with that." I glare at Kalvin. Kyler looks skeptical, and my blood starts to boil. "I could give two shits about your ex!" I hiss at him, anger rearing its ugly head. My eyes roam around the table. "This is nothing to do with anyone but me. I prefer to attend the public school instead of the private one. That's all. I wanted to show you the courtesy of explaining my decision, and now I have." I fling my napkin on the table and rise. "If you'll excuse me."

I try to keep my temper in check as I stride across the room. I doubt Alex would be quick to forgive if I made a scene in front of the hoity-toity crowd. I race down the back stairs and push out through the emergency exit into a dimly lit back alley.

Day has turned to night while we were eating, and I lean back against the wall and gaze at the empty skyline. I inhale and exhale in a slow, deliberate fashion, drawing huge chunks of air into my lungs. The action helps calm my frayed nerves.

I stare at the blank canvas in the sky imagining a myriad of sparkling stars. When I was little, Mum used to say that the stars were God's angels looking down on us, keeping a careful watch over the earth. Dad always laughed—he loved to refute her. He'd point out the various constellations and give me these big, elaborate scientific explanations for how we came to be.

They were an odd match in some ways. Mum always remained true to her Catholic upbringing, while Dad was a self-professed atheist, preferring to believe in the big bang theory rather than the existence of a deity.

I liked how open they were on the topic with me, even from a young age.

I'm not sure what *I* believe in anymore.

If there is a God, why did he do this to me? Why take away the two people I loved most in the world? Why send me here, to a place where money and reputation appear to take priority over love and happiness? My aunt and uncle aren't bad people, but they've lost sense of what's truly important.

Raised voices echo from the far end of the alleyway, and I look cautiously at the three shadowy figures arguing in a corner. One of the guys has his back to me, but the other two are facing frontward. Sporting lethal expressions on their faces, they are staring the other guy down. I don't know if it's working on him, but I'm intimidated as hell. Both wield biceps to rival The Rock and are covered in multi-layers of tattoos. Power and danger lingers around their persona like some paranormal shade.

They are giving me major heebie-jeebies.

"You know who I am. Give me a few more days, and I'll sort it." My entire body tingles in awareness as I recognize the voice.

"You better, Kennedy, or there'll be hell to pay," a gruff voice warns.

Goose bumps the size of golf balls sprout on my arms.

"Here," one of the thugs says.

There's a rustling of paper, and Keven's head dips down. "There are ten names on that list. The agreement was five."

"That was last week," musclehead numero uno says. "Each week that passes will double the list in size."

"What the actual fuck?" Kalvin snarls in my ear, and I nearly jump out of my skin.

"Don't creep up on me like that!" I hiss, punching his arm. "You almost gave me heart failure."

"Come on." He tugs on my elbow. "You shouldn't be out here. And don't let Keven know that you've seen him."

I let Kalvin pull me back inside before I stop him. "Do you know what that was all about?"

"Let's say I have my suspicions and leave it at that." His mouth is set in a displeased line. "It's nothing for you to worry your pretty little head about."

I yank my arm away. "Don't be so bloody patronizing."

His brow creases. "I'm not. I think you've enough to be worrying about as it is."

I do, and it seems like I'm not the only one.

The atmosphere at the table is almost unbearable when we return. Thankfully, everyone has finished eating, so James orders the bill. Keven shuffles back to the table with a deep scowl. Kalvin tries to make eye contact with him, but he keeps his head low. Kyler—scarily observant as ever—watches the interactions with the intensity of a master criminal planning his next big production. James and Alex are deathly quiet, and a level of unspoken stress has descended over the evening.

I exhale gratefully when we finally make our exit. We bid goodbye to Kaden and Keven outside the restaurant, leaving them to make their own way back to Harvard, and the rest of us bundle into the car for the return journey home.

Alex asks to speak to me in private when we arrive at the house, and I follow her and James into the study where we argue for the next half hour. But I'm resolute, and I refuse to back down. Eventually, they both relent but only when I agree to reconsider Old Colonial if I don't settle in Wellesley Memorial.

When Alex asks me if I want to go to Nantucket with her and the boys the next day, I cringe as I decline. They are going to be away until late Friday night, and I can't tell my new boss that I'm unavailable for the next three shifts. Alex accepts my explanation without argument and heads to bed.

I've just changed into my nightie, when a firm rap sounds on my door. Assuming it's Kalvin, I shout out, "Come in." I hope my face doesn't betray my surprise as Kyler walks into the room. He quietly shuts the door, leaning back against the frame. He's rolled the sleeves of his black shirt up to his elbows, and muscles bunch in his arms as he folds them in front of him. His hair has lost some of its slick styling, and a few layers fall casually off his forehead into his eyes. My fingers itch to run between the silky strands, and I have to sit on my hands to dampen the craving.

The now-familiar electrical undercurrent buzzes between us as I regard him warily. "Yes?" I cross my arms over my chest, watching how his eyes track the movement.

"I want to know exactly what you heard in the alleyway tonight."

"And I want to know how to resurrect the dead, but we can't all get what we want," I retort, incensed at the cold, clinical way he is speaking to me.

He scrubs a hand over his stubbly jaw. "Look, I don't want to argue with you. I'm only trying to figure out what kind of trouble my brother has gotten himself into now." Pushing off the door, he walks toward me, his hands hanging loose at his side. "Is it okay if I sit down?" He motions at the space beside me. I didn't know he had it in him to be polite. I toss him a terse nod, and he drops down on the corner of the bed. The heat wafting from his body snakes out in silent invitation.

When I feel my head clouding over in the usual way, I scoot down the bed and create some additional space between us. "Why don't you ask him?" I'm not being a smart mouth. It's the logical next step.

"He'll clam up, and then he'll be extra careful, and I'll never know what's going on."

A jaded look coasts over his eyes, and I take pity on him, telling him what I overheard. "It's not much, I know," I admit, subconsciously tucking my hair behind my ears. "But those guys looked downright scary. The type you don't fall foul of, no matter what. Whatever mess Keven has gotten himself into, it looked serious."

Kyler glances over my shoulder with a frown. I whip my head around in time to see Kalvin slipping into the woods. That isn't the first time I've seen him sneaking about late at night, assuming it was him I spotted that other time. *I wonder what he's up to?* I turn around to ask Kyler that question and find him already striding toward the door. He stops, clearing his throat as he looks over his shoulder at me. "What you did took guts." *Is that a look of ... awe on his face?* "I respect you for making your own decision and standing up to my parents."

My brain has gone numb at the unexpected compliment, and before I can respond, he has walked away.

Chapter Eighteen

The house is eerily quiet the next morning, and I eat breakfast by myself. James arrives downstairs, decked out in clinging white trousers, a white belt, and a dazzling white polo shirt, as I'm finishing my meal. Honestly, words fail me. *Doesn't he have a mirror in his room?*

"Do you have plans for today?" he asks, pouring himself a coffee.

"Yes. I'm going with Rose to meet my new swim coach before my shift."

"Oh, that's good." He snatches a pastry from the counter. "Alex has taken Kalvin and the triplets to Nantucket, and Kyler's already at the track. I'll be playing golf the next few days, but if you need company, say the word and I'll rearrange things."

I scrunch my nose up. "Nah, I'll be grand. I'll probably hang with Rose or mess about in the pool. Don't worry. I'm used to my own company."

"Sit for a minute." He slides onto the bench, and I claim the space across from him. "I've been meaning to talk to you about the Kennedy Charitable Trust. Every year, Kennedy Apparel sets aside a chunk of money to donate to charity. We try to alternate the beneficiaries on an annual basis to share the funds among various different organizations. Our customers can nominate charities, and at the start of every year, the boys have a set amount to donate to a charity of their choice."

I tap my fingers off the tabletop, wondering what this has to do with me.

As if has a direct line to my thoughts, he continues, "You are a part of this family now, Faye, so you need to decide how to allocate your fund." It's starting to sound like a mantra. If Mum were here, she'd clip me around the ear for acting so ungrateful.

"That's not nec—"

He holds up a hand. "As long as you are under our roof, you will be on an equal footing as our sons. I thought Alex and I already explained this to you." He lets out a little sigh. "Plus, it's for a good cause. It's not often we get to help others less fortunate than ourselves. It's one of the nicer aspects of our lifestyle. Just think about what you want to do with your fifty K."

My eyes pop wide. "Did you say fifty thousand? You want to donate fifty thousand in my name?"

He smiles as he rises. "Yes. Time to get your thinking cap on!" He leans in, kissing me cautiously on the head. "There are certain rules regarding charitable donations that we must adhere to, so you only have a week to decide."

"Okay. Thanks." His shoes tap on the floor as he exits the kitchen. "James?" I call after him, and he stops. "Do I have to donate to a charity in America, or can I donate to a charity in Ireland?"

His brows scrunch up. "Good question. I'll check it out and come back to you."

I meet with the swim coach that afternoon and he puts me through my paces while Rose watches from the sidelines. I'm ecstatic when he asks me to attend a tryout with the team once the school term starts back.

Tuesday and Wednesday come and go without incident. Kyler, James, and I are like passing ships in the night, but you won't hear me complaining. Kyler hasn't said one word to me since Monday night, although I've seen him coming and going at various times. Watching him jogging, cycling, swimming, pounding the equipment in the gym, and charging down the driveway like Evel Knievel has left me feeling like a lazy slob, so I purposely squeeze in a few extra laps in the pool each day.

Jill and Rachel are most disappointed that there's no update on the Kyler front, but I'm like a pro as I deflect their attempts to force an admission from me. I'm not admitting to anything, because it can't, and won't, go anywhere, and there's no point entertaining the notion or feeding their need to live vicariously through me.

Thursday rolls around, and I'm surprised to see storm clouds lingering in the gray-tinged sky. I stay in my room for most of the day, reading and doing some further research on suitable charities to "invest" my fund in. James confirmed that the monies have to be donated to charitable organizations in the States so that killed my idea of donating to an Irish orphanage.

James insists on driving me to the diner that night, even coming in to have a quick word with David, my boss. The diner is bustling from the minute I arrive, and I'm immediately thrown into the thick of it, which I love, because the shift whizzes by. Slowly, I'm starting to get to know the other waitresses. They are all friendly, but I don't click with any of them in the way I've clicked with Rose. It's as if we were destined to become best friends. And I have to admit that the thoughts of school on Monday aren't so bad now that I know a couple of girls in my year. I know I've made the right decision, even if my aunt and uncle think I'm missing a few brain cells.

"Welcome to Legends," I say, arriving at the next table as I whip out my pen and pad. "What can I get you?"

"Whatever you're offering," a rich baritone voice says, and I jerk my chin up.

"Jeremy." It pains me to smile at him, but I'm paid to be pleasant, so at least I have an excuse. I hand him a menu. "That'd be whatever's on the menu."

"You didn't call me back," he drawls, taking the menu and flipping it casually on the table.

"I didn't know you'd called," I reply truthfully.

"Kennedy motherfucker. I knew it!" A smug grin tugs up his lips, which I immediately feel an obligation to remove.

"But even if I was aware, I still wouldn't have taken it."

The other boys at the table holler their delight, but Jeremy's smugness clearly knows no bounds. His grin widens and he pins me with a suggestive expression. "Don't knock it 'til you've tried it, sweetheart. You know you want this." He gestures at himself as if he's a prize bull.

Delusional much?

I wiggle my nose in mock disgust. "I plead the fifth. That's what you guys say when you don't want to incriminate yourself, right?"

Jeremy's buddies howl a little louder this time. All semblance of casual indifference flies out the window as Jeremy glares at me. I figure that's me crossed off his little black list, or, at least, I hope it is. "You're a stuck-up bitch, Faye, and I wasn't interested anyway. Don't flatter yourself that this was anything more than a setup."

"Whatever you say, big boy," I tease, on a roll now. "So, what can I get you guys?"

"You handled that well," Rose murmurs as I input their order into the system.

"Hopefully he got the message." I stick my hands into the sink and give them a quick wash.

"Knowing Jeremy, he'll probably only try harder now," a deep voice says.

I whirl around, coming face to face with Brad for the first time since Kalvin explained how he stabbed Ky in the back. He's the only customer sitting at the counter.

"Hi, Faye," he greets me pleasantly. Bringing the drink to his lips, he eyes me over the rim of the glass. It's hard to believe someone with that chiseled, all-American, good-looking, innocent hotness could be so deceptive. On the surface, he's the white to Kyler's black. The light to his darkness. I can understand, on one level, why Addison was drawn to him. He's everything Kyler isn't, but where Kyler may present as the moody bad boy, Brad is the one who acted like it. That act of betrayal showed his true colors.

While Kyler is still in the doghouse as far as I'm concerned, and I don't owe him anything, I despise cheaters. And as Kyler pointed out, outwardly, we need to act like family, so there's no question where my loyalty lies.

In any other circumstance, I'd ignore Brad in a deliberate snub, but I'm in work, and I don't think David would tolerate such rudeness. Pursing my lips, I give Brad a clipped "hi" before heading back out on the floor.

I'm out back on my break, with Rose, later on, when she brings him up. "Judging by that less than enthusiastic greeting you gave Brad earlier,

I'm guessing someone has clued you in?" She takes a long drag of her smoke before offering it to me.

I nod my head. "Kal told me."

Rose takes another drag, leaning her head back against the wall. "I don't get it, at all. Brad is the last person you'd expect to do something like that. I still can't wrap my head around it."

"Well, I have it on good authority that he did."

She twists to face me. "Oh, he did it, all right. There were enough people who saw him and Addison together, but I don't understand how he could throw away his friendship with Kyler for a piece of ass. Or why. It's not like he's short of offers."

I'm unable to add any insight; I don't know the guy.

"I dated him for a while when I first moved here," she admits. "He's a decent guy, from a good family. Although he goes to Old Colonial, and his family is well to do, he isn't from the usual kind of old money. His dad is a well-respected stockbroker with his own firm. I always thought he was different, you know?"

She stubs out her cigarette.

"How come you two broke up?" I hold the door open for Rose to enter ahead of me.

"It wasn't anything serious, we were only kids. It ran its course, that's all."

"You remained friends?" I tie my apron around my waist as I speak.

"Yeah. And when all that shit went down with Addison, I was one of only a handful of people who'd give him the time of day."

"He seems to hover on the fringes, all right."

"He does now, but before all this blew up, Brad was one of the most popular kids in school. When it first came out about him hooking up with Addison, all the guys were like 'you the man' as if cheating with your best friend's girl was badass." She rolls her eyes. "But then Ky weighed in, and the guys all changed their tune. Some of them have no choice but to include him because he's still on the football team, but they don't go out of their way. I feel for him, I do. One wrong move, one bad decision, and he found himself walking the green mile. That's rough."

"Maybe, maybe not." I shrug my shoulders. "He made his bed."

"If he was a deliberately nasty guy, I'd agree with you. But he isn't. He made a mistake, and we're all only human. Maybe I'm a big softie, but if I was Kyler, I'd forgive him. A friendship like that shouldn't be discarded because of a bitch like Addison."

Her words rotate around my head for the next twenty-four hours, and they are still looping through my mind the next night as I step outside the diner at the end of my shift. Max is a little late tonight, and I've no choice but to hang around until he shows. The lights fade to black behind me, and I hear the telltale *beep-beep* of the alarm as David appears on the pavement.

He locks the door and turns to face me. "Can I give you a ride home, Faye? You shouldn't be out here alone." His eyes penetrate mine as he skims a glance over my hair. "You changed your hair?" He's hardly been around all week, and even when he was, he was huddled away in his office.

"Yeah. This is my natural color. I was trialing the red for a while."

He stares at me strangely, and I shift uncomfortably on my feet. "Is that, uh, a problem?"

"Of course not." He smiles, snapping out of whatever weird mood he was in, and I relax. "So, you need a ride?"

"That won't be necessary," a familiar voice says, and I turn toward the sound of approaching footfalls. Kyler walks toward me wearing his usual cutting expression. He looks sinfully good in his jeans, plain white shirt, and black leather jacket. He exudes badassery as if it's a new form of aftershave. "I'm taking Faye home."

"Very well. Goodnight, Faye. I'll see you tomorrow."

I eye Kyler suspiciously. "Where's Max?"

"He's gone to the airport to pick up the others. Come on"—he jerks his head—"my bike is around the corner."

A rush of excitement zips through me, and there's a definite bounce in my step.

He looks at me funnily. "What?"

I give him a quick side-eye. "Nothing."

"You're a strange girl."

I bark out a laugh. "Are you for real? You want to go there?"

"I rest my case."

I groan, as he leads me around the corner. "You put the jerk in jerk-face, and you have the nerve to criticize me? You're unbelievable."

I roll my eyes as he spins around and walks backward in front of me. "I don't pretend to be anything I'm not." I can't tell if he's joking or serious because he's wearing that frustratingly impassive face he loves so much. I wonder if he perfected the mask pre-or-post Addison.

I stop on the spot, anger taking root inside me. "And I do? Is that what you're implying?"

He steps in front of me. "Everyone hides something of themselves."

I fall back, prepared to drop it. I'm far too tired to continue this type of conversation and expect to come out a winner.

A flash of color behind Kyler snags my focus. A couple skips down the steps of the building next door, laughing and joking. My eyes dart to the sign over the entrance. Wellesley Beechwood Hotel is branded in big, gold lettering over the ornate doorway.

The man opens the passenger door to an expensive-looking car. Kyler spots my distraction and turns around.

I don't stop him.

He needs to see this with his own eyes.

James gestures at the stunning blonde in the short, clingy red dress, urging her to get in. Leaning up on her tiptoes, Courtney wraps her arms around his neck, fusing her lips to his.

Chapter Nineteen

Kyler takes my elbow and pulls me down behind the small wall on our right. We crouch low, watching as Courtney and James continue their public snog-fest. I can't believe he's being so open about this, and I wonder if Kyler was already aware. James pins Courtney's wrists together and lifts them above her head as he pushes her back against the car. Her breasts push up with the movement, and James lowers his head, burying his face in her chest. I look away, unable to stomach any more.

The look on Kyler's face paints a thousand pictures. His fists clench and unclench at his side, and I figure he's seconds away from storming over there and doing something he could regret. "Let's get out of here," I whisper, though there's no need. I doubt they can hear us at this distance.

A muscle flexes in his jaw as his gaze stays locked on his dad and his mother's assistant.

Tentatively, I palm one side of his face, turning his head to face me. "Kyler." I peer deep into his storm-filled blue eyes. "We need to get out of here. Now."

He presses his forehead to mine as his breath snakes out in pronounced spurts. His chest rises and falls in painful movements. This must be killing him. Whether he suspected or not, catching his dad in the act is clearly playing havoc with him. Betrayal seems to follow him around, and my heart aches for him.

His eyes are closed as we stay locked in place. His lips are tauntingly close, and I long to bridge the gap and kiss him. It's taking every scrap of willpower to fight the urge to taste him; however, to take advantage of him in a moment of vulnerability would be despicable, and I won't do that.

Blinking his eyes open, he stands up, hauling me with him. He takes a firm hold of my hand and pulls me around the side of an adjacent building and out to an open parking garage at the back. I walk quietly as he guides me to his bike. Wordlessly, he takes my backpack and stuffs it in a hidden compartment under the seat. Extracting a helmet, he fits it down over my head. His fingers brush against my neck as he fixes it in place, and I shiver all over.

"Get on," he commands in a barely restrained voice, securing his helmet and sliding onto the bike.

I've never been on a bike before, so my hands rest lightly against his waist when I hoist myself up behind him. Reaching down, he grips my hands and spreads them firmly across the expanse of his stomach. My thighs slide forward on the leather seat until I'm pressed solidly against his back. All my soft parts meet every delectable hard part of him, and I inwardly swoon. His potent masculinity is enthralling, and it never ceases to draw me in, but it also intimidates me a little. I've never been with any boy who is so alarmingly attractive and so confident in himself and his sex appeal. Kyler totally owns it. I think I could probably orgasm pressed up against him like this.

The engine roars to life, and I grip his waist tighter as he thrusts the bike forward and we take off. By the time we hit the road, his dad and Courtney are nowhere to be seen.

Kyler weaves up and down side roads and alleyways as I attempt to steady my rapidly beating heart. I'm stiff as a board pressed up against him, and it's only when we hit open road and I start to relax a little that I realize my fingers are digging into his skin. I remove the pressure, while still keeping my arms snugly around his warm body. Wind whistles around my neck as Kyler accelerates on the nearly empty roads. I've no idea where we're going, or how long we've been traveling, but after a while, it becomes clear we aren't heading home.

My body hums with vitality and longing, and I don't care where Kyler is bringing me, if I get to stay with him like this. I know I shouldn't be feeling what I'm feeling, but I can't help my body's natural reaction. I like being this close to him, and the danger and anger dripping off him by the bucket load only fuels my desire for him. He's like no one I've ever known, and that excites me more than it should.

Kyler turns off the main road, down a dimly lit dirt track. Little crickets make chirping noises as we pass. Stars glitter in the sky casting an eerie glow over the land below. After a couple of miles, Kyler swerves to the left and pulls the bike to a stop beside a mammoth tree. Reams of overgrown grass sway gently in front of us. Kyler kills the engine and takes off his helmet before helping me with mine. Gripping me by the hips, he lifts me off the bike, setting my feet carefully on the ground. Without uttering a word, he takes my hand and leads me through the tall grass.

We step out of the grass onto a mossy green path. Wildflowers litter the path on both sides. Sounds of lapping water tickle my eardrums, and as we round a corner, a tiny gasp leaves my mouth. Kyler pulls me down on a raised grassy mound, resting his back against the trunk of an ancient tree. I sit beside him, skimming my eyes over the small lake rimmed by woodland on all sides.

"It's beautiful here." I look down at our linked hands, marveling at the feel of his skin against mine. He doesn't respond; he just stares blankly off into space. "What's going through your head?" I ask, determined to get him to open up. I know from experience that bottling things up does no good.

He doesn't say anything for a few minutes, and when he eventually starts talking, his voice is ragged and laced with pain. "I come here when I need to think. It's quiet, peaceful." He looks deep into my eyes. "It calms the madness in my head." I nod, understanding far better than he probably realizes. Air expels from his lungs in an anguished huff. "I knew he was cheating, but I didn't know it was with *her*. I've never warmed to Courtney. At least now I know why."

He drops the veneer, and anguish is clearly legible on his face.

I squeeze his hands. "I'm so sorry you had to find out like that."

"How can he do this to Mom? After everything she's done to provide for this family. This will devastate her." He drags his bottom lip between his teeth. "He's destroying our family, and I don't know what to do. How to stop it." His body trembles powerfully.

I don't know what to say—or if there is anything to say—that'll comfort him, so instead, I scoot closer, wrapping my arms around his waist as I rest my head on his chest.

His arms encircle me immediately, and he holds me close. His heart beats wildly underneath my ear, matching the acceleration of the organ in my own chest. As his fingers drift in and out of my hair, I have to clamp my lips shut to stop from whimpering. "He makes me sick. I hate him." Raw emotion cuts through his tone, and I can hear how much he's hurting. I clutch at his shirt, drawing nearer, wanting to get as close as humanely possible. Heat from his body seeps through my clothes, into my skin, and lodges bone-deep. I shudder as the most intense wave of desire ripples through me.

"Are you cold?" he murmurs, tightening his grip on my waist.

I have a hard time not laughing. I'm the furthest from cold a person could be. If I were any hotter, I'd be Egypt. I can't look up at him, because I know I won't be able to resist capturing his lips. "No," I rasp, nestling into his chest. I can't believe he's allowing this, but I'm not about to look a gift horse in the mouth. He presses tiny kisses into my hair, and I silently melt. He skims his hand up and down my back, and every so often, he squeezes me a little tighter, holding me closer to his chest, almost like he's checking to make sure I'm really there.

Expectation is ripe in the air, but I won't make a move.

It has to be him.

I don't know how long we sit like that before Kyler stirs. "It's late. We should head home."

A pang of disappointment hits me. I don't want to leave, but I know we can't stay here forever. It physically pains me to lift my head off his chest, but I do. I pull myself to my feet, feeling a little chill the minute I separate from Kyler. He stands up alongside me, and I feel his eyes drilling a hole in me. Lifting my chin, I stare into his eyes. Stark emotion shimmers in his gaze, and I can tell he's feeling all the feels too—I'm not in this on my own.

We continue staring at each other, barely breathing, barely aware of our surroundings, and it's one of the most exhilarating moments of my life. My eyes probe his as he explores mine.

Without breaking eye contact, he reels me in close, and his arms wrap firmly around me. My heart is beating furiously in my chest, and sweat coats my palms in a sticky layer. His fingers dip lower on my back, and he brushes the strip of bare skin between the hem of my shirt and the band of my jeans. My skin sizzles from his touch, and an intense shiver zips through me. I think I might be panting. He dips his head, as I rise up to meet him. Stopping an inch from my mouth, his eyes dart from my lips to my eyes and back again. All the breath has left my lungs as I wait for him to close that final gap. My heart feels ready to leap clear out of my chest.

Kiss me, I will him, pleading with my eyes.

Indecision flickers across his face, and disappointment slams into me again. He isn't sure of anything, and nothing can happen between us when he's like this. It would feel wrong, as if I'm taking advantage of the situation. I step back, removing myself from his embrace, negating the temptation. I wrap my arms around my torso to ward off the returning chill and look away. "I think we should go."

"Yeah." I hear the tinge of regret in his voice, but that doesn't do much to soften the rejection.

This time, he makes no move to hold my hand, although his fingers brush gently against my lower back as we walk, silently steering me forward.

I have no choice but to swathe myself around him on the bike ride home. This time, the hum of electricity flaring between our bodies is a teasing, taunting menace.

A reminder of all that is forbidden.

The house is quiet when we arrive back. I presume Alex and the boys are already tucked up in bed, but I've no idea if James is home or not. I'm glad he isn't here because I know I wouldn't be able to keep the disgust off my face. And who knows how Kyler is going to react when he sees his father.

Kyler's silent, larger-than-life presence, as we move quietly through the house, cranks my craving to an all-time high. My fingers twitch restlessly at my side, burning to touch him. I stop at my door and turn to face him. "Will you be okay?" I lightly touch his arm. One fleeting touch and I whip my hand away.

His answering shrug speaks volumes. "Goodnight, Faye." Dipping down, he plants a light kiss on my cheek before walking away.

Whatever progress we made tonight most likely won't mean a thing in the cold light of day. But I can't fault him for that. We shared a moment—that was all. And I'm glad that I was able to provide some comfort to him, no matter how small.

At least we might be more civil to one another from here on out.

"Goodnight, Kyler," I speak softly in the empty corridor before slipping into my room.

Chapter Twenty

I'm still tossing and turning in the bed like a madwoman an hour later. My brain has stretched my limitations beyond over-tiredness and exhaustion, and sleep continues to evade me. The throbbing ache between my legs isn't helping the situation either. I could take care of it myself, but it isn't my touch I crave.

The door creaks open and my heart rate accelerates. Pulling upright in the bed, I watch as Kyler creeps into my room, quietly closing the door behind him. Fierce determination mixes with something darker as he walks toward me. I stare at him open-mouthed as he strides across the floor as if his life depends on it.

He drops onto the edge of the bed, pressing his forehead against mine. Warmth spreads from him to me. Shuttering his eyes, he cups my face with one hand. "I need you." His tone is gruff, his breath heated as it fans across my face. An inner voice urges caution, but I rapidly shut that sucker up. Kyler's eyes open and I gasp. His mask is gone again, replaced by an innocent vulnerability that guts me. He's hurting. So badly. I ingest it as if it's my own pain, and I want to make it go away.

"I'm here for you," I whisper.

He palms the other side of my face. "Can I kiss you?"

I can only nod. My heart is jackhammering in my chest, about to take flight. Blood thrums in my veins, and my entire body is wired tight in anticipation. My limbs have turned to liquefied jelly, and he's barely even touched me yet.

Lowering his head, Kyler brushes his hot mouth against my collarbone, and I shiver all over. Pushing the top of my shirt aside, he deposits tiny kisses all over my upper chest and my shoulder. I clutch his waist for support, and he growls his approval. His mouth grows firmer and more insistent as he secures his lips to that sensitive spot between my shoulder and my neck. A little whimper leaves my mouth, and I can sense his smile.

Heat sweeps over my skin in a fiery trail as his mouth moves up my neck. He stops, briefly, and draws in a long breath as his nose tickles my skin. "You smell so good." He speaks softly and seductively in my ear, and I feel a tingle all the way to my core. He continues worshiping my neck and my collarbone, sucking, licking, and kissing, and edging down toward my chest, but never going quite low enough. It's the most torturous form of seduction, but I'm powerless to resist. He's whipped me into a frenzy of writhing need, and I can barely contain myself. I'm audibly panting, and his mouth hasn't even touched mine yet.

"Kyler," I rasp, need evident in my tone. He chuckles lightly as he kisses my jaw, inching his way slowly toward my mouth. My breath is snaking out in embarrassingly loud spurts but I don't care. I need to taste him. To feel his lips moving against mine. I'm seconds away from pouncing on him and taking what I want. Lifting his head, he pierces me with a horny look that sets my knickers on fire. His dark eyes are smoldering with lust.

Without warning, he crashes his mouth down on mine, and there's an explosion in my pants. An honest to God burst of desire so intense I think I could self-combust. It's the closest I've come to orgasm without being touched down there.

His kiss isn't tender. It's hard and demanding, and it's fueled by sheer lust and raw need. I know, because it's exactly how I'm kissing him back. My lips part, and his tongue plunders my mouth like an invading Viking. He feasts on me, and I eat him up like a starving woman. A desperate, starving woman who doesn't know when she'll get to feast again. Call me greedy, but I'm grabbing all he's offering now. I paw at him like a sex-crazed maniac. Lifting his shirt, I slip my hands underneath, running my fingers urgently over the smooth, defined muscular wall of his chest. He is all muscle and solid mass as I trace the lines of his six-pack.

He presses me down flat on the bed as he stretches out over me, pulling my body flush against his. My hands start an exploration of his ass as his fingers creep up the underside of my shirt. He warms his palms against my skin, and I mewl into his mouth at the contact. Scorching hot desire replaces all sane thought in my brain.

I don't care that this is wrong.

It couldn't be.

Not when it feels so right.

As Kyler caresses me, his fingers sweeping lavishly across my body, I decide I like this feeling. I don't want him to stop. I'll give him whatever he wants so long as he continues to make me feel this way. I arch my back, smashing my breasts into his chest, and he emits a primal moan that fills me with immense satisfaction.

He wants me as much as I want him.

Reaching down, he moves one of my legs around his waist, and I bring my other one up on the other side of his body. Squeezing both legs firmly around his waist, I bring that sensitive, throbbing part of me in direct contact with the hard bulge in his pants.

I leave my body, yet I'm ever-present. It's as if I'm floating above the room looking down at the hot mess in front of me. I watch him lift my shirt up over my head and toss it to the side. I watch myself writhe in sweet agony when his mouth leaves my lips to worship my breasts.

I pop back into my body with an audible gasp. I'm burning up and the desire to shed the rest of my clothes and throw caution to the wind is riding me hard. Kyler is everything. He's all I see. All I want. To hell with the consequences.

I need this.

He needs this.

I mentally lock up logic, secure it into a box, and throw it out the proverbial window.

I fist my hands in his shirt, tugging it frantically up his body. He lifts off me in one lightning-flash move, ripping his shirt up and over his head, and pins me with a sultry look.

My jaw slackens at the sight of his perfect, ripped chest. My hands start an exploration, inspecting every magnificent inch of him. He flinches underneath my touch and I'm loving the power. The tent situation in his jeans is reaching critical mass, so I reach down and cup him through the material. Cursing, he grabs my ass and aligns our bodies perfectly. My legs suction to him like an octopus.

His mouth goes to town again, devouring every inch of me. I'm lost in a world of bliss. A world where there is only Kyler and me and our mutual savage need for each other. He rolls his hips against mine, injecting me with a shot of pure liquid lust.

Beyond caring, I emit a needy moan. We're like wild animals who've just been let out of a cage. We are greedy, clinging, clawing, sucking, and biting, and every touch of his mouth charges the painful ache between my legs. No one has ever made me feel so much, and I'm like putty in his hands. He could have his wicked way with me right here, and I'd be helpless to resist.

But he doesn't overstep the mark, even though I'm sure he wants to as much as I do. His hand slips into my shorts, and he looks up at me, his eyes asking the question. "Touch me. Please," I rasp, breathless and squirming. I'm already primed to explode, and he works me into a frenzy in super-fast time. I shatter, falling over the edge as my body rocks and trembles while he exhausts every last ounce of pleasure.

My heart is thundering in my chest as he crawls up my body, pulling me into his arms. I twist around and strategically place my hand over the bulge in his jeans.

"It's okay." His hand stalls mine. "I don't expect anything."

I prop up on my elbow and stare at him. I've had a long-term boyfriend before, and I know how guys get. He has needs, and I refuse to leave him unsatisfied. Not when he's turned my world upside down.

I'm all about equality.

I brush his hair out of his eyes as I lean down and kiss him gently. "I want to look after *you*." Need radiates in his eyes. "Let me take care of you."

"Are you sure?" He cups my face tenderly.

I give him a teasing smile as I pop the first button on his jeans. I sneak my hand under the band of his boxers, and he curses when my fingers curl around him. I stroke him casually, and he moans. Opening the rest of the buttons, I slide his boxers and jeans down, and I wrap a firm hand around his throbbing length. His head drops back on the pillow as I start pumping, building the pace until he's thrusting into my hand, his whole body tense and ready to rip apart. I bring him over the ledge, reveling in the look of absolute joy on his face and the knowledge that I put it there.

He hauls me up his body, snaring me in his strong embrace. He plants delicate kisses all over my face, and his nose grazes the length of my neck. "Faye." My name is reverential on his tongue, and it does the most amazing things to my insides.

After cleaning up, we continue to share tender, sweet kisses until my lips feel swollen and my jaw starts to ache. Kyler tucks me into his side, and I snuggle into his warmth, relishing the feel of his body alongside mine. Content and happy, I fall into a deep sleep.

Kyler is gone when I wake the next morning, but his smell still lingers on my sheets. Burying my head in my pillow, I inhale his scent like it's oxygen.

There's a quiet knock on my door. I scramble about in the bed, looking for my top while I desperately try to flatten my tangled hair. "Faye," Kyler says in a hushed voice. "It's only me."

"I'm awake," I call out as carefully as I can.

Kyler steps into the room with damp hair and dressed in a clean black shirt and jeans. He looks totally edible, and I want to eat him right up. He carries two mugs in his hands as he advances toward me. I scrutinize his face as I sit up against the headboard, anxious to gauge his mood. I tuck the covers under my armpits as he perches on the side of the bed. Placing the mugs on the locker, he leans down, kissing me sweetly.

A dart of lust whips through me, and I drape my arms around his neck. Inside, the mother of all parties is taking place in my chest. I was anticipating the cold shoulder this morning, so this is most unexpected.

Not that you'll ever hear me complaining when a hot guy shows up at my door, fresh out of the shower, bearing coffee and kisses. "Morning," he mutters belatedly against my lips.

"Hey." I smile against his mouth.

He sits up straighter, putting space between us, and I scowl. A smile curves up the corner of his mouth, and he looks so breathtakingly beautiful in that moment that I can only stare at him in awe. His smile expands, and I'm guessing I look like a total moron, but I don't care.

This guy is to die for.

My heart is fit to bursting point.

Lifting my hand to his mouth, he kisses my palm, and a sudden rush of tingly heat passes from his body to mine. "What?"

"You should smile more. You've no idea how it transforms you." A sudden thought occurs to me, and I sport a sulky expression.

He laughs. "What now?"

"Second thoughts. Don't change. Keep to your usual moody, mean self whenever you're not with me." I sit up on my knees and lean in to kiss him. "Save the smiles for me. Only me." His smile falters a little, and I curse myself for whatever I said to diminish it. "Did I say something wrong?" I bite the inside of my cheek.

He shakes his head as he runs his fingers along my lower lip. "I was wondering if you'd any plans for this morning? Would you like to come to the track with me?"

Chapter Twenty-One

I can't believe he's asked me. This is momentous, and it feels like a breakthrough. He's starting to let me in, and it fills me with so much giddiness. "I've no plans, and I'd love to go to the track with you."

"Yeah?"

"Totally yeah." I lean over and kiss his prickly cheek. "But I need to shower first."

I wrangle him out of the room while I get ready. After showering, I dress casually in jeans and a plain shirt, wrapping a hoodie around my waist. I toe on my runners—I still can't get used to thinking of runners as sneakers, but I know I need to make an effort unless I want to bring a translator with me to school on Monday—and apply my requisite mascara and lip gloss.

Kyler looks surprised when I stroll into the quiet, empty kitchen a few minutes later. "What?" I land my hands on my hips and narrow my eyes.

He grins. "I don't think I've ever known a girl to get ready that quick."

I head straight for the fridge. "I'm not into all that girly shit. I'm fairly low maintenance." Bending down, I snatch a water and some fruit out of the fridge and nudge the door shut with my hip. Spinning around, I meet Kyler's darkening gaze, and I'm immediately suspicious. I purse my lips as recognition dawns. "Were you checking out my ass?"

He leans forward on the table, pinning me with those captivating peepers. He licks his lips, and my mouth feels suddenly dry. "Yep." He grins as he shovels a mouthful of eggs into his gob.

I should probably be disgusted but I'm not.

I'm elated.

Not sure what that says about me.

I unscrew the cap off the bottle as I walk toward the table. "At least you're honest."

"I told you I don't hide who I am." He watches me with penetrating eyes.

I'm tempted to argue with him. To tell him I see the front he wears, but he already knows that, and the fact that I've glimpsed behind it, and observed things he's trying to keep hidden. I could go there, but I don't.

I don't want to ruin this newfound easiness between us. I want to understand him. Challenging him on his bullshit isn't going to further my aim, so I shoot for easy-breezy instead. "Did you like what you see?" I balance a strawberry in my mouth, deliberately swirling my tongue around the outside, before swallowing it whole.

A fire blazes in his eyes and I almost choke. His gaze darkens as he leans over the table, inching closer. He picks a strawberry from my bowl, never once taking his eyes off me. "Hell yeah." He bites the strawberry in half in one quick, fluid movement, gnashing his teeth as he pins me with a look loaded with promise. I forget how to breathe. *Holy moly.* I am completely out of my league with this guy.

"So what are you going to do about it?" I issue the challenge in breathless anticipation.

"Lots." He stands up. "But right now we need to leave. I like to get out on the track early." He walks around the table and stands behind me. Leaning down, he brushes my hair to one side and fixes a lingering kiss on my neck. My eyes close as a flurry of tingles dances over my skin. He grips my hips gently. "Let's go."

I experience another adrenaline rush as I grasp hold of Kyler on the bike. Pressing my face into his back, I soak up every single moment of the ride, committing it to memory.

We pull up in front of two huge gray gates in a remote part of Middleborough. A man with graying hair and a straggly goatee shows up, unlocking the gates and ushering us through. Kyler idles at the entrance, resting his foot on the muddy ground. "The warehouse is open, Ky. I'll meet you out front."

"Thanks, Rick. See you in a few."

Kyler drives toward the large metal structure up ahead. A dilapidated redbrick building resides alongside it. A light flips on and Ky waves to the red-haired lady inside. Her eyes widen in curiosity when she spots me.

Kyler maneuvers the bike inside the giant warehouse, cutting the engine when we reach a spot at the back. He helps me off and removes my helmet. "I need to get my gear on, and check out my bike, but I'll walk you over to meet May first. She'll show you the way to the bleachers, if you want to watch." He takes my hand and guides me forward.

"I'd like that."

We pass a myriad of different bikes as we walk, and I spot an orange and blue one that looks a little familiar. "Is that yours?" I point at it.

"Yeah. I'm storing a couple of my bikes here now. You have a good memory."

"I've always been fascinated by bikes."

He stops, looking at me with a startled expression. "Yeah?"

I shoot him a cautious look. "Why is that so surprising?"

He drags a hand through his hair. "Most girls hate bikes." He gestures around him. "Hate this place."

"Most girls or Addison?" I venture, watching for his reaction.

His shoulders cord into knots as a grim expression spreads across his mouth. "I don't want to talk about her. Come on."

He pulls me forward and that signals the end of our conversation. We slip out of the warehouse, across a narrow grassy stretch, and into the back door of the other building.

It's much larger on the inside than I imagined. We walk past a changing room with lockers, a small gym, a kitchen, and a room kitted out with small chairs and tables, several weathered-looking beanbags, a wall-mounted TV with an Xbox, toys, books, and games. I yank on his hand, drawing him to a halt. "What's this room for?"

"Rick runs sessions for younger kids on the weekends. They usually congregate here for a while afterward. If you're not in a hurry, we can hang around and help out when they arrive."

"Cool."

He eyes me strangely.

"What?"

He shakes his head. "Nothing."

The red-haired lady greets Kyler like a long-lost son when we reach the front of the building. A narrow counter runs along one side with a multitude of framed photos hanging on the wall behind. A glass display cabinet adorns the counter on the other side, stuffed full of trophies. On the opposite side of the room, to the right of the double entrance doors, are several small bistro tables and chairs. Laminated menus stand freely in the center of the tables.

The place is spotlessly clean, but it looks neglected. Paint peels off the walls in spots, and the hardwood floor is heavily scuffed and scratched. Some of the tables have chips in the Formica, and the chairs are a mishmash of colors and styles. A dirty cream-colored blind is pulled across the large window at the front.

"May, this is Faye." Kyler's introduction snaps me out of my inspection. I smile warmly as I accept May's proffered hand. Her handshake is strong, her face kind, as she glances from him to me. "She's my cousin," he adds quickly, and a sinking feeling churns in my gut.

"It's nice to meet you." I keep a smile plastered on my face.

"Can you show her to the bleachers?"

May pats his face affectionately. "Of course, sweetheart. You run along. I'll look after this pretty lady."

"So you're the girl from Ireland?" May inquires as she leads me out the main doors and across the muddy path. My feet squelch in the soft ground, and I'm regretting not wearing my boots.

"That'd be me." I send her a coy smile.

"Kyler told me what happened to your parents. I'm very sorry for your loss."

You could knock me down with a feather, but I cover my reaction well. "Thank you." The usual thorny ball of emotion swells in my throat.

"He's worried about you." The edge of the dirt track arises on our right as I look at her as if she has ten heads. She smiles knowingly. "He's all bark, but underneath he's a big softie."

I think of how he was with me last night and this morning, and I know she's right. "How long have you worked here?" I deliberately attempt to direct the conversation to more neutral territory.

"Rick and I own the track. It's been in his family since the nineteen thirties." A dark cloud passes over her features. "Some of the greatest motocross champions trained in this facility." A note of pride laces her tone.

Taking my elbow, she steers me around to the bleachers. We step up, sliding along a bench at the midway point. There's a good vantage point from this position, and my eyes skim over the track. May leans her elbows on her knees, a sad, faraway look in her eye. For some inexplicable reason, I feel the need to cheer her up. "Tell me what you love most about it."

She sits up straighter. "I love the family atmosphere at the track. A lot of these kids come to us from age four, and they are with us until they turn pro. And even after they leave, they gravitate here whenever they have downtime. Rick and I couldn't have kids, but I never felt like I missed out because of this place. These boys are my family, and I love them all as if they were my own."

I twist around to face her. "I saw you with Kyler. He's like that for you?"

She nods. "He's a sweet boy. A lousy judge of character, but none of us are perfect." My surprise clearly shows on my face. "He talks to me. I know what's happened, but even if he hadn't told me, I would've known. He's been coming here since he was ten, and even though he's always seemed burdened, it's way worse now. He's withdrawn. I figure it's his way of protecting himself, but I worry about all he's missing out on. Apart from the track and his motocross ambition, he doesn't seem to live for much else, and that concerns me enormously."

At that precise moment, Kyler emerges from the warehouse, decked out in blue and white racing gear. He stops to talk to Rick for a few minutes, and they gesture wildly with their hands. Rick slaps him on the back before reentering the warehouse, and Kyler pushes his bike out onto the track.

Swinging his leg over the pillion, he grasps the handlebars in his gloved hands. He's wearing heavy boots that cover his calves, stopping just short of his knees. He pulls the throttle and kicks the bike into gear. His knees and elbows are bent as he stands up and the bike zooms forward.

I can't see his face under the helmet, but his posture screams focus and concentration.

May is watching the expression on my face. "You've never been to a track before?"

My eyes stay locked on Kyler as he picks up speed. "Not a moto-cross one. I used to visit Mondello Park with my dad. It's Ireland's only international racing track. My granddad used to work there when it first opened, building engines for some of the racecars. My dad basically grew up in the place."

I turn and face her, realizing I'm being rude. "He used to take me a few times a year, from when I was this high." I lower my hand in demon-stration. A slow smile adorns my lips. "I loved it. Loved the noise and the crowds. I can still hear the roar of the cars as they prepared to race."

She beams at me. "I can see that. Dirt bikes are a little different, but it's no less exciting. It's become a very popular spectator sport. We don't host races here anymore, it's purely a training facility, but I think you'd like it here."

Kyler glides around the track out of sight at the far end. "Yeah, I think I would. Maybe I'll get Kyler to bring me again."

May's smile appears brittle. When she speaks, her voice breaks a little. "You should do that. I, uh, should get back. Will you be okay by yourself?"

I worry that I've offended her somehow, but rethinking my words, I don't know what I said that might have upset her. "I'll be fine. It was nice talking with you."

"You too, sweetie." She turns to leave but stops at the end of the row. "Ky is a bit lost right now, but he has a good heart. He needs friends, and I think you could be good for him. Be patient."

Our gazes lock and a sort of shared understanding passes between us. I bob my head, and she turns and walks away.

The next hour flies by. I'm mesmerized by Kyler. His passion, dedica-tion, and obvious focus are such a turn-on. As I observe the way in which he commands the bike, and the skill with which he maneuvers his body to work seamlessly with the flow of the bike, it's clear that he's very talented. Now I understand his fixation with exercise and nutrition. Even though I'm no expert, the sport clearly requires huge levels of stamina and fitness.

Kyler leans the bike at the bottom of the bleachers, resting it against the edge of the structure. When he rips off his helmet, his hair is flat on the top of his head, with the longer strands plastered to his sweaty forehead. His skin is red and flushed as he takes the steps two at a time toward me.

My eyes scan the length of him as he shunts down the row toward me, pulling his jersey up and over his head. He plops down beside me, breathless and grinning. Sweat mixes with aftershave in a scent that is uniquely male and completely enchanting. Call me crazy, but I have a sudden urge to bury my head in his neck and soak it up. "You're drooling," he pants out, and I smack his arm.

"Was not," I lie, giving him a look that dares him to challenge me. He unstraps his neck brace and whatever form of chest protection he's wearing until he's sitting beside me in only his multicolored track pants. Morning sunlight glints off his naked chest, highlighting his sweat-slickened abs. Heat darkens my eyes as I ogle him without any pretense. "But I most definitely am now," I admit truthfully.

"You have to stop looking at me like that." His statement lacks substance, and I quirk an eyebrow. "I only have so much restraint."

"Screw restraint." I angle my body into his, running the tip of one finger down his glistening chest. I might be abnormal, but the sight and smell of him like this is hugely arousing.

Without warning, he lifts me sideways onto his lap and smashes his mouth against mine. I scrape my fingers through his hair, tugging on it sharply as he urges my lips apart. His tongue sweeps into my mouth, and his scent surrounds me as I cling to him possessively. Clamping a hand at the back of my neck, he tilts my head to the side and deepens the kiss. Stars explode behind my eyes, and I'm melting under the power of his touch. If feels like my own personal slice of heaven on earth.

Someone loudly clears their throat, and we instantly break apart. May is standing in the row in front, her hands outstretched, her fingers curling around two bottles of water. "I thought you might need to cool down."

Neither of us misses the double entendre. A red flush creeps over my neck and up my face as I slide off his lap and meekly take the offered bottle of water.

"Thanks, May." Kyler probes her face as he accepts the drink.

"Can you stick around? We could use a hand or two." Her disapproving gaze bounces between us. Kyler looks to me.

"I don't mind. I'm not in work until later."

"Count us in." He opens the water and chugs it down his throat.

"Great, thanks."

Kyler stands but she motions for him to sit back down. "The little monsters don't arrive for another hour. Stay." She pins him with a serious look. "Talk." Her gaze flits to me with purpose, and I know she's sending him some silent message. I instantly stiffen, feeling the weight of her dissent. I thought we had gotten along earlier, but now I'm second-guessing myself.

She doesn't approve. That much is blatantly obvious.

May walks off without another word, her lips pinched together. Kyler and I sit in silence for a few minutes. I drink from my water, grappling with my churning mind. Eventually I can take no more of the silence. "What was all that about?"

He smooths his hair off his forehead as he leans back in his seat. Muscles flex and bunch in his chest and his jaw pops in and out, as he stares ahead. I wait patiently for him to speak. "Don't take it personally. I can already tell that May likes you, but I know what she's going to say." He takes a quick slug of his water.

"Spill, Ky." I suspect I know, but I'd rather hear him say it.

A small grin teases the corners of his mouth. "That's the first time you've called me Ky." I pierce him with a deadly look, and he raises his palms in conciliation. "I like hearing it, that's all." He sits up, leaning his elbows on his knees. "It's because we're cousins."

I grimace as he confirms my suspicion. This whole situation is so frustrating. There is nothing in the constitution that says I can't date my cousin, and it's not as if we grew up together. He's a complete stranger to me, and our chemistry is off the charts—if God didn't want us together, why hotwire us to react so explosively to each other's touch?

Although, I'm not naïve, and I can easily imagine how people might judge us. Judgy narrow-mindedness is one of my pet peeves, and this isn't the first time I've been forced to confront reality in such a personal way.

I've guessed this was partly responsible for Kyler keeping his distance, but now I think it's time we laid our cards on the table. "Does that matter to you?" I eyeball him as I wait for his reply.

"That's a bit of a loaded question." He watches me carefully as he tips the bottle into his mouth, draining the last few drops.

"I'm not asking for an in-depth analysis of the legal, social, and moral implications of kissing your cousin. I'm asking how *you feel* about it. Do you think it's wrong?"

He sits up, holding my chin in his hand. "I think you already know how I feel about that. If I wasn't into it, last night or just now wouldn't have happened. That isn't the issue."

"Then what is?"

He cups my face gently. "May is one of the nicest, most tolerant people I know. If she reacts like that, imagine how everyone else would react? People won't approve, especially not in my parents' social circles. My *father*"—he grinds his teeth as he says the word—"told us you were strictly off limits for that very reason."

He releases my face and looks down at his feet. "Maybe we shouldn't start something we can't finish." His Adam's apple jumps in his throat as he looks up at me. "Maybe we should put a stop to this right now."

Chapter Twenty-Two

I stand up, lengthening my spine as I look down at him. "I didn't take you for a coward, but that's exactly what you are. Either you're too chicken to tell me you're not into me, or you're running scared at the first sign of dissent. Either way, it means the same thing. It doesn't matter anyway." I move to walk past him. "We kissed a few times. It's no big deal. Forget about it."

He stands up, taking my elbow and holding me in place. "Don't do that."

"Relax, Kyler. You've made your point and I'm agreeing, so let's move past it and go help May." I try to wriggle out of his grip, but he maintains a firm hold.

"I didn't say I wanted to stop this thing between us, just that it might be the smart thing to do."

I glare at him. "Now you're splitting hairs. Say what you mean and mean what you say." He pins me with a teasing smile, and that pisses me off. "Stop it." Anger starts tunneling to the surface. He grins again, and I nudge him in the ribs. "You're being an ass."

He sweeps his thumb across my lower lip. "You're incredibly hot when you're mad." Hauling me into his body, he leaves his hands hanging loosely against my lower back as he buries his face in my neck.

I shove my hands into his chest and push him away. "Stop fucking with me, Kyler. My head's enough of a mess already. One minute you're saying we should stop this and the next you're flirting? What the hell do you want from me?"

His smile fades. Stepping away, he reaches down to grab his gear. Silence engulfs us. "I don't know," he admits after a bit, looking me straight in the eye. His troubled expression says it all. "I don't know what I want."

I'm disappointed but it's not as if I can tell him what he wants. He's confused, and nothing I say will change that. I have to respect his opinion and accept him at his word. My priority now is protecting my heart from further attack. Tossing the horrible feelings of rejection aside, I face him with a placid expression, determined to be mature about this. "Okay. But until you do, I need you to stay away from me."

The atmosphere is strained when we return to the main building, but if Rick and May notice, they don't say anything. I assist May with registrations while Rick and Kyler help the kids get kitted out and set up on the bikes. The place is utter bedlam as twenty or more kids, all under the age of ten, descend on the front room. I can hardly think over the noise. They chase each other around the room, laughing and giggling, and it's impossible to hold onto my dour mood. I find myself quietly chuckling at their antics.

When the kids are outside, and my ears are functioning normally again, I help May prepare food in the kitchen. We work in silence, initially, but friction is ripe in the air, growing more fraught with each passing second until, eventually, I can't take it any longer. "You disapprove," I say, without looking up from my chopping board.

She sighs, stopping what she's doing. "It's not you, sweetie, and it's not that I disapprove, per se, but"—she gently takes my arm, forcing me to stop working—"I know Ky's folks, and they're good people, but appearance is everything to them. This community does not look favorably on nonconformance." She takes the knife out of my hand, placing it on the counter. Holding both my hands in hers, she fixes her sincere gaze on me. "You are grieving, and Ky is still hurting over Addison and Brad's betrayal. Neither of you need any additional complications. People will not respond well to your relationship, and I worry about what that'd do to both of you."

"We're not in a relationship," I grumble, wanting to at least set her straight on that front. "It's only been a few kisses."

"I've seen enough today to know this is no simple flirtation. I may be past my prime, but I still remember my teenage years. With great fondness, I might add," she says, with a teasing grin. "And I'd bet my last dollar you two have strong feelings for each other."

"But you don't want us to act on that," I paraphrase.

She looks apologetic. "No. I think that's inviting a whole world of trouble."

I chew on the inside of my cheek as I try to compartmentalize my feelings. "I mean no disrespect, May, but that's kind of insulting. You're basically insinuating that neither of us are strong enough to deal with the backlash, and, fair enough, you know Ky, but you don't know me. You have no idea what I can and can't tolerate. The things I've had to endure. Things that could've sent me into a downward spiral if I'd let the situation get the better of me. I'm stronger than you think."

"I've offended you, and I'm sorry about that. I'm only trying to help, because I care about Kyler, and he cares about you. He probably doesn't realize how much, but I see it. And now I see you, and in so many ways, you are perfect for him. You have the power to bring him back, to help him move on. But it could go the other way, too. No matter how you spin it, dating your cousin is taboo around these parts. The backlash would be severe. You could destroy him, and I'm not going to sit back and pretend that I'm comfortable with that. I meant what I said earlier, he's like a son to me."

My spine stiffens, and I remove my hands from hers. "I would never deliberately hurt him, or anyone. You don't see me. You don't see me at all." I step back, reeling, as hurt and anger wage an internal war inside me.

"Faye." She steps toward me, and I raise a hand in warning. "I'm not saying you'd intentionally hurt him. That's not what I meant at all. Can't you see that pursuing this puts both of you at risk? I'm only trying to stop you from making a mistake."

"That's not your call to make," Kyler says gruffly, startling us both. My head whips around. He's standing in the middle of the open doorway, sending daggers at May. He extends his hand toward me. "We're leaving."

May moves toward him, a crestfallen look on her face. "Kyler, I—"

"I don't want to hear it," Kyler says, cutting her off. "I'm way too pissed for this conversation right now, and I don't want to say something I'll regret. Just leave it, May."

Ky takes my hand and pulls me out of the room. Instead of going toward the warehouse like I expect, he guides me out the side door and around the back of the warehouse. Veins protrude in his neck as he drags me up a hilly slope. The sun rests high in the clear blue sky, beating a burning path straight for us. Little beads of sweat break out on my brow, but I don't complain as he steers me to the top of the hill.

He drops down on the ground, and I sit beside him, crossing my legs in front of me. I fan my face with my hands. "Here." He hands me a bottle of water and a sandwich from his backpack.

"Thanks." I gratefully guzzle the water. "How much did you hear?"

"Enough." He bites a large chunk out of his chicken wrap.

"I think she means well."

He surveys the land spread out below us. The kids look like toddlers on dirt bikes from up here. "I know, but she has no right to say any of that stuff to you. Or to dictate what I should and shouldn't do with my life. It's not her decision to make."

I take a sip of water. "It's not that different from what you said earlier, and she wasn't saying it to you. I don't understand why *you're* so mad."

He faces me head-on, and there's a thunderous look on his face. "I'm sick of people trying to manipulate my life! I thought you understood that."

I touch his jean-clad knee. "I do, but this is different. She isn't out to hurt you; she cares about you." Perhaps it's not my place to defend May, and God knows her words hurt me, but this track means so much to Ky. I don't want him to lose that over me. "Her intervention is coming from the right place, for the right reasons, even if it is a little misguided. Don't fall out with her over this."

The storm fades in his eyes. "I know, but she can't say those things to you. And she's got enough on her plate; she shouldn't be worrying about me."

All the cryptic little clues line up perfectly in my brain. "This place is in financial trouble, isn't it? That's what you were talking to your dad about that day in his study."

He scrunches up his wrapper, fisting it in his hand. "Yeah. It's going to close unless they get an injection of cash. I didn't know they were in trouble until recently, and now that bastard won't help. It's punishment for forcing his hand on our allowance."

I pull my knees up to my chest as I twist around to face him. "What do you mean?"

He shoots me a sly grin. "Mom is strict with our allowance, but Dad knows I know about his affair, so he's been slipping all of us more on the side." His grin fades. "But he refused to help Rick and May out because he's trying to reassert his authority. Well, he can fuck off now if he thinks I'm backing down." Determination and spitefulness infiltrates his words.

Tiny hairs lift on my arms. "What are you planning?"

"He's going to fund this track, or I'll tell Mom everything."

I gasp. "You can't blackmail your father!"

"Why the hell not?" He pins me with an incredulous look.

"Because it's wrong. Your mother should know—I agree on that point—but your father is the one who has to come clean. You can't use this situation to your advantage. If you do, you're no better than he is."

His eyes darken and this time it's not with lust. "It wouldn't be solely to my advantage! Take a look around! See all those kids down there"—he jabs his finger in the direction of the track—"what are they going to do without this place? There isn't any other facility that provides this type of opportunity for them. The only other track in the vicinity closed down a few years ago due to …" He visibly pales as he scrapes his hands through his hair. "Well, it's gone, and this is the only place around. Most of those kids come from low-income families who could never afford to indulge their kid's interest in this sport. It's an expensive hobby. Part of the reason why Rick and May have run into so much trouble is because they heavily subside the kids program. This isn't just about me."

His impassioned speech speaks volumes, but he's missing my point. "I understand that, and I'd hate to see this place close, but that doesn't detract from the situation. You cannot blackmail your father into doing this. You can never come back from that! What kind of relationship will you have with him in future if you do that?"

He stands up, flexing his hands into fists at his side. "I want nothing to do with that lying, cheating slime ball, so that's not a concern. If things work out like I've planned, then I won't need his name or his money." He extends his hand to help me up. "Scouts have expressed interest in me. Once I go pro, I'm walking away, and I'm not coming back." He pins me with a laser-sharp look. "Not for anyone."

He storms down the hill, not even glancing behind his shoulder to see if I'm following. I keep a reasonable distance, trailing quietly behind him.

Rick tries to talk to Kyler at the warehouse, but he brushes him off and powers up his motorbike. I climb on behind him even though I'd rather be anywhere but here. His back is rigidly stiff underneath me the entire journey back home.

Once he parks, I slide off the bike and walk into the house without a backward glance.

I'm pissy as all hell as I throw myself down on my bed. A couple of hours later, my anger starts to dissipate. It's one thing knowing your father is having an affair, but it's another matter entirely seeing it with your own eyes. Add in the fact that it's a double betrayal for Alex, and it's probably reopening painful wounds for Ky, too, and I can understand how he is so worked up. Plus, there's this whole uncertainty over "us" and today was only a tiny glimpse of what lies in store *should* we decide to take things further.

I know I'm confused as hell, so I can only assume Ky is too.

Perhaps I was too harsh earlier. I should've been more sympathetic.

I hate leaving things like this between us, and I've an hour until my shift starts, so there's enough time to try to mend things. I knock on Ky's bedroom door but there's no answer. Popping my head into the gym, I frown when I find it empty, too. I wander throughout the house, looking for him. A bout of girlish giggling pricks my ears as I venture outside, and an ominous sense of foreboding sweeps over me.

Stepping onto the patio, I stop dead in my tracks, refusing to believe my eyes. Ky is lying back on a lounge chair looking like the cat that got the cream. Addison is straddling his lap, grinding her hips into his as she leans down to whisper in his ear. Ky smooths a path up and down her spine, his fingers caressing her skin in light strokes. He spies me watching, and a smirk spreads slowly over his mouth. Addison tips her head back and stares at me. A conniving expression creeps over her face as she moves her hand down, in the gap between her and Ky, to cup his junk.

A dart of pain spears me through the heart as nausea travels up my throat. I think I'm going to vomit. Keeping a blank expression on my face, I turn around and scurry back into the house, as Addison's loud peals of laughter follow me in a taunting manner.

Chapter Twenty-Three

My heart is still pumping wildly when I reach the safety of my room. I sit on the edge of my bed, cradling my head in my hands. All manner of confusing thoughts and emotions jumble my mind. My chest heaves visibly as pain slices a clear line through my heart. There has only been one other occasion where I've felt as gullible as I do in this moment.

How could he share intimacy with me last night and then crawl all over another girl the very next day? I feel so cheap, so used. And unbelievably foolish. Old nightmares resurrect to haunt me, and I clutch my stomach, as the usual bout of self-loathing batters me on all sides. Not for the first time in my life, I wish I could rewind time and stop myself from making such an awful mistake.

I don't know what game Kyler is playing, but I'm damned if he's going to use me for some nefarious aim.

As I get ready for work, I curse myself for my naïveté. Ky had no intention of starting anything with me. I was an itch he felt the need to scratch, and I was an idiot to buy into it, to believe it might be going somewhere. I slam my palm against my forehead in frustration.

He played me, and I fell right into his trap.

Well, I won't fall for it a second time. This thing between us is over. Period. And it's clearly for the best. I don't understand why he got so worked up at the track, but that's neither here nor there now.

It's as well I discovered this now before my heart was even more invested.

I grab my bag and yank open the door, almost falling head first into Ky's arms. "Get out of my way," I snarl, pushing at him.

"No." He batters his forearms. "Not until you let me explain."

He starts pushing into the room and I step back. *What the actual fuck?!* "Explain?" I yell. "Your body language gave me all the explanation I need!" I'm incensed beyond all reason, and something snaps inside me. I raise my clenched hand and punch him in the face. Hard. I put every ounce of my hurt and humiliation into the blow, and it pleases me no end when he staggers back, clutching his jaw. He looks shocked as he stares at me, but then the shock gives way to laughter. He's doubled over, clutching his stomach, and an angry red flush steals over my cheeks. How dare he make fun of me! The urge to hit him a second time is strong, but I'm *so* done with this. "Screw you. You deserve that cow. I hope you're both miserable as sin together. Now, get out of my room, get out of my face, and stay the hell out of my life." I roar that last part for extra emphasis.

His laughter withers and dies. He shoots me a terse nod. "Fine. Message understood."

I slump against the wall as he walks away, willing my pounding pulse to settle down.

I'm grumpy as hell at work, and everyone notices. I try to snap out of it, but I can't get the image of Addison grinding on Kyler's lap out of my head. It's the worst form of self-inflicted torture, but short of bleaching my brain, I don't know what else to do. I'm messing up orders left and right, so when David calls me into his office, I figure I'm about to get my marching orders. It's no more than I deserve.

David tells me to take a seat as he plants his butt on the edge of the desk. Concerned eyes meet mine. "Do you want to tell me what's the matter?"

"Nothing's the matter," I lie, sitting up straighter in my chair. I'm not going to air my personal laundry to the boss man.

"Boy trouble?" He astutely guesses, cocking his head to the side as he skims my face for clues.

"I'd rather not talk about it. I should get back." I move to stand, but he shakes his head, keeping me grounded in the seat.

"It's not that busy tonight. You can take off if you like." He pushes off the desk, looming over me.

"I'd prefer to keep working, and I promise no more mistakes."

He bends down, his face coming very close to mine. "I'm a good listener, and I'm here for you anytime you need to talk." He pats my cheek, and I flinch back at the inappropriateness of the gesture.

Sensing my discomfort, he immediately steps back, and I jump to my feet. "Uh, thanks. But I'm fine."

"Very well." He folds his arms across his chest. "You can go back to work."

I'm shaking my head when I return to the floor. "What did he want?" Rose asks.

"He was fishing for info. He wanted to know what was up with me."

"I wouldn't mind knowing the answer to that question either," Rose murmurs.

I sigh. "I'll tell you after our shift ends."

"Okay. Theo and I are heading to a party later. Do you want to come?"

"I'm not sure I'd be the best company."

She lightly touches my elbow. "And that's exactly why you should come. It'll help distract you."

"Maybe. I'll think about it."

I collect orders from a couple of tables and add them into the system. When I turn around, I find a pair of captivating blue eyes watching my every move. Brad is leaning over the counter, flippantly tossing a menu between his fingers. "Hi, Faye," he says pleasantly.

"Hi, Brad. What can I get you?" I remove my notepad, holding my pen aloft. "Nothing, thanks."

I pin him with an inquisitive look. "What are you doing here then?"

He runs a hand through his blond hair. "I wanted to ask you something." I purse my lips, pinning him with a suspicious look. "Don't make it easy or anything," he murmurs with a smile.

"What is it, Brad?"

"Chase is throwing a party tonight, and I wanted to know if you'd go with me."

My brow puckers. "Why?"

His lips curve up at the corners. "Why does any guy ask a girl out?"

My face drops at his sheer nerve. His eyes widen and he reaches out for me. I step back from the counter. "No! Not that. Jeez." He rubs his chin. "That came out wrong. I'm not like that."

"That's not what I've heard."

His features lock down instantly, and he pushes off the stool. "You shouldn't believe everything you hear." Pain flashes in his eyes, and I'm instantly chastised.

"What did you mean if you weren't talking about hooking up?"

"I'd like to get to know you. You seem different to the girls in this town ... hope I guessed right?"

I stare him down as I ponder his words, trying to gauge if he's sincere or playing some angle.

"Okay, I stand corrected. Forget it." He walks toward the exit as I call out to him. Ignoring me, he yanks the door open, almost lifting it from the hinges, and steps outside.

"Go after him," Rose urges, giving me a gentle nudge in the back. "I'll cover for you."

I race out the door after him, wondering why I'm so concerned. Am I that shallow that I don't want him thinking I'm as narrow-minded as the bitches in this place? I'd like to think it's remorse, because he showed his true colors and I could tell that it was a genuine offer, yet I treated him like he deserves his cheating man-slut rep. "Brad, wait up." He's powering along the path in long-legged strides.

He stops and turns around, waiting for me to catch up. "Look," I say, when I reach him. "I'm sorry. I'm new to all this, and so far, mostly everyone who's tried to get to know me has some agenda. But I can tell I was wrong to jump to conclusions about you."

His shoulders loosen a little. "I guess I can understand that. I know this town far too well." He looks away.

"I'm sorry for what I implied back there. Rose told me you're not like that, and she's the only person I trust to be on the level." I no longer trust in anything that Ky has said, so he can take his warning and stuff it where the sun don't shine. The only thing I can fault about Brad is his previous choice in friends and hookups, but everyone deserves a chance to turn over a new leaf.

"Rose is cool, and she's been a good friend. Theo too. So, how about the party? I can pick you up after work."

He looks hopeful, and I don't want to be the one to wipe that from his face. "Sure, why not? I get off at eleven."

He smiles, and I can't help but smile back. "I'll see you then."

Rose gives me the thumbs-up when I relay the gist of our conversation.

As the working night draws to a close, I even find myself getting a little excited. It sure beats the previous heartbroken feeling.

I didn't bring any suitable going-out clothes to work, but luckily, Rose has a few things in her locker belonging to her sister which fit me, and in next to no time, I'm party ready and raring to go. I really feel like letting loose tonight.

"You look gorgeous," Brad says, when I step outside the diner. His eyes skim respectively over my skinny jeans and red halter-top.

"Thanks."

Rose waggles her fingers at me as she hops on the back of Theo's bike. "See you guys out there."

Brad walks me to a silver SUV and opens the passenger door for me. I'm buckling my seat belt when he hops in the driver's side, fixing me with an anxious look. I stop what I'm doing. "What?"

"It's okay if you want to change your mind. I'll understand."

I frown, wondering what kind of vibes I'm giving off. "Why do you think I've changed my mind?"

He grips the steering wheel painfully. "I'm not exactly the most popular guy in this town. Attending with me isn't going to do much to help your cred. I should've thought of that before I asked you."

"You're having second thoughts?"

"Hell no." He twists around in his seat, the leather squeaking with the motion. "I want to go with you, but I don't want to make anything more difficult for you at school. I know what Old Colonial is like."

"Pfft." I dismiss his concern quickly. "I'm the last person to care about that stuff, believe me. And, besides, I'm going to Wellesley Memorial."

His eyes are out on stalks. "You are?"

I eye him skeptically. "Why is that so hard to believe?"

He smiles, shaking his head, as he twists the key and the car powers up. "It's not, actually. It means my first impressions were spot-on. That's great." He flashes me a wide grin. "You're not like other girls. You have no idea how refreshing that is."

He shoves the car in gear, and we glide out onto the asphalt. It feels like the right time to set some ground rules. "Don't go getting any ideas, Brad. I'm not in the market for a boyfriend, or even a hookup, but I'll happily take all the friends I can get."

"I respect that, Faye." He keeps his gaze focused on the road. "And I'll be a perfect gentleman. Scout's honor. Whether you believe me or not, I could really use a friend, so I'm totally cool with that."

Chapter Twenty-Four

The high wrought iron gates open slowly to allow us to pass through. Brad drives up the winding driveway, parking in a line beside a row of flashy cars. "Who is Chase anyway?" I ask, when he opens my door. I slip my hand in his as he helps me out of the car, and his skin is warm but slightly callused, a lot like Ky's. I remember now that Brad is into motocross too, and I wonder if he still trains at Rick and May's track.

"He's on the football team with me." A deep crease furrows his brow, but he shakes it off. "His parents are good friends with your aunt and uncle."

I stumble in my heels on the gravel, and Brad places a steadying hand on my lower back as we walk. Heat seeps into my skin through the sheer material of my top. It doesn't foster the same tingling sensation that Ky's touch invokes, but it's nice all the same.

Rose and Theo are waiting at the side of the house, and she lifts her hand in a wave when she spots us.

"Yay!" Rose says, bounding toward me. "You made it!" She loops her arm in mine and pulls me toward Theo, making necessary introductions. After that, we head around the side of the house, while the boys trail behind us, talking in low voices. "How are you two getting along?" she inquires.

I roll my eyes. "It was only a ten-minute drive, Rose."

"I know, but you can tell he's a decent guy, right?"

I give her a funny look. "Why does it matter so much to you? You still got a thing for him?"

She throws back her head and laughs. "Don't be so silly. I'm crazy about Theo, and I told you me and Brad was only a childish thing, but he's still a good friend, and I worry about him. Everything's changing in his life, and I think you would be good for him. You make a cute couple."

Sounds of laughter are getting louder the farther we walk. "No matchmaking! This isn't that. I've told him already that I only want to be friends. Boys are fuckwits and I don't need any more complications."

She pulls me to the side. "Tell Auntie Rose all about it."

Brad and Theo stop and look at us. "Everything all right?" Theo asks, shooting a loving look at Rose.

"Everything is perfect." I level a gaze at Rose, pleading with her to drop it. I take her arm and pull her forward.

"Later," she whispers in my ear, and I give her a slight nod.

The party is in full swing by a massive pool. Shrieks and cries fill the air as couples mess about in the water. Others are congregated in seating areas, drinking and chatting. Loud music pumps out through huge, mobile speakers. Expansive glass doors are retracted at the side of the house, merging the inside and outside spaces. Lighting is dim inside as Brad guides me through a large living room that has been transformed into a makeshift dance floor. The place is teeming with heaving, sweaty bodies, and Brad has to weave an elaborate path through the crowd in the direction of the kitchen. He keeps a firm hold on my hand as he maneuvers across the room. A few heads turn in our direction. Inquisitive glances dart from Brad to me, but no one makes any effort to greet us.

Emerald green eyes latch on mine, as someone familiar spots me in the crowd. A glimmer of gleeful amusement flickers in Addison's gaze.

"Oh joy."

Brad stops, grimacing as he turns around. "What's up?" He follows my line of sight. Addison notices him for the first time, and the look on her face transforms instantly. She saunters toward us, sashaying her hips in an orchestrated fashion. Her mouth pulls into a provocative pout, and I can't help the snort that escapes my lips. She is such a walking cliché.

Brad moves closer to my side, placing a protective arm across my lower back.

"Well, well," she says, standing in front of us with her hands on her hips. Her gaze hovers from me to Brad and back again. "This is almost too good to be true! The rejected blue blood and the wannabe rich girl! Too funny!" A line of girls form a semi-circle around her, and they all titter at our expense.

"Don't be a bitch, Addison." Brad is uber calm.

"Oh, how the mighty have fallen." She mock tuts, skimming one finger down the front of his shirt. "You've had to downgrade everything, haven't you?" He pales at her words. She tilts her head to the side, and her eyes lock on mine.

The insinuation isn't subtle. Neither is the insult.

"Get lost, Addison," Kalvin demands, coming up on the other side of me. "Can't you tell when you're not wanted?"

"That's not what you were telling me before," she purrs, brushing her chest up against him on purpose.

Are you shitting me?

I gawp at Kalvin, letting him witness the full extent of my disbelief. He stares at me defiantly, stepping back from Addison. "Quit messing around, and stop sniffing near me and my brothers. When are you going to get it into your thick head? We don't want you. We don't even *like* you. Go prey on some other dumb sucker."

Okay, now I'm confused. All these games are tying my brain into knots.

"That's not what Ky was whispering in my ear this afternoon. Ask *her*." She jerks her head at me. "She was there." I visualize myself lunging for her, clawing my nails down her smug face. It helps stem the growing tidal wave of fury taking root inside me.

Kalvin peers into my eyes and he sees the truth. Fixing a dangerous sneer on his face, he bends down so he's at Addison's height. "You listen to me, and you listen good, slut. Stay away from Ky. I fucking mean it. You're not worming your way back in."

Kalvin's low pitch and venomous face state the truth. He isn't joking about. So when Addison pushes him back, and laughs in his face, I have to reluctantly admire her balls of steel. "You, poor, clueless fool. Don't you know that I always get what I want? And you really shouldn't push me. You won't like the fallout."

Kalvin's jaw clenches and unclenches. Turning his back on Addison, he takes hold of my elbow. "I need to speak to you. Right now." His eyes latch on Brad's hand, which is currently loosely draped around my hip. "Get your fucking hand off her."

Brad stands his ground. "You need to chill out, bro."

Kalvin stabs his finger in Brad's chest. "I am not your bro. And Faye's not available to the likes of you."

That's it. I've had enough of this macho-man bullshit. I take hold of Brad's hand. "Let's get a drink." I shove Kalvin's arm away. "You do not dictate who I spend time with. I will talk to you later, after you've calmed down."

I ignore Addison's hoot of laughter, as I let Brad lead the way.

My shoulders sag in relief when we step into the kitchen.

"Wow. That was fun." There is zero humor in Brad's tone or his look.

"You're telling me. These people are flipping crazy."

That brings a smile to his face. "You have no idea."

"Forget about them. I know I want to." I can't decide if I find my cousin's protective streak endearing or plain insulting.

"What's your poison?" Brad asks.

"I'll have a beer. Or ten." So much for steering clear of alcohol.

He smiles as he swipes two from a large ice-filled bucket, handing one to me. "Let's start with one, and see how we go. Do you want to stay in here or head outside?" he shouts over the drone of the music.

"Outside." As far away from Addison is more the sentiment, but that one word will suffice. The heat and the noise die down the second we step out onto a sprawling patio. The crowded pool area is to our left. In front of us, and to our right, small groups and couples converse in private on the expansive lawn.

"Do you want to go sit there?" Brad points out an elevated wooden structure at the far end of the garden, and I nod in agreement.

The large, unoccupied pergola is positioned on top of a raised stone circle. Tiny tea lights hang from little lanterns in the roof. Wicker furniture with soft cream cushions surrounds a low table. Ornate pots of all shapes and sizes are scattered around the space. The setting is very romantic, and now I'm feeling a little uncomfortable. "Don't worry. I won't bite," Brad teases, sitting down on a two-seater couch. I sit down beside him and cross my legs. "So," he says, drumming his fingers off his knee. "What did you do to earn Addison's wrath?"

"I exist." I tip my head back and chug some of my beer.

"I figured as much. Addison strikes quick to neutralize any threat."

"I'm not a threat. I don't want anything she has. She's welcome to it all." *Liar,* a scheming inner devil hisses in my ear. I lean my head back against the soft pillow and stare at the twinkling lights above.

"She wouldn't care to hear that. You are all everyone is talking about, and that's enough to set her blood boiling." He raises the bottle to his lips, and I take the opportunity to slyly study him. I can't reconcile this boy and that bitch. Nope. Don't see it. It doesn't make any sense. Brad seems like a genuinely nice guy, and he's the complete opposite of the Queen B inside.

As I examine his face, I notice the pale shadows under his eyes for the first time. Tired, fine lines crinkle the corners of his eyes, and his pallor is a little off-white. He looks wrecked, as if he's carrying the weight of the world on his shoulders.

"What?" He looks perplexed.

I sit up straighter, realizing my mind had wandered. "What?"

"You were staring; not that I'm complaining." He grins, flashing a set of perfect white teeth. "What are you thinking?"

I pump for honesty. "That I don't understand how you ended up with her. You don't seem the type."

His throat works overtime as he drains his beer in one go. "You and me both." I lean forward on my elbows, waiting for him to continue. "It's complicated. I ..." Brad trails off as he looks over my head.

Feet race across the stone platform and a muscular arm snakes out, lifting Brad up by his shirt. "Keep your filthy paws off her, McConaughey." Kyler growls out a warning. Hostility radiates from him in waves, lifting all the hairs on the back of my neck. A thrill of excitement whips through me, and I'm disgusted at myself. This side of Kyler speaks to the inner demon inside me. I don't want to acknowledge that dark part of me, much less release it. That's why this part of Ky's personality is so dangerous to me. "I don't know what you're up to this time, but you won't hurt my family again."

Brad removes Kyler's hand. "It's not what you think. I'm just looking out for her."

"I'm right here." I feel the need to state the obvious because they're both talking as if I'm not present. Neither of them looks at me. Their faces are locked on one another, and some silent battle is erupting between them. I climb to my feet. "Knock it off, Ky." I tug on his arm, but he doesn't budge. Bunched muscles are rigid under my fingers. Kyler is primed for battle, and all it'll take is one erstwhile comment from Brad to set him off.

"I'd like to leave now, Brad. Can you drive me home?"

He lowers his head to mine. "Of course, Faye. No problem."

"What are you doing?" Kyler pins his dark expression on me. "I told you to stay away from him."

"And I told you to go screw yourself." I lace my fingers in Brad's and jerk my chin up to level a cold look at Kyler. "We done here?"

"I know what you're doing, and it won't work." Kyler scowls, his eyes traveling to our conjoined hands for a brief second.

"I don't know what you're talking about, and I don't care. Come on, Brad." We step around the table, avoiding Kyler. Brad places his arm across my shoulders as he steers us onto the lush grass.

Firm hands seize me from behind, and I'm lifted clear off the ground. Kyler pulls my back against his chest, keeping a tight hold around my midriff. I wriggle in his embrace as he presses his mouth to my ear. "I know you're mad at me, and you've every right to be, but I can explain. Don't do this. You can't trust him." His warm breath seeps over my skin causing me to wither in his arms. Kyler tightens his hold on me, and suddenly I'm hyperaware of his hard body pressed flush against mine. The usual dart of desire ignites instantly, turning my limbs to rubber. I clasp Kyler's arm to stop myself from slithering to the ground. Brad watches me intensely.

"He's not into you," Kyler continues whispering in my ear. "He's using you to get back at me."

A fresh wave of hurt rolls over me. "You'd know all about that."

Kyler stiffens. "What does that mean?" He turns me fluidly around, hanging onto my upper arms.

"You know exactly what I mean," I snap.

"Look, let's not do this here. Let me take you home and we'll talk then." His eyes beseech me to play along, but I owe him nothing.

"No, we won't. Now let me go. I'm leaving with Brad."

He grinds his teeth as he releases me, and I step back, rubbing my arms.

He sighs, running a hand across his stomach. His shirt lifts with the movement, showcasing a tantalizing strip of skin. My eyes linger on his abs a beat too long, and I want to punch myself in the stomach. Either that or gouge out my eyes so they can't betray me anymore.

Kyler smirks knowingly and it's like waving a red flag in my face. My nostrils flare as I take a swing at him. This time, he reacts fast, gripping my wrist before I can make contact. "Hitting isn't very ladylike." He fights to keep the smile off his face, and that only infuriates me further. I lift my knee to his groin, but he bats it away before impact. "That's definitely not very nice."

"Ky," a nauseating voice calls out, and I roll my eyes. "I've been looking for you everywhere." Addison strolls across the grass, shooting me a filthy look. Ky releases me as she circles her arms around him. Brad moves forward, slinging his arm around my waist. I appreciate the show of support.

"Come back inside, Ky," she says, sneaking her hand up under his shirt. She makes a deliberate show of snuggling into him as her hand visibly creeps up over his chest.

How can he stand to have her touch him after what she did? Does he feel superior now that she's sidling up to him in front of Brad? Can't he see her for the opportunist she is?

Red splotches blur my vision, and I'm about to go ninja on her ass. I'm literally two seconds from losing my shit. I grip Brad's hand hard, needing his touch to ground me. "Please get me out of here."

Kyler breaks free of Addison's hold, stepping toward me. "I'll take you home. You're not getting in a car with him."

Addison pouts, fisting a hand in Ky's shirt. "Don't leave. We were only getting properly reacquainted." She loops her fingers in his belt and tugs him toward her. My mouth goes dry as her hand slips under the band of his jeans. Kyler watches me with those penetrating eyes of his, waiting for me to react, and I can't stand it a second longer.

Twirling around, I rest my hands on Brad's chest. He looks down at me, and I see my own hurt and confusion mirrored in his gaze. His arms fasten around my waist, and I don't know if it's the feel of his body against mine, or the shared outrage, or that I need to feel comforted in that moment, but my brain checks out as I lift on my tiptoes and press my lips to his.

His mouth is soft and warm against mine, but his kiss is light and hesitant. I think I may have misread the situation. A surge of embarrassment heats my skin as I start to break away, but he stops me, drawing me in closer to his chest. His arms tighten around me, and he tilts my head, deepening the kiss. His mouth moves confidently against mine, and while his kiss doesn't ignite the same flames that Ky's does, it's still flooding me with gentle warmth.

I'm ripped off him in one fluid movement. Kyler lifts me off the ground, swiftly handing me off to Kalvin who seems to have magically appeared from somewhere. Ky's arm flexes as he throws a concentrated punch at a dazed Brad, glancing the side of his jaw. Brad stumbles but doesn't lose his balance. "Stop, Ky." He deflects a second punch with his raised palm. "I don't want to fight you."

"Tough. You've had this coming for a long while."

Brad stretches his neck from side to side, as he removes his jacket and flings it to the ground. Addison leans back against a tree with a smug look on her face.

"You really want to do this?" Brad asks, rolling up his shirtsleeves. "Fine. Let's do it."

A group advances across the lawn, sniffing a fight.

Brad raises his fists in front of him as Ky approaches. I elbow Kalvin in the ribs, extracting myself from his hold as I jump in the middle of the two would-be brawlers. I raise a hand to each of them. "Stop it. This is not the way to resolve your issues."

"Butt out, Faye," Kyler grits out. "This is nothing to do with you."

"They're fighting over me," Addison says with stupid pride, as if it's some claim to fame. "Did you really think this was about you?" Her eyes scan my body in her usual derogatory fashion.

"You're an idiot if you think this is about you," I say. Her expression sours as she glares at me. Like I care. I show her my back, turning around in time to see Kyler lunge at Brad, thrusting his knotted fist in his face. Brad takes the hit without complaint before jumping Ky and punching him in the nose. Kyler sends him an amused grin, and his fist snakes out again, clocking Brad in the eye.

A large crowd has gathered around the boys now, and they shout out encouragement. Brad lands a blow directly to Ky's mouth, and blood spurts from a cut in his lip. Ky launches himself at Brad, grabbing him in a headlock. They continue to trade successive jabs, as the crowd whoops in delight. Every so often, they share a grin, and I have a sneaky feeling they're actually enjoying this showdown.

I'm utterly disgusted with both of them.

Kicking my shoes off, I snatch them up and take off running. I'm aware of footsteps behind me, but I keep going until I've reached the front of the mansion. "Stay here," Kalvin says, looking down at my bare feet. "I'll get the car."

Chapter Twenty-Five

We don't speak on the way home, and that suits me fine. I'm happy to drown in my turbulent thoughts. I knew I shouldn't have gone out tonight. All I've done is make an awkward situation ten million times worse.

Kalvin eases the SUV into the garage and switches off the engine. He turns to face me. "I'm not going to ask what all that was about tonight."

"Good. Because I couldn't tell you even if I wanted to."

"I don't believe that for a second, but I'll play along." He taps his fingers idly off the steering wheel.

I rest my head against the headrest, closing my eyes. "I shouldn't have kissed Brad."

"Wasn't one of your better moves, but hey, I can't cast stones. I've done *way* worse."

My ears prick up at that. "What did you do?"

His fingers still mid-tap. A reflective look passes over his face. "What haven't I done is probably a better question." He sends me a forced grin, and I narrow my eyes. "We'd be here all week if I was to burden you with details of my sordid past."

"All month, more like." I'm blatantly teasing because I can hardly criticize Kalvin for keeping secrets when I'm doing the same.

He snorts, opening the driver's side door. "I knew there was a reason I liked you."

I hop out, slamming the door shut with more force than necessary.

I follow him into the kitchen. He opens the fridge and bends down, pulling out a few covered bowls. "For what it's worth, I don't actually think Brad is up to anything sinister."

"I don't either," I admit, taking some bread out of the press while Kalvin slices tomatoes. "I know I barely know him, but my gut doesn't usually let me down. Besides"—I plaster mayo on the bread as Kalvin starts loading ham, cheese, and tomatoes on top—"he was Ky's best friend for years, and that's got to count for something."

Kalvin cuts the sandwiches in two and pops them onto plates. "It does." He hands me mine and we walk to the table. "But that only makes the betrayal all that much worse. Brad was closer to Ky than any of us have ever been—they were like blood brothers. They've known each other since they were knee-high. For him to throw that friendship away so easily ..." He stops chewing, shaking his head. "Man, I still don't understand it."

I don't either. "What did he tell Ky about why he did it?" I mumble, in between mouthfuls.

"I haven't a clue. Ky won't talk about it."

"Figures." I sigh. "He'd much rather let his fists do the talking."

I'm brushing my teeth in the en suite bathroom when there's a light rap on my door. I open it and gasp. Blood drips down Ky's face from a gash in his forehead, and the cut on his lip is swollen and caked in dried blood. Hints of a blossoming bruise linger along the side of his jaw, and his nose looks swollen. One arm of his shirt is torn and ripped.

"You should see the other guy."

His attempt at humor dies an immediate death. "This isn't remotely funny."

He rocks back on his heels, looking at me with a more serious expression. "No. You're right. It isn't."

I lean against the doorjamb.

"Can I come in?"

I straighten up. "Why?"

"I owe you an apology." Earnest eyes meet mine, and while I'm suspicious of his motive, I step out of the way, granting him entry.

I walk into the bathroom and wet a facecloth. "Sit," I command, gesturing toward the bed. He does as he's told without argument. I bend over, gently probing his face with the tips of my fingers. He winces when I brush against his jaw. "That's going to be the mother of all bruises."

"Good."

I stand up. "Good?"

He tips his chin up, and his beautiful blue eyes lock on mine. "Dad hates it when I fight, and Mom expects us to be pretty twenty-four-seven."

Crouching down, I dab blood off his forehead. "So this was about your dad?" A muscle pops in his jaw, and I smooth a hand over it to ease the strain. Traces of blood stick to my skin.

"It wasn't about my dad. Brad had that coming."

I move the cloth down to his cheek, mopping up some dried blood. "Feel any better? Is Brad okay?"

His hand curls around my wrist. "Why do you care? Is there something between you?"

I gently press the cloth to his split lip as I respond to his question with one of my own. "What's going on with you and Addison?"

He doesn't shift eye contact as he speaks. "It's not how it looks. I know she's all over me—"

"*Your* hands were all over *her*, earlier at the pool," I viciously cut in.

His eyes soften as he gently tugs me down beside him. "I'm sorry you had to see that."

I look down at my feet. "You hurt me," I whisper. "I don't let just anyone touch me, and you ..." I trail off as an invisible hand constricts my heart. Tears pool in my eyes, and it takes considerable willpower to hold myself intact. I will not cry in front of him.

He takes my hand in his. "And I was a total jerk. And I'm not going to insult your intelligence by saying it wasn't done deliberately. It was"—I flinch and try to pull away from him but he clasps my hand more firmly, keeping me in place—"but not for the reasons you're thinking. Addison is suspicious, and she can't find out about us. I thought the best way of leading her off the scent was to be nasty to you. I'm really sorry, Faye. I didn't want to hurt you. I tried to explain it earlier, but you wouldn't hear me out. Please say you believe me and that you can you forgive me?"

Staring at his pleading expression, I *do* believe him. I know he's telling me the truth. With the tender way he's looking at me, it'd be so easy to get lost in his eyes. Even bloody and swollen, I'm irresistibly drawn to Ky. That unspeakable void in his soul calls out to me, as if we've been carved from the same cloth. An urge to envelop him in my arms is almost overpowering. No matter how much he's hurt me, I can't abandon him.

He needs me, as much as I need him.

He just doesn't know it yet.

I zoom in on his lips, and my stomach does a funny twist. I want to kiss him more than I've ever wanted to kiss any boy before. *How on earth am I supposed to stay away from him?*

The answer is I can't.

And I don't want to.

I draw a deep breath. "I can forgive you if you can forgive me." Even though my kiss with Brad pales in comparison with Ky and Addison's groping fest out by the pool, I can afford to be charitable now I know what was behind it. His method may have been all wrong, but the intent was honorable.

He circles his arm around my back, nudging me into his side. I rest my head on his shoulder. "I wanted to kill him for kissing you. Far worse than I wanted to kill him for sleeping with Addison." His lips brush against my forehead, leaving a fiery imprint behind.

"It wasn't his fault. I pretty much threw myself at him."

He groans. "Don't remind me, and that doesn't really help." He runs his fingers through my hair, and I close my eyes, relishing the tingly sensation.

"Ky," I breathe, nuzzling into his neck. "What are we doing?"

He slides me onto his lap, wrapping his arms around my waist. "I don't know, Faye, but if I don't kiss you right now, I—"

I place my mouth gently against his, savoring the taste of his warm, soft lips. He curls his hand around the nape of my neck, pulling me closer. "Does it hurt?" I whisper, easing back for a second.

"There's only one part of my anatomy hurting right now, and it's not my mouth."

His hardness presses against my ass, verifying his statement. "Wow. You're such a romantic."

He sniggers, sliding his hands in my hair as he draws my head closer. "Kiss me like your life depends on it."

And I do.

Twisting in his lap, I push him flat on the bed as I straddle him. My lips feast on him, and I kiss a trail from his mouth to his chin, around his jaw, and back again. He moans loudly, sending a dart of pure liquid fire straight to my core. I writhe against him, rocking my hips into his, so turned on I think I might self-combust. His lips sweep over my neck as his hands reach under my shirt to cup my bare breasts. I grind into him, and he flips me over so I'm underneath him, pulling my shirt off. Lowering his mouth to my nipple, he grazes his teeth against the swollen tip, and my back arches off the bed. A needy whimper escapes my lips and I grab at his shirt, yanking it up and over his head. My nails dig into the flesh of his back as my legs wrap around his waist. He thrusts into me with a skillful roll of his hips, and even though we still have some clothes covering us, an abundance of tantalizing sensations threatens to send me over the edge.

My hand slips under the band of his jeans, and I wrap my fingers around him. Ky moans his approval as an unwelcome image assaults my mind. Addison's fingers sliding into his jeans are imprinted on my brain, and I go rigid underneath him. He lifts up, surveying me with lust-clouded eyes. "What's wrong?"

The only sound in the room is our joint rapid breathing. Both our chests are moving up and down as if in sync. Dark, smoldering eyes mirror how I feel on the inside.

"What about *her*?"

"You want to talk about her right now?"

My inner demon urges me to forget Addison, but I can't. Logic wins over lust. I won't make the same mistake again. "Yeah, I do." I remove my hand from his jeans. I need to know what he intends to do before we take this any further.

He lets out a frustrated sigh as he lifts off me. His eyes are heavy with desire as he sits on the edge of the bed. "Okay. What do you want to know?"

I'm not having this convo semi-naked, so I grab my top and shimmy it over my head. Kyler never takes his eyes off me. I wrap my arms across my chest, suddenly self-conscious. "What?"

"You have no idea how beautiful you are to me."

Although his words thrill me, I'm not letting them distract me. "Thank you, but we're not changing the subject. What are you doing with her Ky?"

He locks his hands behind his head, sighing again. "I'm going to level with you. I'll tell you our history, and what I have planned, but you're not going to like it."

"I'd prefer honesty." I pull my knees up under my chin as I peer at him.

He twists around to face me. "I thought I loved her." A rancorous look contorts his face. "But I was a total idiot. I have it on good authority that she was cheating on me with several guys for at least the last four months of our relationship." His lips pull together in a grim line. "I knew something was wrong. She was more distant, and her personality started to change. She wasn't always a cheating ho-bag. She used to be so sweet."

I guess I'll have to take his word for it.

He sucks in his cheeks, and I wonder what recollections are replaying in his mind. A part of me is glad to hear this, because I've been wondering how Ky could date such a malicious bitch.

"I knew something was going on with her, at home, but she wouldn't open up. I had a sneaking suspicion that she was going off with other guys, and I was getting ready to confront her when I received an anonymous email." I lift my head up. "The email contained several different pictures of her and Brad, naked, and in the act."

He grabs his head in his hands, and the urge to comfort him is undeniable. But I still don't know everything. "That's an awful way to have your suspicions confirmed. Did you ever discover who sent them to you?"

He shakes his head. "I never bothered trying. They did me a favor, whoever they were. Now do you understand why I can't bear the thought of him kissing you? Him being anywhere near you?"

I nod. "But that still doesn't explain what you are doing with Addison? Do you want to get back with her?"

He barks out a laugh. "As if! The last thing I want is that bitch anywhere near me."

"Could've fooled me. You let her touch you. And you sneered at me, like you didn't care that I was hurting."

He takes my hands in his. "I've already explained and said I'm sorry about that. I had to play the part. She needs to think I'm into her again and that I've no interest in you. If she gets any hint of what's between us, she will make it her mission to destroy you. That's why I need to stay close to her."

Oh, please. Pull the other one.

"So, what, you're fooling around with her as a way of protecting me?" I'm incredulous as I extract my hands from his. This smells like total horseshit, and I'm not buying it.

"It's morphing into that, but I didn't start out with that intention. She played me for an idiot, and I let her. And I'm not talking solely about the cheating. She knew she broke me, and she used the opportunity to gain the upper hand at school. She thinks she's in charge but she's not. She needs to be knocked off her throne, and I'm the one that's going to do it. She isn't the only one who can play head games."

I stand in front of him. "Are you serious? You're doing this to get back at her, and to reclaim some kind of crown at school?" I roll my eyes.

He climbs to his feet. "Yes, and I'm going to bring her down to the gutter, and it's going to feel fucking great."

I shake my head sadly. "No, no, it won't. You'll feel like shit because you'll have sunk to her level." I take his arm gently. "Let it go, Ky. If that is genuinely why you are spending time with her again, just let it go. Hold onto your dignity and regain the respect and trust at school in the right way."

"You don't get it, Faye. You've no idea what you're talking about! I can't imagine stuff like this happened in Ireland."

Anger flares in my gut. "Oh no, because it's all cart horses, leprechauns, and pots of gold in Ireland, isn't it?!" I start pacing the room. "You think we don't have bullies and hierarchies and cheating assholes and whores in Ireland? Don't be so naïve. I know as much about this as you do, more maybe, and trust me when I say I'm speaking from personal experience. Let it go, Ky. Don't let her fuck you up again. She's already taken so much from you."

He goes rigidly still. "What personal experience?"

I stop pacing. "Oh, no," I half-laugh, "This isn't about me, and don't try to change the subject again."

"You're a hypocrite, you know that." He steps toward me, and an angry glare makes an unwelcome reappearance on this face. "You lecture me about honesty when you're keeping things back too!"

"Just because you're opening up about this doesn't mean you're being honest with me. Don't take me for a fool, because I'm not." I step toward him, madder than all hell. "I've seen into that dark, empty part of you. That part that you haven't willingly shared with me, or anyone, I'm guessing." He subtly flinches, but I don't miss it. "So when you're ready to lay it all out on the table, I'll put my cards down too. But until then"—I thump my hand over my heart—"I'm protecting me, and you don't get to call me out on that."

We face off, each of us locked in the pain of our own minds. Tension is thick in the air, and I don't know where we go from here—if anywhere. With every passing second, he is shutting down, withdrawing, and closing himself off to me again. Little by little, the mask is going back on. I see it, as plain as day.

Sudden tiredness overwhelms me, and I'm done. I'm feeling the type of emotional exhaustion that makes physical tiredness pale into insignificance. May's words float to the surface. In a roundabout way, she was right. Neither of us is stable enough to even contemplate starting anything. There is too much anger and grief in both of us for it to ever turn into something good.

"I think May was right," I say, finally breaking the ice. "We *should* stay away from each other. We can't possibly be good together."

He opens his mouth, but I place a finger over his lips to shush him. "You need to find yourself, Ky. You're lost in there somewhere"—I place my hand carefully over his heart, feeling the steady beat thudding under my skin—"and following through on this plan with Addison is not going to help you find the right path. No one can do that for you—it can only be you."

His hand smooths over mine. "I don't know what you went through, and I'm sorry, because it was obviously something painful. But this is different. I don't need to find myself. I already know who I am." He removes my hand, placing it back by my side.

"The problem is, I don't like the person I've become." A tormented look flits over his face.

"Ky, I—" I begin to protest.

He steps back, cutting me off. "I agree that this needs to end now. We're not on the same page. I promise I'll keep my distance." The camouflage is securely in place, completely hiding his feelings. "But you need to promise me that you'll stay away from Brad. Please, Faye. Do this one thing for me?"

"Are you going to stay away from her?"

He squeezes his eyes shut and tilts his head back. After a minute, he lets out a frustrated sigh. "I can't. It has to happen like this."

A heavy pressure bears down on my chest. This is not going to help him, and it feels wrong to be walking away. And he's mistaken. He *is* lost. He just doesn't know it.

But there isn't much more I can do. "Very well, then." I walk toward the door. "I'm making no promises when it comes to Brad." Despite what Kyler has said, I know there's more to this than meets the eye. Brad isn't the devil incarnate, and I'm starting to believe he's as much a victim as Ky is. At this stage, it's only a hunch, and I need to hear his version of events before I start jumping to conclusions. I yank the door open. "Goodnight, Kyler."

He storms out of the room, spinning around before the door has fully closed. "I won't be here to pick up the pieces when he screws you over. I tried to warn you."

"I could say the exact same to you."

His eyes penetrate mine, and I can tell he wants to say more, but he can't, or he won't.

I close the door as he walks away and bury my head in my hands.

Chapter Twenty-Six

I slump to the ground, leaning against the wall, with tears streaming down my face. The floodgates shatter and I allow myself to feel everything I've been fighting. It's an awful ugly mess. Wracking sobs rip from the innermost chamber of my heart, and I give into them, allowing them to fully take over. Pain lances me on all sides, and I bury my head in my knees, giving in to the heartache.

I cry for my parents.

For my lost life.

For the threat that Addison poses, scaring me in ways it shouldn't.

For a boy I can't have and shouldn't want.

For the never-ending gut-wrenching hollow ache in my chest and the soul-crushing loneliness I feel.

Out of everything, I cry hardest for the boy who is so fucked up in the head, he can't help dragging others down with him. I did the right thing by pushing Ky away, because if I didn't, I know he'd only drag me down too. Even still, the acknowledgments hit me hard, ripping my confidence and my resolve to shreds. Heartache collides with selfishness, and I feel utterly confused.

My sobbing grows louder, but I'm powerless to halt it.

The quiet click of the door alerts me to a foreign presence, but I can't even summon the energy to tell Kyler to get lost. Arms wrap around me, hauling me into a warm chest. The crying continues unchecked as I look at Kalvin through blurry, red-rimmed eyes. He lifts me onto his lap, cradling me in his arms. "It's okay. I've got you," he croons, running his hand up and down my back in a soothing gesture.

I nuzzle into his chest, clinging onto him, and gradually the crying lessens until it's only the odd, intermittent pitiful sob. Silently, he hands me some tissues, and I blow my nose and mop up the excess moisture on my skin.

Very gently, he stands—with me still in his arms—and places me on the bed. He helps me under the covers. Tucking the duvet under my chin, he sweeps damp strands of my hair off my face. "I'll be back in a minute."

I nod in zombie-like fashion, shivering under the covers. Kalvin returns a few minutes later with a cup of hot chocolate. Helping me sit up, he holds the cup to my lips and coaxes me into drinking. The warming goodness sits like a lead balloon in my stomach, but gradually it takes the chill away. "Thank you," I whisper.

He looks at me with so much tenderness that it almost opens the well again. "Do you want me to stay? You look like you could use a friend right now."

"Is that what we are?" I whisper.

A sad look crosses his face. "You shouldn't have to ask that. Of course, I'm your friend. More than that, I'm your family."

I retract the covers, unable to speak over the sentimental lump in my throat.

Kalvin holds me in his comforting embrace, and I fall asleep feeling slightly less alone in the world.

Sometime in the early hours of the morning, he slips out of the bed, planting a delicate kiss to my forehead. Still half-asleep, I clasp his fingers and squeeze. I'm drifting off again when the sound of raised voices tickles my ears. But I'm too emotionally drained to care, let alone investigate. Unconsciousness overpowers me and I fall into a deep sleep.

The smell of burnt eggs greets me the second I step foot in the kitchen the next morning. Kalvin is wafting his hand over a smoke-filled pan, scowling in frustration.

I peer into the pan, wrinkling my nose at the congealed, blackened mess. "Shoo." I gently push him. "I'll cook breakfast," I offer, remembering it's Greta's day off.

"You're the best." He smacks his lips across my cheek, and I push him away more forcibly.

"Less of the slobbering if you don't mind." I wipe my sleeve across my cheek.

Keaton chortles from his seat at the table.

Kalvin leans his chin on my shoulder. "I'll have you know that many a girl wishes these lips were attached to their skin."

"I guess some girls just don't know what's good for them," I joke, dumping the ruined pan and retrieving a clean one from the press.

I clutch Kalvin's wrist before he can pull away. Leaning up, I kiss his cheek. "Thank you for last night."

I'm expecting another brazen retort but he surprises me.

"My brother is an ass, and I'm always here for you." He gives me a quick hug. I should correct him. Last night wasn't only about Ky, but I don't want to get into the other stuff.

"What are you two whispering about," Keaton asks, sending me an inquisitive look.

"Nothing," we chime in unison, breaking into a joint laugh. Keaton scowls a little.

I root around in the fridge, and a sudden craving hits me. "Would you guys eat pancakes?" I lean my hip against the door as I face my cousins.

"I'm about ready to eat my hand off, so anything you're offering sounds good to me," Keaton remarks.

"Pancakes it is."

I busy myself at the stove, as the rest of my cousins meander into the kitchen in dribs and drabs. I whip up some scones, on a whim, and shove them into the oven. Tiny, fiery shivers skate across my skin, and I don't need to look up to know that Ky has arrived. My heart rate kicks up, as usual. With a trembling hand, I give the batter one last mix.

"Something smells good."

I look up as Kaden enters the kitchen, rubbing his hands together. "I didn't know you were here."

"I stopped by to have a chat with Ky."

He sends me a loaded look, and I stare back at him. Then the penny drops. "I see." I sense Ky watching us from across the room.

Kaden leans in close to my ear. "You can't get involved. Ky and I will deal with it."

I lift a pancake out of the pan and slide it onto the warmed plate. "So you're onboard with the blackmail plan?" I whisper.

Kaden leans back against the counter, bracing his hands against the edge. Muscles bulge underneath the short sleeves of his shirt. "He told you about that?"

"Yes." I ladle some more batter into the pan.

"I don't agree that's the best way forward, but there are some things you aren't aware of." He dips his head and talks in a low tone. "I'm not happy about this either, but there are legit reasons why Mom can't find out. I'll sort it. It's what I do best."

I flip the pancake over in the pan, pondering his cryptic comment. Pushing wispy strands of damp hair back off my forehead, I turn to face him. "So I'm expected to lie to her face? To pretend like I'm not disgusted with your dad?"

"I know you mean well, Faye, but this kind of crap is minor compared to some of the stuff that's happened in the past. You'll get used to it." He pushes off the counter, licking his lips as he eyes the pancake mountain. "Is there enough for one more?"

And like that, the subject is dismissed.

"Sure. Have a seat. I'm about to serve up."

I place bowls with a variety of toppings in the center of the table, sliding two heaped platefuls of pancakes on either side. "Help yourselves."

"I saved you a seat," Kalvin says, patting the space beside him on the bench. I squeeze in, and he places a protective arm around my shoulder. "This looks awesome. Thanks." He sends a deliberately scathing look at Ky, and I wonder if he's mad at him over last night or if some other drama has come between them.

"You're welcome. Now eat up before it gets cold."

The boys tuck in, demolishing everything in record time.

I'm clearing away the plates when James walks into the kitchen. My eyes immediately wander to Ky, and we exchange a wary look. Kaden stiffens, doing little to hide his abhorrence.

I wish I'd had more opportunity to get to know my eldest cousin, but he scarcely makes an appearance, and when he does, he spends most of his time glowering at his father. I'd love to know exactly what's driving that dynamic. It must be something significant if he can hold onto his animosity for so long.

Ky studies me with inquisitive eyes, and I avert my gaze, snapping out of my pensive inner monologue.

Conversation is subdued around the table now.

"Didn't you boys leave me anything?" James asks, apparently oblivious to the simmering hostility. The triplets and Kalvin are eyeing Ky and Kaden with suspicion.

Kalvin's penetrating gaze meets mine again as I slip on some oven gloves. Crouching down, I remove the baking tray from the oven, sliding the hot goods onto a plate. I push it across the island unit to James. "I made scones if you want one of those." I look at the counter, unable to stomach looking at him.

He lifts a scone and holds it to his nose, sniffing appreciatively. "Saoirse used to make these for me all the time." He's choked with emotion, and it's difficult not to react to that.

Still avoiding his gaze, I glance at my feet as I mumble, "It's Mum's recipe."

"Tastes exactly how I remember it," he adds quietly a couple of minutes later.

Sobs begin to form at the back of my throat, and I flee the kitchen before I break down in front of everyone.

I run outside the house, across the lawn, and race into the woods, aimless and uncaring. My heart is thundering in my chest as I stomp through the forest. I'm still vulnerable after last night, and I can't halt the memories flooding my mind. Successive images of baking with Mum refuse to empty from my brain. Dad is there too, licking his lips and patting his full stomach, heaping praise on both of us. Tears prick my eyes, and I try to shove the visions away. Round and round, they turn on a loop, causing the pain in my heart to notch higher and higher, until I don't think I can bear it any longer. I drop to my knees, desperately sucking air into my lungs.

Breathe, Faye. In and out. In and out.

Depression shrouds me like a thundercloud, and I start to wonder if I'll ever be able to deal with their loss. If the grief will ever become manageable. Trying to shut it up clearly isn't a workable strategy.

Laughter rings out, and I latch onto the distraction with both hands. I scramble to my feet, wiping bits of debris off my hands. I walk in the direction of Lana's bungalow, following the sound of voices. No one answers the door when I knock, so I follow the same path we took the last time and head around the back of the house.

Lana is sitting outside alongside a girl with cropped jet-black hair. A row of studs frames the side of one ear, and she has a stud in her nose and one below her lip. Thick black liner surrounds her brown, almond-shaped eyes—eyes which are currently inspecting me from head to toe.

"Faye!" Lana jumps up. "Come and join us." She motions me over with a flick of her hand.

"Sorry to interrupt. I was out walking, and I heard voices ..." I skip up the steps and take the vacant seat beside the unfamiliar girl. Her gaze flits to mine, and the look she gives me is feral. Pity I'm too numb to care.

"This is Zoe," Lana pipes up. "She goes to my school."

I perk up in my chair. "I'm starting there tomorrow."

"So, it's true?" Lana tucks her legs underneath her. "You *are* slumming it."

I send her a funny look. "Hardly. I went to public school back home." Well, before we relocated to Dublin, that is, but I don't want to get into the specifics.

"Kennedys don't do public," Zoe interjects. There is a distinct lack of warmth in her tone.

"I'm not a Kennedy. I'm a Donovan."

Her cheeks pucker. "Same difference. You're their cousin, right?"

She eyeballs me again, and the cold glare in her gaze pisses me off. "Did my cousins do something to you? Because you're being a bitch, and that couldn't have anything to do with me seeing as I've never met you before."

She pokes her tongue out the side of her cheek, and a slight grin curves up the corners of her mouth.

"Zoe. Stop it," Lana bluntly cautions her.

She slouches in her chair, holding my gaze, and I'm still wondering what her problem is. "Your cousin's a dick."

"Which one?"

"Zoe!" Lana hisses, clearly annoyed. I cast a quick glance in her direction, noting how her mouth is set in a hard line as she glowers at her friend.

"All of them," Zoe replies, turning away from Lana to send me a challenging look.

"That's a little harsh. And don't believe everything you hear."

"What if I'm hearing it from a reliable source?" She slants her head to the side.

Lana jerks her foot out, accidentally knocking a half-empty glass of lemonade all over the place. She jumps up and runs into the kitchen.

I lean forward in my seat, eyeballing Zoe. "Why do I get the sense there's more to your statement than meets the eye?"

"Because there is."

"Zoe. That's enough," Lana grits out, reappearing with a wad of paper towels. She begins mopping up the spillage. "You're being very rude, and Faye has done nothing to deserve your sour attitude. If you can't be polite, don't let the door hit you on the way out."

I hold up my hand. "It's okay. She's entitled to her opinion."

Lana scowls, tossing a bundle of wet towels into the trash.

"How charitable of you." Zoe's tenor is grating.

Is there anyone my cousins haven't had run-ins with?

"That's some serious chip you're carrying. Be careful you don't crumple under the weight."

She stiffens, pointing her finger at me. "Are you threatening me?"

I arch a brow. "Should I be?"

She laughs. "You've got spunk. I might decide to like you after all."

"Am I supposed to be honored or something? You're really weird." I prop my feet up on the edge of the table as she laughs again.

"Speak of the devil," Zoe murmurs under her breath as her head picks up.

Lana's cheeks flush as a familiar form rounds the corner. Kalvin has his trademark smirk firmly planted on his mouth as he ambles toward us, his hands tucked into his khaki shorts. He's bare chested—again—and he has a black cap on backward. A white tee is stuffed in the back pocket of his shorts.

"Did you want something, Kennedy?" Zoe is blunt in the extreme. "Because my tolerance is already waning."

"Do I need to remind you whose property you're on, freak?"

"A Kennedy throwing their weight around. Gee, there's a new concept." She throws up her middle finger, and I disguise my laughter as a cough. I'm starting to like this prickly chick.

Kalvin stalks toward her, putting his face right in hers. "You know what your problem is, Davidson?" She opens her mouth, no doubt to retort, but Kalvin clamps her lips shut. Her face turns puce with barely restrained anger. "You are way too uptight. You need to get laid." Kalvin taps a finger off his chin, pretending to think about it. "But therein lies the problem. No one wants to touch your skanky ass."

"Kalvin!" I grab his elbow, pulling him away from her. "That was downright mean. Apologize."

"She started it!"

"What are you, like, five now?"

He drags his hands through his hair. "I don't need this shit. I only came to fetch you. Mom wants to talk to you."

Every muscle in my back cords into knots. "What about?"

He gives me a quizzical look. "I don't know. You worried?"

I scratch the top of my head. "Nah."

Kalvin throws his arm over my shoulder and spins me around. "Well, let's go then." He doesn't acknowledge the girls as he propels me forward.

"Good riddance, asshole!" Zoe calls out, and I turn around in time to see her flip him the bird again. "Say hi to Addison for me."

I slam to a halt, shooting a stern look at Kalvin. "What's she talking about?"

"Keep walking," he mumbles, propelling me forward with a ferocious look on his face.

I cast a quick glance over my shoulder. Lana's crestfallen look mirrors how I'm feeling inside.

Why do I get the sense that something more is at play here?

And more importantly, why does she look like her world just ended?

Chapter Twenty-Seven

When we reach the edge of the forest, and I'm sure we're a safe distance from Lana's house, I push Kalvin against the side of a tree, placing both my hands firmly on his chest. "Talk. Right now. And don't bullshit me. What was all that about?"

His chest visibly rises. Scrubbing a hand over his jaw, he spits the words out as if they are physically paining him. "I slept with Addison."

I throw my hands in the air. "Why the fuck would you do that?" I'd had an inkling, but I was hoping I was wrong.

"It wasn't intentional!"

I start pacing. "Oh, well, that makes it all right then," I sneer. "I take it Ky doesn't know about this."

"No, and he can't." He reaches out and takes my wrist. "Will you freaking stop!"

"You're an ass." I glare at him. "No, you're much worse than that. I don't think there is a strong enough word in the English language to describe what you are."

"There is no insult you can level at me that I haven't already thrown at myself. I was drunk off my ass when she pounced, and I know I should've tried harder to resist, but—"

I clamp my hand over his mouth. "Please spare me the sordid details."

"I hate myself for it, and I wish I could take it back but I can't."

I start pacing again, my mind churning possibilities. "Why would she sleep with you when she's trying to get Ky back? What is she up to?"

He takes my elbow and steers me out of the woods. "Walk and talk before Mom sends a search party out."

"I can't believe you've done this, Kal. You know you're going to have to tell him."

"No." He shakes his head vehemently. "Absolutely not. It'll kill him."

Keaton appears on the patio, gesturing us forward with a flourish of his hands.

"Kal, he's plotting revenge on her, and she's clearly up to no good. This mess could get so much worse if he isn't aware of the full facts. You can't keep him in the dark."

"Shit." He turns a sickly shade of green. "You might be right." He stops, grasping my arm. "But I need think it through. Please promise me you won't say anything to him. Not yet. Until I try and figure it out."

"I won't, but you have to promise me that you *will* tell him."

He nods, and we start walking again. "One other thing, is something going on with you and Lana?"

"Where'd you get that harebrained idea?" He looks perplexed.

"Call it intuition."

"Well, your intuition needs some fine tuning. There is absolutely nothing going on with Lana and me." His stride picks up, and I have to walk-jog to keep up with him, effectively ending further conversation.

Argumentative voices are waiting to greet us, and we both exchange guarded expressions. Alex is sitting stiffly on a leather recliner in the living room. Kent is staring moodily out the window, and Keaton's foot taps nervously off the ground from his position on the couch. All three heads swivel in our direction. "What are they arguing over this time?" Kalvin asks, his gaze fixed on his mother.

She massages her temples. "Your guess is as good as mine. I don't think they even need a reason anymore." She brings a glass of wine to her lips.

Kalvin looks concerned. "Mom, I don't think—"

She cuts him off dead. "I do not want or need a lecture from you, of all people, on the evils of drinking. It's either do this"—she lifts her glass, swirling it in the air—"or go out there and bash their heads together."

Kalvin's jaw flexes. "Fine, bury your head in the sand. I'm going to find out what's going on."

I race after him. "Don't get involved. Trust me."

He whirls to face me. "You know what it is?"

"I ..." I clam up.

Snarling, he strides with renewed purpose toward the lobby. I catch up with him as Kyler comes bounding down the mezzanine stairs with a face like thunder. Grabbing his jacket, he storms outside without looking at either one of us. The door slams violently in his wake. The telltale roar of an engine can be heard screeching down the driveway a minute later.

Kalvin starts climbing the stairs, two at a time, with a look of fierce determination on his face. Kaden blocks his path at the top. "This doesn't concern you."

"The hell it doesn't!" Kalvin yells. "I'm part of this family too."

"Son," James says, appearing at Kaden's back. "It's only a silly argument." He tugs at his ear in an obvious tell. "There's no need to make a bigger deal of it. Let it go."

I hover at the end of the stairs, and Kaden's enraged eyes meet mine. Subtly, he shakes his head in warning. Kalvin looks between his dad and his brother before huffing and stalking back down the stairs. He shoves past, elbowing me in the shoulder.

"Um, ow!" I massage my sore shoulder.

"Sorry." Kalvin huffs out an insincere apology before stalking toward his bedroom.

Kaden looks his dad up and down with transparent disgust. "You make me sick." Then he bounds down the stairs and straight out the door. I rush down the corridor to my room before James can even make eye contact with me.

A half hour later, Alex comes knocking on my door. She sits at my dresser, facing me. "I'm sorry about all that earlier, Faye. Hormones and tempers flare up from time to time. I tend to steer well clear." She gives me an apologetic smile, but there's lingering sadness behind her eyes. I wonder if it's because she knows more than she's letting on or she knows she's avoiding reality.

She folds her hands neatly in her lap. "I'll be in Milan this week, but I wanted to talk to you before I left. You know I don't approve of your choice regarding Wellesley Memorial, but it's your decision and I respect that. Good luck tomorrow." She gives me a small smile. "I was also wondering if you'd made any decision in relation to the Kennedy Charitable Trust?"

I uncross my legs, planting them on the ground in front of my bed. "Thank you, and yes." I fist clumps of the duvet in my hand. "Is it possible to split my donation between two charities?"

Her eyes blink rapidly as she mulls it over. "I don't see that being an issue. What did you have in mind?"

"I wanted to donate half to the Middleborough Track and half to the local Alcoholics Anonymous center."

She looks surprised. "Kyler's track?"

"Yes. Is that a problem?"

"No, not at all." She splays her fingers over her knees. "I didn't realize you were familiar with it."

"Ky took me yesterday, and I was really impressed with the place, although it's in obvious need of funding. I know they are on the verge of closing down, and it'd be a shame for the children to lose access to the facility."

Worry lines crinkle her eyes. "I didn't know they were in financial trouble. Kyler should've come to me."

Jayzus, was Ky right? Did James stay quiet about this as a twisted form of punishment?

"That seems like a worthwhile cause, and I'm sure Kyler will be delighted," she continues. I nod, even though I'm not doing it for him. Her face softens. "And the donation to the AA is because of your parents?"

I nod again, staring at my feet, uncomfortable under her scrutiny. "If the truck driver who killed my parents had had the support of a group like AA, then maybe he wouldn't have been drunk behind the wheel that night." A single tear leaks out of my eye as I lift my chin to face her. "I'd like to help support their work in the hope that it might save someone else from going through what I went through."

"Oh, honey." She crosses to me, enveloping me in her arms. "I think that's a wonderful idea."

I spend the rest of the day hanging out with Keaton. After he beats my ass playing COD on Xbox—successive times no less—we watch back-to-back repeats of *Gossip Girl* on Netflix in the cinema room. It makes the antics in Chez Kennedy look like child's play in comparison.

I rub my hands over my swollen belly as I groan. "No more." I push the bowl at Keaton. "I don't think I've ever eaten so much popcorn in my life. I feel sick."

He laughs. "Told ya not to overdo it."

"I know. Eyes bigger than my belly."

"Hhm," Keaton says, puckering his lips as he fastens his gaze on my stomach. "I wouldn't be so sure about that."

I grab him into a headlock. "You'll pay for that one, buddy."

He very quickly overpowers me, tickling me until I break into a fit of girlish giggles. I raise my hands in surrender. "Waving the white flag! Stop before I pee my pants."

"Gross visual." Keaton wrinkles his nose as he snickers. My heart swells as I think of how much he's done for me. Without any conscious effort, he helped me settle in here. Made the transition that little bit easier. Of all my cousins, our relationship is the most natural, the most normal. The most cherished.

"Can we be serious for a minute?" His brows flick up curiously. I gulp over the football-sized emotional wedge in my throat. "Thank you so much for being you."

I'm surprised when his eyes turn glassy. "I'm so glad you came to live with us, Faye. Honestly, you've no idea how much. I already feel like you're my best friend." His voice shakes a little, and I'm glad I'm not the only one getting mushy and sentimental.

I pull him into a quick hug. "Me too. I've always wanted cousins, and now I know why."

A choked sob escapes his lips and I hug him tighter. "I love how I can be myself around you without any fear."

I ease back a little, holding him at arm's length. "Why would you be afraid?"

He extracts himself from my embrace, rubbing at his eyes with the corner of his sleeves. "The others all think I'm a joke. They don't see me like you see me."

"I'm sure that's not true. If anything they're probably jealous."

He barks out an incredulous laugh. "Hardly!"

"You are the most levelheaded, and you seem happiest in yourself. Plus, you seem to have a good relationship with your parents, something the rest of them struggle with. You're a great guy, Keaton. Don't let anyone make you feel otherwise."

"Promise you'll always feel like that?" His pleading eyes fail to mask his abject terror and I wonder what's bothering him.

"Hey." I hold his hand. "You will always be my favorite cousin. Nothing or no one will ever change that."

After lunch, Keaton tries several times to get Kalvin to join us, but he continues to sulk in the privacy of his own room. Keanu is out somewhere with that model, Selena, and Kent is MIA as usual. I still haven't figured him out, and I can count on one hand the amount of times he's spoken to me in the last few weeks. Ky doesn't show up either, and I don't even want to think about what he's getting up to, or who he's getting up to it with.

Switching off the lights in my room later that night, I am just pulling the curtains closed when I spot Kalvin creeping across the lawn again. The clock shows it's past eleven, and with school starting tomorrow, I'm surprised he's sneaking out tonight. Not for the first time, I wonder what he's up to.

A hideous thought crosses my mind—is he sneaking out to hook up with Addison? Was he giving it to me straight earlier? Or is there more to this than he's admitted? Briefly, I consider following him. But my recent eavesdropping forays have proven how inept my skills are in that regard.

Besides, I don't think I can stomach watching another one of my cousins slobbering all over that bitch.

No. I'll leave it for now.

But tomorrow, Kalvin will be facing my own personal version of the Spanish Inquisition.

I get up early for a swim the next morning before school. After I've showered and changed, I head straight for the kitchen. My stomach growls its approval. The boys have already left, and Alex is away on business, so I've no choice but to eat breakfast with James.

He tries to make small talk with me but I'm closed off and finding it difficult to look him in the eye. "Don't be too nervous." He sends me a sympathetic look. "I'm sure it'll be fine. And you can always switch to Old Colonial if you don't like it."

I'm happy to let him think my unease is due to school and not the fact that I know he's cheating on his wife. I haven't figured out what I'm going to do with that knowledge yet, and I'd rather avoid confrontation right now. Just as I believed I was starting to get to know my uncle, I realize he's a complete stranger to me. I wonder if this kind of behavior is normal for him—if this character trait had anything to do with my mum distancing herself from him.

I insist that Max drops me around the corner from the school, hell-bent on walking the last half a mile. There's no way I'm rocking up in a chauffeur-driven car on my first day, or any other day for that matter. I make a mental note to ask Lana how she gets to school. Perhaps we can travel together.

I'm approaching the school, when my cell pings with a message from Ky. *Thinking of you. Good luck today.*

This sweet side of him has me tied up in knots. All this hot and cold behavior is playing havoc with my hormones. Shaking my head, I pocket my phone and join the crowd piling into the building.

I collected my locker combination and schedule last week so I walk straight through the main entrance door, pretending I don't notice the curious looks being leveled my way. After a couple of wrong turns, I eventually find my locker.

Throngs of boys and girls swarm the wide corridor. Various groups are clustered around lockers, chatting and laughing. Taunts and insults are shouted at the less popular kids as they scurry down the hallway, heads hanging low, trying to look inconspicuous.

Glancing out the window, I spy a group of dodgy-looking kids congregating around a large tree out front. God only knows what they're doing. It's as if I've walked onto the set of *Pretty Little Liars*, and it couldn't be more different from my last school back home. I never thought I'd ever miss Loreto or the nuns, but in this moment, I'd return to my old school in a heartbeat.

Squashing my oversentimental thoughts, I firmly remind myself that this is my new reality, and I need to get on with it. I doubt I'll find any of this strange or shocking in a couple of days.

I'm sorting out my books when a dark shadow falls over me. Turning around, I confront a familiar face with a shocked gasp. "What are *you* doing here?"

A purplish-yellow bruise is clearly visible on his left cheek, and his right eye is swollen on one side. It's obvious he got a thorough working over. Brad winks with his good eye, giving me an impish smile. "Sorry, didn't get a chance to mention it. This is my school now."

I pull a face. "Why aren't you going to O.C.? And why didn't you say anything the other night?"

"I *was* going to tell you, but then all that other crap happened."

An image of me throwing myself at him jumps up and bites me. I wince. "Yeah, um, about that ..."

The corners of his mouth lift. "It's okay, you don't need to explain."

My brows shoot up. "I don't?"

He leans against the side of my locker. "Nope. And any time you need me to make a point, work away, I'm at your disposal." He grins and I can't work out whether he's on the level or plain making fun of me.

Someone slams into my back, and I'm thrown forward without warning. I crash into Brad, and he stumbles, losing his balance. He falls to the ground with me pinned to his front. He takes the brunt of the fall as I sprawl all over him, but I still feel a jarring movement shooting up my spine. He emits a loud moan as his head slaps off the tiled floor.

"Oh my God, are you okay?"

"I think I'll live," he jokes, tentatively prodding the back of his head.

A few titters ring out, amid a chorus of developing chatter. The click of multiple cell phones snaps me into action. I scramble to my feet with as much grace as I can muster. Extending my hand, I help Brad up.

"Your reputation precedes you, and now I know everything that's been said is true," a shrill, catty voice says from behind me.

I turn around to match the face to the voice.

A stick-thin blonde with dull hazel eyes scans me from head to toe. A sneer contorts her face as she eyes my jeans and blouse combo with a look of obvious distaste. "Don't they teach you how to dress in Ireland?"

A group of girls forms a line at her back, sniggering at her attempt to belittle me.

"Don't they teach you any manners in America?" I shoot back.

"I show respect where respect's due. And that doesn't extend to ho-bags like you."

Her posse purses their lips, tosses their hair, and nods their heads in agreement.

"Funny you should mention ho-bags." I take a slow perusal of her body, noting the short black mini and snug cropped top that clings to her ample chest, baring a wide expanse of flat, tan skin. "Because you look like the stereotypical definition of one. Tell me," I say, planting my hands on my hips, "how many guys have you blown so far today?"

An unattractive sneer creeps over her mouth as she moves all up in my personal space. "You think you're funny? You think you can waltz in here and own the place in a day?" She jabs a pointy finger in my face. "This is my turf. My school. And I call the shots around here."

I thrust her finger back in her face and square up to her. Brad moves closer, placing a cautionary hand on my lower back. Perhaps the smart thing would be to back down, but then they'll think I'm a walkover. And that's when the abuse will start.

I'm starting this as I mean to go on.

"I don't care how you do things here. No one tells me what to do. Certainly not some delusional jumped-up slut with self-esteem issues."

A sly smile spreads over her mouth as she tilts her head back. Then she smashes her forehead into mine with force. Black spots mar my vision as excruciating pain spreads across my skull.

I stagger back, swaying precariously on my feet. *I cannot believe she did that!* Wincing, I palm my sore forehead, hoping I don't have a concussion.

I'm vaguely aware of a strong arm hauling me aside. Brad's citrusy scent invades my nostrils as he pins me in close to his body. "Screw off, Peyton. You've picked the wrong girl to mess with."

I tilt in Brad's arms, struggling to focus my vision. A throbbing headache has taken up residence in my skull, and short jabbing pains stab me behind the eyes. It's the equivalent of a hangover without the nausea and vomiting.

"What is the meaning of this?" an authoritative voice asks. I silently curse.

"Ask the newbie," Peyton responds, sounding slightly dazed. "She started it."

"Faye was minding her own business when you knocked her off her feet," Brad corrects.

"The three of you, into my office. Now."

Chapter Twenty-Eight

I'm having trouble focusing, and Brad props me up as we walk the length of the corridor. Mrs. Carter—the principal, no less—ushers us into her room. "I think Faye needs to see the nurse," Brad supplies when we sit down.

I hold up a hand, blinking excessively as I try to bring my eyesight into focus. "I'm fine." There's no way I'm being carted off for medical treatment. I can't imagine I'd ever live that one down.

Peyton clutches her head in both hands as she sits down. Even if it's not much consolation, I feel some degree of satisfaction knowing she's in pain, too.

Mrs. Carter gives all three of us a stern talking to and a caution that next time we won't get off so lightly.

Try telling that to my pounding head.

"I'm watching you, bitch," Peyton hisses when we're back out in the now-empty corridor. "And that's the only warning you're getting from me." She struts off down the corridor as if she's parading in front of a celebrity crowd on the runway.

"Do I have some sort of invisible brand on my head that attracts bitches?" I ask Brad, as I walk back toward my locker.

He swings his backpack over one shoulder. "You're on everyone's radar because you're new blood. Plus"—he sends me an apologetic look—"Peyton is Addison's cousin, and she goes out with Lance, Memorial's quarterback. They have this place sewn up tight. I'm not sure there was anything you could've done to avoid this. She was always going to target you."

"Cheer me up, why don't ya." I grab my books, stuffing them quickly into my bag. "I never thought I'd miss Sister Mary, but if she miraculously appeared in front of me right now, I'd take a vow of chastity if it meant returning to my old school."

"Hang on here, now, let's not be too hasty." He winks, and I roll my eyes. He slings his arm over my shoulder. "You'll get used to it. And I've got your back."

He walks me toward my math class. "How do you know these kids anyway? Don't the posh snobs turn their noses up at the commoners?"

He sniggers. "That's not far off the mark, but our teams regularly face one another on the sports field, and a lot of the parties are mixed."

I stop at the door to my math class, discreetly peeking inside. Everyone is seated and the teacher is already talking at the top of the class.

Epic.

Not.

"This is me. Wish me luck."

"You don't need it," he says, smiling. "You'll be fine. Wanna meet for lunch?"

"That'd be great."

"Awesome. Give 'em hell." He winks before taking off in the opposite direction.

Drawing a large breath, I curl my fingers around the handle and step into the room.

The morning goes by quite quickly, and I'm grateful. Almost every teacher makes me stand in front of the room and introduce myself. By the fourth class, I could recite it in my sleep. Rose is in my English class, and Brad sits beside me in Science, so it's not as bad as I feared. Most of the other students give me a wide berth, and I'm A-okay with that.

Brad and I walk into the cafeteria together at lunchtime, and virtually every head turns in our direction. "I feel like I'm under a microscope," I say, adding a few things to my tray.

"It comes with the territory when you're a Kennedy." He tries to pay for my lunch, but I won't hear of it.

Rose lifts her hand and waves us over. She's at a table in the far corner with a couple of other girls. Brad and I claim seats across from her as she makes brief introductions. Most of the girls seem to know Brad, and the few who don't look him over with obvious appreciation. The girls are polite but distant toward me.

When Lana and Zoe approach, I wave them over and force Brad to move down a few seats. He sends me an amused grin. "What?" I mouth.

"You're messing with the social hierarchy."

I snort. "As if I give two shits about that."

He laughs before leaning into me. "Keep this up and you'll have every guy in the place falling at your feet."

I scowl at him. "I don't want any guys falling at my feet."

He arches a brow. "You sure about that?" I fix him with a funny look.

Lana drops into the seat beside me, staring at me through vacant, red-rimmed eyes. "Hey." I place my hand on her wrist. "Is everything okay?"

Zoe leans forward, pinning me with a scathing expression that I'm beginning to suspect is just her usual look. "Why did you call us over? What are you playing at?"

I level her with a vicious look all of my own. "I'm not playing any game. I saw you two and wanted to invite you to join us. Shoot me if that's a crime."

"You cannot be this naïve," Zoe scoffs.

"Peyton is going to string you up for this," Lana warns. "I had a few run-ins with her in first year, and she's definitely one to bear a grudge. You don't want to make an enemy of her on your first day."

A strangled laugh slips from my mouth. "I think it's a little late for that, and I don't care. Peyton doesn't scare me. She can go fuck herself."

A shocked silence spreads over our table at my words. I may have stated that a bit louder than intended, but so what.

Rose cracks up laughing, helping to break the tension. "You're exactly what this school needs to break Peyton's hold."

"I don't want to break Peyton's hold. I want to have nothing to do with her. But I'm not going to bow down to that cow either."

"You can't say stuff like that," a girl says at the end of the table. "Even if you are a Kennedy." Her tone carries an awed, reverential quality.

"Why is everyone so obsessed with my cousins? With"—I make little air quotes—"the Kennedys. You'd swear they were actual royalty." I shake my head in consternation.

Now all the girls stare at me as if I've just snorted fire out my nostrils. The girl beside Rose speaks up first. "They basically are around here. The Kennedys epitomize everything we aspire to be. They can make or break you. If you have their support, the world is your oyster."

I almost choke on my salad. "That's the craziest thing I've ever heard. They're only human, same as you and me. And from what I've seen of Wellesley, even their affluence isn't that unusual. I really don't get it."

Brad can't contain the smile on his face. "I'm so glad I transferred to this school. Senior year just got a whole lot more interesting."

I stick out my tongue, and he laughs.

"You're frigging insane," the girl continues. "And stupid not to take advantage of the position you find yourself in. Most girls in this town would kill to be in your shoes."

Her words rub me up the wrong way. "What? Most girls would love to be orphaned, have to ID the mangled bodies of their parents, and move halfway around the world to live in fucking La-La land with you bunch of crazy ass-worshipers?" I stand up, clutching my tray against my chest. "Yeah, I'm sure they would." I doubt I've made any friends with my impassioned speech, but I couldn't care less.

"Nice one, Hayley." Rose glares at her friend as I stride away from the table. Every head in the vicinity swings in my direction, and it's obvious that plenty of people overheard our conversation. Hostile looks come at me from all quarters, but I ignore them as I dump my tray and head outside.

My heart is thudding against my ribcage and my palms are sweaty as I rest against a small stone wall off the main entrance. Brad chuckles as he drops down beside me. "Way to make a first impression."

I spin my head around to face him. "Do you believe all that crap too? You'd swear my cousins were freaking immortal or shit gold out their asses the way everyone goes on."

He roars laughing. "I know them better than most. And, no, I don't have them on a pedestal." His laughter fades away.

"What happened, Brad? Did you really hook up with Addison behind Ky's back because I can't see it."

His shoulders sag, and his Adam's apple lurches in his throat. "I'm guilty as charged, Faye. I betrayed my best friend, and I've lost everything, but I deserve it."

"Everyone makes mistakes at some point in their lives. But it's how they deal with the fallout that matters. And whether they've learned from the experience enough not to repeat the same mistakes."

Brad looks at me with sad eyes. "I would never do that again, and I want to make it up to him, but he's shut me out. And I don't blame him for that. Like I said, I deserve it."

Before I can question him further, the bell rings, and we have to head back to class.

The afternoon passes by in a similar fashion, and before I know it, the bell is hollering, signaling the end of the day.

I made it through my first day of American high school. I'd like to say unscathed, but my head is still throbbing so that'd be an outright lie.

Brad is waiting for me by my locker. "Do you need a ride home?"

"Max is picking me up, but thanks anyway."

"I don't mind picking you up every day if you need a lift."

I shut my locker and start walking. Brad trails alongside me. "You don't need to do that."

"I know, but I don't mind."

I stop, pulling him aside. "Look, I know I kissed you, and I shouldn't have done that, but I meant what I said before that. I'm not looking for anything, so if that's why you're offering ..."

He goes rigidly stiff. "Seriously?" Hurt glimmers in his gaze. "You're really starting to insult me now. I'll see you tomorrow."

Crappers. I run after him, skipping down the steps until I've caught up with him. "Wait, Brad. I'm sorry. You've been nothing but nice to me, and that was totally uncalled for. I'd like to be friends, once we're both on the same page."

He inspects my face and his shoulders relax. "We are. Don't get me wrong; under different circumstances, I'd be all over you." He sends me a meaningful look. "But I hear you loud and clear, and I want to be your friend. In case you hadn't noticed, I don't have too many of those anymore, so I'm not being entirely selfless here."

"It doesn't matter. I like you, and—"

"Do you have a death wish?" a menacing voice asks from behind me, and I shriek.

"Jeez, Ky. Are you trying to give me a heart attack?" I glare at him but his harsh gaze is fixed on Brad. A crowd starts to form around us as everyone picks up on the obvious friction.

"It's not what you think, Ky. We're friends. That's it." Brad holds up his hands in offering.

"You forget that I know exactly how you operate." Ky adopts a protective stance, pulling me behind him.

"I'm not the same person you knew." Brad squares up to him confidently, but there's no aggression or malice in how he carries himself. "Things have changed. I've changed."

Ky harrumphs. "Save it for someone who gives a shit. I won't tell you again, McConaughey. Stay away from Faye."

"Ignore him," I tell Brad, stepping out from Ky's shadow. "I make my own decisions. But I think it's best if you leave." I gesture subtly toward the mob forming a circle around us. "Let's not give them another show."

"Yeah, let's not," Ky interjects before Brad can even respond. "Because half the town is still enjoying the first one." He grinds down on his teeth.

"What?"

Ky thrusts his cell in my hand. "Take a look for yourself."

I press the play button and cringe. Someone posted the earlier incident at my locker online, and it already has several thousand views. I'm sprawled over Brad, both of us laid out on the ground, as if I've jumped him in plain view. *Great.* So much for fading into the background.

Brad curses as he watches over my shoulder. I hand the phone back to Kyler in silence.

"Please tell me you're here to control that slut?" Peyton demands, advancing toward us as the crowd parts to let her through. She stands in front of Kyler with a stupid pout on her mouth. "Someone needs to explain to her how things work around here. If you won't sort it, I will."

Kyler puts the scary mask on and leans into her face. Naked aggression rolls off him in waves. "If you lay a finger on Faye, you'll have me to deal with. Don't try any of your usual bullshit, Peyton. I'll only warn you this once."

Her eyes narrow to slits as a red flush spreads over her chest. The crowd surrounding us waits with bated breath. Bloody brilliant. Ky's called her out in front of the entire school, and she's not going to take that lying down. Tossing her hair over her shoulder, she stares him down. "You're forgetting your place, *Ky-ler*." She enunciates his name slowly, her tone dripping with condescension. "You don't run this joint. I do."

"Pey, back off." A huge guy, with planks for shoulders, strides toward us. "Kennedy." He nods at Kyler.

Ky returns the gesture. "Keep your girl in check, Fielding. Faye's a Kennedy, and she'll be given the respect she deserves, or I won't hesitate to step in."

This is so stupid, and I open my mouth to intervene, when Brad silences me with a subtle nod of his head.

"Message received, Kyler, but you better explain how things work around here, because she needs to respect the way we handle things."

"She understands."

I open my mouth again, but Ky levels a warning glare my way. Dropping keys into my hand, he says, "Get in the car and wait for me." I narrow my eyes as I prepare to give him a piece of my mind.

Brad moves to my side, taking my elbow. "Come on, Faye. I'll go with." I'm sure Ky would love to object, but he's in no position to. Jerking out of Brad's hold, I twist around and walk away. He keeps step alongside me. "He's trying to fix this."

"I don't need or want his help. I can take care of myself." We stop at Ky's SUV, and I slip my bag off my back.

Brad opens the car, placing my bag on the floor. "I know that, and I'm sure Ky does, too, but his public support can't hurt. You don't know these girls like I do. They can make your life hell."

"Been there, done that, bought the T-shirt."

"And you're still not going to explain that, are you?" Ky asks, materializing beside me.

"Are you going to quit with Addison?"

Ky sighs. "You sound like a broken record. Please, just get in." He tosses a mean look at Brad as he rounds the driver side.

I show Ky the middle finger, and it feels great. Leaning over, I kiss Brad sweetly on the cheek. "Thanks for today, and if that offer's still open, you can pick me up at seven thirty in the morning."

He nods. "Sure thing. See you then." With a quick glance at a sullen Ky, he closes the door. I wiggle my fingers at him as I buckle my seat.

"I know what you're doing." Ky thrusts the car in gear and floors it.

I bounce around in my seat. "I don't know what you're talking about." I look idly out the window.

"You're trying to make me jealous, but it won't work."

I look at him through hooded eyes. "So you coming to collect me from school had nothing to do with that video? Nothing to do with Brad at all?"

He grinds his teeth, as he pushes his foot down on the accelerator. "I wanted to make sure you were okay." He casts a quick glance at me. His eyes are brooding, and I know I've touched a nerve.

"Touching, but I don't believe you." I lift my legs onto the dashboard as I lean back in my seat.

"I'm not jealous," Kyler grinds out.

"Of course, you aren't," I say sweetly, pinning him with a smug look. "You're not jealous in the slightest."

Chapter Twenty-Nine

The rest of the week follows a predictable pattern. Brad drives Lana and me to and from school each day. Peyton shoots me daggers in the hallway but keeps her distance. I eat lunch with Brad, Rose, Lana, and Zoe, while most everyone else steers clear of me. Lana is even quieter than usual, while Zoe is more acerbic than ever. My classes are fine, and I've no trouble picking up the curriculum.

Work is almost boring.

Alex is still out of the country, and James has made himself scarce. I hang with Keaton. Kalvin is obviously avoiding me, as I haven't managed to snatch more than the odd few minutes with him, and my questions regarding the exact nature of his relationship with Addison are still unanswered. Kyler has been polite but distant all week.

So, yeah, things are settling into a regular pattern.

The normality is refreshing.

Should've known I'd spoken too soon.

On Friday, Brad drops us off in front of the house and we wave goodbye to him. An unfamiliar sporty blue number is parked in the driveway, sparking my curiosity. I chat to Lana for a bit before she heads home.

Stepping into the hall, I drop my bag on the ground. Someone hisses at me, and I jerk around. Kyler is lurking in the shadows under the stairs, gesturing me forward. He puts a finger to his lips and then points upstairs. The study door is ajar and soft female laughter wafts through the air. Icicles form a line down my back as I recognize Courtney's sultry tone. I tiptoe toward Kyler. "Listen," he mouths as I draw near. He pulls me into his side, and I'm immediately waylaid by the warm, hard lines of his body. Concentrating on eavesdropping becomes a mammoth task. My fingers twitch with the craving to touch him, as if a thousand volts of electricity are coursing through my body. I stare at the back of Kyler's head with pathetic longing. The sides and back of his head are newly shorn, and the thin layer of velvety hair begs to be touched. My eyes trail down his broad shoulders, over his tapered, slim waist, and the taut curves of his ass.

Must. Stop. Drooling.

Except it's no good—I can't resist his charms. Moving closer, I deliberately brush my body against his. His breath falters, and you could hear a pin drop in the space. Courtney's laughter rings out from above as Ky's fingers graze mine, igniting my skin on contact.

"Will you be able to get away this weekend?" Courtney purrs, her voice sounding closer. Ky's fingers entwine fully with mine.

"I'll find a way," James replies. Then it's quiet, and all I hear is the rampant thudding of my heart. Courtney emits a needy moan, and Ky squeezes my hand to the point of pain. His body is rigid with tension. I circle my arms around his waist and rest my head against his back. "We shouldn't be listening," I whisper.

"Now she grows a conscience," he mutters under his breath.

My retort dies on my tongue as more moans waft down the stairs. My insides twist into an acidic knot.

"Oh, James," Courtney rasps. "That feels so good."

Kyler spins around, grabbing me into his arms. He rests his head on my shoulder, and I can hear his heart pounding in his chest. I run my hand up and down his back in a soothing gesture.

"You'd better leave. The kids will be home shortly."

"I hate all this sneaking around, James. You have to tell her."

"Courtney." His loud sigh hints at exasperation. "Not now."

"Or not ever?" I don't need to see her face to imagine the angry look on it.

"We'll talk this weekend."

Ky flattens his back against the wall, holding me flush against his body when they appear at the bottom of the stairs. His hand moves to my hair, and his fingers weave in and out of the thick strands.

"I love you," Courtney states breathlessly. I clamp my lips shut, muzzling my disgust. Kyler tightens his hold on me, and his entire body is one solid, stress-laden mass of pent-up rage. My face is pressed into his neck, and his scent is driving me insane with desire, so I don't hear James' reply, if there is one. The door snicks shut and footsteps ascend the stairs as James disappears into his office.

I lean back and stare at Ky. All manner of emotions is skittering across his face. I cup his face, asking the most universally stupid question ever. "Are you okay?"

Squeezing his eyes shut, he shakes his head. When he reopens them, his gaze has transformed. Prickles spring up all over my skin. Ky moves me to the side and purposefully storms toward the front door. My eyes pop wide as I dash after him.

Courtney is reversing the car when I step outside. She curls her hand around the gear stick, preparing to leave, when she notices Ky making a beeline for her. Ky's poisonous glare is enough to give the game away. A smug smile dances across her lips as she primly tucks her hair behind her ears. I wrap my hand around his biceps, urging him back inside. "Don't. You're playing right into her hands." She's enjoying this, and I don't want to give her the satisfaction.

His fists are clenched so tightly the skin on his knuckles blanches white. "She's trying to destroy my family."

I plant myself in front of him, forcing him to focus on me. "This isn't the way to fight back." I gently place one hand on his chest. "Let her go. Come back inside."

Courtney's eyes narrow suspiciously. "Say hi to Addison," she calls out gleefully as she shoves the car into gear and screeches off down the driveway.

"Ky." I wave a hand in front of his face as he stares, dazed, after the departing car. "Please come back inside."

His gaze is fixated on Courtney, and there's deadly precision in his eyes. "She's lucky she's a woman. That I can't lay a hand on her."

He lets me pull him back into the house. James is at the bottom of the stairs with a frozen look on his face. Kyler drops my hand and lunges at his father, thrusting his fist in his face. James doesn't fight back at first, and Kyler continues to land blows on his face and torso. I spring into action, wrapping my arms around his waist and tugging him back. "Stop, Ky." He tries to shake me free, but I keep my arms locked firmly around his body.

"Kyler. Please." James holds up a hand. "I can explain."

"You disgust me." I feel the fight leave his body, and I remove my hold on him. Kyler steps back, leaning against the balustrade. "You promised you were going to end things. But that was a lie, wasn't it, Dad? You have no intention of finishing with her. Are you going to leave Mom for her?"

James climbs to his feet and faces his son. "No. I'll never leave your mom. I'll make this right, but you need to let me do this my way. There are things you aren't privy to, and believe me or not, I'm doing what I can to protect this family."

Ky's jaw flexes in and out, and I can tell he's close to breaking point. "I meant what I said earlier. If you don't tell Mom, I will. I'm not going to stand by and watch you turn her into a joke. How many other employees has Courtney told about your affair? How many people work side by side with Mom every day knowing her husband is fucking her assistant?" His voice raises a few octaves until he's yelling. "Have you given her any consideration at all?"

"Of course, I've thought about your mother!" He rakes a hand through his hair. "I'm not proud of myself."

"It all makes sense now." Ky flicks his hand in the air. "The hair, and the clothes, going out every night, acting like you're young, free, and single again. Did she put you up to it, or are you stupid enough to think that it'd be enough to keep a slut like Courtney interested when you're past your sell by date?"

"That's enough, Ky. I know I'm in the wrong here, but I'm still your father, and this is my house. You will act respectfully or not speak at all." James surreptitiously nods in my direction.

"This is Mom's house. You haven't worked a day in your life. And like I told you before, I'll give you respect if you ever earn it. But until then"—he

puts his face right into his dad's—"you don't get to tell me what to do."
He grabs his jacket and storms outside, rattling the door in his wake.

"I bet you regret moving here now," James says quietly.

"It's not like I had much choice," I answer honestly.

"I've ruined my relationship with all of them." He hangs his head in shame, and as I look at his sorry ass, anger starts to boil inside me.

"Get over yourself, James." His head jerks up at my stern tone. "I'm not going to indulge your self-pity. You made this mess, and it's up to you to fix it."

"I'm trying."

I step toward him until we're toe-to-toe. "No. You're not. We heard you arranging to meet her this weekend. Ky was right. You have no intention of ending things with her. At least be honest with yourself." I let him see every ounce of disgust on my face, and at least he has the decency to look ashamed. "Do you still love Alex?"

"Of course, I do! She's the one who's turned her back on me." A pained look flits across his features.

"I don't need to know the intimate details, and I'm hardly an expert, but honesty is the cornerstone of trust. You can't have one without the other. If you're not being honest, then the trust is gone too. Is that why Alex looks so sad all the time?"

He buries his head in his hands. "I know you think this is all on me—"

"Oh my God!" I throw my hands in the air. "This *is* all on you! What is wrong with you? You need to man up and take responsibility for your actions. You need to tell Alex, and you need to tell her before Ky does. Don't let your son carry that burden. Not if you hope to have any kind of relationship with him in the future."

He slowly nods. "You're right. Ky's right." He sighs. "I'll speak to her. I'll tell Alex."

"See that you do." I move past him, but he takes my arm, stalling me.

"I'm sorry, Faye."

"I'm not the one you should be apologizing to."

"I owe you an apology too. I've let you down. I've let all you kids down, but I'll make it up to you. I'll make it up to Alex." His voice becomes strangled. "If she'll let me."

The honest regret on his face breaks through the temporary walls I've put up. He needs to understand all that's at stake. He has a choice that I didn't. An opportunity to repair the damage to his family. I need him to understand that, because the man in front of me is scared of facing reality.

"Don't shy away from this, James. Try everything in your power to fix it, because if you lose your family, there's no coming back from that. The pain you will feel inside"—I emit a strangled sob before composing myself—"is like nothing you've ever felt before."

Tears trickle down my face, but I don't try to stop them. James stands uncertainly in front of me, and I can sense the conflict within. He wants to comfort me, but he's afraid to.

"I had no say in the matter," I whisper, hugging my arms around my body. "My family was taken from me overnight without any warning. Without any chance to say goodbye. I thought I'd a lifetime of hugs and kisses to look forward to. An eternity of laughter and shared moments to experience. But it was all gone in the blink of an eye. My mum won't see me graduate. My dad won't get to walk me down the aisle. My parents won't ever get to be grandparents."

Crunching pain ties my stomach into painful knots. "My family is gone. They're never coming back. And I'm trying to find a way of existing when sometimes I feel as dead as them on the inside." Turning, I face him with a fierce look. I wipe my sleeve across my damp face. "So stop feeling sorry for yourself. You fucked up, but it isn't too late to fix it. *Your* family is still here. Fix it, James. Don't let your family trickle through your fingers. Don't blow it." I beseech him with my eyes. "You've only got one family, and if you don't make this right, it'll destroy all of you."

Chapter Thirty

Saturday dawns bright and early. After a leisurely swim, I eat breakfast and then set out on a mission to hunt Kalvin down. I rap loudly on his door three times. "Wakey, wakey, sunshine."

"Get lost!" is the less than cheery response.

Offering up a silent prayer that I don't find him visibly naked on his bed, I open his door and slip inside, shielding my eyes with one hand, just in case.

A pillow whizzes by my head. "It's the butt crack of dawn, woman. Go away and let me sleep." Kalvin's sleep-laden timbre is underscored by a layer of irritation.

I pounce on his bed, and the mattress jiggles. Kal lifts his groggy head, cursing. "What is so urgent that it can't wait?"

"Who are you sneaking out to meet in the woods?"

"Wow. Way to just put it out there." Propping himself up on one elbow, he wipes the remnants of sleep from his eyes. The sheet falls down his body, pooling at his waist and exposing his bare chest.

"Please tell me you're not totally naked under there."

A devilish glint develops in his eye as he rolls flat on his back. "I always sleep naked." He slides a hand under the sheet, palming his junk. "I'll show you mine if you show me yours?" He winks.

"You're gross."

"I'm hot, and you know it." He winks again.

"And so modest, too." I fail to suppress my smile.

"Modesty is for pussies. I've a rocking body, and I know how to use it. I'm not ashamed to admit that. You gotta embrace your talents, you know?" He skims his hand over his crotch as he shoots me a sleazy grin.

"I just puked in my mouth."

"Now, now, don't be mean." He mock pouts. "You wouldn't be saying that if I was Ky."

"I'm not talking about jackass."

He snorts. "You two are hilarious. You should bang and get it out of your system."

"Because sex is the universal answer to every problem," I deadpan.

"I like that idea." He bobs his head up and down.

"You would." I roll my eyes before turning serious. "Quit messing about. I know you're deflecting." I grab his wrist, stalling his movement. "And stop jerking off. It's making me uncomfortable."

Amused eyes meet mine. "If I w—"

"Do not go there again." I momentarily close my eyes in exasperation. "We are not talking about Kyler, or me. We are talking about you and whomever you're hooking up with on the sly. Please tell me it isn't her. Please tell me you're not that stupid."

He scoots up the bed, resting against the sideboard. The sheet slips a little lower, highlighting the V-shaped indents on either side of his hips and the thin trail of hair snaking lower. The bulge under the sheets is too pronounced to go unnoticed.

Hell.

"Admit it," he teases, running his hand under the covers again, "You want this." He starts pumping up and down.

"I swear to God, Kal, if you don't stop that right now I'm going to the kitchen to get a knife and then I'm coming back to castrate you. Don't think I'm joking. If I wanted porn, I'd go download some. So stop being a sleaze, please. It's disgusting."

"Relax, Mary Sue." He holds both hands up in the air. "I'll be a good boy now. But make this snappy so I can attend to business."

I slap a hand across my forehead as air whooshes out of my mouth in frustration.

Finally, he takes pity on me. "Look, I'm not hooking up with Addison so you can chill out, okay?"

"So why you creeping around the woods in the middle of the night?"

"Need to know basis, right?" Reluctantly, I nod. "Well, it isn't anything you need to know. I'm not doing the dirty with Addison in the woods. And"—he holds up a hand—"I haven't talked to Ky yet, but I will. I'm waiting for the right time."

"You know there's no such thing, right? Not when it comes to something like this."

"Okay, okay. Stop busting my balls. You have what you came here for, so I'm kicking you out of my room now. Unless you're offering to help with my … situation?" He flashes me a mischievous grin. Yanking the covers off in one foul swoop, he lies before me in all his glorious nakedness. "Jesus!" I shriek, springing up like there's a rocket up my ass. "Not in this lifetime." I race toward the door trying to rinse the visual from my head.

Pausing, I turn to face him as an idea hits me. Payback time. Quick as lightning, I whip up my top and flash him my bra. His mouth hangs open, and the corners of my mouth curve up. "Wank away, cousin dearest." I'm laughing as I close his door, and crash, face-first, into a warm solid wall. His scent swirls around me and I don't need to open my eyes to know who it is.

"Do I even want to know?" Ky asks softly.

I tip my head up as my hands somehow find their way to his remarkable chest. I press against him, stretching on my tiptoes until our mouths are a hair's breadth from each other. A glimmer of lust bursts in his eyes, and need pulsates between my legs. "No." I rasp, my voice low and husky.

His fingers curl around the back of my neck sending a blanket of warmth cascading down my spine. He brushes a feather-soft kiss against my lips. Unbridled need tries to take command of me, but common sense wins the inner battle.

Resist. Abort. Resist! Resist! Resist!

As much as I crave his mouth on mine, one of us has to show some restraint. I shake my head, stepping out of his embrace. "Don't," I whisper, backing away. "Just don't."

He hangs his head, nodding his acquiescence, and I turn and walk away.

When I reach the lobby, James is coming down the stairs in low-hanging sweats and a white sleeveless shirt. His fascination with holding onto his youth is warped on so many different levels. "Good morning, Faye."

"Morning, James."

"Join me for coffee?" He asks as a loud yawn escapes his mouth.

We take our coffee outside, sitting silently side by side, gazing out onto the imposing lawn. "I wanted to thank you," James says a few minutes later. "For what you said yesterday. I've thought of nothing else all night."

"That's good."

"I'm going to end things with Courtney today, and I'm going to talk to Alex tonight."

I chew on the corner of my mouth. "You're doing the right thing."

He slurps his coffee. "I know, but it's going to hurt her so much. I hate that."

"Maybe you should've thought of that before you started anything with Courtney." My natural curiosity would love to know how long it's been going on and what prompted him to start an affair in the first place, but I know it isn't my place or my business to inquire.

"You think less of me now." His eyes probe mine.

I shrug, unsure how to answer. "We're still only getting to know one another."

My reply doesn't appear to faze him. "I'm proud of you, Faye. You have the courage to stand by your convictions. My baby sister raised you good. I'm proud of her, too." I catch a glimpse of moisture in his eyes before he looks away.

I smile. "They were great parents. Not perfect, but they did their best, and I loved them so much." A solitary tear spills onto my cheek. "I miss them, every damn day."

Hesitantly, he stretches his arm around my back and nudges my head onto his shoulder. It's not as awkward as I would've expected. "What was he like, your dad?"

"He was wonderful." I smile up at him. "He was always there for Mum and me. In a lot of ways, they were completely different, but it worked, you know? They were openly affectionate in front of me, and I know they really loved each other. He was a bit older than her, and his maturity offset her childishness, although he knew how to have fun, too. They were a great team." My eyes trek to the woods, watching the trees sway in the gentle breeze.

"I'm so glad your mother was truly loved. That you had a good upbringing." His voice is congested with emotion. "Never a day went by where I didn't worry about her. Old habits die hard, I suppose. She has shaped my life in so many ways." He grows quieter.

I peer up at him and we share a look. He opens and closes his mouth, as if he's debating saying something. I lift my head off his shoulder and eyeball him. "What?"

He wets his lips. "I think I know why your mom ran away from me."

Everything freezes inside me. "Don't keep me in suspense."

Air whooshes out of his mouth. "She was pregnant with you and she must've been too afraid to tell me."

I scratch the side of my head, frowning. "But she had me when she was nineteen and you said she ran away when she was seventeen?"

Slowly, he shakes his head. "I've checked the dates, Faye. She gave birth to you when she was seventeen."

I hop up. "What?!" My brain is racing at a hundred miles an hour.

He rises. "It's true. I can show you the records." He shuffles on his feet, clearing his throat. "What did she tell you about how she met your father?"

I'm spinning in a million different directions, frantically trying to decipher this latest bombshell.

Jeez, did Mum tell me the truth about anything?

James gently taps my elbow, drawing me out of the hazy mess in my head. "He, um,"—I calm my beating heart and force myself to get it together—"he was working on a construction site in her hometown and they met at a local club." I slap a hand against my forehead as I have a light bulb moment. "Oh my God! That *is* it!" I look deep into his eyes. "I thought Dad was only five years older than her but the age difference was even more pronounced, and if she had me at seventeen, then that means ..." I clamp a hand over my mouth, horrified at the implication.

"That he had unlawful sex with a minor and he could've been jailed," James finishes for me. I plop back down on the seat, completely devastated. James sits down too, speaking softly, as if I might break. "I didn't know she had a boyfriend, and I was insistent on her finishing school, but I'd never have turned her out or handed him over to the authorities. I would have supported her if she'd confided in me."

Tears pool in my eyes. "Has everything been a lie, James? Was anything she told me the truth?" My voice cracks at the end.

Pulling me into his side, he wraps his arms around me. "You know I can't answer that, but my sister loved you, Faye. I see it in the way she raised you and how well she protected you even after her death. She obviously felt she was doing the right thing sheltering you from the truth, or perhaps she had planned to tell you when you were older, when the timing was right."

I sniffle. "Guess we'll never know now."

He smooths a hand over my hair. "I still can't believe she's gone. I can't help thinking of all the wasted opportunities, and of what you said last night. I let your mom down, and I'll never have the chance to change that. But I can with Alex, if she'll let me." He plants a soft kiss to my temple. "I want to have a proper relationship with you, Faye. I can never replace your father, and I don't want to, but I hope in time you can come to rely on me. That you can forgive me for the mistakes I've made. You're very important to me. More so than you can even imagine."

I blink up at him. "I'd like that too."

It's only now I realize how much hearing that means to me.

Chapter Thirty-One

At work later on, I'm a little distracted over the most recent discovery. I'm struggling to find justification for all the lies. I have to believe that Mum was planning to admit the truth at some stage, because otherwise I think I'll stay mad at her forever. I don't want all the good memories stained with the color of her deceit.

I'm so caught up in my mind that I don't notice Jeremy cornering me in the corridor outside the bathrooms. "I've been looking for you, darlin'." Leaning against the wall, he shoots me a sleazy smile. "You're a tricky one to pin down." He winks. "Give me a day and time, right now."

Discreetly, I dig my fingernails into my thigh. "For what?" I feign ignorance, knowing full well what he's implying. Brad was right—Jeremy *doesn't* give up easily.

"Our date."

"I thought our last conversation made everything crystal clear. And, if I remember correctly, you weren't actually interested in going out with me anyway?" I cock my head to the side.

Reaching out, he fists a hand in my hair, tugging me toward him. "I should probably apologize for that, huh?" His large hands hold my face in a firm grip, and I'm instantly uncomfortable.

"Jeremy, let me go." I curl my hand around his wrist, trying to loosen his hold.

"Baby," he rasps, closing his eyes as he inhales deeply. "Don't fight this. You know you'll give in one way or another."

Fear and anger choke me as I raise my knee in preparation.

"Get your fucking hands off her!" Ky's tone is pumped full of explosive rage.

Jeremy slowly releases my face, backing away with a sneer.

Ky pulls me behind him, facing off with Jeremy. Every muscle in his body is on high alert. "Faye isn't interested, so leave her alone." Ice drips down my spine at the hostility in his tone. "Next time, I won't be so understanding."

Jeremy claps him on the shoulder. "Go fuck yourself, Kennedy." Looking down, he fixes his intense gaze on me. "You and me ain't done, Ireland." His eyes smolder with malicious promise. "Not by a long shot." The clumping sound of his boots retreating is like music to my ears, and I release the breath I was holding.

"You need to tell me if anyone is hassling you. Especially that skeeze," Ky glares at me as if this is somehow my fault.

"He hasn't bothered me in ages. I thought he'd lost interest."

"There is no such thing when it comes to Jeremy."

"Well, I'll be ready for him next time."

"I know you can handle yourself, Faye, but Jeremy's got a rep for a reason. Promise me you'll tell me if he gets too much."

Muscles flex and roll under his shirt as he crosses his arms in front of him. His pale blue eyes become storm-filled, and I melt under the power of his gaze. Genuine concern radiates off him in waves and my heart soars in my chest. While I'm more than capable of looking after myself, it feels unbelievably good to know he cares enough to want to protect me. A long-forgotten memory pops into my mind. "I will, thanks." My voice quivers a little.

His thumb swipes over his prickly jawline. "What's going through your head right now?"

"It's nothing." I attempt to shrug it off. "Just remembering something that happened when I was younger."

He lounges against the wall. "Try me."

"It's kind of silly." I pull at the corner of my ear.

A genuine smile graces his lips. "Now I'm intrigued; you have to tell me."

I smooth my hands over my apron as I clear my throat. "We lived in this large estate in Waterford when I was younger, and there were these two brothers who used to tease me relentlessly. They were always giving me a hard time. Mum was fond of saying they had a crush on me, but whatever." I smile at the memory. "During the summers, all the kids used to play water fights on our bikes. It was only supposed to be harmless fun. One time, one of the brothers caught me and absolutely drenched me, soaking every last piece of my clothing. I was hopping mad, so I raced home and filled my bottle with a mix of washing-up liquid and water and went back out and hunted him down. I deliberately squirted it in his eyes, and he totally freaked out, knocking me off my bike and kicking me repeatedly in the stomach. As I was lying on the ground, I remember how much I wished that I had an older brother or a cousin or someone who cared enough to come to my rescue."

Ky's face is a block of stone, and now I definitely feel silly. I shuffle, embarrassed, on my feet. "Your words brought the memory to the forefront of my mind."

Silence engulfs us as we stare at one another. After a bit, he opens his mouth. "I'm not the hero, Faye." A look of repulsion crosses over his face. "And I certainly can't be that for you."

My embarrassing recollection and Ky's words plague me the rest of my shift. No matter what Ky said, his coming to my rescue has touched on a long-held desire. While I don't consider myself to be a damsel in distress, it's nice to know I can count on others to have my back.

It hasn't always been like that.

I still don't know why he came to the diner earlier—whether there was a purpose to his visit or it was just lucky timing. Either way, I'm glad he was there.

Rose comes back to the house with me after work so we can get dolled-up together in my room. My cousins are throwing another party tonight, and even though we can't hear anything from here, I'm assuming it's already in full swing. "Where's Theo tonight?" I ask, wiggling a pair of jeans up my legs.

"Away with his fam for the weekend. He's back tomorrow night." She saunters into my walk-in wardrobe, emitting a low whistle. "Do you think the Kennedys would adopt me if I begged enough?"

I crank out a laugh. "You and Rachel would get on like a house on fire. Borrow whatever you want, Rose."

"I don't get you." She walks out with a swath of black material draped over her arm. "You have the most sought after designer clothes in your closet and you live in jeans. What a waste."

"It's not me." I press my lips together, blotting my lipstick as I peer at my reflection in the mirror.

"You're going to indulge me for one night." Her tone brokers no argument.

I swivel on my seat, raising an eyebrow. "I am?"

"Yep." She flings the black dress at me. "You put that on, and I'll find a dress for me. We're going to rock up to that party and *nail* it."

Twenty minutes later, I'm regretting allowing her to talk me into wearing this pathetic excuse for a dress. The black lace mini clings to my every curve leaving little to the imagination. With thin straps, a dipped neckline, and a shockingly short hem, which barely covers my ass, I'm feeling rather exposed. Thank God, I won the battle of the shoes, and I'm wearing my combat boots and not the sky-high peep-toes Rose wanted me to wear. She's wearing a similar style mini in a floral patterned print that oddly works well with her pink hair.

I insist that we detour to Lana's en route. After several minutes of pleading, I finally get Lana to pinky swear that she'll follow us to the party.

"You two should come with a health warning," Brad jokes, hopping down the steps to greet Rose and me. He gives us a quick once-over, and his smile is appreciative. "You look amazing."

I take in his appearance. Tonight, he's wearing jeans with a plain white tee and a blue-and-red-checkered shirt that's fully unbuttoned. If I wasn't so obsessed with my cousin, I could totally see myself crushing on Brad. "You look good, too."

He leads us through the heaving crowd out toward the back. A few guys reach for me as we pass, but I manage to duck out of their way. Rose continuously flashes her middle finger as a myriad of wolf-whistles are aimed our way. Kalvin grabs me into a headlock the minute I step foot in the kitchen, gleefully messing up my hair. "You're such an ass," I moan, punching him in the gut.

He frees me, palming his sore stomach. "And you've got a real mean violent streak." He looks me up and down. "But I'll forgive you because you've just given me hours' worth of visual stimulation that I'm gonna put to good use." He winks, tapping the side of his head.

"You're grossing me out again." Brad thrusts a wine cooler into my hand, and I smile up at him. Kal stiffens, and I shoot him a cautionary look, but he's not paying any attention to us. Lana has entered the kitchen, scanning the room with anxious eyes. My hand shoots up and I wave her forward.

"What the fuck are you doing here?" Kalvin demands, looming over her with a scowl on his face.

"Back off, asshole," I snap, looping my arm through Lana's and pulling her over to my side. "I invited Lana. She's my friend."

"She's not welcome here," he growls.

"I should leave," Lana mumbles, looking down at her feet.

"You're going nowhere. Stay here while I talk to my *cousin*." It takes considerable effort to call him that and not one of the multiple insults currently flitting through my mind. I gesture to Brad to keep an eye on Lana while I drag my cousin outside.

"You were unbelievably rude to Lana. What the hell is your problem?"

At least he has the decency to look ashamed. "She doesn't belong here, Faye."

"Don't be such a condescending prick! I thought you two used to be friends? How can you treat her like this?"

He hooks his hands in his pockets. "This *is* me being a friend to her."

"That's a cop out! I'd hate to see how you treat your enemies."

"It's not!" He gnashes his teeth at me. "You see those bitches in there?" He points into the house. "They've been horrible to Lana in the past. You've no idea how they've used her to try to get to us. Keeping her away is the best way of protecting her. That's all I'm trying to do."

I suck in my cheeks as I consider his words. "You mean that."

"Yes," he hisses.

"But why do you have to be such a jerk about it?"

He walks around me, opening the door. "Haven't you figured it out yet?"

I shoot him a puzzled look. He leans into my face, and the look of revulsion and self-loathing shocks me. "Because I am a jerk." He pushes into the kitchen, brushing furiously past both Rose and Lana as he storms out.

Lana takes one look at me, her eyes filling with tears, before she runs out of the room.

"Damn it! I'll be back," I shout at Brad and Rose as I race after her, pushing and shoving people out of my way in my haste to catch up with her.

"Lana!" I call after her fleeing figure. "Wait up!"

My tight dress restricts movement, and she makes ground easily, promptly fading from sight. I stop, cursing under my breath. I could murder Kalvin right about now.

Traipsing back to the party, I stop on the bottom step when I catch sight of Addison leaning over the railing, watching everything with those cunning eyes of hers. "Enjoying the drama?" I snap, as I trudge up the stairs.

"Most definitely," she sneers, flicking her blonde locks over her shoulder. "Kennedy parties never fail to enlighten me." She skips into the house ahead of me, grinning as if a genie has just granted her every wish.

Brad hands me a fresh drink when I return to the kitchen. Rose is nowhere to be seen. At that exact moment, Ky shows up in the room with his arm slung protectively around Addison's shoulders. Her arm is wrapped around his back, and she's leaning into his side, purring like a cat. For the second time in a minute, I want to gouge her eyes out with toothpicks. Either that or make a voodoo doll in her likeness to stick pins in.

I can't believe he's doing this. It makes me sick.

Brad leans down and whispers in my ear, "You want to go outside?"

I put my drink down. "I've a better idea. Let's dance." Deliberately avoiding Kyler, I take Brad's hand and pull him into the living room, right into the thick of the teeming crowd. Flicking my hair back, I start swaying to the music, limbering up to the infectious beat. My limbs feel loose and free, and I grin at Brad as he matches my movements.

We dance until sweat coasts down my spine and starts pooling between my breasts. Damp tendrils of hair kiss my forehead, and my mouth feels like something died in there. We head back into the kitchen, and I pull myself up onto the counter, crossing my legs as Brad throws me an ice-cold bottle of water. Dehydrated, I knock it back in one go, my throat working overtime.

A petite girl with masses of red corkscrew curls comes bounding into the kitchen, looking hassled and upset. "Has anyone seen Judy Mills?" Most everyone stares blankly at her. "She looks like me only she's a bit older?" A few people shake their head, and the rest go about their business.

"Crap." She scrunches fistfuls of her hair.

I jump down off the counter. "Are you sure she's here?"

She nods. "She texted me. But what she doesn't know is her boyfriend is on his way here, and if I know Judy ..."

"Gotcha. Did you check the bedrooms?"

She bobs her head vigorously. "I checked the ones on that side"—she gestures to the left—"but I can't check the ones on the other side as you need a key to access the corridor."

"Leave that with me. Stay here and I'll come back."

I drag Brad with me as I locate a sulky Kalvin and retrieve a key. Unlocking the wooden door, I step into the narrow corridor with Brad at my back. The music muffles as the heavy door closes with a thud. Three doors emerge on our left. Loud moans mix with a repetitive thumping noise that appears to be originating from the last bedroom. A female voice cries out, and Brad and I exchange knowing looks as we stop in front of the third door.

I fling it open before I change my mind. The sight that accosts me sends me stumbling back into Brad. He grips my waist, helping to keep me upright. Butterflies swarm my chest in outrage. "Holy fuck. I think I'm going to be sick."

Chapter Thirty-Two

Kent glances over his bare shoulder, leering, completely unashamed, as if this type of behavior is normal. I slap a hand over my lips, forcing myself to swallow the acrid taste in my mouth. He continues to pound into the naked girl underneath him, unconcerned about the audience. His fingers dig into her left hip as he thrusts, and his naked ass cheeks clench and unclench with the motion. I look down at my feet, not wanting that mental image of him etched for eternity in my mind.

Seeing two of my cousins naked in the same day has to be some kind of gross record.

The girl's long, wavy red hair is spread around the pillow like a fan. She emits a passionate moan, and I feel a compelling urge to smack her into next week. "Here to join the private party?" Kent winks. "There's always room for one more. Or two, if you fancy joining in, too, Brad."

"Kent!" the dark-haired girl on the other side of him screams, bucking her hips as his fingers thrust deep inside her. A third girl—this one has poker-straight blonde hair—runs her hands all over his body, jiggling her small breasts at Brad in invitation.

I'm frozen to the spot, utterly disgusted at what I'm seeing. The girls are clearly older than he is. College level, if I had to guess. That only sours my stomach more. Powerful shudders rock my body, as if I was the one being violated. "Kent, you need to stop this right now. You're only fifteen!"

"We like them virile and young," the ignorant blonde says, moving her hands down to slap his butt.

That answers the question of complicity then.

"It's fucking illegal, you imbecile," I fume. If not for the fact that Kent is already in deep doo-doo with the law, I'd call the cops on their skanky asses.

She laughs, and the sound is like a siren call. An inner beast wakes from slumber inside me, clawing at the cage, whispering inducements, begging to be let out. Blood thunders through my veins, and a red haze coats my eyes. My hands clench into fists, and I'm seconds away from charging into the room and inflicting some damage.

Brad senses my mood and hauls me out of the room. "Get Ky. I'll try to talk some sense into him in the meantime. Go."

The beast slithers away, and my blood pressure moderates. While the urge to teach those girls a lesson hasn't dissipated, I know Brad is right. Ky will be able to deal with this more effectively, and right now, the most important thing is extricating Kent from the situation as quickly as possible.

On a hunch, I rush out to the front deck, finding Kyler instantly. Addison is on his lap *again*, grinding against him as her tongue strokes up and down his neck. The beast, only recently tamed, roars inside me, and I'd love to release my pent-up frustration on Addison and her per-fectly formed writhing butt, but this isn't about me. To be fair, Ky is like a statue—motionless and expressionless as Addison gyrates on top of him. Nonetheless, it does little to appease me.

"Ky!" I call out. "You're needed. Right now."

His eyes widen in alarm at my urgent tone, and he lifts Addison off his lap instantly. She starts to protest, and he darts down and kisses her on the cheek. "Stay here. I'll be right back." He takes my elbow and leads me around the other side of the deck, to a quiet spot in the corner. "What's going on?"

"Kent's out of control. He's in one of the bedrooms with three girls. It's ... I"—my speech falters—"I'm no innocent, but I've never seen any-thing so shocking. It's wrong, Ky. You need to stop him."

"Where are they?" His voice is deathly quiet.

"Last bedroom. Brad's there."

"Come on." He leads me back into the house.

Brad steps out of the way as Ky charges into the bedroom. Now that he has this in hand, I turn on my heel and head out in search of the girl's sister. Locating her where I left her in the kitchen, I whisper my discovery. She looks as sick as I feel.

After finding Rose, and explaining I'm calling it a night, I head away, no longer in the mood to party.

I tap timidly on Lana's window, hoping she's still awake. A second later, the blind retracts and the window opens. Lana greets me with tear-swollen eyes, and I want to rip shreds off Kal for upsetting her like this. "Oh, Lana! He didn't mean it."

"He did. He meant every word." She chokes on a sob.

I take her warm hands in my cooler ones. "I know it makes no sense, but he was actually trying to protect you. He's a gobshite for the way he handled it, but his heart was in the right place."

"You genuinely believe that?" she asks, wiping her wet eyes with the hem of her nightie.

"Yeah, I do."

Her features harden. "Well, I don't. That little boy that I knew? The one I thought I loved? He's gone, and all I have are my memories."

I suspected Lana was crushing on Kal, but it seems her feelings ran even deeper. My face softens. "Lana—"

"It's okay, Faye. I'm not sorry I went. I needed closure and now I have it. Kalvin did me a huge favor tonight." She wipes away the last of her tears and faces me with determination. "I'm fine, and it's late. You should go."

"You're sure you're okay?"

She grants me a small smile. "I'm good. Talk to you later?"

"'Kay." Closing the window, she secures the blind in place.

I make my way out of the forest and back toward the main house. I lie down on one of the loungers by the pool, draping a towel over my body to ward off the intense bout of shivering that's taken possession of me. It takes a lot to put me in a funk, but the events of tonight have opened old wounds. I can't stop shivering as unpleasant memories return to haunt me.

And that's how Brad finds me a few minutes later.

"Hey." He sits on the side of the adjoining lounger. "Are you okay?"

"Truth?" I stare into his concerned eyes. "No. I'm not okay. That was ..."

He rests his elbows on his knees. "Insane, I know. Kent was always a little shit but that's on a whole other level." His eyes pin mine. "I'm sensing there's more to your reaction than this. Maybe I'm wrong, and I don't mean to pry, but I'm here if you want to want to talk about it."

I tuck my hands under my cheek. "No offense, but it's a part of my past that I hate reliving."

His spine stiffens, and I reach out for his hand.

"Don't jump to conclusions. I wasn't raped or into orgies or anything. It was a different situation, but seeing Kent like that has brought certain ugly feelings to the surface again." Feelings like helplessness, abandonment, and the accompanying rage. I haven't spent years learning to control my fears and my drivers for it all to unravel in one night.

I pull myself upright, holding my knees snug to my chest. I secure the towel around me as I decide to share what I can. "The worst thing is that he doesn't see his vulnerability. But I do. I see it and my heart aches for him." And that's the truth. At least when I was taken advantage of, I recognized my vulnerability. But Kent doesn't. He thinks he's in control, and that's arguably a more dangerous position to be in.

Brad leans back on his lounger, copying my position. "It seems everyone's family has demons to battle." Arching his head, he stares up at the sky. I could latch onto that and squirrel my way into his mind, plucking all the right strings and diverting focus from me. But I could never manipulate a friend like that, and that's what Brad has come to mean to me. Instead, I bide my time, knowing he'll open up shortly.

I tilt my head and join him, marveling at how peaceful the nighttime canvas looks compared to the turmoil on the ground. Amicable silence descends as we are both lost in our thoughts. I clear my throat after a bit and look sideway at him. "It works both ways, you know." He twists around to look at me. "I'm here if *you* need to talk."

He doesn't say anything for several minutes, and I don't push. I've put it out there that I'm willing to listen. Now the rest is up to him. "I haven't told anyone." A sad look appears on his face. "There hasn't been anyone to tell."

"I'm listening now." We face one another, on our sides.

"Do you promise to keep it to yourself?" His eyes betray a world of pain, and I can see how much he needs to let this out.

"I promise I won't tell another soul. You can trust me."

"There's a warrant out for my dad's arrest" is his startling opening line. "He knew it was coming, and that's why he fled abroad with my mom and sisters three months ago."

I sit up in a flash. "Wait! What?"

"They all left. I stayed because I ... I don't want my future to be jeopardized by his actions. I want to graduate and go to college as planned. Between my grades and my skill on the field, I should be able to score a football scholarship. I couldn't throw all that away."

I stare at him, flabbergasted.

"You think I'm selfish?" He jumps to the wrong conclusion.

I shake my head vehemently. "Definitely not. I'm just shocked that you've been left all alone. How are you coping by yourself?"

He sits up, swinging his legs around, and our knees brush. "I'm still in one piece." He worries his lip between his teeth. "The government is going to seize the house, and they've already frozen most of his assets, but I've got some cash to tide me over, and I have my car, and I'll stay in the house for as long as I can, and then"—he lets loose a shaky breath—"well, I'll figure something out. I can probably move upstate to my aunt's." He sends me a half-hearted smile.

Or move in here.

But I don't say that out loud, tucking it away in a mental cubbyhole for later.

Reaching out, I grasp his hands. "I can't believe you've been living all alone and you said nothing to no one about it. You should've told me."

"I've ostracized myself from most everyone, and I was too embarrassed. Not that it matters now, since it's about to go public. The feds have been keeping a lid on things while they investigate, but soon, everyone will know." He looks off into space.

"What did he do?" I ask quietly.

"Embezzled funds. He's stolen millions from his clients. It's a total shitstorm."

"I'm so sorry, Brad. That's awful. When did you find out?"

"Seven months ago." He gives me a meaningful look, and alarm bells start howling in my ear.

"Does this have something to do with Addison?"

"That time I slept with her was the day I found out. I lost it with my dad, stormed out of the house, and drowned my sorrows in a bottle. I shouldn't have gone to the party without my wingman. Ky was in Nantucket, and Addison was there, alone. I was completely wasted, but I still should've known better. When she came on to me, I didn't refuse her, because I didn't allow myself time to stop and think. I wanted to get out of my head, needed to forget everything, and sex was a welcome distraction. But, the next day, when I realized what I'd done"—he closes his eyes—"I wanted to die, way worse than I had the previous day. Knowing I'd done that to my best friend, I still hate myself for it."

He buries his head in his hands, and I move over to sit beside him, wrapping my arms around his waist. "Brad? Are you saying that you only slept with Addison that one time?"

His head whips up. "Yes. Why?" Recognition dawns on his face. "Ky thinks it was more than that?"

I nod. "You don't even know how he found out, do you?"

He shakes his head. "I figured someone at the party told him. We weren't exactly discreet." A look of self-loathing drifts over his features.

"Someone sent him an anonymous email, and from what he told me, it contained photographic and video evidence of you and her together, and it was more than one occasion. Ky thinks you were cheating with her for months."

He launches himself out of the lounger, his wild eyes meeting mine. "Are you fucking serious?"

I stand up beside him. "Yes. It was definitely only one time?"

"Absolutely. It wasn't a mistake I am ever likely to repeat."

"I believe you." I place my hand on his lower arm. "You two need to talk. Someone's been playing you."

"I've tried talking to him, but he just keeps pushing me away." I can hear the desperation in his voice.

"I'll talk to him."

"It won't work."

"You don't know how resourceful I can be. Leave it with me, okay?" I gently squeeze his arm as I look up at him.

"Thank you." He brushes his lips against my forehead.

"Sorry, am I interrupting?" Ky's blatant sarcasm slices through the moment.

I step away from Brad, turning to face my cousin. "Don't be an ass. Where's Kent? Did you sort it?"

A muscle ticks in his jaw as he nods. "Come inside and I'll tell you."

I look between him and Brad, slightly torn. Brad's poured out his heart to me, and I don't want to toss him aside the second Ky appears on the scene. Especially now I know he's heading home to an empty house. But I don't have to make any decision, because Brad does that for me.

"It's okay, Faye. I was going to head home anyway. Talk tomorrow?"

"Of course." Without examining the wisdom of it, I step into his chest and wrap my arms around him. His hands hover around my waist, uncertainly, and I know he doesn't want to do anything to piss Ky off. But I don't care what Ky thinks right now. Brad needs a friend, and more than ever, I want to be that for him. I squeeze him tighter and finally his arms go around me. I tip my chin up. "Will you be okay?" I mouth.

He presses his mouth to my ear. "I will. Thank you." He kisses the top of my head before pulling away. Giving me a quick wave, he sprints across the lawn toward the forest.

Kyler is stiff as a board, his arms folded sternly across his waist. "Are you two together now?"

"Not that it's any of your business, but no, we're not. We're friends is all. Brad really needs a friend right now." I dare him to challenge me, silently begging him to ask the question, but he doesn't. He does the whole usual sullen moody thing, giving me the silent treatment as he escorts me into the house.

Without asking, I make coffee for both of us, sliding a cup to him over the kitchen counter. "Is Kent okay? I'm worried about him."

He sighs. "That makes two of us." I take a sip of the bitter liquid while I wait for him to elaborate. "I broke it up and gave those girls a piece of my mind. When I came back out, Kent had taken off. Kalvin has gone to look for him." He scratches the top of his head. "You seemed upset, and I wanted to make sure you were all right."

"I'm fine," I answer too quickly.

"Are you ever going to tell me?" He leans forward on his elbows. "I know things are fucked up between us, but I still care. And I'm grateful to you, for being concerned about Kent, for asking me to intervene."

"Why does it all fall on you?" I place my cup down on the counter, resting my face in my hands. "It shouldn't be your responsibility."

"It used to be Kaden, and when he first left for Harvard, I thought Keven would step up, but he's too busy fighting his own demons to look out for his younger brothers."

"So you filled the gap," I add for him.

"Yeah. What else could I do?" His storm-filled eyes reach for mine.

I hold his gaze, burning up from the intensity of it. *Who looks after you?* I want to ask it, but I don't. I'm too afraid that he'll confirm it's no one, and I'll volunteer for the job. Actually, it's way more than that. The extent of my longing to be *that* for him scares the bejesus out of me.

His razor-sharp gaze cracks through my inner shell, penetrating that most precious hidden part of me. Weary and resigned, I let him take his fill, knowing if anyone could understand it, it'd be him.

He rounds the counter, his gaze never drifting from mine. I look up as he stops in front of me, peering down into my eyes with a ferociousness that usually scares me.

But not this time.

The façade is down, and he's inviting me in. Returning the favor. Trusting me as I trusted him. His hand moves to my cheek, caressing me softly. A pool of nurturing warmth blossoms inside me. His eyes pay homage to me, with a look of respect and adoration that has the power to sweep me off my feet if I let it.

When Ky decides to let someone in, she's going to be the luckiest girl in the world, because this boy has a huge heart, and he's capable of enormous feats when it comes to the ones he loves. I see it now, clear as day, as if it's a tangible entity.

Ignoring the surge of tormented longing growing inside me, I rest my hand on his chest, feeling the feverish beating of his heart. I keep my eyes fixated on him as I peer into the chasm within. The cavernous emptiness inside him calls out to me, like a silent mating call. Like one half of a soul recognizing and coveting its equal. That anguished darkness tempts me, crooning and cajoling, begging me to delve inside. To immerse myself in all-too-familiar sensations. To open myself to him and the possibility that he offers.

And it wouldn't be difficult to cross that line with him. To explore our mutual hidden depths. To finally have someone completely understand the person that resides inside.

It's so tempting, almost more than I can bear.

But there are far too many obstacles presently standing in our way.

As if to prove a point, a clanging sound echoes from the lobby, breaking us both out of whatever bubble we were cocooned in. We move without speaking, linking hands as if it's the most natural thing in the world.

The lobby is empty, but I can't shake the eerie feeling crawling over my skin. "It must've been one of my brothers. Wait here," Ky says, "I'll check their rooms." The ominous feeling multiples tenfold as I wait in the silent, dimly lit hallway for Ky's return. My eyes dart around the room, looking for a clue, but everything is as it should be.

"Kent's passed out, fully clothed, on his bed. It was obviously him." He locks one hand around the back of his neck, looking anxiously at me.

Something different is in the air, and it excites me. Although I can't yet put a name to it, it feels like we've reached a pivotal point in our history. I've only caught glimpses of this side of Ky before, and it warms my soul every time he permits me to see into the person he could be. The one he keeps so closely guarded inside.

It's time.

I feel it.

He knows it.

I take his hand and pull him into the living room, tugging him down on the sofa alongside me. Wedging myself into the arm, I face him, drawing my knees to my chest for physical and moral support. "I want to tell you what happened to me."

Chapter Thirty-Three

I draw a large, brave breath and start into my story. "When I was thirteen, I went to my first party, and something happened that night that messed me up pretty bad." I pause, wetting my suddenly bone-dry lips and shuttering my eyes temporarily. Kyler laces his fingers in mine and squeezes. That silent reassurance encourages me to continue.

"I was drinking vodka with my friends, and by the time we started playing Truth or Dare, I was already buzzing. When the bottle spun my way, I chose a dare, and I was challenged to allow this guy, Daniel, to feel my boobs. It all sounds so juvenile now, but back then it was a big deal. He was fifteen and two years ahead of me in school. All the girls had a crush on the guy—me included—but I was still apprehensive about agreeing. Everyone was teasing me over being a prude, so I pushed my nervousness aside and went with him to one of the bedrooms."

I take deep breaths, in and out. No matter how many times I tell this story, it still feels like I'm reliving the moment over and over again. Ky continues to hold my hand firmly, his thumb tracing soothing circles on my skin.

"I developed quite early, and the boys were always making crude jokes, but I was completely innocent. Hadn't even kissed a boy then, so taking my bra off for an older guy was a huge deal." An intense shiver thunders through me. "He was a pig." The usual maelstrom attacks me, but I push on. "He was rough, squeezing my flesh hard, and I closed my eyes, wishing it was over."

I press my lips together as remembered humiliation and discomfort resurfaces. Kyler changes position on the couch, sliding in behind me. His strong arms wrap around me, renewing my courage. I rest my head back on his chest. "That must've been when he took the photo." Ky stiffens underneath me. "I was blocking it all so effectively that I didn't even hear the faint click of his phone. It wasn't until I came back to the main room, greeted by a chorus of obnoxious hollers, that I realized what he'd done. By the next day, the photo had been circulated to everyone in school. The boys wouldn't leave me alone. I was besieged with propositions and wolf-whistles, and random boys would leer at me. Some even tried copping a feel. It was a total free-for-all." A lump builds in my throat.

Kyler holds me tighter, pressing a soft kiss to the side of my head. "But the girls were worse. My friends disowned me. Even though they'd been there, and they knew me and knew how upset I was over the whole thing, they didn't stand up for me. They didn't want to be tarnished by association."

I shake my head sadly. "Complete strangers along with other girls I had known for years shouted insults at me. It was horrendous." I gulp. "I felt so stupid, so foolish, and I couldn't bring myself to tell my parents or any of the teachers in school. I was too ashamed."

Feeling cold, I run my hands up and down Ky's arms, siphoning warmth. "I was depressed, and my parents noticed something was wrong, but I still couldn't tell them. It hurt so much, and even now, I can still feel it. In here." I place my hand over my chest. "I don't think I'll ever forget how violated I felt. Mix that with my self-revulsion, and my head was a very dark place. After a few weeks, I couldn't take much more, and I ... I had a mini breakdown."

Tears glisten in my eyes. "My swimming teacher found me sobbing in the changing room after practice, and she called my parents. I caved. Told them everything."

Kyler's lips brush my cheek.

"My self-esteem was in the toilet, so I started seeing a psychiatrist and began to work through my feelings. My parents insisted on telling the school, and that was when things went to absolute shite. Daniel was suspended for two weeks, and a number of other boys were cautioned. The abuse ramped up a few notches, and 'snitch' was added to the 'slut' taunts. I tried to ignore it but it refused to go away."

I breathe in, inhaling his familiar scent, allowing it to comfort me. "When Daniel returned after his suspension, he waited by my locker every day. He never said a word to me, never so much as looked sideways at me, did nothing concrete that I could report, but that silent intimidation was the worst form of torture. I literally shook walking up the steps to school each morning."

Ky sweeps my hair aside, resting his chin on my shoulder.

"Daniel's girlfriend decided to take matters into her own hands after that. Or maybe he put her up to it." I shrug. "I never found out. But that was when the bullying started in earnest. I'd come out of school to find someone had slashed the tires on my bike. Another time she broke into my locker and destroyed all my books. I'd come out of the pool to find my clothes cut to shreds. She did a bunch of stuff like that, and I knew it was her, but I could never prove it; she always had an alibi. Eventually, even the school was getting sick of the hassle, and I knew they didn't believe me anymore."

I twist in his arms, snuggling into his chest. He presses a kiss to the top of my head. "The twenty-fourth of February 2012 is a day that will be indelibly imprinted on my brain. That's when things came to a head. It was a Friday." I tilt my head back to look at him. His eyes are hard but compassionate. "I knew something was up the minute I stepped into the building. Everyone was laughing and pointing, and I walked toward my locker on shaky legs. Then I saw it plastered across every locker. She had photoshopped my head onto a pornographic image and printed it with 'Hooker for Hire' and my mobile number on it." I blink my eyes shut as a garbled choking sound travels up my throat.

Kyler smooths a hand up and down my back. "I told the principal it was her, but he didn't believe me. He told me they'd investigate it, but I knew she must've covered her tracks. I was like a zombie all day. I blanked everything out. It was the only way I could survive all the insults and disgusting innuendos. She was waiting for me with some of her cronies outside at the end of the day. I can't remember exactly what it was she said to me now, but it was enough to affirm in my mind that she was definitely the one behind it.

I sit up straighter, easing back a little. "I just snapped. It was the final straw. Even though she said it to provoke me, and I should've known better than to respond to it, I was powerless to halt my natural reaction. All the pent-up anger and stress and self-loathing bolted from me like a streak of lightning. Rage, like I've never felt before, consumed me, and I couldn't leash it even if I'd wanted to. But I didn't. I *wanted* to hurt her. To inflict pain so she'd feel what it was like. In that moment, I didn't care what happened to me. I just wanted to make her pay."

"What did you do?" He palms one side of my face.

"I lunged at her, swinging with both fists. I caught her off guard, and she lost her footing on the steep, concrete steps and fell backward, tumbling and crashing to the ground. She was out cold, clearly injured, and I just stood there and laughed. I laughed until my stomach ached. I didn't even feel a twinge of guilt or concern." I hold my head in my hands. "Two ambulances were called. One for her. One for me. I was admitted to the psych ward for evaluation while she was rushed into surgery."

I wrap my arms around his neck. "She suffered a brain injury, Ky, and it was all my fault."

He holds me close. "It was an accident, Faye, and she was hardly blameless. She bullied you to the breaking point, and you retaliated in self-defense. You didn't push her down the steps or deliberately set out that day to inflict damage. She brought it on herself."

I hold his shoulders, leaning back so he can see my face. "I wanted to hurt her, Ky. Like, really, really hurt her. And I didn't feel any remorse when it happened. I *laughed* when she was lying motionless on the ground." The usual bout of self-loathing crawls over my skin like a rash that refuses to go away. "That I could feel such intense rage terrifies *me*. Now I know what I'm capable of doing and it sickens me. I try to stay calm in confrontational situations, but sometimes the need is almost overwhelming. Like back there with Kent. I was so incensed I wanted to storm right in and beat their asses. If Brad hadn't hauled me out of there ..." I look down at my lap, not caring to witness the disappointment that is surely displayed in his eyes.

He tilts my chin up with his finger. "Everyone has a dark side, Faye. A side of them that is downright ugly. *Everyone.*" His eyes burn a hole in mine. "You know *I* know that. But it's what you *do* that counts. The truly evil people in this world can't help but give in to that side of themselves, and they never suffer an attack of conscience. For them, it's as easy as breathing. Then there are those who are weak, those who allow the devil on their shoulder to sway them into doing the wrong thing. The majority of people are strong enough to resist, to know right from wrong, to constantly battle so that good wins out over bad."

He twirls a lock of my hair around his finger. "And then there are people like you. People who are inherently good but who end up in a bad situation. What happened that day was self-preservation. What happened *after* that day is all that matters, and you aren't a bad person, Faye." He shakes his head. "Far from it. You didn't intentionally hurt her, and your natural response is to help others. That's the Faye I've come to know."

I'm quietly contemplative for a few seconds. "I know I would've gotten over it—the photo, I mean. I was embarrassed and humiliated, and I hated the thought that so many people had seen me in such an intimate way, but over the years, I've realized that that wasn't the issue. I could've overcome it, but it's the part that came after that will stay with me forever. The bullying and the loss of friendship and what happened to Vera—that was her name—and the fear that some resident evil conceals itself in the deepest part of me. Now, I have to live with what I've done. With the realization that I'm capable of true evil."

"I'm calling bullshit on that." He pins me with a fierce look. "You defended yourself. It's not the same thing. What exactly happened afterwards?"

"I was in the psych ward for a couple of days. They determined that I'd had a mild break as a result of the excess stress I'd been under. Vera's parents wanted to press charges, but I was a minor. With the psych assessment, and the fact that the school was finally able to pin some of the bullying on Vera, *and* they had caught the entire incident on camera, their solicitor advised them to drop the case. She was in the hospital for a few weeks and I believe her brain injury was minor."

I fiddle with the hem on my dress. "I never saw her again. I never returned to that school. My parents moved us from Waterford to Dublin, and we tried to start over, as if it'd never happened. But I couldn't dismiss it. I couldn't pretend like everything was okay when I felt like I was dying inside. The guilt was destroying me."

"How do you feel about it now?"

"I've spent what feels like a lifetime in therapy, and I've finally learned to manage it. But there are days when I still feel shit about myself. Days where I worry that I might flip again."

"That's not going to happen."

I open my mouth to protest but he silences me with a deadly look. "I've watched you. I *see* you. You're a good person. I think your experiences have proven that fact, because you stand up for yourself and others. You're not a victim or a monster. You fight for what is right, like what went down tonight."

I bite on the inside of my cheek. "I can't stand to see anyone vulnerable being taken advantage of. It reminds me so much of my situation, and no one did anything to help me. My so-called friends all shunned me. I would never do that. And even though Kent doesn't see himself in that light, I do. He's drowning, Ky. I'm no psychologist but even I can see that his behavior is a classic cry for help. Your parents need to do more for him."

He grinds his teeth. "I know. I'll talk to Mom."

"You may need to defer it for a bit. James is planning on telling her about Courtney this weekend."

Ky snorts. "I'll believe it when I see it."

"I spoke with him this morning, and I think he's sincere."

"I guess we'll find out soon enough."

I rest my head on his chest, listening to the steady *thud-thud* of his heart. "You know why we're drawn to one another, don't you?" I twist my fingers in his shirt.

"I know it's not for the reasons you think."

I jerk upright at that. "What do y—"

A massive crash, like the sound of something heavy hitting the ground, halts me mid-sentence. We both scramble to our feet at the same time, running out into the lobby. My eyes fly around the room looking for the source of the noise. A telltale creak emits from upstairs, and Kyler and I lock eyes before he bounds up the stairs, two at a time. I race after him, heart pounding in my chest.

He opens the door to his father's study and slams to an immediate halt. "What the fuck are you doing in here?"

I peer around his taller frame and gasp. A multitude of tiny shards of glass litters the floor around the desk. But it's the sight of Addison, crouched over the desk, with her hands immersed in a bundle of files, that causes all the blood to drain from my face.

Chapter Thirty-Four

Addison raises her palms in a conciliatory gesture, rounding the desk and carefully stepping over the bits of broken glass on the floor. She peers up at Ky, a forced wide-eyed innocent look on her face. "Don't be mad." She juts her lower lip out, and I roll my eyes.

"Why are you in here? What are you searching for?" Ky asks, deliberately stepping sideways. His arm brushes mine.

Addison narrows her eyes suspiciously, as she rakes her gaze over me. "The recording of us."

Ky keeps that well-rehearsed impassive face intact. "What recording?"

She plants her hands on her hips as a deep line creases her brow. "Don't tell me you don't know? It's a vid of us fucking. It looked like the room we used at Jeremy's party." She shoots me a smug look, but I ignore it and her.

"Back up there." Ky holds up his hand. "What are you talking about?"

"At first, I thought Brad was behind the anonymous email I received last week. I know he sent one to you, months ago—to split us up—so I naturally assumed he was up to his old tricks again now that we're back together."

"Bullshit." The words fly out of my mouth like spittle. I whip my head around to Ky. "Brad isn't behind the email you received. Trust me. She's lying."

Addison focuses a concentrated gaze on Ky. "She knows nothing. Brad has been hounding me all year. No matter how many times I tell him that I'm not interested, that it's you I love"—she places her hand on Ky's chest and I feel all territorial—"he just keeps coming back. He deliberately set about breaking us up, thinking I'd fall right into his arms. Why do you think he's feigning interest in her?" Her nostrils flare unattractively. "It's an attempt to make me jealous." She looks down her nose at me. "As if."

"Get to the point, Addison," Ky growls, removing her hand from his chest.

"Brad didn't send me the email, so I moved on to the next likely suspect." Her eyes have a calculating sheen to them.

Ky arches a brow. "Me? You think I sent you some video of us fucking? Why the hell would I do that? Even if I had such evidence, which, for the record, I don't, why would I email it to you?"

"Blackmail, Ky." She says it so sweetly. "And before you say anything else, I didn't think it was you."

Ky glances at me as my eyes widen in realization. *Damn it!* I told Kal he needed to tell Ky before Addison played her hand. Now it's too bloody late.

Addison looks down at her feet, shuffling in a bogus nervous manner. "I thought it was Kal. I didn't think he'd be so stupid as to hide the evidence in his room, so—"

"You thought you'd break into my house and rummage through my father's study?" Ky levels an incredulous look at her.

He's buying this about as much as I am. This reeks of duplicity.

"I know Kal despises you, but he'd never do something like that because of how it would impact me." His razor-sharp eyes lock on Addison as he searches her face for evidence of her lies.

"You don't know everything about your brother," she says softly, and a sympathetic look appears in her eyes.

Her manipulative tone and look chill me to the bone. I swing into action, grabbing her arm at the elbow and hauling her toward the door. "Get out before I call the cops and have you arrested for breaking and entering."

"Get your filthy hands off me." Wriggling, she slaps at my hand, but my hold doesn't budge.

"Wait," Ky commands. "I want to hear what she has to say." My eyes silently plead with him to let this drop. "Let her go, Faye."

Reluctantly, I release her.

She rubs her arm in an exaggerated motion, and I roll my eyes again. "That better not bruise." Her eyes drill a hole in my skull, but I affect my most blasé look.

"Today, Addison." Kyler's impatience is blatant.

Addison leans into Ky. Batting her eyelashes, she peers up at him desolately. "I never wanted it to happen. He took advantage of me."

Ky goes deathly still.

"You're a rotten liar!" I yell, stalking toward her with purpose.

Ky's arm jerks out, holding me back. Pinning fierce eyes on Addison, he demands, "What are you saying, Addison?"

"We slept together, Ky, but I never wanted it. I was drunk, and you were being mean to me, and he swooped in when I was most vulnerable." She forces a tear out of her eye. "And now he's trying to keep us apart by blackmailing me. So now you know why I need that video."

Very slowly, Kyler steps away from Addison, turning to face me. "Wake Kalvin, please, and bring him here."

"Ky." I rest my hand on his arm, feeling bunched-up tendons straining his skin. "She's lying. Kick her out and talk to Kal in private."

A muscle pops in his jaw. "Get him, now, Faye." He batters his forearms, and I can tell there's no reasoning with him.

Fast as my legs will carry me, I race to Kal's room and wake him up. He jumps out of bed the minute I explain, pulling on a pair of sweats, which had been discarded on the floor, and rushing toward the study. His bare feet slip and slide on the polished hardwood floor.

I burst into the room behind Kalvin, watching Addison with hawk-like concentration. Tiny beads of sweat— the only indication that she's nervous—dot her brow. I know this is all a pile of donkey poop, but who knows what Ky is feeling. This girl seems to know exactly what strings to pull.

"I was going to tell you, I swear," Kal says, eyeballing Ky directly. "I was totally trashed, and she came on to me. I tried to push her away, but she took off her clothes and straddled me. I"—he drags a hand through his hair, gulping loudly—"I was a fucking idiot, and I regretted it the second we were done. I'm sorry, man."

Ky is the epitome of cool, calm, and collected as he goes toe-to-toe with his brother. "She claims it happened the opposite way around. That *she* was drunk and you took advantage of her."

"No way, bro. I'm telling you the truth. *She* pounced on *me*." He slants a venomous look at Addison.

Ky nods once before stalking toward Addison.

She stabs her chin in the air, attempting to convey superiority.

"Whatever game you think you're playing ends right now. Do. Not. Test. Me. Again." She takes a step back from his heated glare. "And just so we're clear, I had zero intention of getting back together. Every touch disgusted me."

Addison's nostrils flare, and my lips twitch.

Is it wrong that I'm enjoying this?

"I was playing you, and you were playing me," Ky continues, "so we're done now. Walk away, and I'll do the same. If you don't"—he leans in menacingly, and I spot the telltale vicious glint in his eye—"I *will* ruin you." He straightens up, pointing toward the door. "Now get the fuck out of my house. You're not welcome here, or anywhere near me, ever again."

Slightly rattled—although she's killing herself not to show it—Addison steps around Ky, striding toward the door. At the last second, she turns. A triumphant smile graces her lips. "Not if I ruin you first."

Her threat lacks bite, but I'm still uneasy. I only risk breathing again when I hear the slamming of the front door and I know the Wicked Witch has left the building.

"You fucking imbecile." Ky shoots an angry look at Kalvin.

Kal shifts awkwardly on his feet. "Sleeping with her is unforgivable. I know that. I'm sorry."

"I couldn't give two shits about that!" Ky fumes. "I told you she's less than nothing to me, and I meant it. She's up to something, Kal, and you've exposed yourself, exposed us. Think back. Was there anything she said or did that was suspicious?"

He lifts his eyes to the ceiling and sighs. "I was too wasted to remember much," he admits a minute later. Dipping his head, he looks sheepishly at his older brother.

"Maybe I was a bit hasty. Should've strung her along for a bit longer to find out what she's planning." Ky grips his chin with his thumb and forefinger, staring off into space.

"She's poison. You're well rid." I bend down and carefully start picking up pieces of broken glass.

"I second that, if it's what I think it means." Kal grins, hunkering down to help me. I snort. You'd think he'd be used to my sayings by now.

"Do you think there is a video?" I ask, looking up through my lashes at Ky.

"I hope not." He crouches down alongside me, taking my wrist. "Stop. You'll cut yourself."

I stare into his worried blue eyes, and I'm immediately adrift at sea. A moment passes between us. He checks me out with that penetrating lens of his, his eyes burying into me, making sure I'm okay. I melt on the inside as my lips lift in a smile. A spark flares in his eyes, and a volt of energy electrifies the air. I eye his lips like a vulture waiting to swoop in for the kill.

"I'll, uh, get something to clean this up," Kalvin stutters, most unnaturally. He edges carefully around the shattered glass and ducks out of the room.

Ky pulls me to my feet, sweeping his arm underneath my legs, and carries me over to the seated area in front of the fire. He plunks into one of the red velvet chairs with me in his lap. "What has Brad told you?"

Needing to touch him, I press a kiss to his cheek as my hands wander around his neck. "He didn't know anything about that email you received. Unless he's the best actor on the planet, I'm positive he was telling me the truth. And there's more." I run the tips of my fingers through his hair. Ky leans his head back, and closes his eyes. "He was only with Addison *one* time. At some party. But he swears it was a one-time thing. He was drunk, and it was a mistake. He said he'd never intentionally do something like that to you, and I believe him."

I'm sensing a pattern with Addison.

Ky's eyes flash open. "But the email ..."

"Was clearly doctored," I finish for him. "Someone wanted you to break up with Addison and to fall out with Brad. It's the only explanation that makes sense."

"I agree, but who would do that and why?"

I level determined eyes on him. "That's what we need to find out. Please tell me you kept that email?"

He shakes his head. "Why would I want to keep sexually graphic content of my best bud and my girl getting it on?" Sarcasm is thick like syrup atop his words.

I guess that makes sense. I wouldn't want to keep anything like that either. But our best means of tracking the manipulator is via that email. An idea pops into my head. "What about Keven? He's studying IT, right? Could he retrieve it from your deleted files?"

A slow smile spreads over his mouth. He taps the end of my nose with one finger. "Not just a pretty face." I mock-scowl. "That's a brilliant idea. I'll ask him tomorrow."

"Ask who what?" Kal asks, popping his head cautiously around the door. I arch a brow. "Just checking you weren't dry humping or worse," he jokes, answering my silent question.

"Can you get your mind out of the gutter for five seconds," Ky hisses. "It's that kind of attitude that's going to get you in trouble one of these days."

"Don't act like you're a frigging saint, Ky. You've done your fair share of whoring."

"Enough!" Ky demands. "I need your head on straight if we're to figure out her game plan."

Racing footsteps slap noisily off the porcelain floor downstairs, and we all freeze at once. "Wait! Please!" James calls out, desperation clear in his tone.

"Get your hands off me! I won't ever forgive you!" a clearly emotional Alex screams, charging the stairs amid heaving sobs.

"What now?" Kal sighs as he slants an inquisitive look at us.

I slide off Kyler's lap and he rises behind me. Heat infuses me as I lean back against him.

Alex is a blur of color as she rushes past the study door, oblivious to our presence. James darts past a second later. Kalvin moves to walk after them, but Ky reaches out, holding him back. He shakes his head in silent instruction.

"I want you out!" Alex screams. "Out of this house. Out of my life. Away from *my* boys."

"Please, Alex," James beseeches. "I love you. I'm sorry. I'll spend the rest of my life making it up to you, so, please, please, don't do this."

"Save your breath, James. No amount of begging or false promises will change my mind. Our marriage is over, and you need to leave."

Chapter Thirty-Five

Kal shoves Ky's arm away and marches to the door. We follow hot on his heels. Stepping out onto the small landing, I duck down, as a bundle of clothing flies over my head. Kal isn't quick enough, and a shirt lands on his head. Yanking it off, he peers up at his mom. Alex is standing at the top of the stairs, fisting handfuls of male clothes. Her hair is a tangled mess around her face and judging by her swollen red-rimmed eyes, she's been crying profusely. My heart goes out to her.

"Mom? Are you okay?" Kal asks.

"Go to your rooms, please. Your mom and I need to discuss this in private," James instructs from his position three steps below us.

"They stay." Alex flings the contents of her hands down the stairs. "Do you want to tell them or shall that responsibility fall to me like everything else?" She perches her hands on her slim hips. "I should've known. You've always been fond of lying flat on your back while every-one else did all the heavy lifting."

James winces. "I get it. You want to hurt me, and I deserve that. Do your worst. It won't push me away."

Alex half-laughs, half-cries. "You're a fucking idiot as well as a lousy cheat!" she screams. "I'm not pushing you away. I'm *divorcing* you whether you like it or not."

Kal's worried gaze bounces between his parents.

275

"I won't go." James grips the handrail tightly. "I won't lose my family."

Alex shrieks, bending down and grabbing more fistfuls of clothes. "You should've thought of that before you took my assistant into your bed!"

Kalvin staggers back. "What?" He spins and glares at his dad. "You fucked Courtney?"

James ignores him, devoting his attention to Alex. "Please, Alex. Please don't do this."

A determined look contorts her beautiful face as she stomps down the stairs, halting directly in front of her husband. "Let's get one thing straight, James. *I'm* not doing this. *You* did this. You fucked yourself." She jabs her finger in his chest. "You set this in motion the minute you fucked that slut." Fury radiates off her in waves. She shoves at him, and he stumbles, almost losing his balance. I'm shocked into mute-form. Alex is the quintessential lady, and this is a side of her I haven't seen. Not that I'm casting aspersions. It's understandable, given the situation.

Ky moves to his mom's side, wrapping a sturdy arm around her waist from behind. She crumples, slumping in his embrace. He levels a cold look at his dad as he props his mom up. "If you care about her at all, you *will* leave. Give her some space. You owe her that much."

James looks defeated as he slowly bobs his head. "I owe her much more than that, son."

James turns, shoulders drooping, and descends the stairs, stopping to pick up articles of his clothing on the way. You could hear a pin drop in the room. Kalvin's traumatized gaze lands on mine.

At the door, James spins around, clutching armfuls of clothes. "I'm sorry, Alex. Truly, I am. I'll give you time, but please don't end our marriage, not at least until you've had time to process how you think." He switches his gaze to the boys. "I love you. All of you." His eyes stray to mine, making sure to include me. "Look after your mom."

The door bangs shut behind him, and a tortured cry escapes Alex's lips. She buckles in Ky's arms, and he swoops her up, carrying her up to her bedroom. Her anguished sobs follow me as I head to the kitchen to make her some sweet tea.

When I return a few minutes later, Kalvin is hovering nervously on the stairs, a sad, worried look in his eyes. I touch his arm lightly. "Will you be okay?"

Dazed eyes meet mine. "This is bad, Faye. She's never actually thrown him out before. I can't believe it. My dad's a moron."

"Hopefully they can sort it all out. Try not to worry."

He harrumphs. "Impossible not to."

I give him a quick hug. "You should get some sleep. She's going to need your support in the coming days."

Alex is lying on her side on the top of the bed, a blank, empty expression on her face. Ky is in the en suite bathroom rummaging through the cupboard. I set the tea down on Alex's locker and join him. "What are you looking for?"

He holds a small pillbox in his hand. "These. The doctor prescribes her sleeping tablets on occasion when work stresses keep her up at night."

I nod. "Stay here for a few while I help her get dressed for bed."

Alex is almost comatose as I undress her. Tucking the duvet back over her, I help her sit up against the headrest. She stares numbly ahead, completely unawares. "Ky," I call out softly. "You can come out now."

I perch on the edge of the bed, and Ky rounds the other side. Somehow, he manages to get Alex to take the sleeping tabs, and he supports her trembling form while I help her to take sips of the sweet tea. Gradually, her eyelids grow heavy and she falls asleep in her son's arms. Together, we settle her and turn off her light, tiptoeing down the stairs.

Ky reels me into his arms outside my room, and I wrap myself around him. We don't speak; we just hold each other. After a bit, I lift my head and look up at him. "Are you going to be okay?"

His tongue darts out, wetting his lips. "I'm not important. She is."

I nod. "We'll look after her."

He leans down, planting a feather-light kiss on my lips. "Thank you, for helping her. And for the track." His eyes glisten with unfettered gratitude. "I should've said that sooner. May and Rick are ecstatic."

I smile. "That's great."

His chest heaves up and down. "I'm glad you're here, Faye. So fucking glad. You've no idea."

His words warm part of the frozen spot in my heart. "I'm glad I'm here too." And for the very first time, I mean it. Which is weird, because everything is totally fucked up right now, but it feels like home. Like I'm where I belong. I'm too tired to dissect exactly what that means. As if to prove my point, a loud yawn escapes my mouth.

"Go." Kyler brushes his mouth fleetingly against mine. "You need to sleep. I'll see you in the morning."

I crawl into bed as if I'm half-dead. Exhaustion does a number on me, and I'm out for the count the instant my head hits the pillow.

Sometime during the night, a pair of warm arms snake around my waist and I'm drawn against a firm body. "Is this okay?" Ky whispers, and I mumble something incoherent as I snuggle into his embrace. His faint chuckle is the last thing I hear before I succumb to slumber again.

I'm alone in the bed when I wake the next morning. Rays of golden sunshine stream through the gossamer curtains, bathing the room in glorious light. I scratch my head, wondering if I dreamed Kyler last night. Nuzzling my pillow, I inhale his intoxicating scent as I smile to myself.

He *was* here!

My momentary burst of exhilaration gives way to a bout of anxiety. If James and Alex do end up divorcing, where does that leave me? The thought that I may have to leave here, just as I was starting to envision it as home, is upsetting. But I can't dwell on that now. It's selfish to be concerned with my own future when Alex is so devastated. The thought is sobering.

I wander to the kitchen, enticed by the appetizing smells wafting along the corridor. Kaden is standing in front of the stove, shoveling mountains of bacon and eggs into a large, circular serving dish.

The mood is solemn at the table as everyone sits down to eat. I don't know when Ky found the time to contact Keven and Kaden, but I'm glad they're here. Alex needs all her boys around her.

We eat in silence, and only when the dishes have been cleared does Ky explain everything in more detail to his brothers. Wiping my damp hands along the side of my denim skirt, I drop onto the bench alongside a clearly distraught Keaton. I wrap my arm around him, leaning my head on his shoulder.

Kaden takes immediate charge, warning all his brothers that they are to stay put here today. No one argues, and I'm loving how they are all rallying around their mom in her time of need. Filling a plate with food, he sets out in the direction of Alex's bedroom. The boys converge in the sitting room, and I hover uncertainly on the fringes. Kyler motions me in, but I shake my head and return to the kitchen.

I need a distraction and cooking has always helped center me. Rooting around in the fridge, I do a quick inventory. I pull Kalvin aside and convince him to drive me to the local store where I pick up the items I need.

Hysterical crying greets us upon our return. The triplets and Keven are all cloistered in the lobby, shuffling awkwardly on their feet. "What's going on?" Kalvin drops his keys onto the table.

Keven tucks a sliver laptop under his arm as he shrugs. "She's been like that for the last half hour. Kaden and Kyler are trying to calm her down." He flicks his gaze to me. "Maybe she needs a woman's touch."

"Sure." I hand the bag of groceries to Kalvin. "Can you put the food away?"

I take the stairs two at a time, and Alex's anguished wailing grows louder as I get nearer. When I reach the top, I pause, my heart jackknifing in my chest. Alex is sobbing her heart out, curled in a fetal position on the bed, the tangled bed linen knotted around her thin frame. Ky and Kaden stand on either side of her, looking utterly dejected. Ky's shoulders relax a little when he sees me approaching.

A burst of guilt ambushes me.

I advised James to come clean to his wife, and now everyone is hurting. Perhaps I should've said nothing, but is it better to live in blissful ignorance? To pretend that life is perfect, when it's all a façade and everything is turning rotten underneath? I have some experience of that, and letting things fester only ends up ten times messier in the long run.

The truth always finds a way to out itself.

Alex was destined to be hurt the moment James slipped under the sheets with Courtney.

"Your brothers need you," I murmur to Ky and Kaden. "I'll stay with her."

I kick off my shoes and scoot onto the bed beside Alex. Tentatively reaching out, I stroke her hair in a continual soothing motion, and gradually her sobs subside. She slides in closer to me, wrapping her arms around my waist. We don't speak. I don't think she's capable of forming any coherent words, but I don't mind. I let her lean on me for as long as she needs to.

A while later, she pulls herself upright in the bed, tucking her knees into her chest. "Thank you, Faye," she whispers. Her distressed eyes latch on mine. I didn't do much, but I nod, giving her a gentle smile. "I should speak to the boys."

"Why don't I run you a bath first?" I suggest. She nods and the forlorn look on her face devastates me.

I fill the bath to the brim, adding some drops of scented oil I found in the press to the water. Notes of lavender and thyme swathe the room, mixing with plumes of steam, as I usher Alex into the room. "I'll gather the boys in the living room and tell them to wait for you there. I'm going to cook dinner, so I'll be in the kitchen if you need me."

Alex takes my wrist. "Faye, just because James"—she chokes on his name—"is no longer here, doesn't mean you are any less a part of this family. You should join the boys and wait for me."

It's almost as if she has a hotline to my mind. I give her a quick hug, more grateful than she'll ever know. "I appreciate that, but this is something you need to do with your boys alone. They are worried about you."

It takes me a couple of hours to serve up a traditional roast beef dinner with all the trimmings. It was my dad's favorite dinner, and it's the first time I've made it since he died. Nostalgia is a bitter pill I have to swallow.

During this time, the boys all stay with their mom in the living room. I set the formal dining table, and when they emerge to take their seats, the stress seems to have been somewhat alleviated. Watching how they all fuss over their mother, attending to her every need, brings tears to my eyes. While she may be feeling completely shattered right now, I hope Alex understands how lucky she is to still have so much love in her life.

The next morning, Ky informs me that he's driving me to school every day from now on. I don't object. En route, I broach the thorny subject. "I've been thinking."

"Oh, oh. Should I be worried?"

I slap his arm. "Not funny." I send him a semi-glare. "About Addison." All humor leaves his face. "I don't buy that excuse she gave us for snooping in your dad's office. We need to find out what she's looking for."

Ky maneuvers the SUV into a parking spot in front of my school and snuffs out the engine. "I agree, but I'm not sure where to start looking. Keven took my laptop and he's going to see if he can retrieve that email. Maybe that will give us a clue."

"I hope so." I twist in the seat, the leather making a squelching noise as I do. "You also need to speak to Brad, Ky. Maybe then, we can fit all the pieces together. I'm not excusing his actions, but there's a reason why he was vulnerable the night Addison pounced. And make no bones about it, she targeted him in the same way she targeted Kal."

His face gives nothing away but I press on. "Brad is going through some horrible stuff, and he needs a friend. You do, too." He opens his mouth to object, but I clamp my hand over his lips. "Don't argue. Just trust me. Please."

Slowly, he nods.

"Good. I'll get a lift with him after school, and you can meet us at his house. Just promise me you'll hear him out. Can you do that?"

He presses his lips to my palm. "I'll do it for you."

The meeting at Brad's place turns out even better than I'd hoped. It took a little bit of coaxing, but they both speak freely, finally airing everything.

I sit on the couch beside Brad, and Ky is resting on the edge of the armchair across from us. "I can't believe we wasted the last seven months," Ky says, casting a poignant look in Brad's direction. "I should've at least spoken to you about it, rather than jumping to the obvious conclusion."

"And I should've had the balls to fess up straightaway the next morning," Brad replies. "We both handled it stupidly, but there's no point looking back. What's done is done. I'm more concerned with where we go from here and whether you can trust me again." Brad braces his hands on his knees.

"Now that I know the background," Ky says, sympathy flaring on his face, "I can understand how it happened more easily but it still doesn't excuse it. You don't break the bro code. Not ever."

Brad grows very still. "I know, man. I know." Air knocks out of his lungs. "There's no excuse that will ever make it all right, but I promise I'll never do anything like that again. Your friendship is too important to me." His gaze turns glassy as he stands up and walks over to Ky. "You've always been more like a brother and I've really missed you. I fucked up but it won't happen again. Guaranteed."

Brad extends his hand and it hovers in the air for a second before Ky bumps his fist and they engage in some elaborate form of knuckle touch. Ky springs up and they slap each other on the back. His gaze meets mine over Brad's shoulder, and I smile, though my throat has constricted and tears threaten to spill from my eyes.

"I missed you too, man," Ky admits quietly before taking a step back. "And I feel really shitty that you've been going through all this crap alone." He gestures around the half-empty living room. "I'll talk to my parents. I'm sure they'll cough up the fees so you can return to O.C."

"Don't. They've already done more than enough." Brad rocks back on his heels.

Ky's forehead creases. "What do you mean?"

Brad pinches the bridge of his nose. "Figured they didn't tell you. They found out about the situation with Dad, and they came to offer their help. Off the record."

Ky scratches the line of stubble on his chin. "Of course. They wouldn't want to risk any hint of scandal tarnishing the brand."

"They offered to pay my school fees and ... uh, they wanted me to come and live with you guys—"

"But you said no because of me," Ky cuts in, astutely calling it.

"Yeah. I knew you wouldn't want me anywhere near you." His nose crinkles.

"You can move in now," Ky rushes to reassure him. "I'm sure Mom will have no problem with it."

"Thanks, man, but no. It wasn't just 'cause of that. I don't want to feel like a charity case. Our money is gone now, and I have to learn to get by without it. Plenty of others manage just fine." He gives a lopsided shrug, and my heart swells with pride at his words. I can tell they aren't just for show—he means it.

"I only found out after I joined Memorial that your parents made a massive donation to the school on condition that I was allowed play for the football team. It's breaking all kinds of rules, but somehow they swung it." His eyes glitter with gratitude. "They really shouldn't have done it, but I can't thank them enough. They're good people, and I hope everything works out for them."

The rumor mill is already rife around town, so it's no surprise that Brad has heard something. It's only a matter of time before the press picks up on James' extramarital affair, and then the shit will really hit the fan. At least the heat is off Brad for now—he is all anyone has been talking about these last few days. And that's only down to his change of school and football teams. I can only imagine the type of gossip that'll be bandied about when word filters out about his dad.

Not wanting to intrude any more than I have, I mess about on my cell while Ky fills Brad in on what exactly happened with his parents. They take the opportunity to catch up on some other stuff, too. Watching them covertly from the corner of my eye, I can't help feeling proud of them for opening up to one another and agreeing to move past it—for caring enough to give their friendship another try. I have a sense they won't let anything come between them again.

Genuine friendships are hard to come by and even harder to hold on to.

Real friendship is the sort that lasts a lifetime. The type that can overcome disagreements and differences as if they never happened.

And the real test of friendship? True friendship arises from the ashes of separation stronger and more powerful than before.

Chapter Thirty-Six

The rest of the week follows a similar pattern. Kaden and Keven have to return to Harvard, but the remaining boys barely leave their mother's side. Alex hasn't stepped foot outside the door, choosing to do some work from home instead. James hasn't made an appearance, but he's been in contact with everyone, myself included. His dejected tone speaks volumes, and I can tell he's hurting too.

The extended spell of unseasonably warm weather continues, and Alex decides to head to Nantucket on the weekend. She implores me to come, and this time I can't refuse her. David, surprisingly, agrees to release me from work, and Rose reorganizes the roster so I'm free all weekend.

Thursday is another glorious day, and I'm in super-good humor as I head in to school. While Ky and I haven't put any labels on our relationship, he creeps into my bedroom every night, being careful to return to his room before day breaks. We don't do much more than kiss and sleep clinging possessively to one another, but I've never felt closer to any boy or felt happier despite the lingering sadness that crowds all the empty spaces in the house. Concerns over my future are never far from my mind, but I try not to dwell on it too much. There doesn't seem to be much point until the situation with Alex and James comes to a head.

Peyton has been giving me the stink-eye all week at school, and I get a sense that her cousin updated her on events at the Kennedys' over the weekend. Addison must be running scared though, if she hasn't tried to retaliate yet. Either that or she's planning her attack meticulously, ready to strike at the most opportune time.

"You gonna eat that or just tear it to shreds?" Brad asks, as we sit side by side in the cafeteria, pointing at my plate where I've been absently picking my wrap to bits.

"Have at it." I slide the plate toward him. "I'm not hungry today."

"Is something up?"

"Not really." I take a sip of my water. "Just trying to figure out what Addison's next move will be."

"Don't waste your brain power. Her mind doesn't work like the rest of us. You'll never be able to second-guess her."

"Second-guess who?" Zoe inquires, plunking into the seat across from us. Lana drops quietly into the chair beside her.

"Addison," I confirm.

"She's evil incarnate." Zoe starts digging into her salad. "The Anti-Christ. Satan's lovechild. Hell's most—"

"We got it!" Brad intervenes, raising one hand to stop her. Zoe flips him off, and he sniggers.

"Maybe she's not all bad," Lana pipes up, and three sets of wide eyes spin in her direction. "Perhaps it's the company she keeps." She takes a large bite out of her apple as she eyeballs me.

Zoe scowls in disgust. "Oh, no, you don't. No, no, no." She pins her with a ferocious look. "She may have done you a favor vis-à-vis Douchey-McDouche, but that does not mean she's the good guy. Don't fall for that bull."

Brad and I exchange puzzled looks. A cold, prickly feeling washes over me. "What don't we know?" I ask, looking from Lana to Zoe and back again.

"Nothing," Lana hisses with a scowl, stabbing Zoe with the serrated edges of her agitation.

Some unspoken discussion filters between them.

Zoe flaps her hands in the air. "Fine, fine." She slants her head in our direction. "Private convo. Forget I said anything."

I lean forward in my seat, the blunt edge of the desk digging into my waist. "Addison has declared war on the Kennedys, and if you know something, you should tell me."

Steel and sorrow blur on Lana's face. Her chair screeches as she rises. "Why? What do I owe them? Or you for that matter? I'm done with them and their messed-up morals, their warped loyalties, their fucked-up family. From what I hear, all those boys will end up like James. Bitter, twisted, and disloyal. You should leave, before they ruin you too."

My jaw is still hanging open after she disappears from view. Lana is always so placid. I've never seen her give into anger before. She is obviously hurting over Kalvin, and I'm wondering what exactly she's hiding from me.

Zoe scrambles to her feet, cramming the last few bites of her lunch in her mouth. I tap her arm. "What was all that about? Is she okay?"

"No, I don't think she is. But I got this. Stay out of it." She hightails it after her friend.

"Glad to see O.C. isn't the only educational institution prone to regular diva-esque outbursts," Brad deadpans.

"I thought all American high schools were hotbeds of amateur dramatics," I supply.

He snorts. "You're probably right."

Lana's blow-up plays on my mind for the rest of the day. I was planning to hunt her down after school, but when Brad meets me at my locker at the end of the day, he informs me that we're meeting Ky at the track.

My feet have barely hit solid ground when May rounds on me, yanking me into a constricting hug. "I cannot thank you enough, Faye." She grabs my cheeks firmly. "You're my hero." Her effusive greeting brings a blush to my cheeks, much to Ky's amusement.

"Stop." I gently remove her hands from my sore cheeks. "It isn't me you should be thanking. It wasn't my money."

"You were the lynchpin that made it happen, and you are deserving of our gratitude. So hush up, girlie, and accept it." My cheeks darken, and Ky smirks.

She loops her arm in mine, pulling me forward, as I discreetly flip Ky the bird. He laughs, trailing behind us as we step into the building. Rick is, mercifully, more restrained in his gratitude, clasping my hand in his large one as he mutters a sincere thank you. May explains that they have closed the track down for a couple of weeks to complete the repairs and starts running through the plans with me. Kyler and Brad chat to Rick in the corner of the room before disappearing out the back.

May's incessant chatter trickles out. "I'm glad I got you alone." She knots her hands in her lap. "I owe you an apology, for what I said the last time you were here."

I pat her arm. "It's grand. Forget it."

"I shouldn't have interfered. It's none of my business."

"You care about him, and you don't want to see him hurting again. I respect that."

She gives me a fragile smile. "I don't want to see either of you hurt."

I open my mouth to reply when Brad and Ky reenter the room, clad in tight-fitting overalls that cling to their mutually impressive chests. May's jaw joins mine on the floor.

Ky swaggers toward me. Brushing the side of my mouth with his thumb, he shoots me a wicked smile. "Just cleaning up some drool." Brad sends us a funny look.

I gasp, shoving at him as he wraps his arm around my waist and lifts me into the air. Throwing me over his shoulder, he swats my butt and runs down the corridor. I shout a string of obscenities at him, only shutting up when he places me on the floor in the locker room.

"You're an ass," I say, but he can tell there's little heat behind my words.

"And you're hot when you're pretending to be mad." He nudges me with his body until I'm pressed up against a row of lockers. Leaning down, he nips the corner of my mouth, igniting the liquid lust in my veins.

"We shouldn't do this here. What if someone sees?"

"They won't tell."

I'm not so sure about that, but the instant he plants his hot mouth on my lips, I forget all my concerns.

I grab him to me, lifting one leg up and wrapping it around his waist. He presses into me, growling his approval. His arousal pushes against my lower belly, and an intense surge of self-satisfaction pitches through me. The evidence of his attraction, his desire, thrills me no end.

"Ky." I'm completely breathless. "You've no idea the things you do to me."

"You do the same to me. I'm crazy about you, Faye." He angles my head and kisses each corner of my mouth sweetly. It cranks my hormones into overdrive, and I tug on the back of his head, crashing his lips onto mine, plundering his mouth like an aggressor. I attack him with my body, too, gyrating against him as he drills his hips into mine. We could be anywhere, and all I'd see, all I'd feel, is him. He overpowers everything to the point where I couldn't care less.

I'm panting and clawing at him in frantic need when a loud cough interrupts the moment. We spring apart instantly. "May's wondering if you're planning on painting today or next week?" Rick asks, shuffling uncomfortably. He can't even look us in the eye, and instantly I feel tarnished and dirty, as if we've done something wrong.

"We'll be right out." Ky's tone carries an undercurrent of warning and disappointment as he straightens up my shirt. I hadn't even realized it had ridden halfway up my body, exposing a wide stretch of skin. Rick's rescinding footsteps echo in the silence of the room.

"Well, that was awkward." I shuck out of Ky's embrace.

"Fuck him and his narrow-mindedness." He gives me a sweet kiss. "I'll let you get changed in private." With one last fleeting kiss, he leaves.

Shimmying the tattered overalls on, I can't help grinning to myself despite Rick's obvious disapproval.

Kyler is worth it.

The swirling kernel in my chest expands exponentially every time Kyler is near. Hella, every time I think of him, which, at the moment, is basically every second of every day. I've definitely got Kyler on the brain.

Brad and Ky are splattering more paint on one another than the walls when I return. I secretly watch them from the door. Observing them joke around offers a tiny glimpse into the friendship they once shared. A golf-ball-sized lump lodges in my throat. As they playfully shove and push one another, it's hard to imagine any gulf ever existing between them. But that's guys for you. They can pick up where they left off without unnecessary drama.

"May and Rick are tackling the kid's playroom while we've been left in charge of the main room," Brad offers up, when he spots me lurking in the doorway.

"Cool." Walking to him, I curl my hand around his biceps, pulling him clear across the room. "If we're to make any progress, you two need to separate. There's more paint on you than on the walls." I grin, running my finger through the streak of blue paint smeared across his cheek. "You tackle that one." I point at the peeling expanse at the side of the café area. "Ky can stay where he is, and I'll paint the area around the desk."

"Bossy much?" Brad teases, slapping his brush against the wall.

"You've no idea," Ky retorts.

"Get over yourself. I am not!" I stick my tongue out at him as I bend down to open the lid on the white paint pot.

My instincts kick in a fraction too late, and I jerk to the side just as Ky's hand glances off my butt. I jump up and attempt to rugby tackle him to the ground. He's laughing as he grabs my waist, swinging me around and pinning my back to his front. He holds me firmly, even as I wriggle relentlessly to free myself. "Now, now, Faye. That's no way for a Kennedy lady to act." His mocking has a definite flirtatious edge to it.

Angling my arm, I thrust it back, digging my elbow into his ribs. He grunts, staggering back with a half-laugh. "I never claimed to be a lady."

His boisterous laugh is like music to my ears, and I have to stuff my hands in my pockets to avoid flinging myself at him.

Brad clears his throat. "Are you two … together?"

Ky and I stare at one another as Brad articulates the question of the century. All the air rushes from my lungs as I wait for Ky's response. He locks a hand behind his head as his gaze alternates from me to Brad. With every passing silent second, that swirling kernel inside me loses a little enthusiasm. I'm sure it shows on my face.

Kyler's arms sweep around me unexpectedly, and he hauls me against his delectable body. "She's mine," he snarls, treating Brad to one of his death-glare specials.

No doubt, feminist movements up and down the country would be aghast at his possessive statement, but I'm practically swooning at his feet. This is significant, for all it implies.

"But you're cousins." Brad's face shows his discomfort. "Doesn't it feel … gross?"

Kyler stiffens. "We're not doing anything wrong." His tone is glacial. "And it's anything but gross, I can assure you."

Brad's mouth puckers unpleasantly as his gaze bounces between us. "That's not the way most people will see it."

"We don't care what people think of us. It's none of their business," I interject.

"You say that now, but will you still feel that way when you're fending off hostile looks and innuendos? Dealing with abuse and snide remarks on an hourly basis?"

"We can handle ourselves, and if you won't support us, you can keep your petty opinions to yourself," Ky bites back.

Ky jams the car in gear and swings out of the track. Brad left before us, the air heavy with a multitude of things left unsaid. My earlier euphoria has frayed at the edges, and now I'm wondering if Ky regrets his *"She's mine"* statement. I don't want to come between him and Brad, not when they've just gotten their friendship back on track.

As much as I'd like some assurance with regards to our relationship, there's also a part of me that's terrified to confront it head-on. Addison damaged Ky's trust in girls, and if he commits to me, I need to know that it's because he's in the right headspace and not because he feels backed into a corner. I was serious when I told him he needed to find himself. *Would he have declared his intent if Brad hadn't called him out on it? Does he wish he could take it back? And, more importantly, is he prepared for the backlash if we go public?*

I'd be lying if I said I wasn't feeling a little sore at Brad's reaction. I'd assumed he, of all people, would've shown more empathy. If his reaction is typical, I guess it's going to be harder than I'd envisaged.

We are completely silent on the journey back home, both mulling things over. Except this time, the silence is loaded with unspent words, and the atmosphere is tense.

When Ky parks, I curl my fingers around the handle of the door, ready to leave this hotbed of simmering tension behind.

"Faye. Wait a minute." He unbuckles his seat belt and rests his head back on the leather seat. "Look." He flips his head to the side. "About what Brad said. What I said." He pauses, clearly unsure of himself, and I throw him a lifeline.

"It's fine, Ky. Honestly. You don't need to explain yourself or us. I'm happy with things as they are, and there's no need to make anything formal or official."

Deep lines furrow his brow. He lifts his head off the headrest. "You mean that?"

"Yup." I jump out of the car, holding the door open. "It's cool. We're cool. Don't sweat it."

"Sweet." He exits the car, slamming his door shut with more force than necessary. "Glad we're on the same page," he snarls, stalking into the house as if I've just offended him in the worst possible way.

He fails to make an appearance in my room that night.

And the next morning, Kalvin is waiting to drive me to school.

Chapter Thirty-Seven

"Are you pissed with me?" Brad asks, lounging against my locker when I arrive.

I slam the door shut, narrowly avoiding his fingers. "Why would you think that?" I lay the sarcasm on thick.

"Okaaayy." He pushes off the locker. "I'm going to hazard a wild guess and say that's a yes."

I clutch my books to my chest as Brad falls into step beside me. "I wish you hadn't said anything yesterday."

He takes hold of my arm and turns me to face him. "I've known Ky virtually my whole life, and I can tell when he's messed up, but my intention wasn't to cause any issues between you, I swear."

"You think he's messed up over me?" I spot a few inquisitive gazes as others are forced to walk around us.

"Ky has to sort out his shit before you should even contemplate anything official. He cares about you, I can tell, and I see the way you look at him. You care about him too. But you both need to be solid to deal with the prejudice."

"And you think I don't know that?!" I hiss.

Brad stops outside my class. "Knowing and dealing are two very different things. Are you prepared to be called an inbred, a hillbilly, sick, depraved, a weirdo?"

"Is that what *you* think?"

"I don't know what to think, to be honest." He swallows hard. "I can't quite wrap my head around it."

I clutch the door handle. "I expected more understanding from you."

He winces. "I'll try."

I eyeball him with the door half-open. "For Ky's sake, I hope you do."

Lana is off school sick today and Rose is working on some project, so I avoid the cafeteria at lunchtime, not wanting any further confrontation with Brad.

At the end of the school day, I head to the pool with Rose for my try out. Coach puts everyone through their paces, wanting to gauge my performance against the team. After, he asks me to stay behind for a little while so he can time my individual lengths. When he finally blows his whistle, I leave the pool with aching limbs, happy in the knowledge that I've secured my place.

That exhilarating feeling lasts about 10.5 seconds, or however long it takes me to reach the empty locker room. I search high and low, but my clothes are long gone, along with my towel and sneakers. I hadn't the foresight to stow spares, and considering my cell phone is out of charge, my bag offers little in the way of a solution. I fiddle the locks on all the other lockers, hoping to find one open and praying it contains something I can use. But it's a null score on both counts.

I drop down onto the bench, resting my elbows on my knees as I contemplate my next move. It doesn't take a genius to work out that Peyton's behind this. She's the only one bearing a grudge around here.

My eyes flit to the clock over the door, and I jump up, anxious to catch Brad. Football practice ended ten minutes ago, and I'm hoping he hasn't left yet. While I'm still a bit sore with him, he's currently looking like my only option. I don't relish the thought of rocking up to the boys' locker room in my swimsuit, but it's preferable than having to navigate the parking lot in the same attire.

I edge out into the corridor, my feet squelching off the shiny floor. Loud applause mixes with girlish giggling behind me, and I take a deep breath before I turn and face the mob. Cameras flash in my face, and bile rises up my throat. "I see your sense of fashion hasn't improved," Peyton drawls, sauntering toward me in her finest hooker gear. She eyes me with disgust. "What a boring suit."

"What did you do with my clothes?" I ask as one of her cronies approaches, holding her cell aloft, clearly recording the proceedings. "Turn that thing off." Hell will freeze over before I'll allow any other scandalous pics to become fodder for gossip or grounds for bullying.

"Or what?" Peyton challenges, projecting superiority.

"Or I'll do it for you." I eyeball the girl with the cell. She sends me a simpering look and that gets my back up. I dart forward super-fast and pluck the offending phone from her hand.

"Hey, that's my ..."

She trails off as I throw the offensive cell at the wall, watching it smash into smithereens.

The girl shrieks as Peyton steps into my face. "You really shouldn't have done that."

"Do I look like I give a crap?"

A few other idiots are recording from the sidelines. Pushing Peyton out of my way—none too politely—I make a beeline for them. Two of the girls turn on their heels and make a dash for it, but the third squares up to me, tossing her long hair defiantly over her shoulder. "Delete the recording and I'll leave your cell alone."

"Screw you, bitch."

Making a fist, I clock her right on the nose. She staggers back, screaming, dropping the phone in the process. It clatters noisily to the ground, breaking apart on contact.

My work here is done.

A sharp tug on my hair causes me to wince out loud. Peyton yanks fistfuls of my hair and starts dragging me back across the corridor. I struggle to maintain my balance from this position. Shoving my elbow back, I repeatedly thrust into her stomach, but it lacks substance. She doesn't release me, but it slows her down, and I use that to my advantage. Ignoring the agonizing pull on my hair, I twist around and shove my clenched fist in her face, hitting the side of her jaw with one powerful right jab.

She staggers back, shrieking as she cradles her chin in her hands. Fire burns in her eyes as she kicks her heels off, both shoes flying into the air as she storms toward me. Straightening up, I wiggle my fingers at her. "Bring it."

She charges at me like a bull, and it isn't difficult to slip sideways, out of her way. Before she knows what's happening, I thrust my foot in her back, and she is thrown forward, her face slapping painfully against a locker. When she turns to face me, a trickle of blood seeps out of her nose. Her eyes are wild and out of control as she lunges at me. Screeching, she knocks both of us to the ground. My head smacks off the cold tile, and stars form a dizzy layer over my eyes.

Her hands lock around my throat as she straddles me. Approaching footsteps pick up pace as I arch my body, bucking up and down, flipping her off. Loud masculine shouts ring out around me, but I can see nothing, hear nothing, over the puissant anger coating my insides in liquid fury. I jump up and pounce on her, raining my fists on her face. She reaches up, dragging her claw-like nails across my cheek, ripping skin and unleashing a steady stream of blood. Momentarily distracted, I lose the upper hand. She lifts her head, slamming it into mine, and I fall back, completely dazed. My head is spinning, and shards of pain dance around my skull.

Strong arms lift me up. At the same time, Lance hauls Peyton off the ground, wrapping his bulky arms around her waist to restrain her thrashing form. She's spitting vitriol and bucking violently in his arms, screaming blue murder.

I wriggle in Brad's arms. "Stop, Faye," he whispers in my ear. "Let it go."

As he drags his demonic girlfriend out, Lance snarls something over his shoulder at Brad.

Peyton's posse splits up. Some follow her outside while the remaining girls try to look casual as they ogle the football players surrounding me. "You're shivering," Brad acknowledges, whipping his shirt off without request. He slips it down over my body, and I'm grateful for the cover. A few of the girls salivate at the sight of his naked upper torso, but he pays them no heed, delving into his bag and retrieving a spare shirt which he wastes no time in putting on. Audible grunts of complaint surround us, and it's hard to contain my mirth. Adrenaline still courses through my veins, and I'm feeling wired. It's a strange, jittery, alien feeling.

A warm, soft towel is wrapped around me, and Brad tucks me in under his arm. "Thanks, guys. I've got it from here." I ignore the interested looks from some of the boys and keep my head down as Brad steers me out of the building.

I pull myself into the car, shuddering under the towel.

"She took your stuff?" Brad guesses, sliding the keycard into the slot. The SUV powers up smoothly.

I nod, not trusting myself to speak. Now that my adrenaline rush is dissipating, I just want to get the hell out of here. I'm more shaken than I'd like to admit.

When we move out onto the road, he reaches over and hands me a wad of tissues. "You okay?"

I exhale deeply, telling myself to pull it together. I'm not the same girl I used to be, and this isn't the same situation. I can handle Peyton. Even if this situation develops, it won't be like before. Because I have Brad, Rose, and Lana, and even though I've only known them a short while, I know deep down that I can rely on them.

They won't abandon me.

It won't be like before.

That acknowledgment calms the remaining embers of my frustration. "I'm okay. Thank you—for the shirt and getting me out of there."

"No sweat. I'll drop you home and go back for your bag, and I'll find out what she did with your clothes, too."

"Thanks, but I'm more concerned with the video footage and what she plans to do with it. She's welcome to the clothes." I dab at my cheeks, examining the blood-speckled tissue.

He takes his eyes off the road for a split second. "I'll sort it. Don't worry."

Despite our differences of opinion over my relationship with Ky, I am glad that it doesn't appear to have affected our friendship. It gives me hope that the three of us can work through stuff.

Ky is speeding up the driveway just ahead of us. He swings the car in front of the house, hopping out and running toward Brad's SUV. Ky yanks my door open, and his strong hands grasp my hips, lifting me out of the car. He cradles me in his arms. "Are you okay?" Gently, he touches my injured cheek.

"If it's any consolation, Peyton's nose was gushing blood," Brad says. "Faye gave as good as she got."

"This isn't fucking funny," Ky seethes. "She could've been seriously injured. Peyton is a dangerous bitch. Imagine Addison without the privileges of wealth and esteem, and that's exactly what you're dealing with."

"Gutter Barbie," I murmur, and Brad nearly chokes on his laughter.

Ky carries me up the steps and opens the front door.

I wriggle in his arms. "Put me down."

"Let me take care of you for once," Ky implores, although it's less of a request and more of a demand.

"Remember our surroundings. We have to keep up appearances."

With great reluctance, he puts me down. I don't want to face any of my other cousins looking like this, so I head straight for my room. Brad and Ky talk in hushed voices as they trail me. I push into my room, leaving the main door open as I slip into the bathroom and start the shower.

Both boys are sitting on the edge of my bed looking up at me when I emerge a couple of minutes later wrapped in a towel. "What?" I send them a suspicious look.

"Brad has an idea worth considering." Ky looks miserable as sin.

My eyes flit to Brad's.

"I can pretend to be your boyfriend. If you like," he adds urgently when he spots my wide-eyed look, "and then Peyton will lay off, or Lance will have grounds for convincing her to lay off. There's an unspoken rule amongst players—we don't mess with our own. And it means you could keep your relationship under wraps."

I'm not sure I like the sound of that. "Why would you do that when you don't approve in the first place?"

Brad looks sheepish. "You are still my friends, and I want to help."

"You're into this?" I ask Ky.

"If it means we can be together without any drama, and that you'll be safe, then yeah."

Disappointment flares up at the realization that Ky would rather keep me as his dirty little secret than face up to our dissenters. That's not who I thought he was. And I don't know if that's what I want either.

I instantly disguise my reaction, not wanting either boy to sense how much this upsets me. "How would that work in practice? Will we have to kiss and act all lovey-dovey in public?"

"Like fuck you will." Kyler's jaw is working overtime, popping in and out.

Brad tries, and fails, to hide his grin. "We can work around it, but the odd make-out sesh might be in order."

I swat at his head but he ducks down in time. "Knock it off."

Kyler looks like he's about to go all ninja on Brad's butt, and that goes some way toward appeasing my aching heart.

"Relax, dude." Brad pokes Ky in the arm. "I'm messing with ya. We can appear lovey-dovey without having to do anything intimate. You know this is the best way of protecting her."

"You know I can take care of myself." I glare at them both.

"I saw the state of Peyton, so, believe me, I know." Brad grins. "But it can't hurt to have back up."

When he puts it like that, it's hard to continue the argument. "Okay. We'll give it a go."

After Brad leaves, I make Ky leave too, while I get changed. It affords me some time to get my head together.

I meet him out by the pool, dropping into the lounger beside him. "Are you sure you're okay?" he asks me for the umpteenth time.

"I told you, I'm grand."

He looks around briefly before leaning in and planting a feather-soft kiss on my lips. "When Brad texted me, I almost crashed my car. I was so worried about you."

"I'm not that fragile," I protest. "I know how to defend myself. You shouldn't worry so much."

He takes both my hands in his as he stares sincerely into my eyes. "I like worrying about you, and I want you to know that, to understand that you're not alone anymore. And you never will be. Not as long as I'm around."

I pause considerably before replying, my mind churning at ninety miles an hour. "Only in the background, though, right?" He frowns. "You don't want people to know about us. You'd rather we kept things secret, and I'm not sure that's what I want."

Sitting up, he swings his legs around, leaning forward on his elbows. "That's not my preference, Faye. But you saw how Brad reacted, and he's our *friend*."

I sit up, mirroring his position. "He'll come around, and others will too. It'll be awful for a while, but then it'll blow over. Some other scandal will crop up, and we'll be yesterday's news."

He cups my face. "If I believed that, then I'd say do it. But Brad is right—this sort of prejudice is deep-rooted. It's not something people will forget in the short term. Maybe not ever."

I shake his hand off. "So we hide forever? That's what you're saying?"

He presses his forehead to mine. "Please, baby. I'm trying to protect you here. To spare you all that again. Why can't we just continue on as we are for now?"

I pull my head back, not caring if he can see the tears glistening in my eyes. "Because I don't want to sneak around! I want to be able to kiss you and hold your hand and go on dates and do all the other normal stuff that couples do! Not snatch a few stolen moments here and there behind closed doors!"

Ky pulls me into his arms, resting his chin on top of my head. "I want that too, but we have to be patient." He runs his hand up and down my back, but it's not comforting this time.

The sound of approaching footfall has us jerking apart but not quickly enough.

"What's wrong?" Keaton asks, appearing in front of us just as I shuck out of Ky's embrace.

"Nothing." I shoot him my best replica smile.

"Why are you upset?" A note of suspicion creeps into his tone.

"I had a run-in with some girls at school, and it upset me, but I'm fine now." I hop up, planting another faux smile on my face. I look down at Ky. "Thanks for the chat. It helped."

I walk away, and Keaton calls after me. "Mom said we're leaving in a half hour. You need to pack your stuff."

"On it!" I shout back, sprinting for my room.

I stuff a load of random clothes in my bag and deposit it in the empty lobby on my way outside. I want to call in on Lana before we leave to make sure she's okay.

Greta stonewalls me at the door, not even inviting me in. Her expression is coldly polite. "Lana is sick, and she isn't taking visitors at this time. I'll tell her you called." She moves to close the door in what is a deliberate, rude maneuver.

What the heck?

I plant my booted foot in the door, stopping it from closing. "I hope it isn't serious? Is there anything I can do to help?"

Looking down at my feet, she narrows her lips. "That's very considerate of you, Faye, but Lana needs her rest. It's getting late, and you don't want to miss your ferry. Goodnight." She pushes my foot out and shuts the door in my startled face.

As I walk back through the woods, I can't shake the feeling that a storm is coming.

And I'm not talking about the meteorological kind.

Chapter Thirty-Eight

It's official: I want to relocate permanently to Nantucket. I've been enthralled with the island from the first sighting of the lighthouse as we crested the harbor. Hundreds of yachts bob in the water, fronting magnificent homes that are clustered together, bordered by shrubbery and trees. Elevated American flags waft gently in the breeze.

My nose is glued to the window of the car now, soaking it all up. Quaint old-worldly street lamps bathe the town in a splendiferous glow as we glide by. Charming cobblestone streets sit between elegant buildings and storefronts, rimmed by pristine tree-lined paths as Ky effortlessly maneuvers the car through the main town. Alex sits beside him in the passenger seat, staring vacantly out the window. Every so often, Ky catches my eye in the mirror, and we share a series of loaded looks.

"Someone's getting laid tonight," Kalvin teases in my ear, not properly understanding the situation.

I pinch his thigh hard, and he jumps in his seat. "Shut up."

As we move farther out, the properties become grander and more widespread than the houses down by the harbor.

Kyler stops in front of a shuttered wooden gate, inputting a code on the adjoining keypad. He waits patiently as the gate slowly retracts, granting us entry. We cruise up a gravel-lined driveway that gives way to smooth asphalt as we approach the imposing house. This property is no less striking than the Wellesley house, although the style is completely different.

Set over three levels, the cream- and brown-bricked façade hosts two spherical turrets on each side and a massive circular latticed window in the center. Ky brings the car to a halt in a square courtyard bordered by neat low-level hedging. Bunches of thriving white roses are in flowerbeds under the ledges of all the front windows. Hopping out, he walks around to his mom's side and opens the door, helping her out.

A stout, matronly woman opens the main door of the house. She waits with her hands clasped neatly in front of her.

The boys take the bags out of the boot while I loop my arm in Alex's.

"Good evening, ma'am." The woman extends her hand to Alex.

"Good to see you, Mrs. Beaton. Is everything in order?" Alex shakes her hand and then moves past her into a well-lit hallway.

Tons of family photos adorn the walls as we proceed into the warm kitchen-cum-dining room. Dark stained wooden beams crisscross overhead. A wide marble island unit with stools on both sides rests in the center of the kitchen. Clean, white kitchen cupboards surround it.

Mouthwatering smells tempt me, and my stomach grumbles on demand. Alex leads me to the far end of the kitchen and out to an adjoining conservatory. A long table has been dressed for dinner, but my gaze goes past it to the space outside. Alex smiles at my audible gasp. She gives me a gentle nudge. "Go. Explore while I help Mrs. Beaton serve dinner."

I open the glass double doors and step out onto the beige-stoned patio. A gigantic infinity pool slopes over the edge of the property, the water dappling gently as it curves out of sight. A high wooden railing resides on the other side of the outdoor space, broken only by a steep set of steps leading down to the beach several feet below. It was impossible to tell from the main entrance that the property was this high up and bordering the magnificent sandy beach.

Once again, I'm blown away by the sheer magnitude of the Kennedy fortune.

A warm hand brushes against my lower back, and I instantly know it's Ky. "Well, what's the verdict?"

I tilt my head back and look up at him. "I love it here. The view is beautiful."

"That it is," he intones in that deep, rich, sultry voice of his, looking only at me.

Intense emotion cuts through me at his words and his expression, and I'm reminded once again of how magnetic he is. Kyler puts every other boy I've known to shame. However, it doesn't detract from the fact that we seem to be at an impasse of sorts.

"Dinner's up!" Kal yells, and we move inside to take our seats. Mrs. Beaton has laid out an impressive spread, and while it looks like there's enough to feed twenty, the boys waste little time in demolishing the lot. Kalvin keeps up a steady one-sided stream of chatter the whole way through dinner. Keaton and Keanu are sullen and quiet, like their mother, and the only sentiment Kent displays is animosity as he sends daggers across the table at Ky and me.

Alex divvies out ice cream after dismissing Mrs. Beaton. I had expected her to stick around for the weekend, but Ky explained that they fend for themselves during their stay.

The more I hear about this place, the more I'm falling in love with it.

Keaton gives me a grand tour of the house after dinner. While there's no denying how maze-like the property is, there's a homely quality to this house that is lacking in the Wellesley house. This feels more lived in, and while everything seems to have a place, it's not rigidly organized and expertly color-coordinated. It's a bit of a mish-mash of styles and a blend of luxury and chintz, but it works.

Keaton has been unusually quiet since we arrived, and I sense something is wrong. "Is something up?"

"Why would you ask that?"

I pick up on an edge to his tone. "Have I done something to upset you?"

He stops at the top of the stairs. "I don't know. You tell me—have you?"

The doorbell chimes before I can reply to his leading question. "That's weird," Keaton mumbles, starting to descend the stairs. "I thought Kaden and Keven weren't arriving until tomorrow."

Kent opens the door and curses. James runs a hand anxiously through his hair. "Can I come in, son?"

"Does Mom know you're coming?" He steps aside to let him in.

"No. I thought I'd surprise her."

Kent laughs drily. "It'll be a surprise all right."

I step into the hallway and James notices us for the first time. Keaton stands awkwardly beside me, shuffling on his feet. "Hi, Dad."

"I've missed you all," James admits just as Kalvin and Ky appear in the doorway of the kitchen.

"What are you doing here?" Alex asks, appearing behind her sons. She's a little shaky, and tears glisten in her sad eyes.

"I thought we could talk some more." James' eyes are pleading. "And there is something I need to tell you. It was too urgent to wait."

"Okay." Alex turns to us en masse. "Can you please take a walk while your father and I speak in private?"

We make our way down to the beach in relative silence. Kalvin spots a lit bonfire up ahead, and he steers us off the Kennedys' private beach and out to the next beach. Ky walks beside me, and the triplets take up the rear, talking quietly among themselves.

As we approach the bonfire, I spot several shadowy forms up ahead and hear the contagious beat of music. "You know these people?"

"We know most of these families. Everyone usually only comes here on weekends and for extended vacations. Their parents are all wealthy and successful, like ours. I wouldn't call them friends, but they're fine to hang out with every now and then."

A blustery gust of wind sweeps the length of the beach, and I shiver. I should've thought to bring a jumper—sorry, *sweater*—before I left. Even though we've been enjoying unbelievably warm weather, it's still autumn, and there's a definite chill in the air at night. Add our proximity to the sea and the temps are downright nasty. My flimsy white top is no barrier to the elements.

"I'm going back to grab a hoodie," I tell Ky. "I'll be back in a few."

He pulls his sweater off his head, offering it to me. "Don't bother. Take this."

"Then you'll be cold. It's practically Baltic out here." I thrust it back into his hands. "I'll be quick. You'll barely know I'm missing."

Shucking his sweater back on, he walks back with me. "I'll come with."

I stop dead in the sand. "Stop fussing. Stay. Be with your brothers. I am perfectly capable of walking up and down the beach by myself."

He opens his mouth to argue, no doubt, but clamps his lips shut again, obviously thinking better of it.

I trudge back to the house and head for the bedroom Kyler put my bag in earlier. I root out my warmest sweater and pull it on.

I'm just closing the door behind me, when the sound of arguing reaches my ears. Alex and James are really going for it, shouting at one another without restraint. I don't think it's eavesdropping if you can readily hear every word without trying.

"No way, James! She isn't a part of this family! She doesn't belong, and she certainly doesn't deserve it."

My heart plummets to my toes as her words sink skin-deep.

"I agree, but we don't have much choice. We're over a barrel here. It's legally binding, Alex, and I don't see how we can extricate ourselves from this ..."

A small squeak flies out of my mouth. They can only be talking about me. Agonizing grief presses down on my chest, restricting my breathing. I deliberately blot out the rest of their conversation—I don't want to hear any more.

I race down the stars, desperate to flee as wracking sobs threaten to burst free.

As soon as I step outside, the harsh night air cuts across my cheeks like a knife, matching the slicing, dicing pain slashing my insides to shreds.

How ironic that just as I'm starting to feel like I belong, like I could make this family mine, they've decided they don't want me.

Kyler drops down onto the sand beside me. I feel his penetrating gaze burning a hole in the side of my skull, but I keep my eyes locked on the sea, watching the waves tumble and roll toward the shore. Up the beach, the bonfire burns bright, and the sound of soft laughter tickles my eardrums.

"Faye, it's n—"

I silence him with a shake of my head.

Understanding that I'm not in the mood for talking, he nods, and we sit in amicable silence for a while. I draw strength from his quiet companionship and the warmth he exudes.

A chafing wind swirls through the air, blowing my hair across my face. I shiver, even under my sweater, but I make no move to leave. I don't want to go back to that house. I'd rather freeze my butt off out here than listen to more rejection.

A strong arm creeps around my shoulders, and Kyler pulls me firmly into his warmth. I rest my head on his shoulder and close my eyes. The only time the numbness goes away, the only time I can feel *something* real and true, is when I'm with Ky like this.

I have a strong suspicion it's the same for him.

Although I think we need each other more than either of us would like to contemplate, let alone admit, I can't afford to think like that anymore. It's clear that my days with this family are numbered.

"They weren't talking about you."

"What?" I croak, lifting my head up. I stare into his stunning, earnest eyes.

"You didn't hear the full conversation. They were discussing Courtney."

I twist around in his arm, hating the little nugget of hope that blossoms to life at his words. "That makes absolutely no sense." I pucker my brow.

"I know." He scratches the side of his head. "I didn't hear the start of the conversation, only the part just before you came out of your room, but her name was clearly mentioned, and even if it hadn't been, I would've known they weren't talking about you because we all care about you so much." My heart starts a tentative happy dance. "You are a part of this family now, whether you like it or not."

I shuck out of his arms, sitting up on my knees. "Are you sure they weren't talking about me?"

I hate how desperate I sound, but the prospect of losing this family has brought all my emotions to the surface in stark clarity. Dysfunctional and messed up as they are, they have burrowed their way into my affections. And it's more than this attraction to Kyler. They have all come to mean something to me.

I don't want to leave anymore.

I want to stay.

Kyler takes my hands in his. "I hate that you've been dragged into the middle of this. I didn't want that for you."

A light bulb goes off in my head. "That's what you meant, at the start, when you said I didn't belong." He nods. "You were trying to protect me?" I hear the incredulity in my own tone.

"Yes. Why is that so hard to believe?" A quizzical look passes over his features.

"Because you hardly knew me then."

He shakes his head. "I know you don't really believe that."

Air knocks out of my lungs.

He tucks wayward strands of my hair back behind my ears, leveling an intense look my way. "I saw you that first night, in the same way you saw me." I nod slowly in agreement. "More than that. I felt you reaching into me, pushing through my barrier in a way no one has been able to do before. At first, I panicked, but then I understood. *I felt you too.* I knew instantly you were inherently good, like an angel." He smooths his thumb over my cheek, smiling at me adoringly. "But I saw the emptiness and grief inside you, and I knew all the crap going on in our family had the potential to hurt you. I didn't want that for you. I still don't. And it's the reason why I've been fighting this thing between us."

Sadness stretches over him. "But, ultimately, I'm too Goddamned selfish. I'm tired of trying to stay away from you. You asked me before to find myself. Not to commit until I had. But, the thing is, I can't find myself without you." He cups my face tenderly. "I need you, and you need me. I don't want to deny this anymore. It's killing me. I want to be with you, to cherish you in the way you deserve to be cherished."

My heart swells to bursting.

"I'm yours, Faye. I'm all in. If you'll still have me."

Chapter Thirty-Nine

My insides have melted into a puddle of goo. "I—"

"Wait," Ky interrupts me. "Don't say anything yet. There's more."

Leaning in, I brush my mouth against the corner of his. "I don't need to hear any more. That was pretty perfect."

He winds his hand through my hair, holding me in place by my neck. We're so close our noses are touching. "I'm so sorry, Faye." His voice is soft, barely more than a whisper on the breeze. "For everything." There's no mistaking his sincerity. "For ignoring you and pushing you away. For all that stuff with Addison. For treating you as anything less than the angel you are. You didn't deserve that." His pale blue eyes shimmer in the moonlight.

"I can't get you out of my head," I admit, looking him dead in the eye. "God knows, I've tried, but you are all I think about."

He lifts me onto his lap, and like always, I feel the magnetic pull settling between us. His apology was heartfelt, and I want to believe things can change, but I'm scared to indulge my heart's desire. Our relationship will have to be clandestine, and I don't know if I'm ready to lie to the very people who are starting to mean so much to me.

He traces the contours of my face, eliciting a shockwave of delectable tingles. "I can't stop thinking about you either. It's driving me insane." I part my lips to speak, but he places his fingers against my mouth, shaking his head. "I need to get this out, and it's not easy for me, but I want you to know." He wets his lips, and my eyes follow the movement like a dog eyeing up a juicy bone. "I've wanted you from the very first moment I saw you."

Wait, what? He was *horrible* to me the first time we met.

"I'm crazy about you, Faye. You consume my every waking thought. My unconscious ones, too. You have stolen a piece of my heart, and I like feeling you there." He places a hand over his heart, as my own starts jumping ecstatically in my chest. "It's the only Goddamned thing that feels right in my world. There are a whole host of reasons why we should stay away from one another. But I only care about the one reason that matters." His Adam's apple jumps in his throat. "We belong together. It's as simple as that."

"Do you mean that?"

"I do. I know I've made a mess of everything, but I'll make it up to you, if you'll let me."

Every emotion shows on his face. It's as if his chest is ripped wide open and he's baring his heart and soul for me to see. It's a part of himself I'm certain he doesn't share with many others. I turn to liquid jelly on the inside, but there's a self-protective side of me that's still a teeny bit cautious. "How do I know you won't change your mind? That you won't push me away again?"

"I suppose you'll have to trust me." He caresses my cheek. "I know I've got to work hard to gain your trust, but I'll do whatever it takes to get us to that place."

I'd challenge anyone to hear this and not believe him. He has stripped himself naked, and his vulnerability is the one thing I can trust to be honest and true, even if a part of me is still slightly hesitant. "I don't let many people in, Faye, but once I do, once I've made the decision to go there—and I have with you—there is no going back for me."

Oh my God. This boy has a nurturing hand around my expanding heart, and I know I'm not ever going to be the same. So much emotion is swirling inside me now, and I can barely deal.

A tortured look contorts his beautiful face. "Am I too late? Have I ruined it before it's even begun?"

I hear his pain, and that grounds me. "No, Ky." I place my hands on his chest. "I want you so much it physically hurts. I want everything you're offering, but I'm scared. Because of what happened, I don't let people in all that easily either. What if we only hurt each other more?"

He wraps his arms around me and presses his forehead against mine. "Babe, we'll heal each other."

"You really mean it?" I croak.

"One hundred percent. No more games. No more Addison. No more pushing each other away. We're a team now." I circle my arms around his neck as he reels me into his body. The bitterly cold wind wafts around us but I don't feel it over the blistering heat flaring inside me. "That was very romantic," I murmur. "I think I'm going to like this new you."

"Then that's the benchmark I'll maintain. I want to make you happy."

"Ky," I say, eyeing his lips like a hunter stalking his prey. "You already are. Just shut up and kiss me."

We sneak into my room, carefully easing the door shut. Ky flings me onto the bed, crawling over me. We pick up what we started on the beach, kissing each other ravenously as if our lives depend on it. Clothes rapidly disappear until we're only wearing our underwear. Ky scoots off the bed and swiftly locks the door. The minute he lands on the mattress, I yank him down on top of me and continue feasting. In seconds, we are completely bare, skin to skin.

Every place he touches me alights instantaneously. My back arches off the bed, and a little mewl flies out of my mouth. Ky places his hand over my mouth. "Ssh, baby. We can't make any noise."

"I'll try," I pant, but if I was being brutally honest, I'd tell him how I want to scream my head off whenever he touches me and how I long to just give into everything I feel when I'm with him—to cry out his name when he sends me tunneling into that blissful place.

He lightly chuckles before resuming his exploration of my body. His hot tongue licks a trail across my skin, and my body throbs with undeniable need. I throw my head back as his wicked mouth moves lower and lower. Then he kisses me *there*, and I almost rocket off the bed. He looks up at me through hooded eyes, and his breathing is ragged. "Can I?"

A choked snort rips from me. *Hell yes.* As if saying no is an option. Slowly, I nod and he sends me a devilish grin that forces all the blood to pool in my core. He nudges my legs apart, but I don't feel self-conscious. His tongue is light and tender at first, and then he dives in, worshiping me until I'm a mass of writhing hotness on the bed. I bite down on my lip to stop myself from crying out, drawing blood in the process. My hands fist in the sheets and my toes curl as he sends me over the edge, a wave of pure unadulterated bliss moving through me.

His lips are glossy and swollen as he moves up beside me, his hard length digging into my hip. I slip my fingers down, wrapping around him as I watch his eyelids grow heavy. It's not like me to throw caution to the wind, but nothing has ever felt as right as the two of us do.

In this moment, it feels like fate has brought me to this point, to this boy who already seems so much a part of me. I've never felt more safe or alive or more reassured than I do when I'm with him. I'm almost at a loss to properly describe it myself. But it's an inherent truth. Borne of some precognition buried deep inside me.

This isn't some teenage crush, some fleeting relationship.

This feels like the real deal.

I'm meant to be here with him. I truly believe I was destined to find him. Maybe I'm delusional, or high on lust, but right now, in this second, with every pounding beat of my heart, it feels like the only truth.

Alone, we both suffer in this world.

Together, we can conquer it.

Call me on it if it seems cheesy. I couldn't care less.

"I want to feel you inside me," I tell him, with complete confidence and faith, staring deep into his eyes.

His eyes darken with unbridled lust. "You're not a virgin?"

"Did you think I was?" My hand stops moving.

"We haven't discussed it, and I wasn't sure."

"Well, I'm not. Unless you count born-again virgins?" I half-joke. He props up on an elbow, lifting one brow, and I respond to his silent question. "I had sex one time with my boyfriend." I shudder. "It's an experience I'd rather forget."

"He didn't make it good for you, huh?" His thumb moves over my nipple, and a jolt of red-hot desire surges through me.

"To be fair, we were both pretty clueless."

"I can make it really good for you, Faye. And I want to go there. So badly." He presses into my hand, perfectly illustrating his point. "But I want to make it special for you. Make it everything your first time should've been. So we're not going to sleep together now."

He chuckles at my answering scowl, pressing a searing hot kiss to my lips. "I don't want to rush because I'm scared my parents will come knocking or have to bite back my moans in case someone hears us. I want to worship your body all night long. Make you beg me for more. Hear you screaming out my name." He kisses the top of my nose. "Don't worry. I'll sort something out soon."

There's no way I can argue with his logic, but I'm not letting him leave my room unsatisfied either.

I flip up and push him down flat on his back. His lips curve in antic-ipation. "Now it's my turn to take care of you." I slither down his body, enjoying the feel of every hard, taut muscle pulsing against mine. Wrapping my lips around him, I return the favor. He thrusts his hips upward, the movements becoming more and more frantic, and my actions become faster and faster until soon he's joined me over that heavenly ledge.

I sleep naked and content in Ky's arms until sunrise. Gathering his scattered clothes, he snatches a quick kiss before sneaking back into his room.

Seated with everyone at the breakfast table, it's hard to keep the Joker-like grin off my face. Ky and I share secretive looks whenever we think no one's watching. James is trying to entice his sons into conversation, but he's fighting a losing battle. One-syllable answers and disgruntled mut-terings are the usual response. Alex drinks copious cups of coffee, her fingers shaking like a leaf. Ghastly shadows form rings under her bloodshot eyes, and she looks like someone just told her she has a terminal illness.

Ky and I trade worried expressions.

After breakfast, we bike into town with Kalvin and Keaton. Keanu and Kent have cried off, and James and Alex have holed themselves up in the study. Glorious sunshine beats down on us as we cycle along near-empty roads. A light balmy breeze teases tendrils from my ponytail.

The boys show me their favorite haunts along the route to Surfside Beach. Winds are elevated here but that hasn't stopped the multitude of surfers from braving the boisterous sea. We eat ice cream as we watch them navigate the choppy waters, and a great sense of contentment settles over me.

I shoot sly smiles at Ky whenever the others are distracted, and he finds every opportunity to secretly touch me. When his brothers take a bathroom break, he pounces on me, kissing me with a ferocity that matches my own need. I'm struggling to disguise my rampant breathing when my cousins return.

Kalvin rubs at Ky's mouth, and he slaps his hand away. "What the actual fuck?"

"Lip gloss, bro." Kal winks.

"I don't know what you're talking about." Ky hurriedly tries to dismiss it.

"Oh, please," he says, throwing a diva-like pose. "Anyone with eyes in their head can see you are hot for each other." He drops down on the sand beside me, winking as Ky shoots warning daggers. "Don't worry, it's cool. I won't tell." He makes a zipping movement with his fingers. "These lips are sealed."

"Oh my God." Keaton's shocked look darts between Ky and me. "You two are hooking up?"

My heart pounds frantically in my chest at the look of utmost horror on his face.

Kalvin bursts out laughing, but I fail to see any humor in this scenario. Ky pulls me to my feet, firmly taking my hand. "You have an issue with that?" he asks gently.

Keaton seems fixated on our joined hands. Looking up, he spears me with a hurt-filled expression. "You're related. It's not right." He shakes his head in disgust. "Actually, it's fucking sick."

I flinch at the venom in his tone.

Ky releases my hand, stepping in front of Keaton and planting his hands on his shoulders. "Joker."

Keaton shoves Ky's hands off. "Don't call me that. Don't say another word. You disgust me." Throwing a last shameful look at me, he turns and runs away.

"What's got up his ass?" Kalvin asks, no longer laughing.

"You and your big fucking mouth!" Ky glares at Kalvin.

Kalvin's face goes thunderous. "Don't fucking pin this on me! You two were slobbering all over each other in plain view. He saw you when we were rounding the hill, and I could see he was upset. I threw out all that stuff because I thought if he knew I was okay with it, that he'd be come around. Obviously, I was mistaken."

"I have to go after him." Ky looks to me for confirmation, and I nod my agreement.

"No, let me." Kalvin says, brushing sand off his pants. "I doubt he would listen to either of you."

A muscle tenses in Ky's jaw.

I place my hand on Kal's arm. "Okay, thanks. Go."

He runs off after his brother, and I turn to face Ky. Gripping his upper arms, I force him to make eye contact with me. "It's just the shock of it. He'll come around. Keaton is the most laid-back of all your brothers."

He stares at me, and I see the conflict and confusion in his eyes. Leaning down, he presses his forehead to mine. "What if he doesn't, Faye?" he whispers. "What then?"

Kaden and Keven are at the house when we return, but they may as well be invisible for all we see of them. Kal advises us to steer clear of Keaton until he's had time to calm down. Feigning sudden illness, Keaton withdraws to his room, not even joining us for dinner.

Dinner is another somber affair, and there's a collective sigh of relief when Alex and James retreat to the study once more. Kal, Kaden, and Keven head out to another beach party, but we make excuses and spend a couple of hours in the family room pretending to watch a movie on TV. Huge guilt swamps me whenever I think of Keaton. I'm tempted to go talk to him, but I have to respect his wishes and give him the space he needs.

I'm devastated by his reaction, and it's forced me to rethink everything. If our family and friends are reacting this negatively to our news, it doesn't bode well for the rest of society.

I slip into a depressive funk, and my head's not the happiest of places right now.

Ky must be feeling the same, because he doesn't visit me tonight.

Ky and I don't have much opportunity to talk the next day because James and Alex insist on a family outing, and we're gone for the best part of the day. Keaton is quiet and glum and avoiding both of us at all costs.

It's late Sunday night when we arrive back at the Wellesley house. James isn't with us, having returned to wherever he is staying. It's obvious to everyone that things are still fraught between him and Alex.

Kyler creeps into my bed when the house goes quiet, and some of my anxiety dissipates. We don't talk, but he holds me close, kissing me softly, and I know we'll work things out.

The repetitive chiming of the doorbell wakes me from a deep slumber at the same time Kyler rouses. Rubbing sleepy eyes, he stares quizzically at me. We haul ass, pulling on clothes as if it's a race. Ky swings himself out my window, returning to his bedroom, lest anyone see him coming out of mine.

We meet in the corridor as the triplets stumble, bleary-eyed, from their rooms. "What's going on?" Keaton asks, forgetting he's not supposed to be talking to us. Pounding footsteps approach, accompanied by shrill female protests.

Kalvin joins us, pushing masses of tousled hair out of his sleep-heavy eyes. "'Sup?" He turns a questioning gaze on us as two police officers in black uniforms march toward us.

Kyler pushes me and the triplets behind him and forms a semi-protective wall in front of us. Kalvin steps into place alongside him. "What've you done now, Kent?" he hisses quietly over his shoulder.

I'm wondering if it's anything to do with those girls and the party or if he's been caught shoplifting again.

"Nothing!" Kent snaps. He steps out, facing the advancing officers with a smug grin on his face.

Alex is barking instructions into her cell as she tails the policemen.

"Kalvin Edward Kennedy?" the male officer booms, his eyes jumping between us and the piece of paper in his hand.

Ky steps forward, sheltering his younger brother. "What's this about?"

"Step aside, young man. We need to speak with your brother."

I lace my hand in Kalvin's, squeezing tight. His Adam's apple bobs in his throat as his eyes skitter wildly. Kyler steps right in the policeman's path. "You are not taking my brother."

Alex places her cell against her chest, shaking her head at Ky. "Move aside, Kyler. I'll sort this, but for now, Kalvin has to go with them."

"What?" Kal gulps. "Why?"

Ky reluctantly steps aside as the officer takes Kalvin's wrists and cuffs them behind his back. Kal pulls his mouth into a grim line and stares straight ahead, but I can tell he's freaking out

"Kalvin Edward Kennedy"—the officer begins reading him his rights—"You are under arrest for the sexual assault and rape of Ms. Lana May Taylor."

Chapter Forty

"Are you fucking kidding me?" Ky yells at the officer. "What kind of a sick joke is this? Kalvin didn't rape Lana. Get r—"

"Kyler!" Alex cries. "Stop talking. Right now."

The officer starts leading Kalvin away, and we all follow suit. At the door, Alex turns to address us. "Our attorney will deal with this, and I've notified your father; he's on his way. Do not do anything to make this situation worse for your brother. We will sort this out. Wait here until I return." She grabs her keys and flies out the door after her son.

Kalvin is being lowered into the back of the police cruiser, and I feel so helpless just standing there doing nothing. Worried blue eyes lift to mine, and I try to send him a reassuring look. This is one occasion where money most definitely helps. I'm sure Alex and James will hire the best attorney and have him home before long.

The car door is closed and we watch silently as Kalvin is driven away.

Ky ushers us all inside and closes the door.

"That bitch!" Kent fumes. "I say we storm over there right now and find out what the lying little slut is up to." His fists clench into balls of fury at his side.

"No." Ky's instruction is firm and final. "You heard Mom. We sit tight. This isn't some shoplifting spree. This is a serious accusation. I doubt Dad will be able to pay the cops off in the same way. No one is to do anything. Understood?"

Kent lets loose a colorful volley of curses before reluctantly acquiescing. He skulks back to his room while Keanu and Keaton head into the kitchen.

I make for my room with Ky's quiet footsteps following me. "I'm going to speak to her," I tell him the minute he closes my bedroom door.

"I know, and it has to be us. I don't want the triplets getting mixed up in this. Especially Kent. Not with his track record. Come on." He pushes my window open and jumps out before turning to help me down.

Keeping to the right-hand side of the garden, we take the long route to the forest to avoid triggering the spotlight. Our footsteps crunch on the uneven path as we creep toward Lana's bungalow. The property is lit up like the Fourth of July, and we hang back, scouting the scene.

Lana's parents, Greta and John, are diligently loading cases into a small red Honda. Ky and I trade wary looks. I nudge his shoulder and point around the other side of the bungalow. He motions for me to lead the way, and I tiptoe slowly and carefully through the trees around the other side of the bungalow, coming up at the rear. There's a dim glow coming from Lana's bedroom. The curtains are open offering unrestricted access to the sobbing girl inside.

An ache pierces my chest cavity.

Ky tugs my sleeve, holding me back. "I'll stay here," he whispers, cowering around the corner of the bungalow. "See if she'll talk to you."

I nod and approach the window cautiously, tapping lightly on the glass. Lana jumps ten feet in the air, emitting a tiny shriek. Whipping her head around, she spots me and stills. "Lana, honey, are you okay?" Greta calls out, and I duck my head just in time.

"I'm okay," she says in a muffled voice.

"He's going to pay for this, sweetheart. I promise you."

"But your job ..." she sniffles.

"A job is a job. It's not as important as you. We never should've stayed here this long, not after all those rumors started circulating. And I've known those boys were running amok for some time. Those people have a lot to answer for. I'm so sorry, honey. We've failed you."

Lana hiccups. "It's not your fault."

There's a minute of silence before Greta speaks again, this time in a softer cadence. "Finish packing. We're leaving shortly."

When the *tappity-tap* of footsteps fades, I lift my head, jumping a little when I see Lana with her face pressed firmly to the window above me. She flips the lock and pushes it open. "You shouldn't be here." Her lip wobbles.

The utter devastation on her face almost floors me. "Are you okay?"

A lonely tear trips down her cheek, and my eyes well up. There is so much hurt and pain in her gaze; it's clear something traumatic has happened. I bite back my distress.

It can't be true.

Kalvin is a lot of things, but he's not capable of this. My mind churns in confusion. Something awful has obviously happened to her, but none of this makes any sense. Kalvin wouldn't hurt her. I'd stake my life on it. I chew on the inside of my cheek, utterly conflicted.

"No. I'm not okay," she chokes out.

A sense of dread sweeps through me. "What's going on, Lana? What happened?"

Please tell me it wasn't my cousin, I plead in my head.

No! It wasn't Kalvin. I inwardly chastise myself for even thinking those thoughts.

He wouldn't do this.

"I'm in a bad place, Faye." More tears cascade down her cheeks. "And I hurt so much." There's an anguished quality to her tone that brings tears to my eyes.

I gulp, willing the jittery feeling in my chest to go away. "The police have arrested Kalvin."

More tears erupt, and she wipes her sleeve across her snotty nose. "I know. He hurt me, Faye. He promised me th—"

"Get the hell away from my daughter," Greta demands, cutting Lana off mid-speech as she stomps toward the window. "Leave. Right now, or I'm calling the cops." She pins me with harsh, cold eyes and steely determination.

"I don't think you're in any position to make such demands," Ky supplies, coming up alongside me. "This is our property, our grounds."

"And she's my daughter!" Greta shrieks as her husband materializes beside her. "Leave her alone! You Kennedys have done enough damage."

I glance one more time at Lana, and a myriad of conflicting emotion washes over her face. There's no denying she's wracked with pain, and my heart bleeds for her. Whatever is going on, it's destroying her on the inside—I can tell.

I tug on Ky's arm. "Let's go."

"Please give this to your mother." Lana's father speaks up for the first time, handing Ky a plain white envelope through the open window. Greta trembles, and he throws an arm around his wife's shoulders.

I take Ky's other hand and drag him away. Neither of us speaks on the walk back to the house, but there's a heavy pressure chasing us the entire time.

All is quiet when we return, and the house is in darkness. We slip into my room through the open window and strip to our undies, sliding under the covers together. I rest my head on his bare chest, as his fingers toy with my hair. Everything is such a mess, and all manner of thoughts and ideas flit through my mind.

Concern for Kal competes with questions over my future with Ky. I prop up on one elbow, and peer into his face. "I don't want to hide. Nothing good comes from keeping things secret." James, Kent, and whatever is going on with Kal and Lana is proof of that.

He reaches up, cupping my cheek. "I agree, but we shouldn't rush the decision because of what's happened tonight or Keaton's reaction."

I press my face into his palm, loving the feel of his warm hand on my skin. "I'm not. I've given this plenty of thought. When all that stuff happened to me, I felt ashamed, like I'd done something wrong. It took a while for me to realize that wasn't the case, but I was already walking around like the guilty party. Nearly inviting the taunts and the bullying. I'm not doing that again." I shake my head vigorously. "I want to go out in public with you and hold my head up high, because the only thing I'm guilty of is falling for my cousin. There's nothing illegal about it, and no reason why we can't acknowledge our relationship in front of others. If they choose to look down their nose at us, then that's their issue. Not ours. I won't allow pettiness and narrow-minded prejudice to dictate who I am anymore. I'm not afraid to show my true self in public."

I run my fingers across his cheek. "I want everyone to know I'm your girlfriend." I gaze deep into his eyes, wanting him to see the truth of my words, hoping he can get on this train with me. "We're perfect for each other, and people will see that in time."

He drags my face down and kisses the heck out of me. When he finally releases me, we're both panting. "It's okay if you don't want or feel the same, if y—"

"Ssh," he interrupts me. "I want that. Every part of it. I'm not afraid to go public."

"Are you sure? Because we both need to be on board with this. Both ready to face all the crap."

He sweeps his hand through my hair. "I am. In a way, Keaton did me a favor. At least we'll know exactly what to expect. But I don't care about any of that. I care about you and your happiness. It's all I've been thinking about these last twenty-four hours, and you're right. We are not running and hiding—we're stronger than that. You're the best thing that's ever happened to me, Faye, and I'd happily shout it from the rooftops. The dissenters can screw off."

My grin is so wide it threatens to split my face. "Yeah?"

"Yes, babe. A thousand times, yes."

This time, I lean down and kiss the face off him. When we part, he gazes at me so adoringly that it feels like my heart is about to break free of my chest and dance a salsa. I'm so happy I could burst.

"We need to tell my parents first."

"Of course," I instantly agree. "Now probably isn't the best time ..."

He winces, as if he's only remembering his brother.

To be fair, I had kinda forgotten about Kalvin too, but now it's back on my radar, and my previous concern for his welfare returns with a vengeance. To be thinking about myself, when my cousin is languishing in a jail cell, is probably the most selfish thing I've ever done. "We'll wait a couple of days and then tell them." The previous joy on Ky's face is replaced by grim realization. I rest my head on his chest again, as we both return to that worrisome place.

I wish I could decipher the situation with Kalvin and Lana, because it can't be as it appears.

I know Kalvin has a well-deserved rep, and a dirty mouth to boot, but he isn't a bad guy. It's part bravado, part attention seeking, but never malicious or hurtful. Kal has them lining up outside his door, so why would he ever force himself on a girl? Not that I'm that naïve. I know there is a multitude of reasons why someone forces themselves on another, but my cousin doesn't fit the bill.

I can't believe he would do that. I refuse to believe it.

But something *has* happened to Lana, so why is she lying about it?

"Ky?" I run my hand up his chest as I tilt my chin up to look at him. "Why would Lana make up something like that?"

"I honestly don't know." He drops a sweet kiss on my lips. "She's always been in love with him, and I think, if he was truthful with himself, he'd admit he has deep feelings for her, too. They were virtually inseparable as kids."

My finger makes twirling motions on his bare chest, and he flinches under my ministrations. "She *is* in love with him, but if that's the case, why is she saying this?"

"I hate to say it, but I've been wondering if—"

Ky's words are cut off at the sight of James looming like a ghostly predator in my doorway. Caught off guard, I shriek, my heart pounding wildly against my ribcage. Kyler hauls himself up against the headrest, eyeballing his dad with fierce determination. He pulls me up gently, and his arms fold protectively around my shoulders as I clutch the sheets to my chest. With a healthy dose of trepidation, I watch James stalking toward us. I snuggle into Ky's side figuring there's no point trying to hide what we are to each other now. It's clear from the way James is standing at the edge of the bed with a frozen shell-shocked expression on his face that the game is well and truly up.

Frantic, disbelieving eyes meet mine as his gaze leaps between us. His mouth opens and closes several times but he looks like he's struggling to find the right words. I look at Kyler, my head cluttered with a mixture of apprehension and relief. At least the secret is out in the open now. My heart is still pounding manically in my chest, and I'm half-expecting it to sprout wings and break free of my ribcage.

"What have you two done?" His panicked eyes latch on Kyler's.

"It's none of your business," Kyler grits out. He holds his chin up in a defiant stance.

James looks *horrified* as he stares at his son. A vein throbs in his neck while, simultaneously, his fists clench and unclench at his side. "I told you to stay away from her!" he yells. His face has turned an ugly shade of red as he starts pacing back and forth in front of us. "Damn it all to hell!" he roars, thumping his fist on the top of my dresser. I jump in the bed. He clamps a hand over his mouth as he stares at us again. His face has paled, and he seems to have aged on the spot.

I start shaking—I can't help it. I've never seen him lose control like this, and quite frankly, he's scaring the shit out of me. Kyler reaches out, lacing his fingers in mine. His warm touch helps calm me down, and my trembling subsides a little.

James stops pacing as his eyes fixate on our conjoined hands. He watches Kyler run soothing circles on the back of my hand with his thumb. James scrubs a hand repeatedly across his taut jaw, mumbling curses under his breath. "Have you had sex?" he barks out.

Kyler's wall goes up, and he stares at his dad with his signature blank face. I chicken out, averting my gaze from James altogether.

"Well?" He glares at his son. "Have you?" His gaze flits to me, and I gulp.

Some invisible thief seems to have crept into the room and stolen my vocal cords, because I'm physically incapable of responding or forming any type of denial. I'd like to tell him to sod off and mind his own bleeding business, but the words are stuck in my throat. A dry, sour taste floods my mouth. Something is wrong here, and I've a feeling I'd rather not know.

"Our relationship is nothing to do with you, and I'm not answering that," Kyler snarls. "Mind your own fucking business."

James stalks toward his son, grabbing him roughly by the shoulders. "I am your father, you are living under my roof, and you will answer me! Goddamn it! Have you been inside her, Kyler? I need to know."

I squirm uncomfortably as a red flush creeps up my neck.

"Screw you!" Kyler shoves his father's hands off as he jumps up out of the bed. They face one another with barely an inch of space between them. Kyler eyeballs his dad with a ferocious look. "I love Faye, and there is nothing legally or morally wrong with us being together. And we're done hiding." He looks to me for reassurance.

I think my heart has stopped beating in my chest. Despite the brash waves of hostility emanating from my uncle, I can't keep the smile off my face as I nod at Ky.

He loves me?

I long to fling myself into his arms and return the sentiment, but I don't think James would appreciate the gesture.

James curses again, taking a step back, as he drags his hands through his hair.

"I mean it," Kyler continues, still looking at me. "I love you, and I want everyone to know."

"My God!" James rasps, tugging fiercely on his hair. "This is just like history on repeat."

My stomach lurches unpleasantly, and a nasty taste coats the insides of my mouth.

He fists large tufts of his hair. If he keeps doing that, he'll be bald by morning. He shoots us an anguished look, and my fleeting euphoria has died a rapid death. Butterflies swarm my chest, slamming around my ribcage in sheer panic.

"What?" Kyler looks confused. "What exactly do you mean by that?"

"You shouldn't have had sex with her! You can't be in a relationship with her. I'm sorry, son, but you can't love Faye. Not in that way. You can't." He bridges the gap between them, placing his hand on Kyler's shoulder.

A gnawing hole opens up in my stomach

Kyler thrusts his hand away. "The hell I can't! There's no law that says I can't conduct a relationship with my cousin. You are completely overreacting, as usual."

Wrapping the sheet around my body, I climb out of the bed and walk to Kyler's side. "Ky," I plead, taking his hand in mine. "I'm sure it's still a shock and he needs some time to get used to the idea. Right, James?" I turn imploring eyes on my uncle, hoping he'll throw me a bone, praying that's all this is. I fervently hope my sixth sense is off kilter and he isn't about to drop some massive bombshell.

Momentarily closing his eyes, James shakes his head despondently. "This is my fault. I should've kept a closer eye on you. Should have read the signs instead of being too preoccupied with my own issues." He looks off into space. "This has to end, right now. You can't continue this relationship." The hard set of his jaw indicates there will be no negotiation. His mind is made up. Goose bumps shoot up and down my arms.

Kyler tucks me possessively under his arm. "You don't get to tell me what to do. You lost that right a long time ago. I'm not giving Faye up. Not for you, not for anyone. And you are making far too big a deal of this. She's my cousin. So what? Get over it!"

James looks between us, seemingly contemplating his next words carefully. His breath leaves his body in a loud rush, and everything goes on high alert inside me.

"She's not your cousin."

My eyes are out on stalks as I meet Kyler's equally surprised gaze. Butterflies are throwing the party to end all parties in my chest. "What?" I turn and face my uncle. "Just spit it out. What *are* you saying?"

His eyes soften at the corners, and his chest visibly swells. His Adam's apple bobs in his throat. Reaching out, he holds my wrist gently in his large hand. "Ky isn't your cousin." He gulps, glancing at his son briefly before returning his gaze to me. "He's your half-brother."

I sway on my feet, almost losing my balance along with the ability to breathe, to see, to hear. My head is buzzing. "Wh ... what?" I croak.

"You're my daughter, Faye. I'm your father."

To be continued.

Join the Kennedy Boys mailing list to read exclusive bonus scenes narrated from Kyler's perspective, and to read an exclusive sneak peek of *Losing Kyler*, the next book in the series.

Please type http://smarturl.it/KennedyBoysList into your web browser.

Glossary of Irish Words and Phrases

All her Sundays have come at once » Gotten her heart's desire
Arse » Butt
Bill » Check
Bedside locker » Nightstand
Bleedin'/Bloody » Damn
Boot » Trunk
Chancing his arm » Taking a risk in order to get something you want
Cooker » Stove
Cop on » Realize/Get it together/Figure out
Compel me to up sticks » To go and live in a different place
Do a bunk » Make a hurried or furtive departure or escape
Doolally » Crazy/Insane
Duvet » Comforter
Garda/Guard » Cop
Gawp » Gape
Get out! » No way!
Getting pissed » Getting drunk
Gob » Mouth
Gobshite » Stupid, foolish, or incompetent person
Gobsmacked » Flabbergasted
Grand » Fine

Gutted » Heartbroken
Happy out » Happy/fine
Hoover » Vacuum cleaner
Kitted out » Provide with equipment/clothing to suit a purpose
Knackered » Very tired/exhausted
Knickers » Panties
Lick arse » Ass licker
Mobile/Mobile phone » Cell
Mum » Mom
Press » Cupboard
Ride » Hot/Gorgeous
Ripping the piss » To joke or lie about something in a
humorous manner
Runners » Sneakers
Smart arse » Smart ass
Snog-fest » Make-out session
Sponger » Someone who accepts things from others without giving
anything in return; a moocher/mooch
Tarmac » Asphalt
Trousers » Pants/Dress Pants
Wanker » Jerk/Asshole
Wrecked » Very tired/exhausted

About The Author

Siobhan Davis writes emotionally intense young adult fiction with swoon-worthy romance, complex characters, and tons of unexpected plot twists and turns that will have you flipping the pages beyond bedtime! She is the author of the Amazon bestselling *True Calling* and *Saven* series.

Siobhan's family will tell you she's a little bit obsessive when it comes to reading and writing, and they aren't wrong. She can rarely be found without her trusty Kindle, a paperback book, or her laptop somewhere close at hand.

Prior to becoming a full-time writer, Siobhan forged a successful corporate career in human resource management.

She resides in the Garden County of Ireland with her husband and two sons.

Books by Siobhan Davis

TRUE CALLING SERIES
Young Adult Science Fiction/Dystopian Romance

True Calling
Lovestruck
Beyond Reach
Light of a Thousand Stars
Destiny Rising
Short Story Collection
True Calling Series Collection

SAVEN SERIES
Young Adult Science Fiction/Paranormal Romance

Saven Deception
The Logan Collection
Saven Disclosure
Saven Denial
Saven Defiance
The Heir and the Human
Saven Declaration*
*The Princess and the Guard^*
*The Royal Guard^*
*The Assassin^*

KENNEDY BOYS SERIES
Upper Young Adult Contemporary Romance

Finding Kyler
Losing Kyler*
Keeping Kyler*

MORTAL KINGDOM SERIES
Young Adult Urban Fantasy/Paranormal Romance

*Curse of Gods and Angels**
*Infernal Prophecy^*
*Mortal Ascendance^*

SKYEE SIBLINGS SERIES (TRUE CALLING SPIN-OFF)
New Adult Contemporary Romance

*Lily's Redemption**
*Deacon's Salvation^*

*Coming 2017
^Coming 2018

Acknowledgments

Thank you so much for purchasing my book, and I hope you enjoyed reading it as much as I enjoyed writing it (I had a total blast!)

When I first started out on my self-publishing journey I never imagined so much work goes into creating and publishing a book—believe it or not, the writing is actually the easiest part! It's important to me that I produce the best possible book, to the highest standards, so that my readers have the most enjoyable reading experience. I hope I have delivered on that commitment, and I need to thank a bunch of people who helped make that happen.

Massive thanks to the very lovely Moriah Chavis for all her support and enthusiasm on this project. I would also like to thank my extended beta reading team for this series – Lola, Lillian, Deirdre, Sinead, Teresa, Jennifer, Nelia, Kim, Amanda, Danielle, Karla, Karen, and Candace. Your insights have helped this story to shine!

I feel incredibly lucky to have discovered such a wonderful editor in Kelly Hartigan. Kelly is the consummate professional, and she delivers every time, even when I'm messing up her schedules by asking for extensions! My work is presented in the best possible light because of her input, and I'm eternally grateful.

A big thank you goes out to Fiona Jayde of Fiona Jayde Media for the breath-stealing cover, branding, and graphics she created for this series. I absolutely love them! I especially appreciate how you squeezed this work in during your maternity leave and I hope I didn't test your patience too much!

Tamara Cribley of The Deliberate Page has created some stunning interiors for this book, and it looks so beautiful in my hand. I hope this is the start of a great working relationship.

I need to thank my family and friends, and my dedicated Street and ARC Teams, for all their ongoing support. I also very much appreciate all the lovely bloggers and reviewers who take the time to read my books, write reviews, and help spread the love. You. Rock.

I'd like to give special mention to my author friends all around the world, especially the very lovely Georgia Le Carre, Emigh Cannaday, Elisa S. Amore, Tracey Alvarez, and all the amazing YA authors I've met through the AAYAA group. The Indie Author community is such a wonderful community to be a part of, and I have to pinch myself every day to realize this is my reality.

Big hugs and kisses to my other half, Trevor, and my two boys, Cian and Callum. They sacrifice a lot so I can live my dream and I never forget that. Love you all so much.

A massive THANK YOU to you dear reader. I would not be able to write full time if it wasn't for all the readers who have embraced my work and who support me on this journey. I appreciate each and every one of you.

I love to hear from my readers so don't hesitate to reach out to me – siobhan@siobhandavis.com

28298992R00202

Printed in Great Britain
by Amazon